PENGUIN BOOKS

THE PENGUIN ANTHOLOGY OF STORIES BY CANADIAN WOMEN

DENISE CHONG is the author of the spell-binding memoir *The Concubine's Children: Portrait of a Family Divided.* Translated into seven languages and soon to be made into a feature film, it was awarded the 1995 Edna Staebler Award for Creative Non-Fiction, the 1994 City of Vancouver Book Prize and the Van City Book Prize; it was also shortlisted for a Governor General's Award and the Hubert Evans Non-Fiction Prize. She was a contributor to the anthology *Who Speaks for Canada? Words That Shape a Country.* She lives in Ottawa with her husband and two children.

W9-AUO-026

The Penguin Anthology of Stories by Canadian Women

edited by

Denise Chong

Penguin Books

PENGUIN BOOKS

Published by the Penguin Group

Penguin Books Canada Ltd., 10 Alcorn Avenue, Toronto, Ontario, Canada M4V 3B2

Penguin Books Ltd, 27 Wrights Lane, London w8 5TZ, England

Penguin Putnam Inc., 375 Hudson Street, New York, New York 10014, U.S.A.

Penguin Books Australia Ltd, Ringwood, Victoria, Australia

Penguin Books (NZ) Ltd, cnr Rosedale and Airborne Roads, Albany, Auckland
1310, New Zealand

Penguin Books Ltd, Registered Offices: Harmondsworth, Middlesex, England

First published in Viking by Penguin Books Canada Limited, 1997
Published in Penguin Books, 1998

10 9 8 7 6 5 4

Introduction and Selection copyright © Denise Chong, 1997

*Publisher's note: This book is a work of fiction. Names, characters, places and incidents
either are the product of the author's imagination or are used fictitiously, and any
resemblance to actual persons living or dead, events, or locales is entirely coincidental.*

Manufactured in Canada.

Canadian Cataloguing in Publication Data

Main entry under title:
    The Penguin anthology of stories by Canadian women

ISBN 0-14-026701-8

1. Short stories, Canadian (English) – Women authors.★ 2. Canadian fiction
(English) – Women authors.★ 3. Canadian fiction (English)★ – 20th century.★
1. Chong, Denise.

PS8321.P46 1998   C813'.01089287'09045   C97-931663-4
PR9197.33.W65P45 1998

The acknowledgments on p. 493 constitute an extension of this copyright page.

Visit Penguin Canada's web site at **www.penguin.ca**

Contents

Introduction • ix
Acknowledgments • xv

Cynthia Flood
The Meaning of the Marriage • 1

Marion Engel
Madame Hortensia, Equilibriste • 13

Ann Copeland
Cloister • 24

Alice Munro
Miles City, Montana • 41

Barbara Gowdy
Presbyterian Crosswalk • 66

Mavis Gallant
Voices Lost in Snow • 85

Bonnie Burnard
Crush • 98

Sandra Birdsell
The Midnight Hour • 107

Eden Robinson
Queen of the North • 130

Shani Mootoo
A Garden of Her Own • 157

Monique Proulx
Leah and Paul, for Example • 170

Audrey Thomas
Harry and Violet • 185

Hélène Rioux
Opening Night • 201

Margaret Atwood
Bluebeard's Egg • 211

Dionne Brand
No Rinsed Blue Sky, No Red Flower Fences • 244

Diane Schoemperlen
She Wants to Tell Me • 253

Bronwen Wallace
An Easy Life • 264

Linda Svendsen
White Shoulders • 277

Holley Rubinsky
Rapid Transits • 293

Katherine Govier
Home for Good • 307

Elisabeth Harvor
How Will I Know You? • 318

Joyce Marshall
Blood & Bone • 336

Jane Rule
Lilian • 351

Ethel Wilson
Till death us do part • 358

Isabel Huggan
Secrets • 370

Frances Itani
Marx & Co. • 393

Shirley Faessler
Lucy & Minnie • 400

Sharon Butala
Act of Love • 416

Margaret Gibson
The House that Stan and Rosie Built • 425

Dorothy Speak
Stroke • 449

Carol Shields
Hazel • 463

Jane Urquhart
Storm Glass • 485

Copyright Acknowledgments • 493

Denise Chong

Introduction

"Do not be afraid to go too far, for the truth lies beyond."
—Marcel Proust

To write and be published is to engage in a public life, to invite from critics and readers—most of them complete strangers—questions about *where*, as a writer, you got such and such an idea *from*. The fiction writer is used to being asked about the creative process; the relation of reality to fiction is an old but permanent preoccupation. Not so the non-fiction writer. I confess that, having written about the lives of real people I knew, I stumble over what to say to someone who asks about my work of memoir: "Is it creative?" I'll often say, "It's not made up," which is what I think they want to hear. Usually that ends the exchange, when what I really want to do is hang on to the questioner's arm and say something that exalts the creativity of fiction, to explain that yes, even for the non-fiction writer, fiction sets the example to strive for.

I have always read fiction avidly, mostly in the novel form. Of short story writers, aside from giants like Alice Munro—one of my favourite authors—and Mavis Gallant, I first came across most in anthologies, rather than in collections. I returned intensely to the genre when, as a first-time author, I struggled with how to portray my family in my memoir, *The Concubine's Children*. Acutely aware that writing a book would violate the privacy my grandmother thought she took to the grave with her, and trespass on my mother's past in the everyday life of the old Chinatowns, I felt vindication would come if I captured the truth of their lives. What I meant by truth I wasn't sure. I read to learn about writing. Alice Munro had just written *Friend of My Youth* (1990), and I read and re-read her writings. That led me to other authors of short fiction like Carol Shields and Isabel Huggan. Armed with yellow post-it notes, I furiously marked passages wherever I felt the clear connection between life in reality and life in prose. When I saw that there was hardly a page unmarked, I read for pleasure only.

There is, after all, about fiction a purity of purpose: to discover and register the human condition, to heighten the reality of being. Fiction strives to have within its grasp the eloquence of the universal. In that respect, as a chronicler of a real life, I am humbled knowing that the particulars I enshrine are but a narrow version of the truth. For certain, we writers of non-fiction have no choice but to stay with the facts of a life; someone other than us gave that person life. In contrast, because a fictional life is brought into being as an act of the writer's imagination alone, fiction resonates with truth greater than the particular.

As a reader, I know what I like about the short fiction form. Unlike when I begin a novel, I begin reading a short story relieved of having a bookmark at the ready; I come prepared to hold completely within my imagination from the first word to the last the characters around whom events swirl. I come prepared also to co-exist intensely within the story's domain.

As a writer, I draw lessons from reading short fiction about the possibilities of narrative. Just as it is not possible in real life to know all about a person, neither is it possible to contain a real life within the covers of a book. In that respect, a writer of a real life illuminates only portions of a life, corners of a world, moments of time. As such, a non-fiction rendering of a life, even in the length of a book, has fewer parallels with the completeness of a novel than with the episodic nature of short fiction, where so quickly and intensely are portions, corners, and moments of life intimately brought into being.

Still, how does the non-fiction writer get from here to there, from fact to truth? Early on in the writing of my memoir, I heard a radio interview with Isabel Huggan. The interviewer complimented her ability in her short fiction to evoke the emotional world of childhood. He asked if her own figured in it. When the reply came back yes, the question put was why not write a memoir? "Oh, I couldn't," she replied. "I have such a bad memory!" Contrast Isabel Huggan's verdict on her art with that of the writer to whom success didn't come, who said she was less annoyed at the bad reviews from critics of her first novel than about having "used up" her childhood writing it.

The folly of the second writer was not to see fiction as informed by experience—of which memory is an integral part—*and* imagination. As a writer of memoir, I can attest to the flaws of memory: only ever fragmentary, rarely ordered and captive to the sense attentive at the time. In recounting my family's past, I accepted that I had to adhere to recollection and the reality of the life of my grandmother and of my mother, and the mother–daughter relationship between them. Yet Isabel Huggan breathes "real life" into childhood, not to recreate her own, but to create one recognized by writer and reader alike. I understood: the memoir I wanted to write was less about the ordered facts of certain lives, than about the confusion and contradictions of families, and about making sense of one's origins. It so happened all that played out in a family that was also *mine*. Ultimately what I was doing was fashioning not so much a life, but a text. In that sense, non-fiction can transcend the narrow particulars to sit comfortably where fiction is more commonly entertained, in the reader's imagination.

The act of writing fiction has been explained by Bonnie Burnard as living and working in "an altered state of mind." In 1997, she lectured on the origin of the short story at a symposium at the University of Ottawa. She began by reading aloud what she'd written the night before when she sat down to record a recent experience: on a book tour, she'd arrived at midnight to find the hotel too dank for her comfort. After she finished reading, she confessed that what she'd read was a work of fiction. As usually happened with her writing, the piece had begun in real life when the unexpected occurred. She said, however, that once she starts to write, she begins to see possibilities in the telling. She doesn't change the basic, hard facts of places and events, but starts asking, "What about . . ." of the characters and what she called "clusters" of life that could adhere to them. She starts to see, she said, where "small, helpful lies" would add detail, lend precision.

Even partial truth, for the writer and reader who find it, carries shared meaning; it makes sense of life. Elisabeth Harvor shared a confidence in the 1997 Duncan Campbell Scott lecture: when she first began to write she kept tacked above her desk a note to herself: "A humiliation a day keeps writer's block away." In the realm of fiction, the complexities and minutiae of everyday life come off the page larger than life, appearing more real than life itself. Freed from a fear of limitation, the writer also frees the reader, so that what is ordinary is turned, by an act of imagination, into the extraordinary.

The thirty-two short stories in this anthology are by Canadian women writers, all previously published. I wasn't looking so much for a feminine voice in the short story form, but rather stories in which women figure as central characters, where their points of view dominate. The plot that interested me was life lived in the chaos and uncertainty of everyday happenings and relationships. To intensify that experience for readers, I assembled stories set within living memory and in Canada. None of these criteria imposed much limitation on the selection; the genre in Canada is dominated by women writers—partly, I discovered, because it was an economic form when there wasn't the luxury of time to write more expansively—and writers naturally write about the familiar. So, how I honed my focus was to look for stories with women characters who could be invited easily into the lives of readers. As good short stories do, they also had to surprise and entertain.

The voices in this anthology are mostly established writers. There are some newer writers among them, including Shani Mootoo and Eden Robinson, whose contribution here is taken from her startling debut collection published in 1997. The privilege of doing an anthology is as much in the reading that can't be shared in the selection; I enjoyed many more stories that did not find their way in. Among those that I let slip through the net were some from immigrant voices, often because they were set beyond Canada.

In marshalling my selections, I chose three stories to open the anthology that invite the reader to muse about the lives of women, about the past, about possibilities and alternative destinies. In the varied cast of characters in stories by, respectively, Cynthia Flood, Marian Engel and Ann Copeland are a stepgranddaughter; a mother of six and one-time circus performer; and a nun. The rhythm of a life lived is evoked by the order of the stories that follow, bounded by a story by Alice Munro about parental love and instinct, and one by Jane Urquhart, about the affirmation of a good life in the face of death.

In between these authors are stories of the lives of girls and women. The stories enter a girl's world, painted in contrasts by Barbara Gowdy and Mavis Gallant. Sexual awakening is portrayed by Bonnie Burnard, the certainty and ignorance of adolescence by Sandra Birdsell and spent youth by Eden Robinson. Life matures into adult relationships and responsibilities. Shani Mootoo writes of a lonely bride, Monique Proulx illustrates the knowledge of love and betrayal, Margaret Atwood the ignorance of both, and Audrey Thomas and Hélène Rioux, the practicalities of love. Women living in isolation, physical and emotional, appear in stories by Dionne Brand, Diane Schoemperlen and Bronwen Wallace. Families unravelling are intensely rendered by Linda Svendsen and Holley Rubinsky. Katherine Govier has a story of moving on, in this instance, after an affair. Elisabeth Harvor captures the singularity of being a woman. In stories of encounters between women, there is longing: sexual, as in Jane Rule's lesbian theme; for understanding, as expressed in Joyce Marshall's portrayal of a young woman's first meeting with her birth mother; and for friendship, rendered sympathetically by Ethel Wilson, gently by Frances Itani, spiritedly by Shirley Faessler. Isabel Huggan spills unwanted secrets between a mother and a daughter. The lengthening past brings forth memories, as in an account of a once forgotten rape in a story by Sharon Butala, and acceptance and regret, contrasted by the emptiness of old age in Margaret Gibson's fiction and tenderness in Dorothy Speak's. An end can also be a beginning, attested to in Carol Shields' character Hazel, a widow who comes into her own demonstrating cookware in department stores.

A caveat to the short stories in this anthology, as in all books of fiction, would read: "This is a work of fiction. Names, characters, places and incidents are either the product of the author's imagination or are used fictitiously. Any resemblance to actual events, locales or persons living or dead is purely coincidental."

I nod in deference to fact, yet I also shake my head, because I know that what abounds in fiction is the truth of life itself. In these many fictional lives, I hope the reader will have, from time to time, as I did, a frisson of recognition: "That was *my* life."

Denise Chong
June 1997

Acknowledgments

The writers in this anthology gave me great reading pleasure; I'm honoured to share their stories with others. I wish to thank several people at Penguin, including Wendy Bush-Lister, whose idea it was, Cynthia Good, who encouraged me, and Jem Bates, who saw it through. For their research and help, I thank Charlotte Engel and John Sweet. Most of all, I'd like to thank Meg Masters, who keeps fresh the joy of reading and as well, for me, the joy of writing. Thanks also to Larry Wong and Johanne Riverin.

Cynthia Flood

The Meaning of the Marriage

Mrs. Perren marries my grandfather on a Tuesday after-noon, late, so providing a wedding meal is unnecessary. The guests simply drink tea and eat pound cake. On the Tuesday morning, Mrs. Perren comes with her sister to inspect my grandfather's house. (I don't know where he is.) They find everything very clean. The oak floors shine, as do the thin high windows. Mrs. Perren's sister is enthusiastic about a man who keeps house so. (My grandfather is a saddler.) The two women see the bedroom prepared for the motherless little girl, my mother, who is now to leave her grandparents' house and come to live with her father, because he will again have a wife.

The sisters end their tour in the kitchen. Glass-fronted cup-boards go right up to the ceiling, so Mrs. Perren stands on a chair to inspect the topmost shelves. From her altitude she sees out to the back yard, where a nasty box-headed tomcat rolls about in the sun-dappled shade of the maple. She sends the sister out with a broom. Then the two leave my grandfather's house to go along to the village dressmaker.

During the many fittings of her wedding dress, the bride has been narrowly inspected, for she is not local; this unknown woman is to replace my dead grandmother and to "take on" my mother, aged five. Mrs. Perren's wedding garment is of mauve silk, for she has been a widow long enough to finish with black and dove-grey in their turn. The dress is the bride's "best" for some time after the ceremony; it moves then through a sequence of annual demotions which lead to temporary burial in the rag bag, but thence it rises to magnificent resurrection in the crazy quilt on the spare room bed. Mrs. Perren was a notable quilter.

Of the rite I know only that it was Methodist, though Mrs. Perren, I believe, adhered to a harder covenant. I don't know if my mother was at the wedding, to carry flowers for her new step-mother. At the little reception, did she chatter and clown to get the attention she was accustomed to? How did my grand-father feel on his wedding night? He was after all a veteran. His first wife had died after childbirth, taking twin girls with her to the grave, and his second, my grandmother, proved no more durable. A beautiful twenty-six, she fell victim to the same "childbed fever" as her predecessor... but her offspring survived.

Looking at my grandmother's photograph, taken in the year of her marriage and death, made me feel strange when I turned twenty-six. Years later I told my mother so. For her, she said, the strangest time had been when she herself was fifty-two. These jumping years unnerve me. Two days after my first daughter's birth, my body's temperature rose. I lay cold and sweating, could not eat, wept feebly on the nurse when she arrived at last. *Chills, headache, malaise, and anorexia are common.* In no time flat I was out of the ward, into isolation, on antibiotics. *Treatment consists of debridement by curettage and administration of penicillin;* I don't remember being debrided. The baby ran a fever too. Nobody named the poison in us.

Could my grandmother's family bring themselves to attend the wedding? My great-grandmother did make the pound cake for the occasion. I know, because over the years Mrs. Perren was repeatedly plaintive to her new husband and his little girl about its impropriety: "A fruit-cake would have been seemlier." Perhaps Mrs. Perren felt that the rite hadn't really "taken." How did my great-grandmother feel as she mixed the butter and sugar and flour, a pound of each? And did she and my great-grandfather witness the wedding that featured the same bridegroom as in their daughter's ceremony and was held in the same church? There also my grandmother's funeral had been conducted, with, as my mother always says, "the entire village in tears." This is a direct quotation from my great-grandparents, who told and retold to my mother the terrible story of their daughter's death. The narrative shaped the ends of their lives. My great-grandparents also told my mother, repeatedly, that their dead daughter was a joyful woman. My mother still repeats this to me. Her voice lingers with the phrasing. "My mother made everyone laugh with her," she says. The pound cake suggests that my great-grandmother tried to wish the marriage well (not perhaps so well as to merit candied fruit).

That is all I have for the story's opening.

Next comes a story set in the same polished kitchen that Mrs. Perren and her sister saw on the wedding morning. (I never heard a thing else about that sister.)

My mother is now nine, and wears a green checked dress. Her dark hair shines and her eyes are hazel like mine, like her dead mother's. Her cheeks are hot. In her hands is a small box, dark blue leather. The clasp is stiff, my mother's fingers determined, and the opening lid reveals a set of miniature ivory-handled cutlery. Oh perfect, she sees, for raspberries on leaf plates with girlfriends in the back yard, for imaginary cat-banquets with the strays watching lickerishly from the lower branches of the maple…The little things exactly fit her hands. (My mother now looks with disbelief at her arthritic digits.)

Who has given her this present? Its extravagance suggests

grandparents. My mother has never said. I don't think she cares. The cutlery's fate is far more important than its provenance. My step-grandmother snatches the box away. She throws it into the wood stove. With the toasting fork, she rams the gift well down into the flames. "Sinful waste," says Mrs. Perren, "and for a wicked girl like you." Burning leather smells dreadful.

Why didn't my grandfather stop her? He isn't there, in the story.

Then did my mother tell him, crying, when he came home from work? Why didn't he do something then? Or later?

Mrs. Perren did not approve of pets—I believe she was originally a farm woman—and so my mother played with the neighbours' cats and dogs, and with strays. Mrs. Perren said they were all "dirty beasts." One such was the box-headed tomcat, which turned out to have been a female rolling about desirously in heat; Tipsy's kittens caused the first full confrontation between step-mother and step-daughter. Yet my mother has always been vague about this story, never releasing details about how "she got rid of them." When—rare—she talks about her step-mother, she usually tells about the poison.

This story begins in an act of straightforward evil: Some person or persons unknown leave gobbets of raw meat daubed with strychnine up and down the village lanes. Dying cats and dogs writhe and yowl and froth. Now thirteen years old, my mother is frantic to hold the dying animals, stroke, comfort. Not unreasonably (in her narrative, my mother is always careful so to characterize the action), my step-grandmother refuses permission.

What Mrs. Perren does instead is to walk my mother out to the back lane and hold her there, forcibly, to watch one of the cats complete its death. She does this to convey to my mother the meaning of the expression "tortures of the damned," for, as Mrs. Perren says to the thirteen-year-old girl, "You do not know yet that you are wicked, and it is my business to teach you."

I can never bear this part, and break in, "But your father, why didn't he do something so she wouldn't be so mean to you?"

The answer never satisfies. "Well," my mother says mildly, "*she* was looking after me, you know. I was her job. And everybody said I was very spoiled. My grandparents—they were broken-hearted, you see. I looked exactly like my mother. My step-mother probably told my father I was difficult. I suppose I was. And he was a quiet man."

A twenty-year gap comes between this story and the next.

My mother, thirty-three years old and now really a mother, drives out from Toronto to the village with her little son, my older brother. She drives out on a pretty spring day to visit my step-grandmother. Why?

Mrs. Perren is a widow again. My grandfather died when my mother was twenty-six.

Why does my mother, fully-orphaned now, make this journey?

I still think of Mrs. Perren as Mrs. Perren; she doesn't feel like a relative. Recently, it came to me that I don't even know her first name. She must have come *from somewhere* when she and her sister walked up to that thin clean house on that Tuesday. What happened to Mr. Perren? Why were there no little Perrens? Why did she remarry, at forty? My grandfather presumably sought the stability of husband-hood and of having a mother-substitute for his child; losing *this* wife to puerperal fever was unlikely. If age was one of Mrs. Perren's charms, what were those of a middle-aged saddler with two dead wives and a young wilful child? What were her options?

My mother drives out to see her step-mother.

All I know of my step-grandmother, this woman who has so influenced my own life and my brother's, lies in these stories and questions. I tack them together into the rough shape of Mrs. Perren's ignorance and hate; as a dress for the tale, they suffice. But *he* is missing. The man is missing—my grandfather. Where is he? I do not know one single story about him. The space where he should be is a blatant absence that magnetizes me.

My mother tells me about my *great*-grandfather, about a time when he goes to England, I don't know why. While there, he makes a purchase for my great-grandmother and her five sisters: beautiful silk. (Every decent woman must have her good black dress.) To get the goods past Canadian customs, my great-grandfather wraps the gleaming yardage around his waist and so passes, unscathed though bulky, under authority's eye. This story, pleasingly, takes the edge off the intimidating probity of my fore-bears. I like to imagine my great-grandfather in his stateroom as the ship pulls in to Quebec, breathing heavily, winding the stuff round and round himself and pinning it firmly at his sides. Fur-ther back, I like to see him in the English shop—in London? in a textile city of the Midlands? —looking at the black shining rivers of fabric. "Yes, this is good. Rachel will like this."

Those sisters—my great-great-aunts, are they?—I know sto-ries about them too. One has a daughter, Sarah, who dithers in her selection of a husband until my great-great-aunt loses patience and declares, "Sarah! you will go round and round a bush and choose a crooked stick at last!" I even know that Sarah's marriage in fact turns out well. And I know that another great-great-aunt, designated to teach my mother tatting, finally takes away from her the small circle of grubby botched work and issues the verdict: "Some are not born to tat."

But I have not even a little story like these about my grand-father.

Mrs. Perren did not like the story about the smuggled silk. (In what context did she hear it?) My mother says simply, "My step-mother disapproved." Of the purchase itself? Of the deceit? Yet she used strips of that silk to edge the splendid crazy quilt she created for the spare room in my grandfather's house. How did the scraps get to Mrs. Perren? Perhaps my great-grandmother and great-great-aunts sent them along as a compliment, intended to soften; competent needlewomen themselves, they recognized, but did not possess, the talent required to conceive such an extraordinary bedcovering as my mother describes. To follow a pattern—log-cabin or wedding ring or Texas star—is one thing; to create *ex nihilo*, quite another. Buying material would be dreadful waste. No. The quilt-maker must use whatever has come to her rag bag through the years, and thence generate a design that exploits those random colours and textures, displays them to their utmost brilliance. Thus she is midwife to a metamorphosis. In her quilt, the scraps and bits and tatters fuse and then explode into a shapely galaxy of shattered stained glass.

Perhaps my great-grandmother and my great-great-aunts hoped, through this gift, to win influence over Mrs. Perren, to move her towards a gentler treatment of my mother. They must have mourned to see the little girl, beloved both for her resemblance to the dead and for her own living sweetness and dearness, unhappily exiled in that mother-loveless dwelling. But perhaps I'm just making up that supposition; perhaps none of them even knew how my mother felt—my mother, another scrap sent from house to house. Did she ever speak of her misery, then? I don't know—but for those women I can imagine possibilities, scenes, expressions. My grandfather's face I cannot see.

So now my mother is thirty-three. Her visit to Mrs. Perren may be intended to say, "You taught me I was evil. You did all you could to stop me from living my life, yet I have won. I am educated, a trained teacher. I have travelled. I am married, pretty, happy. I have borne a beautiful healthy son." The subtext is clear: "None of this is true of you, step-mother." Yet that is not the story she tells of the visit.

She only told me the full story once, when I was young. Now my mother wants me to tell her how the story ends.

During the visit, my brother is noisily vigorous, running about the neat back yard and stomping in the kitchen and wanting to throw his ball in the living room.

Mrs. Perren says to my mother, "Take him away."

My mother is angry, but she does not leave. Instead she leads my brother upstairs, to show him mummy's room when she was a little girl. Mrs. Perren does not go upstairs any more (arthritis), has not for some years; a bed has been placed for her in the dining room. So she sits, alone again, in the chair by the window. How does she pass the time today, any day? She can no longer quilt. No novels—devil's work. Perhaps Mrs. Perren reads the Bible, looks out the window and disapproves of passersby.

I can imagine thus about my step-grandmother, my great-grandfather, my great-great-aunts. I cannot imagine about my grandfather, because my imagination requires a toehold on the known world, and I know no stories about him.

Up the stairs go my mother and my brother, in the story, and as they climb they smell the musty acrid odour of stale cat excrement, stronger and stronger, nearer and nearer. In the spare room, a branch, from the maple tree beloved in my mother's youth, has pierced the window. The wind has shaken out big shards of glass, the tree has kept on growing, and now a convenient cat-bridge leads to shelter and relative warmth. Right now, as my mother and brother enter the room, they find two animals dozing on the quilt. Silk and velveteen and grosgrain and muslin and polished cotton and gingham and corduroy and chintz, triangles and rhomboids and squares in all the colours—all are smeared, all stained, rumpled. Cat fur lies thick. A drift floats, airborne, as one cat rushes out the broken window into safe leafiness. The other purrs under my delighted brother's pats. The floor is littered, sticky, with feces. The down pillows drip urine. My mother goes quickly into the other rooms on this upper floor. The cats have been everywhere.

My mother no longer remembers what she did next. In her memory, she can only find what she thought of doing.

One choice is to tell Mrs. Perren, perhaps even to help her make arrangements for pruning, glazing, cleaning. (My mother wonders if undiluted Javex would work.)

The other choice is to say nothing, to leave her step-mother stewing in her stink. My mother worries about getting my brother's co-operation, so he will not cry excitedly to Mrs. Perren, "Kitties pee on floor!" Surely, she thinks, the coming summer heat will eventually let the old nose know. Or some other visitor will come. (She herself never went to that house again.)

My mother asks me now, "Which did I do?" But I don't remember. Nor does my brother. Neither of us can tell her what she wants to know.

I wish I could tell her, but for me as a child that story had little to do with the solitary woman waiting downstairs or the sharp resentful voice saying, "Take him away." I did not care, either, about the reeking sodden floorboards in the spare room, the precious quilt ruined, the golden double featherstitching frayed. No. What I loved was the branch to the spare room, the branch where the cats ran back and forth in the moony night and through the green leaves of the day. Perhaps if that branch were sturdy, the window-hole big enough, a child might travel thus and hide in the heart of the tree, with the furry cats purring and snoozing and stretching their lithe long selves?

For me, this cat-story was just one of many from Before Me, stories told and retold by my mother and my brother, like the one about Slippers the calico, who in her first pregnancy follows my mother from room to room, sleeps on her lap and on her bed. Her labour begins as my mother prepared for a dinner party; my brother strokes and soothes the cat as my mother finishes dressing, takes up her cloak. (This wonderful garment is purple velvet, cast-off church curtains. How has my agnostic mother come by this fabric? The purple is limp, the nap gone in parts, but my mother takes scrim and shapes a high dramatic collar to show off her high-piled hair.)

Slippers struggles up and follows my mother, mewing, one scarcely-born kitten left behind in the basket and another's nose sticking out of her vagina. My brother retrieves the cat, but Slippers writhes and yowls and my brother, fearful, drops her. She runs after my mother and halfway down the stairs delivers her second kitten. My mother stops. She gathers cat and kitten into her cloak. She brings them back to the basket in her bedroom. My brother has to go downstairs and tell my father, waiting impatiently in the living room with the fire going out, that she isn't coming. She settles down with Slippers, and the kittens are born in peace. When all are safely curled by their mother, she does go to the party, where she makes a fine story out of the event and my father almost forgives her.

And another story is of the cat Johnny-come-lately, of a winter's dusk, thick snow falling, my brother by the living-room window gazing, half-dreaming with the white movement of the flakes. A red car comes along—an uncommon colour in 1930s Toronto—and stops by our house. My brother calls, "Mum, come look at the red car." The moment she appears at the window, the car opens, a black kitten is flung out, and the car flees scarlet down the street, with rooster tails of snow and exhaust whirling behind it. Johnny, who lived with our family for years, was the first animal whose death I grieved.

My mother wants me to tell her the ending of the story about the visit so she will know whether she did right or wrong. Did she obey duty or desire? Which was which? Without the memory, she cannot judge herself.

I want other knowledge. I want to know why my mother forgot my grandfather. She has never in my presence pronounced the term *Dad*, never used the words, "I remember when my father…" No snapshot or painting is extant. No letters survive, account books, diaries. No stories. But a beautiful joyous woman married him; she must have had her reasons, and I wish I knew what they were.

Did my mother feel such abandonment that when she grew up she simply obliterated him from the stones of memory? Did she unilaterally declare herself fatherless as well as motherless? Her mother was always dead, a person who existed only in stories, none told by her father. None of his words have survived. Nor has he. At this point in the story, I have said every single thing I know about him.

I'll try to imagine. Let us suppose that after my mother's birth my grandfather sits by my grandmother's bedside, looking down at her lovely face, seeing with delight his living daughter. Likely he goes away then, to tell family and friends, perhaps to thank his God for the safe deliverance this time, to sleep at night and wake joyful in the morning. But by then the dirt, the poison, is thick in her blood. She feels unwell. The doctor comes. The milk stops. The baby cries. The smells begin. *The patient is toxic and febrile, the lochia is foul-smelling, and the uterus is tender....* The young woman lies quietly. *Chills, headache, malaise, and anorexia are common. Pallor, tachycardia, and leukocytosis are the rule.* This rule holds. So as she dies my grandmother does not scream and writhe and froth like the cat, but slowly dazes and drifts, descending into a poisoned stupor (*Hemolytic anemia may develop.... With severe hemolysis and coexistent toxicity, acute renal failure is to be expected*) and so to her death. The mortality rate is then about fifty percent. But then there was neither debridement nor penicillin, so that rate did not apply.

The father sends the child off to live with her grandparents. What else to do? My great-grandparents love the baby, painfully. They live nearby. He cannot be a saddler and care for an infant on his own. Paid help is not possible. So for five years the little girl lives thus. Then—inexplicably, to such a young child—comes the alleged reunion, which is in truth a meeting with a cold bitter woman who resents her step-daughter even before they meet, who burns her present and makes her witness the agony of the cat.

In his third marriage, how came my grandfather to make such an error in judgement?

In my fifteenth summer, our plump tabby cat Mitzi with the extra toes dies on the operating table as she is being spayed. My mother collapses with grief, self-blame, rage at herself and my father for having determined that this cat should not kitten. "She mewed all the way in the car," my mother shouts, weeping, her sweating face contorted. "She didn't want to go. I made her. Because I was bigger and stronger. I took her to her death." My mother falls on the sofa and shoves her head into the cushions and hits the sofa arm repeatedly. My father and I look at each other. I start to leave the room. "You can't run away from this," he says, gripping my arm hard. "Come back to her."

Somehow the afternoon comes to its end. My mother does not make any dinner, and this is very difficult for me because my father likes no cooking but hers. Early in the evening, she goes up to the spare room in the attic and closes the door. She stays there overnight. We hear her crying from time to time, and shoving at the stiff window; finally it surrenders to her strength, with a harsh scraping rattle of glass against wood. In the spare room are stored non-working lamps, moth-nibbled blankets, magazines that my brother will sort through someday. The bed is not made up. Faded chenille covers its lunar surface. The heart of the house beats in the wrong place that night, and, though the spare room is next to mine, I gain no comfort from my mother's nearness. Thinking of her there disturbs me still.

Marian Engel

Madame Hortensia, Equilibriste

I'm all right now, though I've had my uncomfortable patches. I have six children, and I hide behind them. They're very good about it. Every year I line them up in front of the picket fence and the privet hedge and take pictures of them, which we stick in the album. They're very good about it, except Amy. Not everyone is born with a happy nature.

Sometimes I get restless and think, I'll have to be moving on, but this year, I think, I'll be spared.

The only ones of the children who know about me are the oldest, the twins Yolande and Roland. They think it's fascinating; they want to get my old albums out, and read my life like a story, but I won't let them. It's bad luck to have ambition, I tell them. It's exercising overweening pride. It's taken me all these years to get humdrum. Don't spoil it.

"Yolande," I say, when I see her posing in front of the mirrors—she's pretty as one of Charlie's Angels and she knows it, but in a nice way—"don't get ideas about yourself. The only happy people here are the ones who are ordinary." She looks at me impishly, as if I'm an old woman who doesn't know any more which end is up, but she's sweet, she always says, "Okay, Mum," and buckles down to a little school work, not too much. I don't allow them to distinguish themselves unless they can't help it.

But I get uneasy. I don't want them to know about me. I don't want them to get spoiled. I want them to lead ordinary lives, as if they were the children of some ordinary woman. Mrs. Wiggs of the Cabbage Patch, say.

We live on the outskirts of town, and it's a very small town. I don't see many people. I send the kids to the stores or phone to have what I need delivered. I call myself Mrs. Robinson. I always liked Robinson Crusoe. The only indulgence I've allowed myself is their lovely garland of names, Yolande and Roland, Amy and Gwendolyn, Abel and Fortunatus (William Fortunatus, so he won't be beaten up at school).

Mr. Robinson left some years ago, feeling somewhat overwhelmed by children and undermined by my fortune. It wouldn't have helped the children if I'd given my fortune away, so I kept it. We need it now. It's not as much as it seemed in the days when everyone was poor but me, and it wasn't my fault.

Goodness, I sound like Cardinal Newman, needing to apologize for myself. But the papers say we're in for another wave of over-achievers again and I can't bear the idea of people competing and rising above each other once more. All that battling and tattling. I'm old enough, just old enough, to see history repeating itself. Old enough too, that there won't be another Mr. Robinson. (Once there were so many. I wonder now why.) So I might as well spend my evenings writing my story down. I wish the Cantcurl carbon wouldn't roll up in the rain.

Gwendolyn won the typewriter in a colouring contest. She's out at her ballet lesson. I didn't want her to take it but they're giving them free at the Public Library now. I said I wouldn't go to the recital.

Yolande and Roland are upstairs studying for their exams. Fortie's at band rehearsal, Abel's out delivering for the drug store, Amy's the only one at home tonight. Upstairs sulking. Squeezing blackheads, likely. That's her style. She hasn't worn anything but black satin for two years. She's mourning her lost childhood, she says. They're a lovely, rowdy cheerful gang except for her. Nice normal kids.

I wish Yolande didn't want to go to Radcliffe.

I was born in St. Thomas, Ontario, the town where Jumbo died, in 1930. My parents were on the verge of being elderly, and although my tiny little father kept a tiny little shop on Main Street next to the Kineto Theatre, we did not live in St. Thomas. We only used the hospital. In fact, I have no idea whether the main street of St. Thomas is called Main Street, and someone recently informed me that the theatre was called the Kineto for one month only; it was so called during the time when I was vouchsafed my only visit to The Glovery, where my father sold handkerchiefs, kid gloves and ladies' haberdashery—underwear—exquisite as himself. It was about six feet square, a miniature emporium crammed next to the theatre marquee, and he presided over it in a morning coat and grey moleskin spats, as dapper and tidy as his white moustache.

I don't know much about my parents. They eventually vanished as one's parents do, but without leaving much documentation behind them. I don't remember any cosiness with them, they were more like indulgent grandparents; they're like "the little old lady and the little old man" in a fairy tale when I think of them, not like the gritty slip-strap mothers and shirt-sleeve fathers of Canadian fiction.

They called me Mireille.

They were old when they had me. I suppose she—her name was Sylvia, which seems unmotherly to me—was forty-five when I was born, in 1930. And he was a good ten years older.

And they lived out in the country, on the edge of a little village, quite apart from the community. He commuted to his store in a big purring Packard with a net in the roof, as grey, outside, as his spats.

They were lovely people, tiny and silver and delicate. Lovely, and it seemed to me, always in love with each other. Everything they had was dainty and soft. Even if I was only their little half-chick, they called me, as I said, Mireille, and I grew up in their house like Tom Thumb in his little nutshell of a bed, covered and clothed with cobwebs. In those days there was no business of trying to bring up the abnormal as if they were like everyone else.

I was spoiled, and I was very happy. It was hard for me to learn to walk, but nurses and doctors didn't come into it. A man in St. Thomas made me the most beautiful little contraption, half cane, half crutch, trimmed with bits of leather and silk so that it looked a little like a parasol. I hopped around the front lawn behind the cedar hedge, pushing it ahead of me. In no time at all I was mobile.

I don't think it was because of me that they lived quite apart from the community. I can't imagine them participating in the gross functions of an ordinary Canadian town, and the thought of Father putting his birthday pennies in the Rotary Box or marching in the 12th of July parade is grotesque.

They were from Toronto. Legend had it that they had met while working in office buildings across Adelaide Street from each other and had fallen in love like two toys in facing plate-glass windows. They had had, in their words, to scrimp and save in order to marry, but by the time I "came along" Father was doing well. Lacy handkerchiefs and fine underlinen were much in demand in St. Thomas, even during the Depression.

All our visitors, except for Miss Mitcham, the Anglican minister's daughter who educated me, were from Toronto: stately men and women, hatted and gloved, soft voiced; though one of my mother's sisters, Aunt Zinnia, sometimes raised her voice and hooted with laughter when she said they'd meant to call my mother not Sylvia but Salvia.

Until I was sixteen, we were very happy.

Mother was what is known as frail. Her heart was as fragile as her floating chiffon afternoon dresses. Her wrists were too fine and thin to knit the heavy khaki socks required by the Red Cross for the war effort. She worked on complicated cobwebby layettes, and otherwise devoted herself to instructing Mrs. Ruddy, the housekeeper, and a series of country girls, in the delicate maintenance of the house. She took a great many naps. Our only forays into the outside world took us to the movies. She was fond of both Shirley Temple and Myrna Loy. Esther Williams was a source of wonder to her. We went at night, chauffeured by Father. I think he spent the time playing poker, but I was not aware of the fact at the time.

I was not aware of many facts at the time.

When I was sixteen, my father was what they called "stricken" by a heart attack. I went to his funeral in a wheelchair with a plaid car rug over my knees. A number of men in black suits arrived at the house. Mother collapsed in tears. Miss Mitcham turned her whole attention to her resuscitation and my education came to an end. Soon the rest of the happy dream faded, for my mother outlived my father by only six months.

Curiously, I did not mind. I was involved in my own dream.

Cosseted, sheltered, and protected, I was yet a child, and not many children like to be sheltered. I had seen little of the world beyond the hedge, for little of it filtered into our house. We received one Toronto newspaper (which was extravagant of us, as Father's executors pointed out), *Maclean's* magazine, and *The New Yorker*. My mother's reading tended to be old romances like *The Rosary* and *Captain Blood*, copies of which sat in the glass-front bookcase in the parlour. She also liked Browning and Elizabeth of *Elizabeth and Her German Garden*. Miss Mitcham had taught me Ovid and Hesiod, a few poems of Goethe and Schiller, and how to read enough French to plough through *La Porte étroite* and *L'Education sentimentale* (Miss Mitcham's taste was sophisticated for her time and place). A little botany. A little Euclid. Mother's taste in movies was unreal to say the least, though throughout the war, news films supplied some sense that there was something beyond our hedge. And the country girls invariably smuggled magazines like *True Confessions* and *Photoplay* into the house, to read on the toilet when they were supposed to be making the beds.

The Public Library did not exist for my parents, but it did for Miss Mitcham, who was kind enough to supply me with a certain number of her favourite authors. I read Scott and Stevenson, Jane Austen and George Eliot, Virginia Woolf and Edith Wharton. Of the Canadians, Grey Owl, Marjorie Pickthall, and Archibald Lampman. We discussed the matter of E. Pauline Johnson and decided she was not refined. I think Miss Mitcham shied away from anything too athletic. I had read Mother's copies of *Freckles* and *A Girl of the Limberlost* but not been impressed by them; they were from my world.

But I was, in my strange way, athletic. I could not spend my whole time doing lessons and reading. I had no talent for knitting and embroidery and the piano was out because I could not use the soft pedal comfortably and Mother had Headaches. Unless we were having company, which we seldom did, all the afternoons of my life were free, and I set about to use them.

Where does the child acquire this impulse to distinguish herself, set herself up above other people? Especially a child who has rarely met another child, knows no one of her own age?

We had a beautiful set of tea plates for use on special occasions. They were thin and white and gold banded and in the centre there were exquisite coloured engravings of acrobats: Mme Hortensia was the one I loved; Mme Hortensia in a scarlet corset, standing on one foot on the back of a horse; Mme Hortensia, *équilibriste*. For whose profession, it seemed to me, I was admirably suited.

During those years my father came and went like a lovely silver shadow.

Equilibriste. I had to be someone, distinguish myself somehow. I could not become a musician, that was clear, for I was not allowed piano lessons. I did water-colours with Miss Mitcham and made a mess of them. My handwriting was poor. How could I be a great beauty with a frizz of carroty hair which even Mrs. Dodger, who came to the house each week to do Mother and me, couldn't make lie down without smelly pomades? I couldn't be Esther Williams. Myrna Loy. "Capitalize on your assets, Mireille," Miss Mitcham was always saying. "You have linguistic ability; use it." But I had no desire to be a writer. Nothing, perhaps, to say.

In those days, everyone, to avoid tuberculosis, went down for a nap after lunch. We lived on the edge of the village, almost in the country. I was forbidden to go beyond the hedged front lawn, but behind the house there were outbuildings, old stables and barns, and an orchard. It was in the abandoned barn, in the orchard, and along the top of the wall that separated the orchard from the farm next door that I became Mademoiselle Mirella, Equilibriste. Nobody ever saw me, or at least nobody ever told. Perhaps we were a local mystery and there was no one to tell.

Mother's little half-chick, protected and cosseted, hopped outdoors for her exercise at naptime. Clearly, she was not dying of consumption. Mother's little half-chick went into the barn and shed her long, protective skirts. Mother's little half-chick, first on the saw-horse, then on the beam, then on the hanging rope another lot of children had used for a swing…

Mother's little half-chick tailored herself scarlet corsets from an old Chinese dressing-gown; saliva'd her eyebrows and rouged her cheeks; found in the attic a frilly parasol.

Birdcage in one hand, parasol in the other, exquisite in pink silk stockings she found in a trunk: really, Mireille!

No one ever saw and no one ever knew. And then they died.

Oh, I had read Dickens, too.

Being an orphan was not what it was cracked up to be. I went to live in Toronto in a very dull house in a very dull neighbourhood. My cousin Dick worked in a bank. He had everything sold and put into trust for me. There was a good deal of money. He called my father the Jew Bootlegger.

His sisters, my cousins Betty and Nancy, tittered when I went hop-hop-hop. Aunt Zinnia put all my fragile clothes in the washing machine and ruined them. She grumbled that I used her like a maid.

In the end, I had to take matters into my own hands. I had an allowance of five dollars a week and spent it taking a taxi to a theatrical impresario. Hop-hop-hop.

This is not a moral story. It simply is not done in this country—in most countries, in fact—to succeed in one's aims almost without trying. In addition, to live almost totally cut off from the world, then to tackle its most cynical side head-on and to survive almost without injury is very immoral indeed. It's as bad as turning ploughshares into swords. Why was I not broken on the rack? I suppose because I didn't know I was supposed to be. My parents had called me Mireille and I escaped from my thick-headed cousins (though not from my cousin Dick's investment advice) before they had a chance to teach me the techniques of defeat.

From the day I met Mr. Zambala, everything was easy. He was extraordinarily kind and interested in my special abilities. He passed me along to his friend Mr. Borodino, manager of a number of night club performers, because, as he said, for a person of my refinement it was important to avoid the carny shows.

Mr. Borodino had a large, bouncing, happy family, and he took me home to live with them while we planned my career. The problem of my age was quickly solved with the discovery that my birth had never been registered; it was easy to lie about my age. Finances were a small problem, for my mother had given me her jewellery before her death, and it was good jewellery.

I had hated so-called "family" life at Aunt Zinnia's; with the Borodinos it was different. There were six children, all busy and buzzing with ideas. Chrissie was nearest my age. Unable to decide between being a seamstress and a nurse, she became my dresser and remained with me for ten years. We are still good friends.

I opened in Buffalo in October 1947, as Madame Hortensia, Equilibriste. I was supposed to be a French war widow. We thought it was better not to mention St. Thomas because of Jumbo.

Buffalo led to better things—New York, then Hollywood. In those pre-television days America was hungry for sensations, and America found them. I cut across the public imagination at just the right points and was written up in *Life* magazine.

Mr. Borodino and I spent a lot of time working up material, for it was important to avoid the grotesque. Chrissie and I fabricated costumes that were delicate and discreet. It was important to maintain an image that embodied these characteristics.

In all, my performing life lasted, as I said, for ten years. I loved most of it, for I no longer felt cut off from what I have always called "the outside world," and I received a good deal of praise. In addition, for some reason I cannot fathom, men were crazy about me: I was sent flowers and candy and invitations after every performance and grew agile at hopping away from greasy Lotharios.

All good things come to an end, however, and by 1957, my popularity waning, Chrissie dying to leave me to live with her true love, I decided to marry.

This is where my lack of experience of the real world tripped me up: I was a poor picker.

The story of my life with George ought to be veiled in obscurity. It began well and ended very, very badly. He was handsome and spoiled and for a while he called me his Dresden doll. After Yolande and Roland arrived, he began to call me his freak. At heart a good little Victorian, I could not imagine that my marriage, like so many others contracted in the fifties and sixties, would end. I began to drink and soon found that the world was eager to shut its doors on a popular curiosity. The warbling little voice I had worked up for the stage sounded obscene when I bleated my banal tragedy into telephones. Friends disappeared in droves.

Fortunately, George, revivified by freedom, was too busy with a series of new girlfriends (a lion-tamer, a theatrical agent, a blind chanteuse) to claim the children. Just as I was collapsing in a sticky puddle of self-pity, Chrissie and my lawyer persuaded me to take Roland and Yolande home to Canada and count my blessings.

I hated the idea at first, but with my savings and a stipend from George, I settled not in the modest sordidness of Aunt Zinnia's quarter, but on the edge of the Rosedale Ravine. I changed my name and took to making my forays on the outside world in a wheelchair, to avoid exhibiting my extraordinary talents. I was still attractive to men—odd how some of us have sex appeal and others don't and neither of us makes the choice—and met and married my Mr. Robinson, producing with great rapidity Gwendolyn, Amy, Abel, and Fortunatus before he left for younger pastures.

When I look back on it all, I am amazed, but I also see what is wrong. Perhaps it was the Women's Liberation Movement that taught me this. To be different, to set oneself up above other people, even to chase the Borodino boys around the edge of a Buffalo billiard table, is to become an object, a freak. As my parents' little Mireille, I was a person; as Madame Hortensia, I was as unreal, as objectified, as one of the little figures on the Porcelain de Paris plates, as people on talk shows.

My children are splendidly normal, free of the birth defects Mr. Robinson and George constitutionally feared. I live in the country now, at the edge of a small town with a good school system and plenty for the children to do. If you've seen one night club act, you've seen them all. I can no longer painlessly imagine myself hopping in disguised lingerie over the patrons' martini glasses. I do not know whence my desire to do so arose, but I wish it hadn't, for it caused me great and unnecessary pain. It is better to be plain Mrs. Robinson with one's children in front of one like a privet hedge, a picket fence. I keep my acrobatics to myself, now, and Amy worries me with her black satin.

Ann Copeland

Cloister

She hated going for permissions. One would have thought that, like most repeated exercises in any life, she would have got used to this one. She, too, had originally thought that over the years, kneeling in front of superior after superior, reciting her needs, receiving her requests, giving an account of her regularity of observance, she would have got used to it—like other rituals that originally had been a hurdle in religious life: chanting a lesson at Matins, being first chorister, preparing for chapter, reading in the refectory. But none of these, absolutely none, made her stomach churn like this monthly exercise. She was happy when the superior was sick—though she knew she shouldn't be and she felt a bit guilty about it. She was happy when the superior was away. She was happy, in fact, when any turn of Providence interfered with her obligation to summarize herself verbally to her superior and await the response.

As she sat in line outside Reverend Mother's office—any Reverend Mother, though there were better and worse—she sometimes felt she might vomit. Gradually she had developed a range of strategies for coping. Basic was that she not think of the encounter about to occur; basic also was that she not try to read. She saw others making their spiritual reading as they waited, and she wondered at her own inability. Didn't they mind this impossible task? Were they really as placid as they appeared when they emerged from the office, nodded, and headed into chapel to say the penance imposed for this month's faults? Was she the only one whose insides contracted, who felt dampness gather along her spine?

The door opened. Sister Joanne limped out, a trifle flushed, nodded toward her, and passed by into the chapel. She stared a moment at the closed office door, grasped her notebook firmly, and got up to knock.

"Yes, Sister?"

The voice from within.

Acting rapidly as she had learned was wisest, she opened the door and shut it tightly behind her. Then she knelt silently beside the superior's desk.

"Reverend Mother, may I please have your blessing?"

The slight indentation of a cross pressed on the crown of her head as the superior bent forward in response.

"I humbly beg you to renew my permissions for the following…" She moved rapidly through her list of requests for things needed: toothpaste, deodorant, an extra supply of notecards and a file for her research, a new winter nightgown, Aspirin. This part was easiest: simple material needs. The answer was yes or no. Invariably it was yes.

"Yes, Sister." Reverend Mother sat quietly, hands folded loosely in her ample black lap. Long tapering fingers with perfectly groomed nails—they always drew your attention. Hands that seemed unacquainted with manual labour.

"And Reverend Mother"—looking up from her notebook—"I have felt especially fortunate this month. My prayer life has been peaceful. I'm meditating on the gospel text for each day, as that seems most fruitful." She hated the sound of her voice. Sometimes when she got to this section of the renewal formula, she reported no graces. But she had learned it was wisest to have a few now and then; declaring one's desolation of soul had proved more nuisance than it was worth. In her curious moments she wondered what personal graces the worst community characters noted and reported; more often she regretted a prevailing sense of irony within herself that undercut her own attempts at simplicity.

"I'm glad, Sister. Meditating on the gospel always brings us close to Our Lord. And if you are experiencing a period of consolation, thank God. But remember, God sometimes allows dryness in those who are His favourite souls. We must be prepared to accept all from His hand with gratitude."

The pale elegant hands resting before her magnetized her attention momentarily until she willed to look upward, directly into the small deep-set blue eyes behind Reverend Mother's thick glasses. How could she admit that it was absolutely impossible for her to stay awake for the hour from six to seven these cold mornings, that the most dramatic New Testament texts left her dull of mind and heavy with sleepiness, longing for Father to arrive for Mass so they could move about legitimately, assemble in their places, and prepare the hymns.

"I would like to ask your permission to see Father Purcell, Reverend Mother. It's been quite a few months and I do feel the need."

She did not elaborate that need. Superiors differed. With most it was wiser to leave needs acknowledged but undetailed. For an instant her eyes slid to the fully clothed figure of the Infant of Prague on the tall filing cabinet behind Reverend Mother's desk. It had been carried in solemn procession the previous day for a special community intention. Fortunately, classroom duties had made her late for the procession so that she arrived only for the final litany in the small chapel near Reverend Mother's office. Even as a child she had disliked dolls, and this devotion—replete with costume changes for the Infant for each liturgical season—repelled her. It was one of Reverend Mother's favourites.

"Well, Sister..." The pause was long. "Let's see. You have been out quite a bit lately. And we must never become careless about our rule of cloister, difficult as that may be in today's world." She looked at the kneeling nun significantly, implying they both understood that magic measure of time out and time in that constituted a well-balanced religious life in the year of Our Lord 1965. "Would you wish to go this week? Holy Week is a particularly busy time for everyone. And you know Father will be saying Mass here on Holy Thursday."

Her heart sank. She did not want to see him there. She knew well the difficulties of maintaining any kind of private life within the cloister. Not that anyone would comment openly. But inevitably there was curiosity. Beneath its palpable silence and discretion, the house breathed a lively alertness to sounds and voices from the guest parlour. The kitchen would be notified. Ginger ale and cookies for Father. A paper doily on the plate. Reverend Mother would stop by to greet him.

"Yes, I know, Reverend Mother. But there will be so much commotion here on Holy Thursday. The procession, reposition, the special dinner. He'll have enough to think of then without my adding to it." A motive of charity—that should do it.

"True. How would you get over to see him at the university then? Can you find a companion?"

"There is a car going over tomorrow." She had checked it all out and knew that technically there was little Reverend Mother could object to in her request. Other nuns would be in the car; they would qualify as companions. Her right to a spiritual director was guaranteed by the Constitutions—a right which the

Order did not, in fact, encourage her to exercise. Not that she actually claimed Father Purcell as a spiritual director. Nothing that grandiose. He was simply an intelligent priest, one of the best educated and most understanding persons she knew. He seemed to embody a freedom of spirit; at least she felt that must be what made him so attractive to many in the Order, old and young. And he served them with astonishing fidelity: early Mass every morning, confessions before Mass, sermons—memorable ones—on Sunday. He had been doing it for years and was by now a familiar figure to most of the nuns in the province. Over the past two or three years he had done the retreat circuit in the province and somehow he could make even the Exercises come to life for those eight days. When he interpreted them, the Ignatian metaphors of warfare made sense—no small feat.

"Well, if you feel that for the good of your soul this is the time you should go, Sister, then see if there is room for you in the car. You can let me know tomorrow after breakfast, or just drop a note in my box."

Reverend Mother sat very still, hands resting quietly. She peered through her glasses, waiting. Sister Claire was familiar with that pause and she steadied herself to resist. It was the invitation to confide. She was not obliged, strictly speaking, but she was encouraged. Her inner life was her own personal affair—the Order recognized that—but then again, they had been trained since the earliest novitiate days to see all superiors as God's representatives and more—spiritual mothers whose care it was to guide their subjects toward sanctity. How could that be done without mutual trust?

"Thank you, Reverend Mother." She scanned her notes on regularity of observance, notes that fatigued her with their cumulative innocuousness. They were allowed to report only external faults. Sin was reserved for the confessional.

"Reverend Mother, I have failed in several ways this month

in observing the Rule and Constitutions. I feel I've given in to my curiosity and disedified my sisters by carelessness in religious modesty. Especially during Office I have looked around a good bit."

"Yes, Sister. A few of your sisters have mentioned this to me." Reverend Mother leaned forward slightly, raising one hand to touch the wooden crucifix in her cincture. "It is very easy to become careless about mortification of the senses. Yet Our Lord rewards those who curb their curiosity about the outer world by speaking to them within. Unless we quiet worldly curiosity and mortify the tendency to look about, we shall never hear Him when He speaks."

Sister Claire held her expression steady. The inner voice. She thought of Saint Bernard looking the other way as he passed the beauties of Lake Desanzano, Saint Somebody spitting out his tongue at the temptress. She remembered Keats' nightingale and Stevens' Ursula. God was about, that she believed. Where should they look to find Him?

"Also, Reverend Mother, I've become a bit careless about silence, especially Great Silence." Again, she did not elaborate. She knew how important these two items of Rule were to Reverend Mother: religious modesty and silence.

"Yes, Sister. Is there anything else?"

Sister Claire saw her glance at the clock on the desk. The line outside was long; that might help her cause.

"I've been wondering if you and Reverend Mother Provincial have decided whether I may accept the invitation to the Eastern Linguistics Conference in June?"

Once more she resisted the urge to elaborate her request. The invitation had come weeks ago. It was an honour. She was one of two religious invited; the others were secular scholars from name universities in the East. This meant nothing to Reverend Mother, that she well knew. In fact too much attention to such distinction could be seen as vanity or worldliness. She had to be cautious.

"I noticed last Monday, Sister, that you received a request in the mail for final acceptance or rejection. It's June when, did you say?" She picked up the small desk calendar from her blotter and carefully turned over the pages to June.

"June fifteenth to twentieth, Reverend Mother." Her right knee had begun to tingle. She had given all this information to Reverend Mother weeks ago. Shifting her weight slightly, Sister Claire fought a rising sense of irritation.

"Right during retreat. Father McDonald arrives the fourteenth."

She willed a clamp on the surge of anger exploding within. She had known right along the answer would probably be no. She had written one courteous note to the chairman apologizing for her delay and implying a conflict of plans yet to be settled. How could she say that the Provincial was a chronic procrastinator, that Reverend Mother was prone to distrust motives and see her desire to attend as self-seeking? All outgoing mail was put in Reverend Mother's box unsealed. Improprieties of tone never passed. So her letter had been brief and non-committal: then she had waited. Bided her time and bitten her tongue. She was beginning to feel acutely embarrassed about the whole affair.

"Should I notify them no, Reverend Mother?" In a way it would be a relief to be done with it all, though she wanted to attend.

"Mother Provincial will be here on Sunday, Sister. We should surely have a definite decision for you by then. Is there anything else?" She began to finger her crucifix.

"No, I don't think so, Reverend Mother. I humbly beg you to give me a penance."

"Say three Hail Mary's, Sister."

Again, the light pressure of a cross on her head. Then Sister Claire opened the door and nodded to the next in line; she headed for chapel to say the penance immediately.

The next afternoon, waiting outside Father Purcell's office, she sat quietly on the straight chair and watched the secretary. Obviously an expert in mediating between Father and both his worlds, academic and religious, she typed efficiently, ignoring Sister Claire. The telephone rang.

"No, I'm sorry, Father Purcell is busy all afternoon. Would you care to try again in the morning? He should be in after his nine o'clock class. Thank you."

Laconic replies, thought Sister Claire, so no one waiting could glean whether Father, in the inside office, is dealing with matters of soul or modern languages.

As chairman of the university's modern language department, he was highly regarded. His active professional life gave him access to a variety of thresholds and he crossed these with enviable ease. Sister Claire respected that, as did his colleagues. Several of his books were in the convent library signed with his distinctive flourish. Yet, considerable professional acclaim did not seem to have affected his religious commitment. His sermons—brief, explicit, based on the gospel—always contained some kernel of human meaning that reached her. She thought of their many laughs over breakfast—his breakfast, during the year she had been charged with serving him after he finished saying morning Mass.

The first time had been a nightmare. She had never had that charge before and although she was not particularly shy, contact with priests had been strictly limited to confessional, retreats, or Mass. She had never been sacristan.

The day before she was to take over the charge, she left Mass early and followed her predecessor through the routine. They put coffee on immediately in the tiny pantry outside the priests' dining-room.

"Father likes it *hot*," emphasized Sister Marion as she carried a small pitcher of cream from the little refrigerator into the dining-room and set it by his cereal bowl. "He'll drink three cups, the last with his cigarette after breakfast. He likes to be left alone for that. If he wants company, he'll make it clear."

They hurried downstairs to the kitchen for eggs. The cook was primed to have them ready for 7.40: two, easy over, yokes unbroken. She never failed. At Christmas and Easter Father sent for her to congratulate her in person and she loved it.

"He likes them soft but not runny," whispered Sister Marion as they panted back up the stairs and down the long, empty corridor to the priests' dining-room. "I try to make it back up here before the nuns leave chapel. Otherwise you'll get stuck on the stairs waiting for the line to pass, and the eggs get cold."

Back in the pantry she plugged in the toaster with one practised hand, took the cover off the eggs with the other, then hurried in to Father. He was halfway through his cereal. Sister Claire heard guffaws of laughter as she waited outside in the pantry buttering his toast, preparing his coffee, and mentally rehearsing her debut the following morning.

That morning had been a disaster. She had somehow got herself trapped on the staircase. As she stood there waiting for the silent black line to pass, she could almost feel the heat leaving the carefully prepared eggs. Back then to the pantry. He was already in the dining-room. She knocked lightly on the door frame and hurried in, carrying the pitcher of cream she had forgotten to put on the table after she started the coffee. Obviously, he had been waiting; the cereal was untouched.

"Good morning, Father." Not really looking at him.

"Well!" He set down his cigarette, exhaling slowly. "So you're the new one." Looking her up and down attentively, he laughed shortly. "I'm difficult, you know. But you'll grow to like me."

The cream pitcher clattered against the saucer as she set it near his right hand. A large hand, she couldn't help noticing, with blunt clean nails and blond hairs covering its back. It expertly tapped the accumulated ash from the cigarette it held.

"I'll get your eggs, Father. My name is Sister Claire."

"Yes, I know," he replied. "Don't worry. Marion primed me about you."

Hurrying back to the pantry, she grabbed the eggs and coffee in confused haste. Toast would have to wait. "Marion." For that she had not been prepared. *Marion!* Would he call her Claire? How should she respond? It irritated her not to know. The good-humoured masculine sound of his voice in the confessional before morning Mass had always pleased her with its subtle blend of intimacy and respect. This was somehow different.

She had bungled through that morning—burnt toast, cold eggs, embarrassed inexperience—and had escaped as fast as she could, angry at herself and at him. Bristling. She couldn't stand him. She had not been prepared to feel anything in executing her charge except the usual nervousness at beginning something new. Instead, he bothered her. He teased her, making her feel awkward and embarrassed. His tone struck her as annoyingly familiar, and she left the dining-room feeling hot, confused, vaguely troubled or exhilarated, relieved to be done with it for the morning. Then the pressures of the school day would claim her consciousness—until the next morning came and she knelt through Mass with half her mind anticipating what was to come afterward.

Yet, as days passed and she got beyond the toast-burning stage, he grew strangely deferential. He asked her opinion. He refused to let her be overly serious, but when they discovered a common interest in linguistics, he talked about it with her. They discussed new approaches to language. He seemed to respect her mind. Gradually she concluded that his initial aggressiveness had been a manoeuvre to shake her preconceptions so that he might talk to her simply as a person, regardless of her habit. Or perhaps her own judgment of what constituted aggressiveness was not to be trusted. She was inexperienced in such areas; she distrusted her responses, for she was aware of her own highly conditioned outlook.

His approach flattered her. She began, gradually, to look forward to those brief daily encounters, planning ahead what she might talk to him about the next day. Then, after a year, her charge had been changed. Now no longer the easy casualness of assigned task and daily meeting: she had to ask permission and make appointments. *That* she hated.

"Father will see you now, Sister Claire." The secretary nodded toward the closed door and resumed her typing.

When she entered he was leaning way back in his chair, feet on the desk. It was a small office, rather dark, lined with crammed bookcases and filing cabinets. A faint smell—the mixture of newsprint, tobacco, and other indefinable odours—met her. Next to his feet, the desk was littered with loosely stacked papers, batches of mail, unemptied ash-trays, a telephone. On the floor beside the desk lay a newspaper folded carelessly, as if just dropped there.

"Come on in, Claire." He waved her toward the straight chair near the desk. "Make yourself comfortable." Then he surveyed her a bit closely through the smoke he was calmly exhaling. "Want a cigarette?"

It was a joke between them. She laughed and quickly sat down, remembering that yes she had shut the door behind her. Surely the secretary knew how off-hand Father could be. Still, it was habit with her to remember what doors she had shut and which were still open.

"Mmmmm." He drew deeply on the cigarette with exaggerated pleasure. "Few satisfactions like it, Claire. You women don't know what you're missing. It helps one love one's neighbour to see him through a cloud of smoke!" Three perfectly symmetrical rings glided softly upward. She understood that if she said yes he would simply give her one and light it gallantly for her. This knowledge alone freed her of any such desire. Besides, she had never been a smoker.

"Well, Claire, you're looking a bit peaked. How's life treating you?"

His way of asking disarmed her momentarily and made her want to talk.

"Really, Father, you know just about how it goes. I'm still waiting for the answer about the Conference."

He slammed down both feet and stood up abruptly. "That's part of it, is it? By God I wish they'd wake up!" Moving out from behind the desk and rustling the newspaper as he brushed by it, he stalked about the small office. "Do you mean to say that Provincial of yours still hasn't made up her mind about such a simple request? Why on earth is there any problem?"

She felt again the ridiculous explosion of hopelessness and anger within. She had thought it well under control—had, in fact, prayed hard to be spared showing how strongly she felt about this. Why had she brought it up immediately? It was stupid to get so upset. Yet the fact was that she could not reconcile herself just to writing off the whole matter as God's Will.

What galled her especially was the Order's apparent blindness to its own best interests. "Make unto yourselves friends of the mammon of iniquity...." Not that this was the mammon of iniquity. Used wisely, however, the Conference could be a great help to the Order in planning future programs for its own schools as well as developing contacts with the larger professional world outside. She knew that probably Father Purcell had put in a good word for her. Surely it was ultimately due to him that she had been invited. Of course he never told her this outright; he was delicate about such matters. But she surmised.

"You know how it is with us, Father. And you know only too well the limits of Mother Provincial. To her it's simply not important. She's busy preparing her report for the next General Chapter." She rested one elbow on the desk and succumbed to a sudden rush of weariness. It was all out of proportion to the question at hand and she knew it, but she felt intensely tired and discouraged.

"Look, Claire"—he stopped squarely in front of her—"it isn't a case of a religious principle being at stake. It's just a question of common sense. Are they afraid they'll lose you if they let you out?"

She did not answer. The question did not really seem to touch her. What did touch her was the overpowering sense of hollowness that yawned inside her—like the hunger that came after the long Lenten fast, or the strange silent blank that opened within her at the end of the school year when she went back to clean her classroom. Empty desks, empty closets, nameless faceless room. Cherished identities vanished, personal challenge dead. It was too suddenly quiet, too totally empty. Later on in the summer that emptiness would turn a different way and begin to feel familiar and deeply peaceful to her. Then, even the tiny particles of dust suspended lazily in the slats of late afternoon sun across empty varnished desks would become warm silent friends of her own summer solitude. But that came later. Before that stage there was this kind of emptiness....

Deep inside she could feel now the beginning of tears and she prayed for composure. His understanding touched her; blindness was easier to handle.

"Well, anyway...." She stopped, swallowing. The lump in her throat felt monstrous. There must be another topic, some way to turn their attention from her. She felt him looking at her and longed for instant invisibility. He was a big man, squarely built. Early middle age seemed only to have intensified the impression of solid strength his body conveyed. She felt the power of that body. "There's not a thing more I can do, so we might as well forget about it. How are things over here? Have you settled your plans for the European trip this summer?" Gulping desperately, she wrenched her mind to another focus. It infuriated her to be held in such a vise of emotion. Had she expected it, she never would have come.

He glanced at her quickly, then started moving about the office again as he lit another cigarette. "It's pretty well set. First the conference in Lucerne—that looks promising. Spatz will be there to elaborate his new theory of vowel development. And after that I'm on my own. I plan to spend a lot of time in Spain this trip."

She thought herself kneeling before Reverend Mother wondering if she would get permission to travel ten miles for an official visit with a friend. Beneath clanging emotions lay the other dull familiar ache of consciousness—the consciousness of irony.

"Do you have friends there?"

"One or two. One especially interesting one...." He paused in front of her, blew out the smoke, and grinned again broadly. "Met her during my last sabbatical. I never dreamed she'd be in Spain six years later. But there she is! So we'll look her up at some point. Then there are several friends from the scholasticate, God help us. We'll find out what we've all turned into." He swung away again. "That's what you need, Claire! A European trip. Fat chance." He snorted and stopped behind her.

It was too much. The lump in her throat grew larger and heavier—first like a wad of cotton she could manage with care, then a marble, then an orange, then a rock that would neither melt nor budge. It would all be over shortly. Bending her head slightly forward, she rested it on her clenched fist and closed her eyes. The tears came—burning, rapid. Hot all over with embarrassment and the effort to control, she sensed his silent form behind her and couldn't bear to look. Just to breathe was a struggle.

"I'm, I'm sorry." Hearing her own ugly choking sound, she gave up.

The silence in the room, heavy and smothering, was broken only by her gasping movements. The hard wood of the desk's surface pressed against her elbow, while from outside came the faint rat-a-tat-tat of the secretary's typing. Tears ran down her plastic guimpe and she thought briefly of what a mess she would be when it was over. Then, through thick emotions, the lump sticking in her throat, the gulps for breath, through her perspiring sense of disintegrating order and clumsy discomfort, she felt a prop. Gently, it held her fast. Closing over her fist so that it grazed her cheek, she felt the rougher texture of a firm, comforting hand, a hand whose male tobacco smell penetrated even her clogged consciousness. The arm was tight around her from behind.

Two swings of response vibrated wildly through her tautness—spiralling, subsiding, rising again, fading in a confused blur of contradiction and longing: comfort, panic, comfort. First, a welcome relenting of strained will. Then, a stiffening again beneath the wakeful eye of consciousness that warned: be careful, be careful. She felt his strength holding her and she tried to relent or resist. Impossible either way.

"Now, Claire." The voice was gentle, understanding. She remembered the early morning confessional. It had something of that intimacy, but more. She felt herself a cumbersome confusion of starch and veil. Beneath that—real panic. She could not answer. Nothing was clear. Stilling the urge to react openly, she waited to see.

"Claire." He came around in front of her, bending down, looking close at her messy face. On the breath, tobacco. She could feel it, faintly warm. And some other smell, vaguely sweet and very clean. "You're too tense."

She barely grasped the words; her panic was too deep. Then, on her back, she felt the slightest pressure. He had slipped his other hand under her veil and it pressed beneath her shoulder blades, large and steady. Through the thickness of serge, its power and warmth seemed to press reassurance into her.

As if some secret spot had been touched, some unsuspected reserve spot of her own, resistance rushed through her body, just enough to act. She pushed him back urgently and tried to stand up. Only one thought drummed now at her pounding temples and made her powerful. He did not resist; in fact, after a swift glance at her, he stood back and waited for her to move.

It was embarrassing. There was little to say. Was he merely offering comfort? That question she could not ask. It was not comfort. She took out her white handkerchief and silently mopped, straightening her headdress as she did so.

He had turned away and was walking toward the window, lighting another cigarette. It was over. She sensed his reading of her profound rejection. It was over.

"Anyhow…" Somehow the burden was on her to pick up the thread. She stood up and grasped the edge of the desk, trying to feel and look in command. Perspiration trickled down her back and her stomach churned. "I do hope you have a good trip." It sounded lame. Stupid. Silly. She heard it. What did it matter?

He stood, back to her, rhythmically exhaling, and giving her time to compose herself. She glanced at the black breadth of shoulders and briefly felt their enigma. She knew she had to go. Quickly.

"Okay, Claire." He turned. His face was serious, quiet, slightly flushed. He came toward her, one hand in his pocket, the other holding the cigarette. She was already at the door. Opening it deftly for her, he nodded toward the secretary outside as she glanced up inquiringly.

"I'll send you a card from Spain." His voice was steady and kind. Why did she feel so angry?

"Thank you, Father." She was aware of the secretary's listening presence. "Have a good trip." Her voice, she could hear it, was barely under control. Thin and light, it was the sound of a stranger from far off hollowing through the opposite end of a tube.

As she turned and walked past the secretary's desk, she missed hearing the closing click of his office door and she registered vaguely that he must have business in the outside office.

Then she glanced at her watch. In fifteen minutes the car would be leaving. There was just time to find a ladies' room and clear away the outer traces of turmoil, lest she feel the pressure of her companions' discretion as they carefully looked away from her red eyes and smudges.

Tightening her cincture as she went, she moved purposefully down the long corridor. Her steps grew quicker and quicker. Near the end, she paused before a door marked by the silhouette of a female. Then, grasping its handle, she pushed open the door and went in.

Alice Munro

Miles City, Montana

My father came across the field carrying the body of the boy who had been drowned. There were several men together, returning from the search, but he was the one carrying the body. The men were muddy and exhausted, and walked with their heads down, as if they were ashamed. Even the dogs were dispirited, dripping from the cold river. When they all set out, hours before, the dogs were nervy and yelping, the men tense and determined, and there was a constrained, unspeakable excitement about the whole scene. It was understood that they might find something horrible.

The boy's name was Steve Gauley. He was eight years old. His hair and clothes were mud-coloured now and carried some bits of dead leaves, twigs, and grass. He was like a heap of refuse that had been left out all winter. His face was turned in to my father's chest, but I could see a nostril, an ear, plugged up with greenish mud.

I don't think so. I don't think I really saw all this. Perhaps I saw my father carrying him, and the other men following along, and the dogs, but I would not have been allowed to get close enough to see something like mud in his nostril. I must have heard someone talking about that and imagined that I saw it. I see his face unaltered except for the mud—Steve Gauley's familiar, sharp-honed, sneaky-looking face—and it wouldn't have been like that; it would have been bloated and changed and perhaps muddied all over after so many hours in the water.

To have to bring back such news, such evidence, to a waiting family, particularly a mother, would have made searchers move heavily, but what was happening here was worse. It seemed a worse shame (to hear people talk) that there was no mother, no woman at all—no grandmother or aunt, or even a sister—to receive Steve Gauley and give him his due of grief. His father was a hired man, a drinker but not a drunk, an erratic man without being entertaining, not friendly but not exactly a trouble-maker. His fatherhood seemed accidental, and the fact that the child had been left with him when the mother went away, and that they continued living together, seemed accidental. They lived in a steep-roofed, grey-shingled hillbilly sort of house that was just a bit better than a shack—the father fixed the roof and put supports under the porch, just enough and just in time—and their life was held together in a similar manner; that is, just well enough to keep the Children's Aid at bay. They didn't eat meals together or cook for each other, but there was food. Sometimes the father would give Steve money to buy food at the store, and Steve was seen to buy quite sensible things, such as pancake mix and macaroni dinner.

I had known Steve Gauley fairly well. I had not liked him more often than I had liked him. He was two years older than I was. He would hang around our place on Saturdays, scornful of whatever I was doing but unable to leave me alone. I couldn't be on the swing without him wanting to try it, and if I wouldn't give it up he came and pushed me so that I went crooked. He teased the dog. He got me into trouble—deliberately and maliciously, it seemed to me afterward—by daring me to do things I wouldn't have thought of on my own: digging up the potatoes to see how big they were when they were still only the size of marbles, and pushing over the stacked firewood to make a pile we could jump off. At school, we never spoke to each other. He was solitary, though not tormented. But on Saturday mornings, when I saw his thin, self-possessed figure sliding through the cedar hedge, I knew I was in for something and he would decide what. Sometimes it was all right. We pretended we were cowboys who had to tame wild horses. We played in the pasture by the river, not far from the place where Steve drowned. We were horses and riders both, screaming and neighing and bucking and waving whips of tree branches beside a little nameless river that flows into the Saugeen in southern Ontario.

The funeral was held in our house. There was not enough room at Steve's father's place for the large crowd that was expected because of the circumstances. I have a memory of the crowded room but no picture of Steve in his coffin, or of the minister, or of wreaths of flowers. I remember that I was holding one flower, a white narcissus, which must have come from a pot somebody forced indoors, because it was too early for even the forsythia bush or the trilliums and marsh marigolds in the woods. I stood in a row of children, each of us holding a narcissus. We sang a children's hymn, which somebody played on our piano: "When He Cometh, When He Cometh, to Make Up His Jewels." I was wearing white ribbed stockings, which were disgustingly itchy, and wrinkled at the knees and ankles. The feeling of these stockings on my legs is mixed up with another feeling in my memory. It is hard to describe. It had to do with my parents. Adults in general but my parents in particular. My father, who had carried Steve's body from the river, and my mother, who must have done most of the arranging of this funeral. My father in his dark-blue suit and my mother in her brown velvet dress with the creamy satin collar. They stood side by side opening and closing their mouths for the hymn, and I stood removed from them, in the row of children, watching. I felt a furious and sickening disgust. Children sometimes have an excess of disgust concerning adults. The size, the lumpy shapes, the bloated power. The breath, the coarseness, the hairiness, the horrid secretions. But this was more. And the accompanying anger had nothing sharp and self-respecting about it. There was no release, as when I would finally bend and pick up a stone and throw it at Steve Gauley. It could not be understood or expressed, though it died down after a while into a heaviness, then just a taste, an occasional taste—a thin, familiar misgiving.

Twenty years or so later, in 1961, my husband, Andrew, and I got a brand-new car, our first—that is, our first brand-new. It was a Morris Oxford, oyster-coloured (the dealer had some fancier name for the colour)—a big small car, with plenty of room for us and our two children. Cynthia was six and Meg three and a half. Andrew took a picture of me standing beside the car. I was wearing white pants, a black turtleneck, and sunglasses. I lounged against the car door, canting my hips to make myself look slim.

"Wonderful," Andrew said. "Great. You look like Jackie Kennedy." All over this continent probably, dark-haired, reasonably slender young women were told, when they were stylishly dressed or getting their pictures taken, that they looked like Jackie Kennedy.

Andrew took a lot of pictures of me, and of the children, our house, our garden, our excursions and possessions. He got copies made, labelled them carefully, and sent them back to his mother and his aunt and uncle in Ontario. He got copies for me to send to my father, who also lived in Ontario, and I did so, but less regularly than he sent his. When he saw pictures he thought I had already sent lying around the house, Andrew was perplexed and annoyed. He liked to have this record go forth.

That summer, we were presenting ourselves, not pictures. We were driving back from Vancouver, where we lived, to Ontario, which we still called "home," in our new car. Five days to get there, ten days there, five days back. For the first time, Andrew had three weeks' holiday. He worked in the legal department at B.C. Hydro.

On a Saturday morning, we loaded suitcases, two thermos bottles—one filled with coffee and one with lemonade—some fruit and sandwiches, picture books and colouring books, crayons, drawing pads, insect repellent, sweaters (in case it got cold in the mountains), and our two children into the car. Andrew locked the house, and Cynthia said ceremoniously, "Goodbye, house."

Meg said, "Goodbye, house." Then she said, "Where will we live now?"

"It's not goodbye forever," said Cynthia. "We're coming back. Mother! Meg thought we weren't ever coming back!"

"I did not," said Meg, kicking the back of my seat.

Andrew and I put on our sunglasses, and we drove away, over the Lions Gate Bridge and through the main part of Vancouver. We shed our house, the neighbourhood, the city, and—at the crossing point between Washington and British Columbia—our country. We were driving east across the United States, taking the most northerly route, and would cross into Canada again at Sarnia, Ontario. I don't know if we chose this route because the Trans-Canada Highway was not completely finished at the time or if we just wanted the feeling of driving through a foreign, a very slightly foreign, country—that extra bit of interest and adventure.

We were both in high spirits. Andrew congratulated the car several times. He said he felt so much better driving it than our old car, a 1951 Austin that slowed down dismally on the hills and had a fussy-old-lady image. So Andrew said now.

"What kind of image does this one have?" said Cynthia. She listened to us carefully and liked to try out new words such as "image." Usually she got them right.

"Lively," I said. "Slightly sporty. It's not show-off."

"It's sensible, but it has class," Andrew said. "Like my image."

Cynthia thought that over and said with a cautious pride, "That means like you think you want to be, Daddy?"

As for me, I was happy because of the shedding. I loved taking off. In my own house, I seemed to be often looking for a place to hide—sometimes from the children but more often from the jobs to be done and the phone ringing and the sociability of the neighbourhood. I wanted to hide so that I could get busy at my real work, which was a sort of wooing of distant parts of myself. I lived in a state of siege, always losing just what I wanted to hold on to. But on trips there was no difficulty. I could be talking to Andrew, talking to the children and looking at whatever they wanted me to look at—a pig on a sign, a pony in a field, a Volkswagen on a revolving stand—and pouring lemonade into plastic cups, and all the time those bits and pieces would be flying together inside me. The essential composition would be achieved. This made me hopeful and lighthearted. It was being a watcher that did it. A watcher, not a keeper.

We turned east at Everett and climbed into the Cascades. I showed Cynthia our route on the map. First I showed her the map of the whole United States, which showed also the bottom part of Canada. Then I turned to the separate maps of each of the states we were going to pass through. Washington, Idaho, Montana, North Dakota, Minnesota, Wisconsin. I showed her the dotted line across Lake Michigan, which was the route of the ferry we would take. Then we would drive across Michigan to the bridge that linked the United States and Canada at Sarnia, Ontario. Home.

Meg wanted to see, too.

"You won't understand," said Cynthia. But she took the road atlas into the back seat.

"Sit back," she said to Meg. "Sit still. I'll show you."

I could hear her tracing the route for Meg, very accurately, just as I had done it for her. She looked up all the states' maps, knowing how to find them in alphabetical order.

"You know what that line is?" she said. "It's the road. That line is the road we're driving on. We're going right along this line."

Meg did not say anything.

"Mother, show me where we are right this minute," said Cynthia.

I took the atlas and pointed out the road through the mountains, and she took it back and showed it to Meg. "See where the road is all wiggly?" she said. "It's wiggly because there are so many turns in it. The wiggles are the turns." She flipped some pages and waited a moment. "Now," she said, "show me where we are." Then she called to me, "Mother, she understands! She pointed to it! Meg understands maps!"

It seems to me now that we invented characters for our children. We had them firmly set to play their parts. Cynthia was bright and diligent, sensitive, courteous, watchful. Sometimes we teased her for being too conscientious, too eager to be what we in fact depended on her to be. Any reproach or failure, any rebuff, went terribly deep with her. She was fair-haired, fair-skinned, easily showing the effect of the sun, raw winds, pride, or humiliation. Meg was more solidly built, more reticent—not rebellious but stubborn sometimes, mysterious. Her silences seemed to us to show her strength of character, and her negatives were taken as signs of an imperturbable independence. Her hair was brown, and we cut it in straight bangs. Her eyes were a light hazel, clear and dazzling.

We were entirely pleased with these characters, enjoying the contradictions as well as the confirmations of them. We disliked the heavy, the uninventive, approach to being parents. I had a dread of turning into a certain kind of mother—the kind whose body sagged, who moved in a woolly-smelling, milky-smelling fog, solemn with trivial burdens. I believed that all the attention these mothers paid, their need to be burdened, was the cause of colic, bed-wetting, asthma. I favoured another approach—the mock desperation, the inflated irony of the professional mothers who wrote for magazines. In those magazine pieces, the children were splendidly self-willed, hard-edged, perverse, indomitable. So were the mothers, through their wit, indomitable. The real-life mothers I warmed to were the sort who would phone up and say, "Is my embryo Hitler by any chance over at your house?" They cackled clear above the milky fog.

We saw a dead deer strapped across the front of a pick-up truck.

"Somebody shot it," Cynthia said. "Hunters shoot the deer."

"It's not hunting season yet," Andrew said. "They may have hit it on the road. See the sign for deer crossing?"

"I would cry if we hit one," Cynthia said sternly.

I had made peanut-butter-and-marmalade sandwiches for the children and salmon-and-mayonnaise for us. But I had not put any lettuce in, and Andrew was disappointed.

"I didn't have any," I said.

"Couldn't you have got some?"

"I'd have had to buy a whole head of lettuce just to get enough for sandwiches, and I decided it wasn't worth it."

This was a lie. I had forgotten.

"They're a lot better with lettuce."

"I didn't think it made that much difference." After a silence, I said, "Don't be mad."

"I'm not mad, I like lettuce on sandwiches."

"I just didn't think it mattered that much."

"How would it be if I didn't bother to fill up the gas tank?"

"That's not the same thing."

"Sing a song," said Cynthia. She started to sing:

"Five little ducks went out one day,
Over the hills and far away.
One little duck went
'Quack-quack-quack.'
Four little ducks came swimming back."

Andrew squeezed my hand and said, "Let's not fight."

"You're right. I should have got lettuce."

"It doesn't matter that much."

I wished that I could get my feelings about Andrew to come together into a serviceable and dependable feeling. I had even tried writing two lists, one of things I liked about him, one of things I disliked—in the cauldron of intimate life, things I loved and things I hated—as if I hoped by this to prove something, to come to a conclusion one way or the other. But I gave it up when I saw that all it proved was what I already knew—that I had violent contradictions. Sometimes the very sound of his footsteps seemed to me tyrannical, the set of his mouth smug and mean, his hard, straight body a barrier interposed—quite consciously, even dutifully, and with a nasty pleasure in its masculine authority—between me and whatever joy or lightness I could get in life. Then, with not much warning, he became my good friend and most essential companion. I felt the sweetness of his light bones and serious ideas, the vulnerability of his love, which I imagined to be much purer and more straightforward than my own. I could be greatly moved by an inflexibility, a harsh propriety, that at other times I scorned. I would think how humble he was, really, taking on such a ready-made role of husband, father, breadwinner, and how I myself in comparison was really a secret monster of egotism. Not so secret, either—not from him.

At the bottom of our fights, we served up what we thought were the ugliest truths. "I know there is something basically selfish and basically untrustworthy about you," Andrew once said. "I've always known it. I also know that that is why I fell in love with you."

"Yes," I said, feeling sorrowful but complacent.

"I know that I'd be better off without you."

"Yes. You would."

"You'd be happier without me."

"Yes."

And finally—finally—racked and purged, we clasped hands and laughed, laughed at those two benighted people, ourselves. Their grudges, their grievances, their self-justification. We leapfrogged over them. We declared them liars. We would have wine with dinner, or decide to give a party.

I haven't seen Andrew for years, don't know if he is still thin, has gone completely grey, insists on lettuce, tells the truth, or is hearty and disappointed.

We stayed the night in Wenatchee, Washington, where it hadn't rained for weeks. We ate dinner in a restaurant built about a tree—not a sapling in a tub but a tall, sturdy cottonwood. In the early-morning light, we climbed out of the irrigated valley, up dry, rocky, very steep hillsides that would seem to lead to more hills, and there on the top was a wide plateau, cut by the great

Spokane and Columbia rivers. Grainland and grassland, mile after mile. There were straight roads here, and little farming towns with grain elevators. In fact, there was a sign announcing that this county we were going through, Douglas County, had the second-highest wheat yield of any county in the United States. The towns had planted shade trees. At least, I thought they had been planted, because there were no such big trees in the countryside.

All this was marvellously welcome to me. "Why do I love it so much?" I said to Andrew. "Is it because it isn't scenery?"

"It reminds you of home," said Andrew. "A bout of severe nostalgia." But he said this kindly.

When we said "home" and meant Ontario, we had very different places in mind. My home was a turkey farm, where my father lived as a widower, and though it was the same house my mother had lived in, had papered, painted, cleaned, furnished, it showed the effects now of neglect and of some wild sociability. A life went on in it that my mother could not have predicted or condoned. There were parties for the turkey crew, the gutters and pluckers, and sometimes one or two of the young men would be living there temporarily, inviting their own friends and having their own impromptu parties. This life, I thought, was better for my father than being lonely, and I did not disapprove, had certainly no right to disapprove. Andrew did not like to go there, naturally enough, because he was not the sort who could sit around the kitchen table with the turkey crew, telling jokes. They were intimidated by him and contemptuous of him, and it seemed to me that my father, when they were around, had to be on their side. And it wasn't only Andrew who had trouble. I could manage those jokes, but it was an effort.

I wished for the days when I was little, before we had the turkeys. We had cows, and sold the milk to the cheese factory. A turkey farm is nothing like as pretty as a dairy farm or a sheep farm. You can see that the turkeys are on a straight path to becoming frozen carcasses and table meat. They don't have the pretence of a life of their own, a browsing idyll, that cattle have, or pigs in the dappled orchard. Turkey barns are long, efficient buildings—tin sheds. No beams or hay or warm stables. Even the smell of guano seems thinner and more offensive than the usual smell of stable manure. No hints there of hay coils and rail fences and songbirds and the flowering hawthorn. The turkeys were all let out into one long field, which they picked clean. They didn't look like great birds there but like fluttering laundry.

Once, shortly after my mother died, and after I was married—in fact, I was packing to join Andrew in Vancouver—I was at home alone for a couple of days with my father. There was a freakishly heavy rain all night. In the early light, we saw that the turkey field was flooded. At least, the low-lying parts of it were flooded—it was like a lake with many islands. The turkeys were huddled on these islands. Turkeys are very stupid. (My father would say, "You know a chicken? You know how stupid a chicken is? Well, a chicken is an Einstein compared with a turkey.") But they had managed to crowd to higher ground and avoid drowning. Now they might push each other off, suffocate each other, get cold and die. We couldn't wait for the water to go down. We went out in an old row-boat we had. I rowed and my father pulled the heavy, wet turkeys into the boat and we took them to the barn. It was still raining a little. The job was difficult and absurd and very uncomfortable. We were laughing. I was happy to be working with my father. I felt close to all hard, repetitive, appalling work, in which the body is finally worn out, the mind sunk (though sometimes the spirit can stay marvellously light), and I was homesick in advance for this life and this place. I thought that if Andrew could see me there in the rain, red-handed, muddy, trying to hold on to turkey legs and row the boat at the same time, he would only want to get me out of there and make me forget about it. This raw life angered him. My attachment to it angered him. I thought that I shouldn't have married him. But who else? One of the turkey crew?

And I didn't want to stay there. I might feel bad about leaving, but I would feel worse if somebody made me stay.

Andrew's mother lived in Toronto, in an apartment building looking out on Muir Park. When Andrew and his sister were both at home, his mother slept in the living room. Her husband, a doctor, had died when the children were still too young to go to school. She took a secretarial course and sold her house at Depression prices, moved to this apartment, managed to raise her children, with some help from relatives—her sister Caroline, her brother-in-law Roger. Andrew and his sister went to private schools and to camp in the summer.

"I suppose that was courtesy of the Fresh Air fund?" I said once, scornful of his claim that he had been poor. To my mind, Andrew's urban life had been sheltered and fussy. His mother came home with a headache from working all day in the noise, the harsh light of a department-store office, but it did not occur to me that hers was a hard or admirable life. I don't think she herself believed that she was admirable—only unlucky. She worried about her work in the office, her clothes, her cooking, her children. She worried most of all about what Roger and Caroline would think.

Caroline and Roger lived on the east side of the park, in a handsome stone house. Roger was a tall man with a bald, freckled head, a fat, firm stomach. Some operation on his throat had deprived him of his voice—he spoke in a rough whisper. But everybody paid attention. At dinner once in the stone house—where all the dining-room furniture was enormous, darkly glowing, palatial—I asked him a question. I think it had to do with Whittaker Chambers, whose story was then appearing in the *Saturday Evening Post*. The question was mild in tone, but he guessed its subversive intent and took to calling me Mrs. Gromyko, referring to what he alleged to be my "sympathies." Perhaps he really craved an adversary, and could not find one. At that dinner, I saw Andrew's hand tremble as he lit his mother's cigarette. His Uncle Roger had paid for Andrew's education, and was on the board of directors of several companies.

"He is just an opinionated old man," Andrew said to me later. "What is the point of arguing with him?"

Before we left Vancouver, Andrew's mother had written, "Roger seems quite intrigued by the idea of your buying a small car!" Her exclamation mark showed apprehension. At that time, particularly in Ontario, the choice of a small European car over a large American car could be seen as some sort of declaration— a declaration of tendencies Roger had been sniffing after all along.

"It isn't that small a car," said Andrew huffily.

"That's not the point," I said. "The point is, it isn't any of his business!"

We spent the second night in Missoula. We had been told in Spokane, at a gas station, that there was a lot of repair work going on along Highway 2, and that we were in for a very hot, dusty drive, with long waits, so we turned onto the interstate and drove through Coeur d'Alene and Kellogg into Montana. After Missoula, we turned south toward Butte, but detoured to see Helena, the state capital. In the car, we played Who Am I?

Cynthia was somebody dead, and an American, and a girl. Possibly a lady. She was not in a story. She had not been seen on television. Cynthia had not read about her in a book. She was not anybody who had come to the kindergarten, or a relative of any of Cynthia's friends.

"Is she human?" said Andrew, with a sudden shrewdness.

"No! That's what you forgot to ask!"

"An animal," I said reflectively.

"Is that a question? Sixteen questions!"

"No, it is not a question. I'm thinking. A dead animal."

"It's the deer," said Meg, who hadn't been playing.

"That's not fair!" said Cynthia. "She's not playing!"

"What deer?" said Andrew.

I said, "Yesterday."

"The day before," said Cynthia. "Meg wasn't playing. Nobody got it."

"The deer on the truck," said Andrew.

"It was a lady deer, because it didn't have antlers, and it was an American and it was dead," Cynthia said.

Andrew said, "I think it's kind of morbid, being a dead deer."

"I got it," said Meg.

Cynthia said, "I think I know what morbid is. It's depressing."

Helena, an old silver-mining town, looked forlorn to us even in the morning sunlight. Then Bozeman and Billings, not forlorn in the slightest—energetic, strung-out towns, with miles of blinding tinsel fluttering over used-car lots. We got too tired and hot even to play Who Am I? These busy, prosaic cities reminded me of similar places in Ontario, and I thought about what was really waiting there—the great tombstone furniture of Roger and Caroline's dining room, the dinners for which I must iron the children's dresses and warn them about forks, and then the other table a hundred miles away, the jokes of my father's crew. The pleasures I had been thinking of—looking at the countryside or drinking a Coke in an old-fashioned drugstore with fans and a high, pressed-tin ceiling—would have to be snatched in between.

"Meg's asleep," Cynthia said. "She's so hot. She makes me hot in the same seat with her."

"I hope she isn't feverish," I said, not turning around.

What are we doing this for, I thought, and the answer came—

to show off. To give Andrew's mother and my father the pleasure of seeing their grandchildren. That was our duty. But beyond that we wanted to show them something. What strenuous children we were, Andrew and I, what relentless seekers of approbation. It was as if at some point we had received an unforgettable, indigestible message—that we were far from satisfactory, and that the most commonplace success in life was probably beyond us. Roger dealt out such messages, of course—that was his style—but Andrew's mother, my own mother and father couldn't have meant to do so. All they meant to tell us was "Watch out. Get along." My father, when I was in high school, teased me that I was getting to think I was so smart I would never find a boyfriend. He would have forgotten that in a week. I never forgot it. Andrew and I didn't forget things. We took umbrage.

"I wish there was a beach," said Cynthia.

"There probably is one," Andrew said. "Right around the next curve."

"There isn't any curve," she said, sounding insulted.

"That's what I mean."

"I wish there was some more lemonade."

"I will just wave my magic wand and produce some," I said. "Okay, Cynthia? Would you rather have grape juice? Will I do a beach while I'm at it?"

She was silent, and soon I felt repentant. "Maybe in the next town there might be a pool," I said. I looked at the map. "In Miles City. Anyway, there'll be something cool to drink."

"How far is it?" Andrew said.

"Not so far," I said. "Thirty miles, about."

"In Miles City," said Cynthia, in the tones of an incantation, "there is a beautiful blue swimming pool for children, and a park with lovely trees."

Andrew said to me, "You could have started something."

But there was a pool. There was a park, too, though not quite the oasis of Cynthia's fantasy. Prairie trees with thin leaves—cottonwoods and poplars—worn grass, and a high wire fence around the pool. Within this fence, a wall, not yet completed, of cement blocks. There were no shouts or splashes; over the entrance I saw a sign that said the pool was closed every day from noon until two o'clock. It was then twenty-five after twelve.

Nevertheless I called out, "Is anybody there?" I thought somebody must be around, because there was a small truck parked near the entrance. On the side of the truck were these words: "We have Brains, to fix your Drains. (We have Roto-Rooter too.)"

A girl came out, wearing a red lifeguard's shirt over her bathing suit. "Sorry, we're closed."

"We were just driving through," I said.

"We close every day from twelve until two. It's on the sign." She was eating a sandwich.

"I saw the sign," I said. "But this is the first water we've seen for so long, and the children are awfully hot, and I wondered if they could just dip in and out—just five minutes. We'd watch them."

A boy came into sight behind her. He was wearing jeans and a T-shirt with the words "Roto-Rooter" on it.

I was going to say that we were driving from British Columbia to Ontario, but I remembered that Canadian place names usually meant nothing to Americans. "We're driving right across the country," I said. "We haven't time to wait for the pool to open. We were just hoping the children could get cooled off."

Cynthia came running up barefoot behind me. "Mother. Mother, where is my bathing suit?" Then she stopped, sensing the serious adult negotiations. Meg was climbing out of the car—just wakened, with her top pulled up and her shorts pulled down, showing her pink stomach.

"Is it just those two?" the girl said.

"Just the two. We'll watch them."

"I can't let any adults in. If it's just the two, I guess I could watch them. I'm having my lunch." She said to Cynthia, "Do you want to come in the pool?"

"Yes, please," said Cynthia firmly.

Meg looked at the ground.

"Just a short time because the pool is really closed," I said. "We appreciate this very much," I said to the girl.

"Well, I can eat my lunch out there, if it's just the two of them." She looked toward the car as if she thought I might try to spring some more children on her.

When I found Cynthia's bathing suit, she took it into the changing room. She would not permit anybody, even Meg, to see her naked. I changed Meg, who stood on the front seat of the car. She had a pink cotton bathing suit with straps that crossed and buttoned. There were ruffles across the bottom.

"She *is* hot," I said. "But I don't think she's feverish."

I loved helping Meg to dress or undress, because her body still had the solid unselfconsciousness, the sweet indifference, something of the milky smell, of a baby's body. Cynthia's body had long ago been pared down, shaped and altered, into Cynthia. We all liked to hug Meg, press and nuzzle her. Sometimes she would scowl and beat us off, and this forthright independence, this ferocious bashfulness, simply made her more appealing, more apt to be tormented and tickled in the way of family love.

Andrew and I sat in the car with the windows open. I could hear a radio playing, and thought it must belong to the girl or her boyfriend. I was thirsty, and got out of the car to look for a concession stand, or perhaps a soft-drink machine, somewhere in the park. I was wearing shorts, and the backs of my legs were slick with sweat. I saw a drinking fountain at the other side of the park and was walking toward it in a roundabout way, keeping to the shade of the trees. No place became real till you got out of the car. Dazed with the heat, with the sun on the blistered houses, the pavement, the burned grass, I walked slowly. I paid attention to a squashed leaf, ground a Popsicle stick under the heel of my sandal, squinted at a trash can strapped to a tree. This is the way you look at the poorest details of the world resurfaced, after you've been driving for a long time—you feel their singleness and precise location and the forlorn coincidence of your being there to see them.

Where are the children?

I turned around and moved quickly, not quite running, to a part of the fence beyond which the cement wall was not completed. I could see some of the pool. I saw Cynthia, standing about waist-deep in the water, fluttering her hands on the surface and discreetly watching something at the end of the pool, which I could not see. I thought by her pose, her discretion, the look on her face, that she must be watching some byplay between the lifeguard and her boyfriend. I couldn't see Meg. But I thought she must be playing in the shallow water—both the shallow and deep ends of the pool were out of my sight.

"Cynthia!" I had to call twice before she knew where my voice was coming from. "Cynthia! Where's Meg?"

It always seems to me, when I recall this scene, that Cynthia turns very gracefully toward me, then turns all around in the water—making me think of a ballerina on point—and spreads her arms in a gesture of the stage. "Dis-ap-peared!"

Cynthia was naturally graceful, and she did take dancing lessons, so these movements may have been as I have described. She did say "Disappeared" after looking all around the pool, but the strangely artificial style of speech and gesture, the lack of urgency, is more likely my invention. The fear I felt instantly when I couldn't see Meg—even while I was telling myself she must be in the shallower water—must have made Cynthia's movements seem unbearably slow and inappropriate to me, and the tone in which she could say "Disappeared" before the implications struck her (or was she covering, at once, some ever-ready guilt?) was heard by me as quite exquisitely, monstrously self-possessed.

I cried out for Andrew, and the lifeguard came into view. She was pointing toward the deep end of the pool, saying, "What's that?"

There, just within my view, a cluster of pink ruffles appeared, a bouquet, beneath the surface of the water. Why would a lifeguard stop and point, why would she ask what that was, why didn't she just dive into the water and swim to it? She didn't swim; she ran all the way around the edge of the pool. But by that time Andrew was over the fence. So many things seemed not quite plausible—Cynthia's behaviour, then the lifeguard's—and now I had the impression that Andrew jumped with one bound over this fence, which seemed about seven feet high. He must have climbed it very quickly, getting a grip on the wire.

I could not jump or climb it, so I ran to the entrance, where there was a sort of lattice gate, locked. It was not very high, and I did pull myself over it. I ran through the cement corridors, through the disinfectant pool for your feet, and came out on the edge of the pool.

The drama was over.

Andrew had got to Meg first, and had pulled her out of the water. He just had to reach over and grab her, because she was swimming somehow, with her head underwater—she was moving toward the edge of the pool. He was carrying her now, and the lifeguard was trotting along behind. Cynthia had climbed out of the water and was running to meet them. The only person aloof from the situation was the boyfriend, who had stayed on the bench at the shallow end, drinking a milkshake. He smiled at me, and I thought that unfeeling of him, even though the danger was past. He may have meant it kindly. I noticed that he had not turned the radio off, just down.

Meg had not swallowed any water. She hadn't even scared herself. Her hair was plastered to her head and her eyes were wide open, golden with amazement.

"I was getting the comb," she said. "I didn't know it was deep."

Andrew said, "She was swimming! She was swimming by herself. I saw her bathing suit in the water and then I saw her swimming."

"She nearly drowned," Cynthia said. "Didn't she? Meg nearly drowned."

"I don't know how it could have happened," said the lifeguard. "One moment she was there, and the next she wasn't."

What had happened was that Meg had climbed out of the water at the shallow end and run along the edge of the pool toward the deep end. She saw a comb that somebody had dropped lying on the bottom. She crouched down and reached in to pick it up, quite deceived about the depth of the water. She went over the edge and slipped into the pool, making such a light splash that nobody heard—not the lifeguard, who was kissing her boyfriend, or Cynthia, who was watching them. That must have been the moment under the trees when I thought, Where are the children? It must have been the same moment. At that moment, Meg was slipping, surprised, into the treacherously clear blue water.

"It's okay," I said to the lifeguard, who was nearly crying. "She can move pretty fast." (Though that wasn't what we usually said about Meg at all. We said she thought everything over and took her time.)

"You swam, Meg," said Cynthia, in a congratulatory way. (She told us about the kissing later.)

"I didn't know it was deep," Meg said. "I didn't drown."

We had lunch at a take-out place, eating hamburgers and fries at a picnic table not far from the highway. In my excitement, I forgot to get Meg a plain hamburger, and had to scrape off the relish and mustard with plastic spoons, then wipe the meat with a paper napkin, before she would eat it. I took advantage of the trash can there to clean out the car. Then we resumed driving east, with the car windows open in front. Cynthia and Meg fell asleep in the back seat.

Andrew and I talked quietly about what had happened. Suppose I hadn't had the impulse just at that moment to check on the children? Suppose we had gone uptown to get drinks, as we had thought of doing? How had Andrew got over the fence? Did he jump or climb? (He couldn't remember.) How had he reached Meg so quickly? And think of the lifeguard not watching. And Cynthia, taken up with the kissing. Not seeing anything else. Not seeing Meg drop over the edge.

Disappeared.

But she swam. She held her breath and came up swimming. What a chain of lucky links.

That was all we spoke about—luck. But I was compelled to picture the opposite. At this moment, we could have been filling out forms. Meg removed from us, Meg's body being prepared for shipment. To Vancouver—where we had never noticed such a thing as a graveyard—or to Ontario? The scribbled drawings she had made this morning would still be in the back seat of the car. How could this be borne all at once, how did people bear it? The plump, sweet shoulders and hands and feet, the fine brown hair, the rather satisfied, secretive expression—all exactly the same as when she had been alive. The most ordinary tragedy. A child drowned in a swimming pool at noon on a sunny day. Things tidied up quickly. The pool opens as usual at two o'clock. The lifeguard is a bit shaken up and gets the afternoon off. She drives away with her boyfriend in the Roto-Rooter truck. The body sealed away in some kind of shipping coffin. Sedatives, phone calls, arrangements. Such a sudden vacancy, a blind sinking and shifting. Waking up groggy from the pills, thinking for a moment it wasn't true. Thinking if only we hadn't stopped, if only we hadn't taken this route, if only they hadn't let us use the pool. Probably no one would ever have known about the comb.

There's something trashy about this kind of imagining, isn't there? Something shameful. Laying your finger on the wire to get the safe shock, feeling a bit of what it's like, then pulling back. I believed that Andrew was more scrupulous than I about such things, and that at this moment he was really trying to think about something else.

When I stood apart from my parents at Steve Gauley's funeral and watched them, and had this new, unpleasant feeling about them, I thought that I was understanding something about them for the first time. It was a deadly serious thing. I was understanding that they were implicated. Their big, stiff, dressed-up bodies did not stand between me and sudden death, or any kind of death. They gave consent. So it seemed. They gave consent to the death of children and to my death not by anything they said or thought but by the very fact that they had made children—they had made me. They had made me, and for that reason my death—however grieved they were, however they carried on—would seem to them anything but impossible or unnatural. This was a fact, and even then I knew they were not to blame.

But I did blame them. I charged them with effrontery, hypocrisy. On Steve Gauley's behalf, and on behalf of all children, who knew that by rights they should have sprung up free, to live a new, superior kind of life, not to be caught in the snares of vanquished grownups, with their sex and funerals.

Steve Gauley drowned, people said, because he was next thing to an orphan and was let run free. If he had been warned enough and given chores to do and kept in check, he wouldn't have fallen from an untrustworthy tree branch into a spring pond, a full gravel pit near the river—he wouldn't have drowned. He was neglected, he was free, so he drowned. And his father took it as an accident, such as might happen to a dog. He didn't have a good suit for the funeral, and he didn't bow his head for the prayers. But he was the only grownup that I let off the hook. He was the only one I didn't see giving consent. He couldn't prevent anything, but he wasn't implicated in anything, either—not like the others, saying the Lord's Prayer in their unnaturally weighted voices, oozing religion and dishonour.

At Glendive, not far from the North Dakota border, we had a choice—either to continue on the interstate or head northeast, toward Williston, taking Route 16, then some secondary roads that would get us back to Highway 2.

We agreed that the interstate would be faster, and that it was important for us not to spend too much time—that is, money—on the road. Nevertheless we decided to cut back to Highway 2.

"I just like the idea of it better," I said.

Andrew said, "That's because it's what we planned to do in the beginning."

"We missed seeing Kalispell and Havre. And Wolf Point. I like the name."

"We'll see them on the way back."

Andrew's saying "on the way back" was a surprising pleasure to me. Of course, I had believed that we would be coming back, with our car and our lives and our family intact, having covered all that distance, having dealt somehow with those loyalties and problems, held ourselves up for inspection in such a foolhardy way. But it was a relief to hear him say it.

"What I can't get over," said Andrew, "is how you got the signal. It's got to be some kind of extra sense that mothers have."

Partly I wanted to believe that, to bask in my extra sense. Partly I wanted to warn him—to warn everybody—never to count on it.

"What I can't understand," I said, "is how you got over the fence."

"Neither can I."

So we went on, with the two in the back seat trusting us, because of no choice, and we ourselves trusting to be forgiven, in time, for everything that had first to be seen and condemned by those children: whatever was flippant, arbitrary, careless, callous—all our natural, and particular, mistakes.

Barbara Gowdy

Presbyterian Crosswalk

S ometimes Beth floated. Two or three feet off the ground, and not for very long, ten seconds or so. She wasn't aware of floating when she was actually doing it, however. She had to land and feel a glowing sensation before she realized that she had just been up in the air.

The first time it happened she was on the church steps. She looked back down the walk and knew that she had floated up it. A couple of days later she floated down the outside cellar stairs of her house. She ran inside and told her grandmother, who whipped out the pen and the little pad she carried in her skirt pocket and drew a circle with a hooked nose.

Beth looked at it. "Has Aunt Cora floated, too?" she asked.

Her grandmother nodded.

"When?"

Her grandmother held up six fingers.

"Six years ago?"

Shaking her head, her grandmother held her hand at thigh level.

"Oh," Beth said, "when she was six."

When Beth was six, five years ago, her mother ran off with a man down the street who wore a toupee that curled up in humid weather. Beth's grandmother, her father's mother, came to live with her and her father. Thirty years before that, Beth's grandmother had had her tonsils taken out by a quack who ripped out her vocal chords and the underside of her tongue.

It was a tragedy, because she and her twin sister, Cora, had been on the verge of stardom (or so Cora said) as a professional singing team. They had made two long-play records: "The Carlisle Sisters, Sea to Sea" and "Christmas with the Carlisle Sisters." Beth's grandmother liked to play the records at high volume and to mouth the words. "My prairie home is beautiful, but oh …" If Beth sang along, her grandmother might stand next to her and sway and swish her skirt as though Beth were Cora and the two of them were back on stage.

The cover of the "Sea to Sea" album had a photograph of Beth's grandmother and Aunt Cora wearing middies and sailor hats and shielding their eyes with one hand as they peered off in different directions. Their hair, blond and billowing out from under their hats, was glamorous, but Beth secretly felt that even if her grandmother hadn't lost her voice she and Cora would never have been big stars because they had hooked noses, what Cora called Roman noses. Beth was relieved that she hadn't inherited their noses, although she regretted not having got their soft, wavy hair, which they both still wore long, in a braid or falling in silvery drifts down their backs. Beth's grandmother still put on blue eye shadow and red lipstick, too, every morning. And around the house she wore her old, flashy, full-length stage skirts, faded now—red, orange or yellow, or flowered, or with swirls of broken-off sequins. Beth's grandmother didn't care about sloppiness or dirt. With the important exception of Beth's father's den, the house was a mess—Beth was just beginning to realize and be faintly ashamed of this.

On each of Beth's grandmother's skirts was a sewed-on pocket for her pencil and pad. Due to arthritis in her thumb she held the pencil between her middle finger and forefinger, but she still drew faster than anyone Beth had ever seen. She always drew people instead of writing out their name or their initials. Beth, for instance, was a circle with tight, curly hair. Beth's friend Amy was an exclamation mark. If the phone rang and nobody was home, her grandmother answered it and tapped her pencil three times on the receiver to let whoever was on the other end know that it was her and that they should leave a message. "Call," she would write, and then do a drawing.

A drawing of a man's hat was Beth's father. He was a hard-working lawyer who stayed late at the office. Beth had a hazy memory of him giving her a bath once, it must have been before her mother ran off. The memory embarrassed her. She wondered if he wished that she had gone with her mother, if, in fact, she was supposed to have gone, because when he came home from work and she was still there, he seemed surprised. "Who do we have here?" he might say. He wanted peace and quiet. When Beth got rambunctious, he narrowed his eyes as though she gave off a bright, painful light.

Beth knew that he still loved her mother. In the top drawer of his dresser, in an old wallet he never used, he had a snapshot of her mother wearing only a black slip. Beth remembered that slip, and her mother's tight black dress with the zipper down the back. And her long red fingernails that she clicked on tables. "Your mother was too young to marry," was her father's sole disclosure. Her grandmother disclosed nothing, pretending to be deaf if Beth asked about her mother. Beth remembered how her mother used to phone her father for money and how, if her grandmother answered and took the message, she would draw a big dollar sign and then an upside-down v sitting in the middle of a line—a witch's hat.

A drawing of an upside-down v without a line was church. When a Presbyterian church was built within walking distance, Beth and her grandmother started going to it, and her grandmother began reading the Bible and counselling Beth by way of biblical quotations. A few months later a crosswalk appeared at the end of the street, and for several years Beth thought that it was a "Presbyterian" instead of a "Pedestrian" crosswalk and that the sign above it said Watch for Presbyterians.

Her Sunday school teacher was an old, teary-eyed woman who started every class by singing "When Mothers of Salem," while the children hung up their coats and sat down cross-legged on the floor in front of her. That hymn, specifically the part about Jesus wanting to hold children to His "bosom," made Beth feel that there was something not right about Jesus, and consequently it was responsible for her six months of anxiety that she would end up in hell. Every night, after saying her prayers, she would spend a few minutes chanting, "I love Jesus, I love Jesus, I love Jesus," the idea being that she could talk herself into it. She didn't expect to feel earthly love; she awaited the unknown feeling called glory.

When she began to float, she said to herself, "This is glory."

She floated once, sometimes twice a week. Around Christmas it began to happen less often—every ten days to two weeks. Then it dwindled down to only about once a month. She started to chant "I love Jesus" again, not because she was worried any more about going to hell, she just wanted to float.

By the beginning of the summer holidays she hadn't floated in almost seven weeks. She phoned her Aunt Cora who said that, yes, floating was glory all right, but that Beth should consider herself lucky it had happened even once. "Nothing that good lasts long," she sighed. Beth couldn't stop hoping, though. She went to the park and climbed a tree. Her plan was to jump and have Jesus float her to the ground. But as she stood on a limb, working up her courage, she remembered God seeing the little sparrow fall and letting it fall anyway, and she climbed down.

She felt that she had just had a close call. She lay on her back on the picnic table, gazing up in wonder at how high up she had been. It was a hot, still day. She heard heat bugs and an ambulance. Presently she went over to the swings and took a turn on each one, since there was nobody else in the park.

She was on the last swing when Helen McCormack came waddling across the lawn, calling that a boy had just been run over by a car. Beth slid off the swing. "He's almost dead!" Helen called.

"Who?" Beth asked.

"I don't know his name. Nobody did. He's about eight. He's got red hair. The car ran over his leg and his back."

"Where?"

Helen was panting. "I shouldn't have walked so fast," she said, holding her hands on either side of her enormous head. "My cranium veins are throbbing." Little spikes of her wispy blond hair stood out between her fingers.

"Where did it happen?" Beth said.

"On Glenmore. In front of the post office."

Beth started running toward Glenmore, but Helen called, "There's nothing there now, everything's gone!" so Beth stopped and turned, and for a moment Helen and the swings seemed to continue turning, coming round and round like Helen's voice saying, "You missed the whole thing. You missed it. You missed the whole thing."

"He was on his bike," Helen said, dropping onto a swing, "and an eyewitness said that the car skidded on water and knocked him down, then ran over him twice, once with a front tire and once with a back one. I got there before the ambulance. He probably won't live. You could tell by his eyes. His eyes were glazed." Helen's eyes, blue, huge because of her glasses, didn't blink.

"That's awful," Beth said.

"Yes, it really was," Helen said, matter-of-factly. "He's not the first person I've seen who nearly died, though. My aunt nearly drowned in the bathtub when we were staying at her house. She became a human vegetable."

"Was the boy bleeding?" Beth asked.

"Yes, there was blood everywhere."

Beth covered her mouth with both hands.

Helen looked thoughtful. "I think he'll probably die," she said. She pumped her fat legs but without enough energy to get the swing going. "I'm going to die soon," she said.

"You are?"

"You probably know that I have water on the brain," Helen said.

"Yes, I know that," Beth said. Everyone knew. It was why Helen wasn't supposed to run. It was why her head was so big.

"Well, more and more water keeps dripping in all the time, and one day there will be so much that my brain will literally drown in it."

"Who said?"

"The doctors, who else?"

"They said, 'You're going to die'?"

Helen threw her an ironic look. "Not exactly. What they tell you is, you're not going to live." She squinted up at a plane going by. "The boy, he had . . . I think it was a rib, sticking out of his back."

"Really?"

"I *think* it was a rib. It was hard to tell because of all the blood." With the toe of her shoe, Helen began to jab a hole in the sand under her swing. "A man from the post office hosed the blood down the sewer, but some of it was already caked from the sun."

Beth walked toward the shade of the picnic table. The air was so thick and still. Her arms and legs, cutting through it, seemed to produce a thousand soft clashes.

"The driver was an old man," Helen said, "and he was crying uncontrollably."

"Anybody *would* cry," Beth said hotly. Her eyes filled with tears.

Helen squirmed off her swing and came over to the table. Grunting with effort, she climbed onto the seat across from Beth and began to roll her head. "At least I'll die in one piece," she said.

"Are you really going to?" Beth asked.

"Yep." Helen rotated her head three times one way, then three times the other. Then she propped it up with her hands cupped under her chin.

"But can't they do anything to stop the water dripping in?" Beth asked.

"Nope," Helen said distantly, as if she were thinking about something more interesting.

"You know what?" Beth said, swiping at her tears. "If every night, you closed your eyes and chanted over and over, 'Water go away, water go away, water go away,' maybe it would start to, and then your head would shrink down."

Helen smirked. "Somehow," she said, "I doubt it."

From the edge of the picnic table Beth tore a long sliver of wood like the boy's rib. She pictured the boy riding his bike no-hands, zigzagging down the street the way boys did. She imagined bursting Helen's head with the splinter to let the water gush out.

"I'm thirsty," Helen sighed. "I've had a big shock today. I'm going home for some lemonade."

Beth went with her. It was like walking with her grandmother, who, because of arthritis in her hips, also rocked from side to side and took up the whole sidewalk. Beth asked Helen where she lived.

"I can't talk," Helen panted. "I'm trying to breathe."

Beth thought that Helen lived in the apartments where the immigrants, crazy people and bums were, but Helen went past those apartments and up the hill to the new Regal Heights subdivision, which had once been a landfill site. Her house was a split-level with a little turret above the garage. On the door was an engraved wooden sign, the kind that Beth had seen nailed to posts in front of cottages. No Solicitors, it said.

"My father is a solicitor," Beth said.

Helen was concentrating on opening the door. "Darn thing's always stuck," she muttered as she shoved it open with her shoulder. "I'm home!" she hollered, then sat heavily on a small mauve suitcase next to the door.

Across the hallway a beautiful woman was dusting the ceiling with a mop. She had dark, curly hair tied up in a red ribbon, and long, slim legs in white short shorts.

To Beth's amazement she was Helen's mother. "You can call me Joyce," she said, smiling at Beth as though she loved her. "Who's this lump of potatoes," she laughed, pointing the mop at Helen.

Helen stood up. "A boy got run over on Glenmore," she said.

Joyce's eyes widened, and she looked at Beth.

"I didn't see it," Beth told her.

"We're dying of thirst," Helen said. "We want lemonade in my room."

While Joyce made lemonade from a can, Helen sat at the kitchen table, resting her head on her folded arms. Joyce's questions about the accident seemed to bore her. "We don't need ice," she said impatiently when Joyce went to open the freezer. She demanded cookies, and Joyce poured some Oreos onto the tray with their coffee mugs of lemonade, then handed the tray to

Beth, saying with a little laugh that, sure as shooting, Helen would tip it over.

"I'm always spilling things," Helen agreed.

Beth carried the tray through the kitchen to the hallway. "Why is that there?" she asked, nodding at the suitcase beside the front door.

"That's my hospital suitcase," Helen said. "It's all packed for an emergency." She pushed open her bedroom door so that it banged against the wall. The walls were the same mauve as the suitcase, and there was a smell of paint. Everything was put away—no clothes lying around, no games or toys on the floor. The dolls and books, lined up on white bookshelves, looked as if they were for sale. Beth thought contritely of her own dolls, their tangled hair and dirty dresses, half of them naked, some of them missing legs and hands, she could never remember why, she could never figure out how a hand got in with her Scrabble letters.

She set the tray down on Helen's desk. Above the desk was a chart that said "Heart Rate," "Blood Pressure" and "Bowel Movements" down the side. "What's that?" she asked.

"My bodily functions chart." Helen grabbed a handful of cookies. "We're keeping track every week to see how much things change before they completely stop. We're conducting an experiment."

Beth stared at the neatly stencilled numbers and the gently waving red lines. She had the feeling that she was missing something as stunning and obvious as the fact that her mother was gone for good. For years after her mother left she asked her father, "When is she coming back?" Her father, looking confused, always answered, "Never," but Beth just couldn't understand what he meant by that, not until she finally thought to ask, "When is she coming back for the rest of her life?"

She turned to Helen. "When are you going to die?"

Helen shrugged. "There's no exact date," she said with her mouth full.

"Aren't you afraid?"

"Why should I be? Dying the way I'm going to doesn't hurt, you know."

Beth sat on the bed. There was the hard feel of plastic under the spread and blankets. She recognized it from when she'd had her tonsils out and they'd put plastic under her sheets then. "I hope that boy hasn't died," she said, suddenly thinking of him again.

"He probably has," Helen said, running a finger along the lowest line in the chart.

The lines were one above the other, not intersecting. When Beth's grandmother drew one wavy line, that was water. Beth closed her eyes. Water go away, she said to herself. Water go away, water go away ...

"What are you doing?" The bed bounced, splashing lemonade out of Beth's mug as Helen sat down.

"I was conducting an experiment," Beth said.

"What experiment?"

More lemonade, this time from Helen's mug, poured onto Beth's leg and her shorts. "Look what you're doing!" Beth cried. She used the corner of the bedspread to dry herself. "You're so stupid sometimes," she muttered.

Helen drank down what was left in her mug. "For your information," she said, wiping her mouth on her arm, "it's not stupidity. It's deterioration of the part of my brain lobe that tells my muscles what to do."

Beth looked up at her. "Oh, from the water," she said softly.

"Water is one of the most destructive forces known to mankind," Helen said.

"I'm sorry," Beth murmured. "I didn't mean it."

"So what did you mean you were conducting an experiment?" Helen asked, pushing her glasses up on her nose.

"You know what?" Beth said. "We could both do it." She felt a thrill of virtuous resolve. "Remember what I said about chanting 'water go away, water go away'? We could both chant it and see what happens."

"Brother," Helen sighed.

Beth put her lemonade on the table and jumped off the bed. "We'll make a chart," she said, fishing around in the drawer of Helen's desk for a pen and some paper. She found a red pencil. "Do you have any paper?" she asked. "We need paper and a measuring tape."

"Brother," Helen said again, but she left the room and came back a few minutes later with a pad of foolscap and her mother's sewing basket.

Beth wrote "Date" and "Size" at the top of the page and underlined it twice. Under "Date" she wrote "June 30," then she unwound the measuring tape and measured Helen's head—the circumference above her eyebrows—and wrote "27½." Then she and Helen sat cross-legged on the floor, closed their eyes, held each other's hands and said, "Water go away," starting out in almost a whisper, but Helen kept speeding up, and Beth had to raise her voice to slow her down. After a few moments both of them were shouting, and Helen was digging her nails into Beth's fingers.

"Stop!" Beth cried. She yanked her hands free. "It's supposed to be slow and quiet!" she cried. "Like praying!"

"We don't go to church," Helen said, pressing her hands on either side of her head. "Whew," she breathed. "For a minute there I thought that my cranium veins were throbbing again."

"We did it wrong," Beth said crossly. Helen leaned over to get the measuring tape. "You should chant tonight before you go to bed," Beth said, watching as Helen pulled on the bedpost to hoist herself to her feet. "Chant slowly and softly. I'll come back tomorrow after lunch and we'll do it together again. We'll just keep doing it every afternoon for the whole summer, if that's what it takes. Okay?"

Helen was measuring her hips, her wide, womanly hips in their dark green Bermuda shorts.

"Okay?" Beth repeated.

Helen bent over to read the tape. "Sure," she said indifferently.

When Beth got back to her own place, her grandmother was playing her "Sea to Sea" record and making black bean soup and dinner rolls. Talking loudly to be heard over the music, Beth told her about the car accident and Helen. Her grandmother knew about Helen's condition but thought that she was retarded—in the flour sprinkled on the table she traced a circle with a triangle sitting on it, which was "dunce," and a question mark.

"No," Beth said, surprised. "She gets all A's."

Her grandmother pulled out her pad and pencil and wrote, "Don't get her hopes up."

"But when you *pray*, that's getting your hopes up," Beth argued.

Her grandmother looked impressed. "We walk by faith," she wrote.

There was a sudden silence. "Do you want to hear side two?" Beth asked. Her grandmother made a cross with her fingers. "Oh, okay," Beth said and went into the living room and put on her grandmother's other record, the Christmas one. The first song was "Hark! the Herald Angels Sing." Beth's father's name was Harold. The black bean soup, his favourite, meant he'd be home for supper. Beth wandered down the hall to his den and sat in his green leather chair and swivelled for a moment to the music. "Offspring of the Virgin's womb ..."

After a few minutes she got off the chair and began searching through his wastepaper basket. Whenever she was in here and noticed the basket hadn't been emptied, she looked at what was in it. Usually just pencil shavings and long handwritten business letters with lots of crossed-out sentences and notes in the margins. Sometimes there were phone messages from his office, where he was called Hal, by Sue, the woman who wrote the messages out.

"PDQ!" Sue wrote. "ASAP!"

Today there were several envelopes addressed to her father, a couple of flyers, an empty cigarette package, and a crumpled pink note from her grandmother's pad. Beth opened the note up.

"Call," it said, and then there was an upside-down v. Underneath that was a telephone number.

Beth thought it was a message for her father to call the church. Her mother hadn't called in over four years, so it took a moment of wondering why the phone number didn't start with two fives like every other phone number in the neighbourhood did, and why her father, who didn't go to church, should get a message from the church, before Beth remembered that an upside-down v meant not "church" but "witch's hat."

In the kitchen Beth's grandmother was shaking the bean jars to "Here We Come a-Wassailing." Beth felt the rhythm as a pounding between her ears. "My cranium veins are throbbing," she thought in revelation, and putting down the message she pressed her palms to her temples and remembered when her mother used to phone for money. Because of those phone calls Beth had always pictured her mother and the man with the toupee living in some poor place, a rundown apartment, or one of the insulbrick bungalows north of the city. "I'll bet they're broke again," Beth told herself, working up scorn. "I'll bet they're down to their last penny." She picked up the message and crumpled it back into a ball, then opened it up again, folded it in half and slipped it into the pocket of her shorts.

Sticking to her promise, she went over to Helen's every afternoon. It took her twenty minutes, a little longer than that if she
left the road to go through the park, which she often did out of
a superstitious feeling that the next time she floated, it would be
there. The park made her think of the boy who was run over. On
the radio it said that his foot had been amputated and that he
was in desperate need of a liver transplant. "Remember him in
your prayers," the announcer said, and Beth and her grandmother did. The boy's name was Kevin Legg.

"Kevin *Legg* and he lost his *foot!*" Beth pointed out to Joyce.

Joyce laughed, although Beth hadn't meant it as a joke. A few
minutes later, in the bedroom, Beth asked Helen, "Why isn't
your mother worried about us getting your hopes up?"

"She's just glad that I finally have a friend," Helen answered.
"When I'm by myself, I get in the way of her cleaning."

Beth looked out the window. It hadn't occurred to her that
she and Helen were friends.

Beth's best friend, Christine, was at a cottage for the summer.
Amy, her other friend, she played with in the mornings and
when she returned from Helen's. Amy was half Chinese, small
and thin. She was on pills for hyperactivity. "Just think what I'd
be like if I *wasn't* on them!" she cried, spinning around and slam-
ming into the wall. Amy was the friend that Beth's grandmother
represented with an exclamation mark. Whatever they were
playing, Amy got tired of after five minutes, but she usually had
another idea. She was fun, although not very nice. When Beth
told her about Helen dying, she cried, "That's a lie!"

"Ask her mother," Beth said.

"No way I'm going to that fat-head's place!" Amy cried.

Amy didn't believe the story about the doctor ripping out
Beth's grandmother's tonsils, either, not even after Beth's grandmother opened her mouth and showed her her mutilated
tongue.

So Beth knew better than to confide in Amy about floating. She knew better than to confide in anybody, aside from her grandmother and her Aunt Cora, since it wasn't something she could prove and since she found it hard to believe herself. At the same time she was passionately certain that she had floated, and might again if she kept up her nightly "I love Jesus" chants.

She confided in Helen about floating, though, on the fifteenth day of *their* chanting, because that day, instead of sitting on the floor and holding Beth's hands, Helen curled up on her side facing the wall and said, "I wish we were playing checkers," and Beth thought how trusting Helen had been so far, chanting twice a day without any reason to believe that it worked.

The next day, the sixteenth day, Helen's head measured twenty-seven inches.

"Are you sure you aren't pulling the tape tighter?" Helen asked.

"No," Beth said. "I always pull it this tight."

Helen pushed the tape off her head and waddled to the bedroom door. "Twenty-seven inches!" she called.

"Let's go show her," Beth said, and they hurried to the living room, where Joyce was using a nail to clean between the floorboards.

"Aren't you guys smart!" Joyce said, sitting back on her heels and wiping specks of dirt from her slim legs and little pink shorts.

"Come on," Helen said, tugging Beth back to the bedroom.

Breathlessly she went to the desk and wrote the measurement on the chart.

Beth sat on the bed. "I can't believe it," she said, falling onto her back. "It's working. I mean I *thought* it would, I *hoped* it would, but I wasn't absolutely, positively, one hundred per cent sure."

Helen sat beside her and began to roll her head. Beth pictured the water sloshing from side to side. "Why do you do that?" she asked.

"I get neck cramps," Helen said. "One thing I won't miss are these darn neck cramps."

The next day her head lost another half inch. The day after that it lost an entire inch, so that it was now down to twenty-five and a half inches. Beth and Helen demonstrated the measurements to Joyce, who acted amazed, but Beth could tell that for some reason she really wasn't.

"We're not making it up," Beth told her.

"Well, who said you were?" Joyce asked, pretending to be insulted.

"Don't you think her head *looks* smaller?" Beth said, and both she and Joyce considered Helen's head, which *had* looked smaller in the bedroom, but now Beth wasn't so sure. In fact, she was impressed, the way she used to be when she saw Helen only once in a while, by just how big Helen's head was. And by her lumpy, grown-up woman's body, which at this moment was collapsing onto a kitchen chair.

"You know, I think maybe it *does* look smaller," Joyce said brightly.

"Wait'll Dr. Dobbs sees me," Helen said in a tired voice, folding her arms on the table and laying her head down.

Joyce gave Helen's shoulder a little punch. "You all right, kiddo?"

Helen ignored her. "I'll show him our chart," she said to Beth.

"Hey," Joyce said. "You all right?"

Helen closed her eyes. "I need a nap," she murmured.

When Beth returned home there was another message from her mother in her father's wastepaper basket.

This time, before she could help herself, she thought, "She

wants to come back, she's left that man," and she instantly believed it with righteous certainty. "I *told* you," she said out loud, addressing her father. Her eyes burned with righteousness. She threw the message back in the wastepaper basket and went out to the back yard, where her grandmother was tying up the tomato plants. Her grandmother had on her red blouse with the short, puffy sleeves and her blue skirt that was splattered with what had once been red music notes but which were now faded and broken pink sticks. Her braid was wrapped around her head. "She looks like an immigrant," Beth thought coldly, comparing her to Joyce. For several moments Beth stood there looking at her grandmother and feeling entitled to a few answers.

The instant her grandmother glanced up, however, she didn't want to know. If, right at that moment, her grandmother had decided to tell her what the messages were about, Beth would have run away. As it was, she ran around to the front of the house and down the street. "I love Jesus, I love Jesus," she said, holding her arms out. She was so light on her feet! Any day now she was going to float, she could feel it.

Her father came home early that evening. It seemed significant to Beth that he did not change into casual pants and sports shirt before supper, as he normally did. Other than that, however, nothing out of the ordinary happened. Her father talked about work, her grandmother nodded and signalled and wrote out a few conversational notes, which Beth leaned over to read.

After supper her father got around to changing his clothes, then went outside to cut the grass while Beth and her grandmother did the dishes. Beth, carrying too many dishes to the sink, dropped and smashed a saucer and a dinner plate. Her grandmother waved her hands—"Don't worry, it doesn't matter!"—and to prove it she got the Sears catalogue out of the cupboard and showed Beth the new set of dinnerware she intended to buy anyway.

It wasn't until Beth was eating breakfast the next morning that it dawned on her that if her mother was coming back, her grandmother would be leaving, and if her grandmother was leaving, she wouldn't be buying new dinnerware. This thought left Beth feeling as if she had just woken up with no idea yet what day it was or what she'd just been dreaming. Then the radio blared "... Liver ..." and she jumped and turned to see her grandmother with one hand on the volume knob, and the other hand held up for silence. "Doctors report that the transplant was a success," the announcer said, "and that Kevin is in serious but stable condition."

"Did they find a donor?" Beth cried as the announcer said, "The donor, an eleven-year-old girl, died in St. Andrew's hospital late last night. Her name is being withheld at her family's request."

Her grandmother turned the volume back down.

"Gee, that's great," Beth said. "Everybody was praying for him."

Her grandmother tore a note off her pad. "Ask and it shall be given you," she wrote.

"I know!" Beth said exultantly. "I know!"

Nobody was home at Helen's that afternoon. Peering in the window beside the door, Beth saw that the mauve suitcase was gone, and the next thing she knew, she floated from Helen's door to the end of her driveway. Or at least she thought she floated, because she couldn't remember how she got from the house to the road, but the strange thing was, she didn't have the glowing sensation, the feeling of glory. She drifted home, holding herself as if she were a soap bubble.

At her house there was a note on the kitchen counter: a drawing of an apple, which meant that her grandmother was out grocery shopping. The phone rang, but when Beth said hello, the person hung up. She went into her bedroom, opened the drawer of her bedside table and took out the message with her mother's phone number on it. She returned to the kitchen and dialled. After four rings, an impatient-sounding woman said, "Hello?" Beth said nothing. "Yes, hello?" the woman said. "Who's calling?"

Beth hung up. She dialled Helen's number and immediately hung up.

She stood there for a few minutes, biting her knuckles.

She wandered down to her bedroom and looked out the window. Two back yards away, Amy was jumping off her porch. She was climbing onto the porch railing, leaping like a broad jumper, tumbling on the grass, springing to her feet, running up the stairs and doing it again. It made Beth's head spin.

About a quarter of an hour later her grandmother returned. She dropped the groceries against a cupboard door that slammed shut. She opened and shut the fridge. Turned on the tap. Beth, now lying on the bed, didn't move. She sat bolt upright when the phone rang, though. Five rings before her grandmother answered it.

Beth got up and went over to the window again. Amy was throwing a ball up into the air. Through the closed window Beth couldn't hear a thing, but she knew from the way Amy clapped and twirled her hands between catches that she was singing, "Ordinary moving, laughing, talking..."

She knew from hearing the chair scrape that her grandmother was pulling it back to sit down. She knew from hearing the faucet still run that her grandmother was caught up in what the caller was saying. Several times her grandmother tapped her pencil on the mouthpiece to say to the caller, "I'm still listening. I'm taking it all down."

Mavis Gallant

Voices Lost in the Snow

Halfway between our two great wars, parents whose own early years had been shaped with Edwardian firmness were apt to lend a tone of finality to quite simple remarks: "Because I say so" was the answer to "Why?," and a child's response to "What did I just tell you?" could seldom be anything but "Not to"—not to say, do, touch, remove, go out, argue, reject, eat, pick up, open, shout, appear to sulk, appear to be cross. Dark riddles filled the corners of life because no enlightenment was thought required. Asking questions was "being tiresome," while persistent curiosity got one nowhere, at least nowhere of interest. How much has changed? Observe the drift of words descending from adult to child—the fall of personal questions, observations, unnecessary instructions. Before long the listener seems blanketed. He must hear the voice as authority muffled, a hum through snow. The tone has changed—it may be coaxing, even plaintive—but the words have barely altered. They still claim the ancient right-of-way through a young life.

"Well, old cock," said my father's friend Archie McEwen, meeting him one Saturday in Montreal. "How's Charlotte taking life in the country?" Apparently no one had expected my mother to accept the country in winter.

"Well, old cock," I repeated to a country neighbour, Mr. Bainwood. "How's life?" What do you suppose it meant to me, other than a kind of weathervane? Mr. Bainwood thought it over, then came round to our house and complained to my mother.

"It isn't blasphemy," she said, not letting him have much satisfaction from the complaint. Still, I had to apologize. "I'm sorry" was a ritual habit with even less meaning than "old cock." "Never say that again," my mother said after he had gone.

"Why not?"

"Because I've just told you not to."

"What does it mean?"

"Nothing."

It must have been after yet another "nothing" that one summer's day I ran screaming around a garden, tore the heads off tulips, and—no, let another voice finish it; the only authentic voices I have belong to the dead: "... then she *ate* them."

It was my father's custom if he took me with him to visit a friend on Saturdays not to say where we were going. He was more taciturn than any man I have known since, but that wasn't all of it; being young, I was the last person to whom anyone owed an explanation. These Saturdays have turned into one whitish afternoon, a windless snowfall, a steep street. Two persons descend the street, stepping carefully. The child, reminded every day to keep her hands still, gesticulates wildly—there is the flash of a red mitten. I will never overtake this pair. Their voices are lost in snow.

We were living in what used to be called the country and is now a suburb of Montreal. On Saturdays my father and I came in together by train. I went to the doctor, the dentist, to my German lesson. After that I had to get back to Windsor Station by myself and on time. My father gave me a boy's watch so that the dial would be good and large. I remember the No. 83 streetcar trundling downhill and myself, wondering if the watch was slow, asking strangers to tell me the hour. Inevitably—how could it have been otherwise?—after his death, which would not be long in coming, I would dream that someone important had taken a train without me. My route to the meeting place—deviated, betrayed by stopped clocks—was always downhill. As soon as I was old enough to understand from my reading of myths and legends that this journey was a pursuit of darkness, its terminal point a sunless underworld, the dream vanished.

Sometimes I would be taken along to lunch with one or another of my father's friends. He would meet the friend at Pauzé's for oysters or at Drury's or the Windsor Grill. The friend would more often than not be Scottish- or English-sounding, and they would talk as if I were invisible, as Archie McEwen had done, and eat what I thought of as English food—grilled kidneys, sweetbreads—which I was too finicky to touch. Both my parents had been made wretched as children by having food forced on them and so that particular torture was never inflicted on me. However, the manner in which I ate was subject to precise attention. My father disapproved of the North American custom that he called "spearing" (knife laid on the plate, fork in the right hand). My mother's eye was out for a straight back, invisible chewing, small mouthfuls, immobile silence during the interminable adult loafing over dessert. My mother did not care for food. If we were alone together, she would sit smoking and reading, sipping black coffee, her elbows used as props—a posture that would have called for instant banishment had I so much as tried it. Being constantly observed and corrected was like having a fly buzzing around one's plate. At Pauzé's, the only child, perhaps the only female, I sat up to an oak counter and ate oysters quite neatly, not knowing exactly what they were and certainly not that they were alive. They were served as in "The Walrus and the Carpenter," with bread and butter, pepper and vinegar. Dessert was a chocolate biscuit—plates of them stood at intervals along the counter. When my father and I ate alone, I was not required to say much, nor could I expect a great deal in the way of response. After I had been addressing him for minutes, sometimes he would suddenly come to life and I would know he had been elsewhere. "Of course I've been listening," he would protest, and he would repeat by way of proof the last few words of whatever it was I'd been saying. He was seldom present. I don't know where my father spent his waking life: just elsewhere.

What was he doing alone with a child? Where was his wife? In the country, reading. She read one book after another without looking up, without scraping away the frost on the windows. "The Russians, you know, the Russians," she said to her mother and me, glancing around in the drugged way adolescent readers have. "They put salt on the window sills in winter." Yes, so they did, in the nineteenth century, in the boyhood of Turgenev, of Tolstoy. The salt absorbed the moisture between two sets of windows sealed shut for half the year. She must have been in a Russian country house at that moment, surrounded by a large Russian family, living out vast Russian complications. The flat white fields beyond her imaginary windows were like the flat white fields she would have observed if only she had looked out. She was myopic; the pupil when she had been reading seemed to be the whole of the eye. What age was she then? Twenty-seven, twenty-eight. Her husband had removed her to the country; now that they were there he seldom spoke. How young she seems to me now—half twenty-eight in perception and feeling, but with a husband, a child, a house, a life, an illiterate maid from the village whose life she confidently interfered with and mismanaged, a small zoo of animals she alternately cherished and forgot; and she was the daughter of such a sensible, truthful, pessimistic woman—pessimistic in the way women become when they settle for what actually exists.

Our rooms were not Russian—they were aired every day and the salt became a great nuisance, blowing in on the floor.

"There, Charlotte, what did I tell you?" my grandmother said. This grandmother did not care for dreams or for children. If I sensed the first, I had no hint of the latter. Out of decency she kept it quiet, at least in a child's presence. She had the reputation, shared with a long-vanished nurse named Olivia, of being able to "do anything" with me, which merely meant an ability to provoke from a child behaviour convenient for adults. It was she who taught me to eat in the Continental way, with both hands in sight at all times upon the table, and who made me sit at meals with books under my arms so I would learn not to stick out my elbows. I remember having accepted this nonsense from her without a trace of resentment. Like Olivia, she could make the most pointless sort of training seem a natural way of life. (I think that as discipline goes this must be the most dangerous form of all.) She was one of three godparents I had—the important one. It is impossible for me to enter the mind of this agnostic who taught me prayers, who had already shed every remnant of belief when she committed me at the font. I know that she married late and reluctantly; she would have preferred a life of solitude and independence, next to impossible for a woman in her time. She had the positive voice of the born teacher, sharp manners, quick blue eyes, and the square, massive figure common to both lines of her ancestry—the West of France, the North of Germany. When she said "There, Charlotte, what did I tell you?" without obtaining an answer, it summed up mother and daughter both.

My father's friend Malcolm Whitmore was the second god-parent. He quarrelled with my mother when she said something flippant about Mussolini, disappeared, died in Europe some years later, though perhaps not fighting for Franco, as my mother had it. She often rewrote other people's lives, providing them with suitable and harmonious endings. In her version of events you were supposed to die as you'd lived. He would write sometimes, asking me, "Have you been confirmed yet?" He had never really held a place and could not by dying leave a gap. The third god-parent was a young woman named Georgie Henderson. She was my mother's choice, for a long time her confidante, partisan, and close sympathizer. Something happened, and they stopped see-ing each other. Georgie was not her real name—it was Edna May. One of the reasons she had fallen out with my mother was that I had not been called Edna May too. Apparently, this had been promised.

Without saying where we were going, my father took me along to visit Georgie one Saturday afternoon.

"You didn't say you were bringing Linnet" was how she greeted him. We stood in the passage of a long, hot, high-ceilinged apartment, treading snow water into the rug.

He said, "Well, she is your godchild, and she has been ill."

My godmother shut the front door and leaned her back against it. It is in this surprisingly dramatic pose that I recall her. It would be unfair to repeat what I think I saw then, for she and I were to meet again once, only once, many years after this, and I might substitute a lined face for a smooth one and tough, large-knuckled hands for fingers that may have been delicate. One has to allow elbow-room in the account of a rival: "She must have had something" is how it generally goes, long after the initial "What can he see in her? He must be deaf and blind."

Georgie, explained by my mother as being the natural daughter of Sarah Bernhardt and a stork, is only a shadow, a tracing, with long arms and legs and one of those slightly puggy faces with pulled-up eyes.

Her voice remains—the husky Virginia-tobacco whisper I associate with so many women of that generation, my parents' friends; it must have come of age in English Montreal around 1920, when girls began to cut their hair and to smoke. In middle life the voice would slide from low to harsh, and develop a chronic cough. For the moment it was fascinating to me— opposite in pitch and speed from my mother's, which was slightly too high and apt to break off, like that of a singer unable to sustain a long note.

It was true that I had been ill, but I don't think my godmother made much of it that afternoon, other than saying, "It's all very well to talk about that now, but I was certainly never told much, and as for that doctor, you ought to just hear what Ward thinks." Out of this whispered jumble my mother stood accused—of many transgressions, certainly, but chiefly of having discarded Dr. Ward Mackey, everyone's doctor and a family friend. At the time of my birth my mother had all at once decided she liked Ward Mackey better than anyone else and had asked him to choose a name for me. He could not think of one, or, rather, thought of too many, and finally consulted his own mother. She had always longed for a daughter, so that she could call her after the heroine of a novel by, I believe, Marie Corelli. The legend so often repeated to me goes on to tell that when I was seven weeks old my father suddenly asked, "What did you say her name was?"

"*Votre fille a frôlé la phtisie*," the new doctor had said, the one who had now replaced Dr. Mackey. The new doctor was known to me as Uncle Raoul, though we were not related. This manner of declaring my brush with consumption was worlds away from Ward Mackey's "subject to bilious attacks." Mackey's objections to Uncle Raoul were neither envious nor personal, for Mackey was the sort of bachelor who could console himself with golf. The Protestant in him truly believed those other doctors to be poorly trained and superstitious, capable of recommending the pulling of teeth to cure tonsillitis, and of letting their patients cough to death or perish from septicemia just through Catholic fatalism.

What parent could fail to gasp and marvel at Uncle Raoul's announcement? Any but either of mine. My mother could invent and produce better dramas any day; as for my father, his French wasn't all that good and he had to have it explained. Once he understood that I had grazed the edge of tuberculosis, he made his decision to remove us all to the country, which he had been wanting a reason to do for some time. He was, I think, attempting to isolate his wife, but by taking her out of the city he exposed her to a danger that, being English, he had never dreamed of: this was the heart-stopping cry of the steam train at night, sweeping across a frozen river, clattering on the ties of a wooden bridge. From our separate rooms my mother and I heard the unrivalled summons, the long, urgent, uniquely North American beckoning. She would follow and so would I, but separately, years and desires and destinations apart. I think that women once pledged in such a manner are more steadfast than men.

"*Frôler*" was the charmed word in that winter's story; it was a hand brushing the edge of folded silk, a leaf escaping a spiderweb. Being caught in the web would have meant staying in bed day and night in a place even worse than a convent school. Charlotte and Angus, whose lives had once seemed so enchanted, so fortunate and free that I could not imagine lesser persons so much as eating the same kind of toast for breakfast, had to share their lives with me, whether they wanted to or not—thanks to Uncle Raoul, who always supposed me to be their principal delight. I had been standing on one foot for months now, midway between *frôler* and *falling into*, propped up by a psychosomatic guardian angel. Of course I could not stand that way forever; inevitably my health improved and before long I was declared out of danger and then restored—to the relief and pleasure of all except the patient.

"I'd like to see more of you than eyes and nose," said my godmother. "Take off your things." I offer this as an example of unnecessary instruction. Would anyone over the age of three prepare to spend the afternoon in a stifling room wrapped like a mummy in outdoor clothes? "She's smaller than she looks," Georgie remarked, as I began to emerge. This authentic godmother observation drives me to my only refuge, the insistence that she must have had something—he could not have been completely deaf and blind. Divested of hat, scarf, coat, overshoes, and leggings, grasping the handkerchief pressed in my hand so I would not interrupt later by asking for one, responding to my father's muttered "Fix your hair," struck by the command because it was he who had told me not to use "fix" in that sense, I was finally able to sit down next to him on a white sofa. My godmother occupied its twin. A low table stood between, bearing a decanter and glasses and a pile of magazines and, of course, Georgie's ashtrays; I think she smoked even more than my mother did.

On one of these sofas, during an earlier visit with my mother and father, the backs of my dangling feet had left a smudge of shoe polish. It may have been the last occasion when my mother and Georgie were ever together. Directed to stop humming and kicking, and perhaps bored with the conversation in which I was not expected to join, I had soon started up again.

"It doesn't matter," my godmother said, though you could tell she minded.

"Sit up," my father said to me.

"I am sitting up. What do you think I'm doing?" This was not answering but answering back; it is not an expression I ever heard from my father, but I am certain it stood like a stalled truck in Georgie's mind. She wore the look people put on when they are thinking, Now what are you spineless parents going to do about that?

"Oh, for God's sake, she's only a child," said my mother, as though that had ever been an excuse for anything.

Soon after the sofa-kicking incident she and Georgie moved into the hibernation known as "not speaking." This, the lingering condition of half my mother's friendships, usually followed her having said the very thing no one wanted to hear, such as "Who wants to be called Edna May, anyway?"

Once more in the hot pale room where there was nothing to do and nothing for children, I offended my godmother again, by pretending I had never seen her before. The spot I had kicked was pointed out to me, though, owing to new slipcovers, real evidence was missing. My father was proud of my quite surprising memory, of its long backward reach and the minutiae of detail I could describe. My failure now to shine in a domain where I was naturally gifted, that did not require lessons or create litter and noise, must have annoyed him. I also see that my guileless-seeming needling of my godmother was a close adaptation of how my mother could be, and I attribute it to a child's instinctive loyalty to the absent one. Giving me up, my godmother placed a silver dish of mint wafers where I could reach them—white, pink, and green, overlapping—and suggested I look at a magazine. Whatever the magazine was, I had probably seen it, for my mother subscribed to everything then. I may have turned the pages anyway, in case at home something had been censored for children. I felt and am certain I have not invented Georgie's disappointment at not seeing Angus alone. She disliked

Charlotte now, and so I supposed he came to call by himself, having no quarrel of his own; he was still close to the slighted Ward Mackey.

My father and Georgie talked for a while—she using people's initials instead of their names, which my mother would not have done—and they drank what must have been sherry, if I think of the shape of the decanter. Then we left and went down to the street in a wood-panelled elevator that had sconce lights, as in a room. The end of the afternoon had a particular shade of colour then, which is not tinted by distance or enhancement but has to do with how streets were lighted. Lamps were still gas, and their soft gradual blooming at dusk made the sky turn a peacock blue that slowly deepened to marine, then indigo. This uneven light falling in blurred pools gave the snow it touched a quality of phosphorescence, beyond which were night shadows in which no one lurked. There were few cars, little sound. A fresh snow-fall would lie in the streets in a way that seemed natural. Side-walks were dangerous, casually sanded; even on busy streets you found traces of the icy slides children's feet had made. The red-dish brown of the stone houses, the curve and slope of the streets, the constantly changing sky were satisfactory in a way that I now realize must have been aesthetically comfortable. This is what I saw when I read "city" in a book; I had no means of knowing that "city" one day would also mean drab, filthy, flat, or that city blocks could turn into dull squares without mystery.

We crossed Sherbrooke Street, starting down to catch our train. My father walked everywhere in all weathers. Already mined, colonized by an enemy prepared to destroy what it fed on, fighting it with every wrong weapon, squandering strength he should have been storing, stifling pain in silence rather than speaking up while there might have been time, he gave an impression of sternness that was a shield against suffering. One day we heard a mob roaring four syllables over and over, and we turned and went down a different street. That sound was starkly terrifying, something a child might liken to the baying of wolves.

"What is it?"

"Howie Morenz."

"Who is it? Are they chasing him?"

"No, they like him," he said of the hockey player admired to the point of dementia. He seemed to stretch, as if trying to keep every bone in his body from touching a nerve; a look of help-lessness such as I had never seen on a grown person gripped his face and he said this strange thing: "Crowds eat me. Noise eats me." The kind of physical pain that makes one seem rat's prey is summed up in my memory of this.

When we came abreast of the Ritz-Carlton after leaving Georgie's apartment, my father paused. The lights within at that time of day were golden and warm. If I barely knew what "hotel" meant, never having stayed in one, I connected the lights with other snowy afternoons, with stupefying adult conversation (Oh, those shut-in velvet-draped unaired low-voice problems!) compensated for by creamy bitter hot chocolate poured out of a pink-and-white china pot.

"You missed your gootay," he suddenly remembered. Estab-lished by my grandmother, "*goûter*" was the family word for tea. He often transformed French words, like putty, into shapes he could grasp. No, Georgie had not provided a *goûter*, other than the mint wafers, but it was not her fault—I had not been announced. Perhaps if I had not been so disagreeable with her, he might have proposed hot chocolate now, though I knew bet-ter than to ask. He merely pulled my scarf up over my nose and mouth, as if recalling something Uncle Raoul had advised. Breathing inside knitted wool was delicious—warm, moist, pun-gent when one had been sucking on mint candies, as now. He said, "You didn't enjoy your visit much."

"Not very," through red wool.

"No matter," he said. "You needn't see Georgie again unless you want to," and we walked on. He must have been smarting, for he liked me to be admired. When I was not being admired I was supposed to keep quiet. "You needn't see Georgie again" was also a private decision about himself. He was barely thirty-one and had a full winter to live after this one—little more. Why? "Because I say so." The answer seems to speak out of the lights, the stones, the snow; out of the crucial second when inner and outer forces join, and the environment becomes part of the enemy too.

Ward Mackey used to mention me as "Angus's precocious pain in the neck," which is better than nothing. Long after that afternoon, when I was about twenty, Mackey said to me, "Georgie didn't play her cards well where he was concerned. There was a point where if she had just made one smart move she could have had him. Not for long, of course, but none of us knew that."

What cards, I wonder. The cards have another meaning for me—they mean a trip, a death, a letter, tomorrow, next year. I saw only one move that Saturday: my father placed a card face up on the table and watched to see what Georgie made of it. She shrugged, let it rest. There she sits, looking puggy but capable, Angus waiting, the precocious pain in the neck turning pages, hoping to find something in the *National Geographic* harmful for children. I brush in memory against the spider-web: what if she had picked it up, remarking in her smoky voice, "Yes, I can use that"? It was a low card, the kind that only a born gambler would risk as part of a long-term strategy. She would never have weakened a hand that way; she was not gambling but building. He took the card back and dropped his hand, and their long intermittent game came to an end. The card must have been the eight of clubs—"a female child."

Bonnie Burnard

Crush

It's Thursday morning and it's hot, hot, hot. The girl is painting the kitchen cupboards. The paint stinks up the room, stinks up the whole house. Her summer-blonde ponytail and her young brown shoulders are hidden in the cupboards, and a stranger coming into the kitchen, seeing only the rounded buttocks in the terrycloth shorts and the long well-formed legs, might think he was looking at part of a woman.

She's tired. She babysat last night. It's not the best job she can get; there are other kids, easier kids. She takes the job because of him, for the chance to ride alone with him in the dark on the way home. She thinks she's in love.

She remembers him at the beach, throwing his kids around in the water, teaching them not to be afraid. She doesn't try to imagine anything other than what she has seen, because it's already more than enough. His back and thighs she will remember when she is seventy and has forgotten others.

Her mother stands over the ironing board just inside the dining room door. Thunk, hiss, thunk, hiss. The kitchen table separates them. It has been piled impossibly high with dishes and cans of soup and corn and tea towels and bags of sugar and flour and pickling salt. Spice jars, pitched here and there, rest askew in the crevices of the pile. The cupboards are hot and empty. She has nearly finished painting them.

Neither the girl nor her mother has spoken for over an hour. It is too hot. She leans back out of the cupboards, unbuttons her blouse and takes it off, tossing it toward the table. It floats down over the dishes. She wants to take off her bra, but doesn't.

Her mother doesn't lift her head from the ironing. "You be careful Adam doesn't catch you in that state, young lady. He'll be coming through that door with the bread any minute." Her sleeveless housedress is stained with sweat. It soaks down toward her thick waist.

Maybe I want him to, the girl thinks.

"Have you picked out the bathing suit you want?" Her mother glances up at her. The bathing suit is to be the reward for the painting. "It's time you started to think about modesty. It's beginning to matter."

"No." The girl watches the fresh blue paint obliterate the old pale green. She's lying. She has picked out her suit. It's the one on the dummy in the window downtown, the one the boys gather around. She knows she won't be allowed to have it. Mrs. Stewart in the ladies shop wouldn't even let her try it on, said it wasn't suitable for her. But it is. It's the one she wants.

She hears the scream of the ironing board as her mother folds it up and then she hears again her mother's voice.

"I'm going downtown for meat. You put that blouse on before I leave. Get it on. I'm as hot as you are and you don't see me throwing my clothes off."

Her mother stands checking the money in her billfold, waiting until the last button is secure before she moves toward the back door. "I'll bring you some cold pop." The screen door bangs.

The girl steps down from the paint-splattered chair. She goes to the sink and turns the water on full, letting it run to cold. She opens the freezer door, uses her thumbs to free the tray of ice-cubes. She fills a peanut butter glass with ice and slows the tap, watches the water cover the snapping cubes. She sips slowly, with her jaw locked, the ice bumps cold against her teeth as she drinks. She lifts a cube from the glass and holds it in her hand, feels it begin to soften against the heat of her palm. She raises her hand to her forehead and rubs the ice against her skin, back into her hair, down her cheek, down over her throat. The ice-cube is small now, just a round lump. Her hand is cold and wet.

His hand was wet when he danced with her at the Firemen's dance. Not the same wet though, not the same at all. His buddies stood around and hollered things about him liking the young stuff and everyone laughed, even the wives. She laughed too, pretending she understood how funny it was, his touching her. But she can still feel the pressure of his hand on her back, any time she wants to she can remember how it steadied her, how it moved her the way he wanted her to move. It should have been hard to move together, but it was easy, like dreaming.

She wonders how close he is to their house. She dries her hand on the tea towel hanging from the stove door. She undoes the top button of her blouse, then the next, and the next, and the next. It slips from her shoulders and lands in a heap on the floor. She unfastens her bra, eases it down over her brown arms, drops it.

She climbs back up on the chair and begins to paint again. Although the paint is thick and strong, she can't smell it any more. She works slowly, deliberately, the chair solid under her feet. The stale green paint disappears beneath the blue.

She turns at his sudden, humming entrance, the bang of the screen door no warning at all. He stands on the mat with the tray of fresh baking slung round his neck, shifting his weight from one foot to the other, suddenly quiet. She comes down from the chair, steps over the heap of her clothes and stands in front of him, as still as the surface of a hot summer lake.

"Jesus," he says.

"I wanted to show you," she says.

He backs out the door quickly, doesn't leave Thursday's two loaves of white and one whole wheat.

The girl can hear her mother's voice through the open back door. It sounds uneasy and unnaturally loud. She bends down and picks up her bra, although she knows there won't be time. She knows, too, that she will be punished, and in some new way.

He's in the truck and he's wishing he had farther to go than the next block. Lord, he thinks. What the hell was that?

He checks his rearview mirror. Her mother could come roaring out after him any minute. She could be forgiven for thinking there was something going on. He's a sitting duck in this damned truck. Just deliver your bread, he thinks. And then, Shit. A drive. He'll go for a drive. To clear his head.

He goes out past the gas station, past the beer store, out of the town onto a side road bordered by fence-high corn. He drives a few miles with the window down, letting the hot breeze pull the sweat from his face and arms. He eases the truck over to the shoulder.

He knows his only hope is that she tells her mother the truth. Which could be unlikely. Shit. If her mother decides he was in on it, there'll be phone calls, there'll be hell to pay. His wife won't believe it. He doesn't believe it and he was there. Maybe the smart thing to do is just lie low and hope, pray, that her mother is embarrassed enough to keep her mouth shut. If it's going to come up, it'll come up soon and he'll just have to say it was a surprise, a real big surprise, and they can give him a lie detector on it if they want.

The girl has never given him even one small clue that she was thinking in those terms. And he can certainly see a clue coming. When he picks her up and drives her home, she always hides herself behind a pile of schoolbooks hunched up tight against her sweater. She's a good sitter, the kids love her. He likes talking to her and he always makes a point of being nice to her. And she helped him teach the kids to swim because his wife wouldn't, and he didn't even look at her, can't even picture her in a bathing suit.

So damned hot. He leans back in the seat, unbuttons his shirt and lights a Player's. The sight of her drifts back through the smoke that hangs around him. It's been a long time since he's seen fresh, smooth, hard breasts. Not centrefold stuff, not even as nice as his wife before the kids, but nice just the same. Yeah. Nice. He shifts around in his seat. Damn.

It's like she just discovered them. Or maybe she got tired of being the only one who knew. Now he knows and what the hell's he supposed to do about it? Man, this is too complicated for a Thursday morning.

The picture drifts back again and this time he holds it for a while. He's sure they've never been touched. He thinks about dancing with her that once and how easy she was in his arms. Not sexy, just easy. Like she trusted him. He can't remember ever feeling that before. They sure didn't trust him when he was seventeen, had no business trusting him. And what he gets from his wife isn't trust, not exactly.

She could be crazy. She's the age to be crazy. But he remembers her eyes on him and whatever it was they were saying, it had sweet all to do with crazy.

Back the picture comes again, and he closes his eyes and the breasts stay with him, safe behind the lids of his eyes. He can see a narrow waist, and squared shoulders. He hears words, just a few, although he doesn't know what they are, and he feels a gentleness come into his hands, he feels his cupped hands lift toward her skin and then he hears a racket near his feet and he opens his eyes to see a wretched crow on the open floor of the truck beside the bread tray; it's already clawed its way through the waxed paper, it's already buried it beak. He kicks hard and waves his arms and yells the bird away and he throws the truck in gear and tells himself out loud, "You're crazy, man, that's who's crazy."

The mother stands watching the girl do up the top button of her blouse. She holds the package of meat in one hand, the bottle of pop in the other. The pale brown paper around the meat is dark and soft where blood has seeped through. She walks over to the fridge, puts the meat in the meat keeper and the pop beside the quarts of milk on the top shelf. She closes the fridge door with the same care she would use on the bedroom door of a sleeping child. When she turns the girl has climbed up on the chair in front of the cupboards and is lifting the brush.

"Get down from that chair," she says.

The girl rests the brush across the top of the paint can and steps down.

"I could slap you," the mother says, calmly. This is not a conversation she has prepared herself for. This is not a conversation she ever expected to have. She cannot stop herself from looking at the girl's young body, cannot stop the memory of her own body and the sudden remorse she feels knowing it will never come back to her. She longs to feel the sting of a slap on her hand and to imagine the sting on the girl's cheek. But she pushes the anger aside, out of the way. She pulls a chair from the table, away from the mess of cupboard things piled there, and sits down in the middle of the room, unprotected.

"Sit down," she says.

The girl sits where she is, on the floor, her brown legs tucked under her bum as they were tucked through all the years of listening to fairy tales. The mother can smell her fear.

"How much did you take off?"

The girl does not answer. She looks directly into her mother's eyes and she does not answer.

The mother begins the only way she knows how.

"I had a crush on your father. That's how it started with us, because I had a crush on him. He was only a little older than me but I think it's the same. I don't know why it should happen with you so young, but I'm sure it's the same. The difference is I didn't take my clothes off for him. And he wasn't married. Do you understand? It's wrong to feel that way about someone if he's married and it's wrong to take your clothes off." She remembers other talks, remembers pulling the girl into her arms and carrying her up to bed.

The girl picks at a crusty scab on her ankle.

"The way you feel has got nothing to do with the way things are. You've embarrassed him. I could tell at the gate that he was embarrassed. You won't be babysitting for them any more. He'll tell his wife and they'll have a good laugh about it. You've made a fool of yourself." Oh, she thinks, don't say that.

"You will feel this way from now on. Off and on from now on. You have to learn to live with it. I wish it hadn't happened so soon. Now you just have to live with it longer. Do you understand?"

The girl shrugs her shoulders, lifts the scab from her skin.

"Women have this feeling so they will marry, so they will have children. It's like a grand plan. And you've got to learn to live within that plan. There will be a young man for you, it won't be long. Maybe five years. That's all. You've got to learn to control this thing, this feeling, until that young man is there for you."

The mother gets up from the chair and goes to the fridge. She takes out the pop and opens it, dividing it between two clean glasses which she takes from a tray on top of the fridge. She hands one to the girl, insisting.

"If you don't control it, you will waste it, bit by bit, and there won't be a young man, not to marry. And they'll take it from you, any of them, because they can't stop themselves from taking it. It's your responsibility not to offer it. You just have to wait, wait for the one young man and you be careful who he is, you think about it good and hard and then you marry him and then you offer it."

The girl gets up from the floor and puts her glass, still almost full, on the counter by the sink.

"I'd like to go now," she says.

The mother drains her glass. She feels barren. She is not a mother any more, not in the same way. It is as if the girl's undressing has wiped them both off the face of the earth.

The girl has run away from the house, out past the gas station and the beer store, onto a grid road that divides the cornfields. She is sitting in a ditch, hidden, surrounded by long grass and thistles.

She knows she's ruined it, knows the babysitting days are over. Not because he was embarrassed. He wasn't embarrassed, he was afraid. It's the first time she's ever made anyone afraid. She will find a way to tell him that she didn't mean to scare him.

She wishes her mother had just slapped her. She hears again the feelings her mother had about her father in some other time, some other century. She covers her ears. She hated having to hear it, it was awful, and that stuff about holding back and then getting married some day, she knows all about that. That's what all the women do, and it's likely what she'll end up doing because there doesn't seem to be any way to do anything else.

Except maybe once in a while. If she can learn not to scare people.

She feels absolutely alone and she likes it. She thinks about his back and his dark thighs and about standing there in the kitchen facing him. It's the best feeling she's ever had. She won't give it up.

She crosses her arms in front of her, puts one hand over each small breast and she knows she isn't wrong about this feeling. It is something she will trust, from now on. She leans back into the grass, throws her arms up over her head and stares, for as long as she can, at the hot July sun.

Sandra Birdsell

The Midnight Hour

Christina prefers the direct approach. She would like to go into her mother's room, drop a book on the floor to wake her and say, For your information: I'm going suntanning in Assiniboine Park with Pam and Lisa. Not ask, just tell. But she knows what complications can arise from being face to face, and so she'll leave a note instead. *Dear Unit. Have gone to the park to suntan with Pam and Lisa,* she writes. She began calling her parents "my parental unit" when recently it became certain they were going to split up. They never caught the irony in it, never really listened to how she said it. Going to the park, Lorraine would say, you mean hang around, don't you? And so Christina picks up the felt marker and adds, *and to hang around.*

She flips a cassette into her Walkman, puts the earphones on, and sticks the note under a butterfly magnet on the refrigerator door just as Yo-Yo Ma begins bowing his cello. Lorraine is suspicious of Pam and Lisa. "They don't look me in the eye," she says. What do their parents do? Christina doesn't know because Grant Park isn't like junior high where everyone complains constantly about parents' bitching and curfews. At Grant Park the kids talk about being grounded for a week as though it's a reward and joke about ruining their parents' social lives. Pam and Lisa write notes to each other about complications of break-through bleeding on the pill and yeast infections. Never about parents.

Will you please reason with the other half of my parental unit? Christina asked her father last night when he telephoned to wish her a happy birthday. She couldn't understand why wanting to go to the park was such a big deal. She was pleased that he remembered her birthday and then wondered if Georgina had reminded him. He asked what she wanted. He was going to the lake for the weekend, he said, and was sorry, his bum had been smack against the wall all week, and he hadn't got anywhere near a shopping mall. His gift would be a tad late. That's okay, Christina told him. She understood, she said, and reached for her flip-flop to squash a spider crawling up the wall towards the window and its nest of webs clotted with husks of insects.

—So, is everything okay?

—I've grown out of my jeans. I need new ones.

—Okay.

—I'm thinking about getting my hair streaked?

—How's your mother?

—Okay.

—How much do you think that would cost? Jeans and hair?

—About a hundred and fifty.

—I can't promise.

—Pam's dad? He works for Air Canada?

—Who's Pam?

—He's taking Pam to Hawaii for Christmas if her marks are good.

Christina heard one of Georgina's boys shouting in the background and Georgina's shrill reply. She heard her father sigh.

—I'll see what I can do, Chris. But no promises.

—Calvin committed suicide.

—Who?

—My friend Calvin. With his dad's gun.

Yo-Yo Ma isn't bad, Christina thinks as she spoons yoghurt into a bowl and sprinkles it with Harvest Crunch. She thinks the sound of the cello is deep, a purple sound. It makes her think of the suicide note her friend Calvin left behind in the bathroom sink and, beside it, a picture of Jennifer. He sat on the toilet to do it, had hooked his toe into the trigger and, like the man she'd seen in a movie, a man who failed to make boot-camp training, all Calvin's memories, every idea he'd ever had, splashed against the wall behind him. Here, take a listen to this, Christina wants to tell Lorraine. Listen to this music and tell me what it makes you think about. But Lorraine is still sleeping, repairing her mind, she calls it, because it's like pulling teeth from her brain, she says about the script she's presently working on.

Once Christina thought that nothing would ever happen to her, that she was doomed to a boring life, embedded like a bug in amber, at age thirteen. Since they'd moved to the four-plex, what passed for excitement happened only once. A transformer blew up on the telephone pole outside their building and the boom of it had woken her from a deep sleep. She stood on her bed looking out the window and saw the air arcing with white light as recoiling wires spurted electricity, lashing against the fence and threatening to incinerate Lorraine's swimming pool. Still in her nightgown, Christina had run out to save it, had dragged the plastic pool across the yard and through the back door into the kitchen.

"You silly fool," Lorraine said, crying and grabbing her in a hug. "You could have been electrocuted," she said, making, as usual, a big issue out of a small one.

"Your mother has this imagination," her father said. "You know." Yes, she knows too well how the smallest misdemeanour becomes a full-scale production in her mother's mind that ends with Christina winding up behind bars in prison. She suspects her mother had stood at the door, watching her rescue the pool, writing the obituary, choosing music for the funeral service at the same time.

But she's fifteen today and it seems that, lately, too much happens. The mouse mattresses every month, for example. The irritating wad of sanitary napkins between the legs. And her height. She's shot up six inches in a year, and the marks of the growth spurt climb up the kitchen door in ink smudges they'll have to paint over when Lorraine, if ever, saves enough money so they can move. She's noticed, too, how the world seems to be going faster. Masses of people wander in deserts, starving; airports are exploding. She has stopped watching the news. "It's wrong," she told Lorraine, "how they're trying to make me face up to things that aren't my fault." She refuses to watch starving children, their swollen bellies, and not enough common sense to brush away the flies crawling across their dumb eyes. "We're poor, too," she said. Their house went to the divorce settlement, to pay off credit cards, car loans, bad debts. She has to bang the side of the television to stop its picture from rolling. She chose for her Social Studies newspaper project the topic of rock stars involved in car accidents, instead of Ethiopia. A one-armed drummer is tragic, too, she thinks.

She hears the droning of an electric can opener in the suite above and then cat's claws clicking against the floor. She can't get used to the sound of people going about their lives beside her and above her. She needs to concentrate, to think before she goes to the park. What did Diamond Dave say? "I used to have a drug problem, but now I can afford it." Diamond Dave again: "I had to quit jogging because the ice cubes kept falling out of the glass." She stayed up late last night copying the quotes into her journal after she and Lorraine had returned from the failed birthday dinner. She went down into her room and put Billy Idol on loud so she wouldn't hear the television or think about her mother huddled in front of it, mascara ground to a black smudge beneath her eyes. Lorraine, reaching across Christina in the parking lot outside the four-plex for the glove compartment, tossing the gift-wrapped cassette of Billy Idol into her lap.

—Why do I even bother to try?

—Just tell me what I did.

—Happy birthday, sweet fifteen.

—What did I do?

—I'm going inside. Lock your door.

—We don't communicate.

—What you mean is, I don't agree with everything you say.

Christina went downstairs, propped pillows against the wall and copied the Diamond Dave quotes in her journal. Then she lay on the floor and listened to Billy Idol as the street light slanted down into her basement room illuminating the poster of Baryshnikov. She had gone to see *White Nights* three times. She wanted to see the dancer suspended in air and try to discover how he did it. Around the ballet dancer, the Mötley Crüe grimaced at her, made funny faces, devil's horns with their fingers. She cradled a pillow and thought about her father and his bum always being against the wall. She imagined his boat sinking and herself, cutting through the water, kicking down into its depths and grabbing for her father, dragging him to the surface.

Footsteps thump against the ceiling in the kitchen and a dish thuds against it, bounces twice. Christina pulls the earphones out and listens. Chris? You're not going to the park and that's that. The absence of her mother's voice makes the room feel dead, like the sudden silence when the television is turned off, the picture collapsing into itself. She pushes aside the bowl of yoghurt, full suddenly and craving a cigarette. The wallpaper does it to me, she told Lorraine. Its positive ugliness makes her itch to smoke. What do you think? Lorraine said, pulling Christina through the rooms of the suite, trying to make her feel as though finding it was a gift from God. I think ugly. Forget the wallpaper, she said. It's temporary. Their stay will be for only as long as it takes her to get enough money for a down payment on another house. Christina doesn't want another house. She wants the old one back. Lorraine hung travel posters over the wallpaper, and now lime-green and orange flowers bleed through matadors sticking bulls, a tropical forest rimming a crescent of white beach.

Lorraine's cigarettes aren't in their usual place on the refrigerator. Smoking in bed, she'll kill us one of these days, Christina thinks, as she inches her mother's door open. She sees her tucked up in one corner of the futon, a pillow jammed against her stomach and dark head curled into her chest. Christina listens to the soft purr of her mother's breathing, the squeak of bedsprings as the tenant in the apartment above rolls over in bed. Sometimes Christina comes upstairs in the night to go to the bathroom, and finds Lorraine seated at the kitchen table in the dark, smoking. Waiting, Christina knows, for the couple upstairs to be finished making love. She saw the squiggly line drawings in her mother's journal when she left it lying open beside the bed. Lines that formed a woman's face, wild hair, tears squirting from the eyes and all over the page; and nipples, dark, accentuated, as though she'd pressed hard on the pencil when she drew them, and the shape of an open vulva.

They'd had a window booth at Grapes for the birthday supper the night before, had watched the traffic rolling by on Route 90; ate Mediterranean salads, barely speaking. Lorraine absent, worrying because they had not been satisfied with the most recent draft of her script. "They" being the people who pay the rent, she explained. She ate as though starved, tearing apart huge shrimps with her fingers. She had pulled the blue butterfly clips from her hair and it drooped around her face, making her look wilted.

"So, ladies, which one of you is fifteen today?" the waiter asked.

Lorraine laughed. "I wonder," she said, and fiddled with the sand dollar hanging from her neck.

As the waiter reached across the table for her plate, Christina felt him staring at her breasts. She looked up and saw Lorraine watching, faint surprise rising in her eyes that became dread as she frowned and ground her cigarette out in the ashtray, as though she was in danger of starting a forest fire, performing a complicated task that demanded her complete attention. "Cheeky twit," she said after he had left. "I don't think we should come here any more." After that, their conversation, while more animated, had gone downhill.

—I'm thinking about going on the pill.

—What, in god's name, for?

—There's this guy at school? He looks like Diamond Dave.

—So?

—So I think I'm going to have sex with him.

—And?

—I thought you might want to know.

—Why can't you just sneak around like your sister did?

—You want me to lie, then?

—Let's just say that I don't want a blueprint of your future sexual activity. And I don't think much of your new friends. And your schoolwork is going down the tube. An incomplete in your Social Studies newspaper project. Chris. Just what is this about, anyway?

—They give it away, you know. I can go on the pill without your consent.

—You'll put on weight. Become bloated. Your breasts will be sore and swollen. Get even larger.

A clutter of magazines, a half-eaten cheese sandwich, pages of notes, an overflowing ashtray litter the floor around Lorraine's futon. Christina stoops, about to slide a cigarette from its package.

Lorraine's legs scissor through the blankets. "You're not going to the park," she says. She flings her pillow aside and rises onto an elbow and the strap of her nightgown slides down a shoulder, to her upper arm, its skin dimpled beneath a deep tan.

"I hate that place," Lorraine says, meaning Assiniboine Park. "Bunch of creeps hanging around, flashing their noodles."

"It's Sunday. There's nothing else to do." Christina is gratified by the wince of guilt in Lorraine's dark eyes. Though they have the right to use the cabin at the lake, they haven't gone once in two summers.

"At least I can talk to Pam and Lisa." She shuffles through the pile of magazines with her foot. Lorraine's journal lies on top, opened to a column of figures, her attempt to predict how much she needs to sock away for income tax. Every several pages of notes stop for figures with different titles: WHAT I NEED. INCOME HOPED FOR. EXPENDITURES.

"You'd kill me if my room looked like this."

Lorraine groans, flops back onto the bed, pulls a floral sheet over her head. The smell of coconut cream rises, thick, too heavy, like the lard aftertaste of the icing on mass-produced birthday cakes. "Oh, Chris." A sigh, and the sheet puffs out around her mouth. "Now what?"

"I'm pregnant."

The sheet collapses around Lorraine's face as she inhales deeply.

"What if I was? What would you do?"

Lorraine rolls over, faces the wall, pretends to be asleep.

"I could get mother's allowance, you know. Raise it myself. At least it wouldn't be so boring around here."

Still Lorraine feigns sleep.

Christina has clear memories of walking upstairs to her bedroom in their house, and feeling as though her feet never touched the steps. She rides past the house on her bicycle often to check for changes. New curtains. A cedar deck. If the evergreen seedling she brought home from a field trip has grown. She saw a young couple walk up the front sidewalk holding hands. She wonders if the air inside the house has cleared. Believes someone should invent a spray bomb, like a new-car scent, that covers spillage, emotions erupting, hostility. She wonders if the new owners found her name. She had got a wood-burning set one Christmas and had burned her name into the hardwood floor under her bed.

Where they live now is called a four-plex, and better than an apartment because it has a yard, Lorraine says. Christina hasn't told her that she's found messages written on water pipes near the ceiling in her bedroom. F.A. LOVES B.D. L.A. IS A DYKE. She thought the misspelling made the person sound pathetic. She'd found the word HELP! And sometimes she thinks she hears the word whispered. Once the building was a home for girls, the landlord said. On nights when she can't fall asleep it's because she feels she's being watched. In this new room, she dreamed of being a baby. Of seeing herself curled in a strange mist, and receding, falling backwards and becoming smaller, a curled pink shrimp about to disappear, until she kicked out at it, yelled away her own disappearance.

"Well, if you won't have a baby," she tells Lorraine, "then I will."

"I don't even have a boyfriend, for god's sake."

"No wonder." Christina slams the bedroom door behind her.

She stands in the kitchen, fists clenched against the window, against a knot in her throat. Lorraine is not going to ruin this day.

"You're not going to the park," Lorraine says through the door. Then Christina hears her mother's step against the floor. "And I'll thank you to stay out of my cancer sticks."

Through the kitchen window Christina sees the wind lift paper and whisk it about the knees of a boy crossing the parking lot beside McDonald's. The glare of sunlight is reflected in the windows of the restaurant. Across from it, Grant Park High squats in a broad field. Inside it all year, boys back girls into lockers, trap them with wiry arms laid across their shoulders. When someone backs Christina into a locker and says, How about you and me fucking? she punches him, and says, Sorry, but I'm totally devoted to the man I love. Sometimes she wishes this were true, but she has doubts. She's seen what can happen when Pam and Lisa became totally devoted over and over and wind up being totally miserable.

She saw Calvin's brains, like flecks of porridge, all over the photograph of Jennifer.

"I'm quitting school," Christina says as Lorraine enters the kitchen.

"Oh, Chris," Lorraine says, as she struggles with the zipper on her shorts. "You're crying again. It must be that time of month."

"I can't stand it."

"It'll pass," Lorraine says, and pats Christina lightly on the buttocks as though she is still five years old and just swallowed a penny.

She wheels her bicycle out into the blast of hot air that makes the day smell used and already spent. A styrofoam container cupping splashes of relish and ketchup tumbles across the yard and nestles against the leg of Lorraine's chaise longue. Dishes clatter in the sink as Lorraine rushes about in shorts and halter, trying to make up for the hours of lost sunlight. The window slides open.

"Make sure you stay away from the bushes, and be home no later than five."

"I'll try." The words are covered by the sudden drone of an air conditioner. Lorraine caved in too easily, Christina thinks, as she bounces the bicycle down the steps. She'd got up her strength to batter down a door and it opened just as she put her shoulder to it.

Damned garbage again, Christina thinks, as the bike's wheel meets a plastic Zellers bag on the bottom step. But as she reaches for it, she knows, from the look of it, how the bag's opening is tucked under neatly, that it's been set there. She sees the hurried dash of her name on an envelope inside it.

The birthday card has a picture of a mirror and large XXXOOO's ETC. written in lipstick across it and red letters below that say, "Especially the etc." "A little something for someone sweet." Her father's tight printing adds to the card's message. Inside the bag is a round tin of assorted toffee. A hurried, last-minute gift, she thinks, while Georgina shopped for steak and barbecue sauce. She slits the plastic seal and pries off the lid. Just what she needs; mondo fat, she thinks. She sifts through the candy, enjoys the slippery feel of the cellophane-wrapped swirls. Her favourite. She remembers the sheet of Mackintosh's toffee, her father putting it in the freezer until it was as hard as glass, then smashing it with a hammer and pressing crumbs of it with his finger onto her tongue. The wind blows too hot against her neck. Forget it, she thinks, she won't go to the park. I've changed my mind, she'll tell Lorraine. Instead, she'll sit in the dark coolness of her room, Randy Rhoads and Nikki Sixx watching as she tries on clothing, ties scarves around her breasts, draws hearts on her cheeks, and then she will practise her ballet, will stretch and bend into the sound of Yo-Yo Ma's cello.

"What in god's name did you spill in the kitchen?" Lorraine calls from the window. "I'm sticking to the floor."

She's been watching, Christina realizes. She puts the tin of candy into her knapsack and wheels across the yard. Lorraine watching. Lorraine telephoning on the hour whenever she has to go out at night, checking, listening carefully to Christina's answers to determine if anything has changed.

Christina pedals down the wide street bordering Assiniboine Park, Yo-Yo Ma working hard on her ears. She passes by graceful stone houses, lawn sprinklers twisting out rainbows. She doesn't know why she likes the music, because sometimes it's confusing. The cello has so many sounds, it seems to work around the melody, to hide its message. And then suddenly, the melody pushes through the confusion, clear, easy to follow. She was with Pam and Lisa in Eaton's when they stole the tapes. Pam, more certain of herself, took her time and got exactly what she wanted. Lisa, too obvious with her purple hair, grabbed the first tape she came to. This is it: the Elgar Cello Concerto, Opus 85. Yo-Yo Ma playing the cello.

"I hate that place," Lorraine said about the park, because once she'd been flashed there. She tried to act casual, Lorraine, up on her feet demonstrating the man's shuffle, how he swung his walking-stick, and each time she told the story she added a detail, a white moustache, patent-leather shoes, a red handkerchief in his blazer pocket, but always ended by saying, "And his pathetic little dink, dangling from his unzipped pants, like a piece of old leather." Building something that will likely appear somewhere, later. Making a big issue out of nothing. As Christina enters the park's stone gates, she feels the welcome of cooler air, anticipates how the trees beside the river harbour deep shadows.

"'I'm a very family-oriented person. I have personally been responsible for starting about seven families this year,'" Christina says, quoting Diamond Dave.

"He's an animal!" Lisa shrieks. Her knees uncurl as she falls backwards onto the blanket. Her hair, purple and maroon flames, licks at the grass.

"That's an old one," Pam says.

Lisa rises to her knees, arms raised as she stretches, and a whistle rises up from a car passing by. The two girls were already stripped to their bathing suits when Christina finally found them in a clearing below the Pavilion. Her black T-shirt sucks up the heat of the sun and sticks to her back, but she won't take it off. You can see through my bathing suit when it's wet, she explained. But we're not going anywhere near water, Pam says with a flicker of annoyance. Christina envies their short bodies. She can't find jeans that fit. Her problem, Lorraine says, is an extra-long torso. And her bathing suit isn't long enough, either. She hangs out over it on top, and bulges out below.

Lisa runs fingers through her hair, shakes it loose across her shoulders. "I think Tod's still mad at me," she says, collapsing suddenly. "He still hangs up when I call."

"What did you expect?" Pam says.

"He's too serious. Thinks he owns me."

"Like Calvin and Jennifer," Christina says. For weeks they picked it apart. Jennifer should have waited to dump Calvin until things got better for him at home; that his parents are wrong to blame her, cruel even. It's not fair, they reassured Jennifer, and invited her to sit with them at their table at McDonald's, the one they usually occupied during study periods. Until Calvin shot himself, Pam and Lisa didn't know Jennifer existed, Christina thinks, as she makes a pillow of her knapsack and lies down.

A yellow Frisbee arcs across the sky, through the jangle of music playing from car radios. She watches a man; tall, his hair shines orange in the sunlight as he chases after it. There is something close to loser about a person who plays Frisbee alone, she thinks. She thought she would feel different when she turned fifteen, but here she is still wearing Lorraine's knobby knees and must lie on her stomach to hide them. Her face is in the process of deciding who she will look like, Lorraine said. It takes time. Right now, her nose is her father's. Strong, her mother says, a handsome nose that she will grow into. Unfortunately, she also has inherited her father's caterpillar eyebrows. The park swims with heat and the man playing Frisbee becomes a spot of colour wavering against a watery wall.

When Christina wakes up, the girls are gone. She watches as the ribbons of a kite sway above the trees. The hoarse toot of a miniature train signals its entry into the tunnel. Beyond, children yank at parents' hands, drawing them towards the sound.

—Oh look! See the tunnel, the tunnel! We're going into the tunnel now.

—Here it comes! Here comes the tunnel, Chris. Duck!

An island of trees emerged, a deer in the underbrush reared its head, watching them pass through a forest of muskeg and the sprinkling of pink and blue wild asters alongside the tracks. Her father's hand gripped hers, tight, squeezing, he more excited than she.

—Oh, Chris! Here it comes! Here comes the tunnel!

A girl runs towards Christina, hair streaming and, pulling her face taut, becomes a moving picture stopped in frame, action suspended, and her eyes are blank and flat. It seems to Christina that the light changed. It became flat, too, and she feels she's turning pages in a book, looking at a picture of a girl playing in a park, and that she's the only one who is real.

She can't go home yet. It isn't quite five o'clock. Lorraine will be cooling off in the wading pool, towel, suntan lotion, diet-drink cans, the columns of figures lying on the lounge chair. And she will pry with questions as though she suspects oncoming illness. Christina sits cross-legged, cradling the tin of candy, when she spots Lisa, her hair, the iridescent flare of colour, as the girls run backwards down a grassy incline, hands flailing at the air.

Then she sees Pam emerge from the shadows of an ivy trestle beside the Pavilion. She strides across the open field with a certain hard knowledge in her punchy, determined movement. Then she turns and beckons, and a man with orange hair, wearing a red vest, steps out from the ivy trestle. It's the man who played Frisbee with himself, Christina realizes, as Lisa scoops up a yellow Frisbee, and sprints towards her. She drops onto the blanket beside Christina, chest heaving and collar-bone slick with perspiration. "You are not going to believe this guy. He is so incredibly gorgeous. I can't stand it."

Pam begins stuffing towels and cosmetics into a bag. "We went for a walk," she says, avoiding her gaze. "We didn't think you'd want us to wake you."

Black beads swing against the man's chest as he stands at the edge of the blanket, his body blocking out the sun. "Who's she?"

"Christina," Pam says, "this is Darren."

"So, it's Christina. Listen, when I said you should come and see my room, I hadn't planned on a party."

"I have to go," Christina tells them. She pulls on her jeans, turns away as she sucks in her stomach and yanks at the zipper. Damned jeans. She will call her father, put the pressure on Georgina every day until he comes through. She will go home, turn on the television, and let the world blow up.

Darren whistles. "Holy, an Amazon. No, wait," Darren says as Christina turns, a fist balled. "I like Amazons." He grins and cracks his knuckles. Gold crosses dangle from his ears. "I guess I am having a party," he says. "You dudes like monkey's lunch?" The tattoo of a woman's face ripples on his forearm. She has a red star in the middle of her forehead, hair whipped by the wind. The tattoo, his hair, the gold crosses in the ears look familiar.

"What's monkey's lunch?" Lisa wants to know.

"You've never heard of monkey's lunch?"

"And so what?" Pam snaps.

He bangs his fist against his forehead. "Lordy. Bunch of Ethiopians coming to my party." He smiles suddenly, as though the pain they'd caused is gone. "It's okay," he says. "I'm used to it."

"Definitely strange," Pam says as they wheel their bicycles behind him. He strides, his red vest flapping. "But interesting."

"You coming?" they ask Christina.

Lorraine will be waiting, her small frame coiled and humming with pent-up energy.

Darren turns and, leaping up, grabs a tree branch and swings down in front of her. "Of course she's coming."

He punches the air as he walks, lips moving constantly, as though he's plugged into music, Christina thinks.

He lives in a house on one of the streets that border the park, in a tall stone house with diamond-shaped bevelled glass in its windows. Like the houses she and Lorraine sometimes cruise past, Lorraine hoping to catch glimpses of rooms, see how the other side lives, she says.

"You rich or something?" Lisa asks.

"Don't give him the satisfaction," Pam mutters.

They pass through a stone archway to the back of the house. Christina feels as though it's night and she is home alone, listening for a knock at the door, feeling the danger of opening it, the danger compelling her forward.

They climb up cedar stairs to a second-floor deck with white canvas chairs and a table with a yellow umbrella. Christina thinks of Lorraine draped over the edges of the wading pool, her body lying in six inches of water, misting her body with water in a Windex bottle.

"Shoes," Darren says and points to their feet.

"This is getting boring," Pam says, but takes off her runners.

Keys jangle as he unlocks the door. "You're breathing on me," he says to Pam.

Christina follows them into a room that's completely blue. Plush blue carpet brushes against her bare feet. A blue couch rests against a wall, its plump cushions creaseless as in a furniture advertisement. The only thing in the room not blue is a refrigerator.

Darren walks to the wall, spreads his arms, and sliding doors open; on the other side, more blue.

"There was a sale on paint," Pam says.

"Far out," Lisa says as she steps into the bedroom. The bed flashes with navy blue satin sheets. On each side of it are upholstered platforms in crushed velvet, on one, a television set and vcr. Pam pokes the bed. It undulates with water.

"I did it myself," Darren says. "The couch is custom-built."

"I never would have guessed," Pam says.

Darren fake-punches her on the chin. "And I'll bet your hole is lined with glass," he says.

Lisa giggles nervously.

"I've only got two rules," Darren says. "No tampons in the toilet, and don't pop zits on the mirror. Can't have any of those little white spots, can we?"

"A preppy in disguise," Pam says, as she circles the room. Except for a raised platform and speakers mounted above it, one end of the room is completely bare. A row of stuffed animals lines a wall along the floor and she stops and nudges them with her foot.

Darren enters carrying a tray with glasses, thick brown cream jiggling against their sides. "Over there," he says. They are to sit on the floor, along with the rest of the animals, he says. As he kneels beside Christina, she feels his breath on her neck. "It's your birthday?" he asks, and holds up the birthday card.

"You were in my knapsack."

"Okay, that's it. We're out of here," Pam says.

"Wait," Darren says. He springs to his feet. "I had to check. You could be terrorists, for all I know."

"I didn't know it was your birthday," Lisa says.

"It's no big deal."

"You're wrong," Darren tells her. "It is a big deal. A very big deal. I'll be right back."

Brown cream rims Lisa's mouth and she licks it away. "It's not a milkshake, that's for sure. Definitely not."

"Weirder and weirder," Pam says, as the light in the room begins to dim and a faint circle of light grows on the wall above the platform, becoming wide, sharp, and bright. Pulsing staccato music taps against Christina's breastbone. The rhythmic slide of a snare drum and cymbal dies to a guitar that rises suddenly, screaming up the scale. Darren leaps into the spotlight and punches the air with a black gloved hand. He becomes Billy Idol singing to Christina. What had set her free and brought her to him? In the midnight hour, he sang, as though he knew that she had been down in her basement room for two years watching the grass grow outside the window. She wants more, too, like him. She wants more than Lorraine, more than a basement view, a tin of toffee, watching the world blow up on TV. She wants to know, most of all, what it is she wants. Not knowing gives her heart-cramps.

"It's not really him," Pam shouts. "He's lip-syncing."

"Who cares?" Lisa says. She gets up and begins swaying and clapping to the beat.

Christina's arms grow heavy, and it seems that a weight sits on top of her head, presses her into the floor, keeps her fixed on Darren's contorted face, and what she thinks are tears rolling in his eyes. The song ends, but he is into another one immediately, and then another, his energy frantic, unfaltering, until, finally, just when Christina thinks her head will cave in, the show ends. He drops to his knees, presses his forehead into the blue shag. Christina gropes for the wall, slides her hands along it until she finds the bathroom door.

"You're great," Lisa says.

Behind Christina, the bedroom fills with light and she sees her face in the bathroom mirror. She runs water into the sink, scoops its coolness against her cheeks. When she looks up she sees him in the mirror, his orange spiky head bending towards her.

"Happy birthday," he says.

She grabs him, and presses her cheek into his hot one. "I know what you feel," she tells him.

His crab-like arms become a vice, squeezing her, flattening her breasts against his ribs. "And what do I feel?" he asks.

"Like there's too many radios playing at the same time, all on different stations."

Darren takes her hand and sets it against the lump in his jeans. "What would you say if I jumped you?"

"She'd say, no thanks." Pam stands in the doorway, her hand searching for the light switch. Fluorescent lights bounce off the mirror and wall tiles.

"Get lost," Darren says. Perspiration trails down his face, leaving pale tracks through his deep tan. Christina sees the tinge of blue whiskers. She pushes him away. She notices that his hair is thinning on top and she sees through it to the black roots at his pink scalp.

"You okay?" Pam asks.

"Okay." Christina's eyes meet Pam's hand at the switch.

"Look," she says. The switch is the shape of an erect penis; red, ridiculous-looking.

Pam's face cracks open with laughter. "I am going to wet my pants," she says, and, taking Christina by the wrist, leads her from the bathroom. "Let's get out of here."

But they don't leave. Pam dances around the room, jeering and laughing, and Christina follows. The two of them leap onto the bed, wind themselves in satin sheets and dance. *With a rebel yell*, they chant, *we want more, more, more.* Lisa joins in, and the stuffed animals bounce off the blue walls. Then Christina remembers her knapsack. "Food fight," she says, and as they had seen in a video of an old movie, and had once begun to do in McDonald's, they grab handfuls of toffee, pelt one another. Darren stands in the bathroom doorway, white-faced, stricken.

"My room," he says. "Get out of here, you animals. You're ruining my fucking room."

She has only two gears left on her bicycle, high and low, and the muscles in her legs knot as she pedals up an incline in the street. "Fucking room, I'll bet," Pam said. "He couldn't get it up, I'll bet." There is something about Pam she doesn't like, Christina thinks, as Pam and Lisa pedal across an open parking lot and disappear behind an apartment building. But she isn't sure what it is. She coasts down the street, passes through blocks of shadows cast by the sun hanging low behind the houses. Yo-Yo Ma's music makes her think of a wolf, now. In one of those wilderness films, a wolf standing on an outcrop of rock, howling at the moon.

And then the music is full and charged, like a suicide note that is romantic and terrible, but sad, too, because the person is gone and can't have the satisfaction of knowing that people have cried. Or know that their writing has been analysed, words remembered forever. It's not fair, she thinks, that you have to die before people pay that kind of attention. She looks for Calvin in the streets. Long hair, black Johnny Walker T-shirt, looking like a hundred others at Grant Park High. Slippery skin, because all he ate was French fries. Once he bummed a cigarette from her. If she'd known, she would have given him the whole package.

On the cover of the cassette there is a picture of Yo-Yo Ma. He is a small person who curls around the cello as he plays, eyes closed in concentration behind glasses, the music the only living thing for the moment. Like Lorraine, keening over Christina's bed most mornings. "Christina, Christina, honey. Are you awake? Christina, wake up, please. You'll be late. Good morning, Christina, honey bun."

When she wheels her bicycle into the yard, she sees Lorraine's chaise longue resting against the stair railing, folded up and chained to it. The wading pool is upended against the wall beneath the kitchen window. She smells the smoky remains of barbecues on the balconies of the high-rises towering above their four-plex on three sides. A mixture of spicy sauce and singed meat. Someone strums awkwardly at a guitar. Lorraine's shadow passes the kitchen window and, moments later, the back door flies open.

"Chris? That you?" She's still in shorts and halter, and its strap droops, reveals a wedge of untanned flesh set against the gentle curve of her sun-freckled breast. "You're late. Good job. That's the thanks I get, eh?"

Christina smells coconut as she passes Lorraine in the doorway.

"Well? What have you got to say?" Lorraine follows Christina into the kitchen. Pink candles circle a cake, a circle of light centred on the table that she'd spread with a white cloth. Christina frees her arms, lets the knapsack drop to the floor, and for a moment, for the moment it takes to absorb the presence of the cake, its lit candles, she wants to grab Lorraine, to wind her arms about her mother's neck and cradle her head against her.

"Well?" Lorraine waits, hands at her hips. "So that's the thanks I get. First time I let you go, and look what happens."

Christina thinks that if you didn't know Lorraine as well as she does, you could be fooled and taken in by her eyes. They are always bright, huge discs of light with questions in them, or filled with the reflections of the people she talks to, reflections of their sadness, or happiness, reflections of the programs she watches on television. But if you look further, to her mouth, for instance, you will see a dryness at the corners of her lips, a withering that could be taken for meanness. But it's more a drying up from caring than from meanness, Christina thinks.

"The minute I get home, you're on my case."

"I have the right."

"And if I were you, I wouldn't wear short shorts."

"Really."

"I wouldn't. You've got cellulite on the backs of your legs."

"Take a hike, kiddo. Was that nice?" Lorraine's voice follows Christina down the stairs. "We need to talk, you and I."

"Be up in ten," Christina says, thinking, Hah, you mean you'll do the talking and I'll do the listening.

June 22, Christina writes in her journal as, overhead, Lorraine slams cupboard drawers and cutlery clinks down into place on the table. She would like to write a poem, something for Calvin, call it Opus 85. But instead she writes, *Life is dull and boring and sometimes I think that if Lorraine doesn't get off my case, I'm going to take off. I have places to go*, she writes, because she suspects that Lorraine reads her journal.

"Sorry to report, Unit, no flasher in the bushes," Christina says as she comes up the stairs. May as well help, she thinks, or else have to put up with Lorraine the martyr.

"It's not them I worry about," Lorraine says, as Christina enters the kitchen.

Changed into her jeans, Christina notices. Good.

"Or white-slave traders, either."

"There's a movie on, later," Christina says.

"I'll make popcorn," Lorraine says.

"Should I open up the hide-a-bed? Okay?"

"Okay," Lorraine says. "Happy birthday, honey."

Their lips touch, a quiver of hope passes between them.

Eden Robinson

Queen of the North

Frog Song

Whenever I see abandoned buildings, I think of our old house in the village, a rickety shack by the swamp where the frogs used to live. It's gone now. The council covered the whole area with rocks and gravel.

In my memory, the sun is setting and the frogs begin to sing. As the light shifts from yellow to orange to red, I walk down the path to the beach. The wind blows in from the channel, making the grass hiss and shiver around my legs. The tide is low and there's a strong rotting smell from the beach. Tree stumps that have been washed down the channel from the logged areas loom ahead—black, twisted silhouettes against the darkening sky.

The seiner coming down the channel is the *Queen of the North*, pale yellow with blue trim, Uncle Josh's boat. I wait on the beach. The water laps my ankles. The sound of the old diesel engine grows louder as the boat gets closer.

Usually I can will myself to move, but sometimes I'm frozen where I stand, waiting for the crew to come ashore.

The only thing my cousin Ronny didn't own was a Barbie Doll speedboat. She had the swimming pool, she had the Barbie-Goes-to-Paris carrying case, but she didn't have the boat. There was one left in Northern Drugs, nestling between the puzzles and the stuffed Garfields, but it cost sixty bucks and we were broke. I knew Ronny was going to get it. She'd already saved twenty bucks out of her allowance. Anyway, she always got everything she wanted because she was an only child and both her parents worked at the aluminum smelter. Mom knew how much I wanted it, but she said it was a toss-up between school supplies and paying bills, or wasting our money on something I'd get sick of in a few weeks.

We had a small Christmas tree. I got socks and underwear and forced a cry of surprise when I opened the package. Uncle Josh came in just as Mom was carving the turkey. He pushed a big box in my direction.

"Go on," Mom said, smiling. "It's for you."

Uncle Josh looked like a young Elvis. He had the soulful brown eyes and the thick black hair. He dressed his long, thin body in clothes with expensive labels—no Sears or Kmart for him. He smiled at me with his perfect pouty lips and bleached white teeth.

"Here you go, sweetheart," Uncle Josh said.

I didn't want it. Whatever it was, I didn't want it. He put it down in front of me. Mom must have wrapped it. She was never any good at wrapping presents. You'd think with two kids and a million Christmases behind her she'd know how to wrap a present.

"Come on, open it," Mom said.

I unwrapped it slowly, my skin crawling. Yes, it was the Barbie Doll speedboat.

My mouth smiled. We all had dinner and I pulled the wishbone with my little sister, Alice. I got the bigger piece and made a wish. Uncle Josh kissed me. Alice sulked. Uncle Josh never got her anything, and later that afternoon she screamed about it. I put the boat in my closet and didn't touch it for days.

Until Ronny came over to play. She was showing off her new set of Barbie-in-the-Ice-Capades clothes. Then I pulled out the speedboat and the look on her face was almost worth it.

My sister hated me for weeks. When I was off at soccer practice, Alice took the boat and threw it in the river. To this day, Alice doesn't know how grateful I was.

There's a dream I have sometimes. Ronny comes to visit. We go down the hallway to my room. She goes in first. I point to the closet and she eagerly opens the door. She thinks I've been lying, that I don't really have a boat. She wants proof.

When she turns to me, she looks horrified, pale and shocked. I laugh, triumphant. I reach in and stop, seeing Uncle Josh's head, arms, and legs squashed inside, severed from the rest of his body. My clothes are soaked dark red with his blood.

"Well, what do you know," I say. "Wishes do come true."

Me and five chug buddies are in the Tamitik arena, in the girls' locker room under the bleachers. The hockey game is in the third period and the score is tied. The yells and shouting of the fans drown out the girl's swearing. There are four of us against her. It doesn't take long before she's on the floor trying to crawl away. I want to say I'm not part of it, but that's my foot hooking her ankle and tripping her while Ronny takes her down with a blow to the temple. She grunts. Her head makes a hollow sound when it bounces off the sink. The lights make us all look green. A cheer explodes from inside the arena. Our team has scored. The girl's now curled up under the sink and I punch her and kick her and smash her face into the floor.

My cuz Ronny had great connections. She could get hold of almost any drug you wanted. This was during her biker chick phase, when she wore tight leather skirts, teeny weeny tops, and many silver bracelets, rings, and studs. Her parents started coming down really hard on her then. I went over to her house to get high. It was okay to do it there, as long as we sprayed the living room with Lysol and opened the windows before her parents came home.

We toked up and decided to go back to my house to get some munchies. Ronny tagged along when I went up to my bedroom to get the bottle of Visine. There was an envelope on my dresser. Even before I opened it I knew it would be money. I knew who it was from.

I pulled the bills out. Ronny squealed.

"Holy sheep shit, how much is there?"

I spread the fifties out on the dresser. Two hundred and fifty dollars. I could get some flashy clothes or nice earrings with that money, if I could bring myself to touch it. Anything I bought would remind me of him.

"You want to have a party?" I said to Ronny.

"Are you serious?" she said, going bug-eyed.

I gave her the money and said make it happen. She asked who it came from, but she didn't really care. She was already making phone calls.

That weekend we had a house party in town. The house belonged to one of Ronny's biker buddies and was filled with people I knew by sight from school. As the night wore on, they came up and told me what a generous person I was. Yeah, that's me, I thought, Saint Karaoke of Good Times.

I took Ronny aside when she was drunk enough. "Ronny, I got to tell you something."

"What?" she said, blinking too fast, like she had something in her eye.

"You know where I got the money?"

She shook her head, lost her balance, blearily put her hand on my shoulder, and barfed out the window.

As I listened to her heave out her guts, I decided I didn't want to tell her after all. What was the point? She had a big mouth, and anything I told her I might as well stand on a street corner and shout to the world. What I really wanted was to have a good time and forget about the money, and after beating everyone hands down at tequila shots that's exactly what I did.

"Moooo." I copy the two aliens on *Sesame Street* mooing to a telephone. Me and Uncle Josh are watching television together. He smells faintly of the halibut he cooked for dinner. Uncle Josh undoes his pants. "Moo." I keep my eyes on the TV and say nothing as he moves toward me. I'm not a baby like Alice, who runs to Mommy about everything. When it's over he'll have treats for me. It's like when the dentist gives me extra suckers for not crying, not even when it really hurts.

I could have got my scorpion tattoo at The Body Hole, where my friends went. A perfectly groomed beautician would sit me in a black-leather dentist's chair and the tattoo artist would show me the tiny diagram on tracing paper. We'd choose the exact spot on my neck where the scorpion would go, just below the hairline where my hair comes to a point. Techno, maybe some funky remix of Abba, would blare through the speakers as he whirred the tattoo needle's motor.

But Ronny had done her own tattoo, casually standing in front of the bathroom mirror with a short needle and permanent blue ink from a pen. She simply poked the needle in and out, added the ink, and that was that. No fuss, no muss.

So I asked her to do it for me. After all, I thought, if she could brand six marks of Satan on her own breast, she could certainly do my scorpion.

Ronny led me into the kitchen and cleared off a chair. I twisted my hair up into a bun and held it in place. She showed me the needle, then dropped it into a pot of boiling water. She was wearing a crop top and I could see her navel ring, glowing bright gold in the slanting light of the setting sun. She was prone to lifting her shirt in front of complete strangers and telling them she'd pierced herself.

Ronny emptied the water into the sink and lifted the needle in gloved hands. I bent my head and looked down at the floor as she traced the drawing on my skin.

The needle was hot. It hurt more than I expected, a deep ache, a throbbing. I breathed through my mouth. I fought not to cry. I concentrated fiercely on not crying in front of her, and when she finished I lay very still.

"See?" Ronny said. "Nothing to it, you big baby."

When I opened my eyes and raised my head, she held one small mirror to my face and another behind me so I could see her work. I frowned at my reflection. The scorpion looked like a smear.

"It'll look better when the swelling goes down," she said, handing me the two mirrors.

As Ronny went to start the kettle for tea, she looked out the window over the sink. "Star light, star bright, first star—"

I glanced out the window. "That's Venus."

"Like you'd know the difference."

I didn't want to argue. The skin on the back of my neck ached like it was sunburned.

I am singing Janis Joplin songs, my arms wrapped around the karaoke machine. I fend people off with a stolen switchblade.

No one can get near until some kid from school has the bright idea of giving me drinks until I pass out.

Someone else videotapes me so my one night as a rock star is recorded forever. She tries to send it to *America's Funniest Home Videos*, but they reject it as unsuitable for family viewing. I remember nothing else about that night after I got my first hit of acid. My real name is Adelaine, but the next day a girl from school sees me coming and yells, "Hey, look, it's Karaoke!"

The morning after my sixteenth birthday I woke up looking down into Jimmy Hill's face. We were squashed together in the backseat of a car and I thought, God, I didn't.

I crawled around and found my shirt and then spent the next half hour vomiting beside the car. I vaguely remembered the night before, leaving the party with Jimmy. I remembered being afraid of bears.

Jimmy stayed passed out in the backseat, naked except for his socks. We were somewhere up in the mountains, just off a logging road. The sky was misty and grey. As I stood up and stretched, the car headlights went out.

Dead battery. That's just fucking perfect, I thought.

I checked the trunk and found an emergency kit. I got out one of those blankets that look like a large sheet of aluminum and wrapped it around myself. I searched the car until I found my jeans. I threw Jimmy's shirt over him. His jeans were hanging off the car's antenna. When I took them down, the antenna wouldn't straighten up.

I sat in the front seat. I had just slept with Jimmy Hill. Christ, he was practically a Boy Scout. I saw his picture in the local newspaper all the time, with these medals for swimming. Other than that, I never really noticed him. We went to different parties.

About midmorning, the sun broke through the mist and streamed to the ground in fingers of light, just like in the movies when God is talking to someone. The sun hit my face and I closed my eyes.

I heard the seat shift and turned. Jimmy smiled at me and I knew why I'd slept with him. He leaned forward and we kissed. His lips were soft and the kiss was gentle. He put his hand on the back of my neck. "You're beautiful."

I thought it was just a line, the polite thing to say after a one-night stand, so I didn't answer.

"Did you get any?" Jimmy said.

"What?" I said.

"Blueberries." He grinned. "Don't you remember?"

I stared at him.

His grin faded. "Do you remember anything?"

I shrugged.

"Well. We left the party, I dunno, around two, I guess. You said you wanted blueberries. We came out here—" He cleared his throat.

"Then we fucked, passed out, and now we're stranded." I finished the sentence. The sun was getting uncomfortable. I took off the emergency blanket. I had no idea what to say next. "Battery's dead."

He swore and leaned over me to try the ignition.

I got out of his way by stepping out of the car. Hastily he put his shirt on, not looking up at me. He had a nice chest, buff and tan. He blushed and I wondered if he had done this before.

"You cool with this?" I said.

He immediately became macho. "Yeah."

I felt really shitty then. God, I thought, he's going to be a bragger.

I went and sat on the hood. It was hot. I was thirsty and had a killer headache. Jimmy got out and sat beside me.

"You know where we are?" Jimmy said.

"Not a fucking clue."

He looked at me and we both started laughing.

"You were navigating last night," he said, nudging me.

"You always listen to pissed women?"

"Yeah," he said, looking sheepish. "Well. You hungry?"

I shook my head. "Thirsty."

Jimmy hopped off the car and came back with a warm Coke from under the driver's seat. We drank it in silence.

"You in any rush to get back?" he asked.

We started laughing again and then went hunting for blueberries. Jimmy found a patch not far from the car and we picked the bushes clean. I'd forgotten how tart wild blueberries are. They're smaller than store-bought berries, but their flavour is much more intense.

"My sister's the wilderness freak," Jimmy said. "She'd be able to get us out of this. Or at least she'd know where we are."

We were perched on a log. "You gotta promise me something."

"What?"

"If I pop off before you, you aren't going to eat me."

"What?"

"I'm serious," I said. "And I'm not eating any bugs."

"If you don't try them, you'll never know what you're missing." Jimmy looked at the road. "You want to pick a direction?"

The thought of trekking down the dusty logging road in the wrong direction held no appeal to me. I must have made a face because Jimmy said, "Me neither."

After the sun set, Jimmy made a fire in front of the car. We put the aluminum blanket under us and lay down. Jimmy pointed at the sky. "That's the Big Dipper."

"Ursa Major," I said. "Mother of all bears. There's Ursa Minor, Cassiopeia…" I stopped.

"I didn't know you liked astronomy."

"It's pretty nerdy."

He kissed me. "Only if you think it is." He put his arm around me and I put my head on his chest and listened to his heart. It was a nice way to fall asleep.

Jimmy shook me awake. "Car's coming." He pulled me to my feet. "It's my sister."

"Mmm." Blurrily I focused on the road. I could hear birds and, in the distance, the rumble of an engine.

"My sister could find me in hell," he said.

When they dropped me off at home, my mom went ballistic. "Where the hell were you?"

"Out." I stopped at the door. I hadn't expected her to be there when I came in.

Her chest was heaving. I thought she'd start yelling, but she said very calmly, "You've been gone for two days."

You noticed? I didn't say it. I felt ill and I didn't want a fight. "Sorry. Should've called."

I pushed past her, kicked off my shoes, and went upstairs.

Still wearing my smelly jeans and shirt I lay down on the bed. Mom followed me to my room and shook my shoulder.

"Tell me where you've been."

"At Ronny's."

"Don't lie to me. What is wrong with you?"

God. Just get lost. I wondered what she'd do if I came out and said what we both knew. Probably have a heart attack. Or call me a liar.

"You figure it out," I said. "I'm going to sleep." I expected her to give me a lecture or something, but she just left.

Sometimes, when friends were over, she'd point to Alice and say, "This is my good kid." Then she'd point to me and say, "This is my rotten kid, nothing but trouble. She steals, she lies, she sleeps around. She's just no damn good."

Alice knocked on my door later.

"Fuck off," I said.

"You've got a phone call."

"Take a message. I'm sleeping."

Alice opened the door and poked her head in. "You want me to tell Jimmy anything else?"

I scrambled down the hallway and grabbed the receiver. I took a couple of deep breaths so it wouldn't sound like I'd rushed to the phone. "Hi."

"Hi," Jimmy said. "We just replaced the battery on the car. You want to go for a ride?"

"Aren't you grounded?"

He laughed. "So?"

I thought he just wanted to get lucky again, and then I thought, What the hell, at least this time I'll remember it.

"Pick me up in five minutes."

I'm getting my ass kicked by two sisters. They're really good. They hit solidly and back off quickly. I don't even see them coming anymore. I get mad enough to kick out. By sheer luck, the kick connects. One of the sisters shrieks and goes down. She's on the ground, her leg at an odd angle. The other one loses it and swings. The bouncer steps in and the crowd around us boos.

"My cousins'll be at a biker party. You want to go?"

Jimmy looked at me like he wasn't sure if I was serious.

"I'll be good," I said, crossing my heart then holding up my fingers in a scout salute.

"What fun would that be?" he said, revving the car's engine.

I gave him directions. The car roared away from our house, skidding a bit. Jimmy didn't say anything. I found it unnerving. He looked over at me, smiled, then turned back to face the road. I was used to yappy guys, but this was nice. I leaned my head back into the seat. The leather creaked.

Ronny's newest party house didn't look too bad, which could have meant it was going to be dead in there. It's hard to get down and dirty when you're worried you'll stain the carpet. You couldn't hear anything until someone opened the door and the music throbbed out. They did a good job with the sound-proofing. We went up the steps just as my cousin Frank came out with some bar buddies.

Jimmy stopped when he saw Frank and I guess I could see why. Frank is on the large side, six-foot-four and scarred up from his days as a hard-core Bruce Lee fan, when he felt compelled to fight Evil in street bars. He looked down at Jimmy.

"Hey, Jimbo," Frank said. "Heard you quit the swim team."

"You betcha," Jimmy said.

"Fucking right!" Frank body-slammed him. He tended to be more enthusiastic than most people could handle, but Jimmy looked okay with it. "More time to party," he said. Now they were going to gossip forever so I went inside.

The place was half-empty. I recognized some people and nodded. They nodded back. The music was too loud for conversation.

"You want a drink?" Frank yelled, touching my arm.

I jumped. He quickly took his hand back. "Where's Jimmy?"

"Ronny gave him a hoot and now he's hacking up his lungs out back." Frank took off his jacket, closed his eyes, and shuffled back and forth. All he knew was the reservation two-step and I wasn't in the mood. I moved toward the porch but Frank grabbed my hand. "You two doing the wild thing?"

"He's all yours," I said.

"Fuck you," Frank called after me.

Jimmy was leaning against the railing, his back toward me, his hands jammed into his pockets. I watched him. His hair was dark and shiny, brushing his shoulders. I liked the way he moved, easily, like he was in no hurry to get anywhere. His eyes were light brown with gold flecks. I knew that in a moment he would turn and smile at me and it would be like stepping into sunlight.

In my dream Jimmy's casting a fishing rod. I'm afraid of getting hooked, so I sit at the bow of the skiff. The ocean is mildly choppy, the sky is hard blue, the air is cool. Jimmy reaches over to kiss me, but now he is soaking wet. His hands and lips are cold, his eyes are sunken and dull. Something moves in his mouth. It isn't his tongue. When I pull away, a crab drops from his lips and Jimmy laughs. "Miss me?"

I feel a scream in my throat but nothing comes out.

"What's the matter?" Jimmy tilts his head. Water runs off his hair and drips into the boat. "Crab got your tongue?"

This one's outside Hanky Panky's. The woman is so totally bigger than me it isn't funny. Still, she doesn't like getting hurt. She's afraid of the pain but can't back down because she started it. She's grabbing my hair, yanking it hard. I pull hers. We get stuck there, bent over, trying to kick each other, neither one of us willing to let go. My friends are laughing their heads off. I'm pissed at that but I'm too sloshed to let go. In the morning my scalp will throb and be so tender I won't be able to comb my hair. At that moment, a bouncer comes over and splits us apart. The woman tries to kick me but kicks him instead and he knocks her down. My friends grab my arm and steer me to the bus stop.

Jimmy and I lay down together on a sleeping bag in a field of fireweed. The forest fire the year before had razed the place and the weeds had only sprouted back up about a month earlier. With the spring sun and just the right sprinkling of rain, they were as tall as sunflowers, as dark pink as prize roses, swaying around us in the night breeze.

Jimmy popped open a bottle of Baby Duck. "May I?" he said, reaching down to untie my sneaker.

"You may," I said.

He carefully lifted the sneaker and poured in some Baby Duck. Then he raised it to my lips and I drank. We lay down, flattening fireweed and knocking over the bottle. Jimmy nibbled my ear. I drew circles in the bend of his arm. Headlights came up fast, then disappeared down the highway. We watched the fireweed shimmer and wave in the wind.

"You're quiet tonight," Jimmy said. "What're you thinking?"

I almost told him then. I wanted to tell him. I wanted someone else to know and not have it locked inside me. I kept starting and then chickening out. What was the point? He'd probably pull away from me in horror, disgusted, revolted.

"I want to ask you something," Jimmy whispered. I closed my eyes, feeling my chest tighten. "You hungry? I've got a monster craving for chicken wings."

Bloody Vancouver

When I got to Aunt Erma's the light in the hallway was going spastic, flickering like a strobe, little bright flashes then darkness so deep I had to feel my way along the wall. I stopped in front of the door, sweating, smelling myself through the thick layer of deodorant. I felt my stomach go queasy and wondered if I was going to throw up after all. I hadn't eaten and was still bleeding heavily.

Aunt Erma lived in east Van in a low-income government housing unit. Light showed under the door. I knocked. I could hear the familiar opening of *Star Trek*, the old version, with the trumpets blaring. I knocked again.

The door swung open and a girl with a purple Mohawk and Cleopatra eyeliner thrust money at me.

"Shit," she said. She looked me up and down, pulling the money back. "Where's the pizza?"

"I'm sorry," I said. "I think I have the wrong house."

"Pizza, pizza, pizza!" teenaged voices inside screamed. Someone was banging the floor in time to the chant.

"You with Cola?" she asked me.

I shook my head. "No. I'm here to see Erma Williamson. Is she in?"

"In? I guess. Mom?" she screamed. "Mom? It's for you!"

A whoop rose up. "Erma and Marley sittin' in a tree, k-i-s-s-i-n-g. First comes lust—"

"Shut up, you social rejects!"

"—then comes humping, then comes a baby after all that bumping!"

"How many times did they boink last night!" a single voice yelled over the laughter.

"Ten!" the voices chorused enthusiastically. "Twenty! Thirty! Forty!"

"Hey! Who's buying the pizza, eh? No respect! I get no respect!"

Aunt Erma came to the door. She didn't look much different from her pictures, except she wasn't wearing her cat-eye glasses.

She stared at me, puzzled. Then she spread open her arms.

"Adelaine, baby! I wasn't expecting you! Hey, come on in and say hi to your cousins. Pepsi! Cola! Look who came by for your birthday!"

She gave me a tight bear hug and I wanted to cry.

Two girls stood at the entrance to the living room, identical right down to their lip rings. They had different coloured Mohawks though—one pink, one purple.

"Erica?" I said, peering. I vaguely remembered them as having pigtails and making fun of Mr. Rogers. "Heather?"

"It's Pepsi," the purple Mohawk said. "Not, n-o-t, Erica."

"Oh," I said.

"Cola," the pink-Mohawked girl said, turning around and ignoring me to watch TV.

"What'd you bring us?" Pepsi said matter-of-factly.

"Excuse the fruit of my loins," Aunt Erma said, leading me into the living room and sitting me between two guys who were glued to the TV. "They've temporarily lost their manners. I'm putting it down to hormones and hoping the birth control pills turn them back into normal human beings."

Aunt Erma introduced me to everyone in the room, but their names went in one ear and out the other. I was so relieved just to be there and out of the clinic I couldn't concentrate on much else.

"How is he, Bones?" the guy on my right said, exactly in synch with Captain Kirk on TV. Captain Kirk was standing over McCoy and a prone security guard with large purple circles all over his face.

"He's dead, Jim," the guy on my left said.

"I wanna watch something else," Pepsi said. "This sucks."

She was booed.

"Hey, it's my birthday. I can watch what I want."

"Siddown," Cola said. "You're out-voted."

"You guys have no taste at all. This is crap. I just can't believe you guys are watching this—this cultural pabulum. I—"

A pair of panties hit her in the face. The doorbell rang and the pink-haired girl held the pizza boxes over her head and yelled, "Dinner's ready!"

"Eat in the kitchen," Aunt Erma said. "All of youse. I ain't scraping your cheese out of my carpet!"

Everyone left except me and Pepsi. She grabbed the remote control and flipped through a bunch of channels until we arrived at one where an announcer for the World Wrestling Federation screamed that the ref was blind.

"Now this," Pepsi said, "is entertainment."

By the time the party ended, I was snoring on the couch. Pepsi shook my shoulder. She and Cola were watching Bugs Bunny and Tweety.

"If we're bothering you," Cola said. "You can go crash in my room."

"Thanks," I said. I rolled off the couch, grabbed my backpack, and found the bathroom on the second floor. I made it just in time to throw up in the sink. The cramps didn't come back as badly as on the bus, but I took three Extra-Strength Tylenols anyway. My pad had soaked right through and leaked all over my underwear. I put on clean clothes and crashed in one of the beds. I wanted a black hole to open up and suck me out of the universe.

When I woke, I discovered I should have put on a diaper. It looked like something had been hideously murdered on the mattress.

"God," I said just as Pepsi walked in. I snatched up the blanket and tried to cover the mess.

"Man," Pepsi said. "Who are you? Carrie?"

"Freaky," Cola said, coming in behind her. "You okay?"

I nodded. I wished I'd never been born.

Pepsi hit my hand when I touched the sheets. "You're not the only one with killer periods." She pushed me out of the bedroom. In the bathroom she started water going in the tub for me, poured some Mr. Bubble in, and left without saying anything. I stripped off my blood-soaked underwear and hid them in the bottom of the garbage. There would be no saving them. I lay back. The bubbles popped and gradually the water became cool. I was smelly and gross. I scrubbed hard but the smell wouldn't go away.

"You still alive in there?" Pepsi said, opening the door.

I jumped up and whisked the shower curtain shut.

"Jesus, don't you knock?"

"Well, excuuuse me. I brought you a bathrobe. Good thing you finally crawled out of bed. Mom told us to make you eat something before we left. We got Ichiban, Kraft, or hot dogs. You want anything else, you gotta make it yourself. What do you want?"

"Privacy."

"We got Ichiban, Kraft, or hot dogs. What do you want?"

"The noodles," I said, more to get her out than because I was hungry.

She left and I tried to lock the door. It wouldn't lock so I scrubbed myself off quickly. I stopped when I saw the bathwater. It was dark pink with blood.

I crashed on the couch and woke when I heard sirens. I hobbled to the front window in time to see an ambulance pull into the parking lot. The attendants wheeled a man bound to a stretcher across the lot. He was screaming about the eyes in the walls that were watching him, waiting for him to fall asleep so they could come peel his skin from his body.

Aunt Erma, the twins, and I drove to the powwow at the Trout Lake community centre in East Vancouver. I was still bleeding a little and felt pretty lousy, but Aunt Erma was doing fundraising for the Helping Hands Society and had asked me to work her bannock booth. I wanted to help her out.

Pepsi had come along just to meet guys, dressed up in her flashiest bracelets and most conservatively ripped jeans. Aunt Erma enlisted her too, when she found out that none of her other volunteers had showed up. Pepsi was disgusted.

Cola got out of working at the booth because she was one of the jingle dancers. Aunt Erma had made her outfit, a form-fitting red dress with silver jingles that flashed and twinkled as she walked. Cola wore a bobbed wig to cover her pink Mohawk. Pepsi bugged her about it, but Cola airily waved good-bye and said, "Have fun."

I hadn't made fry bread in a long time. The first three batches were already mixed. I just added water and kneaded them into shapes roughly the size of a large doughnut, then threw them in the electric frying pan. The oil spattered and crackled and steamed because I'd turned the heat up too high. Pepsi wasn't much better. She burned her first batch and then had to leave so she could watch Cola dance.

"Be right back," she said. She gave me a thumbs-up sign and disappeared into the crowd.

The heat from the frying pan and the sun was fierce. I wished I'd thought to bring an umbrella. One of the organizers gave me her baseball cap. Someone else brought me a glass of water. I wondered how much longer Pepsi was going to be. My arms were starting to hurt.

I flattened six more pieces of bread into shape and threw them in the pan, beyond caring anymore that none of them were symmetrical. I could feel the sun sizzling my forearms, my hands, my neck, my legs. A headache throbbed at the base of my skull.

The people came in swarms, buzzing groups of tourists, conventioneers on a break, families, and assorted browsers. Six women wearing HI! MY NAME IS tags stopped and bought all the fry bread I had. Another hoard came and a line started at my end of the table.

"Last batch!" I shouted to the cashiers. They waved at me.

"What are you making?" someone asked.

I looked up. A middle-aged red-headed man in a business suit stared at me. At the beginning, when we were still feeling spunky, Pepsi and I had had fun with that question. We said, Oh, this is fish-head bread. Or fried beer foam. But bullshitting took energy.

"Fry bread," I said. "This is my last batch."

"Is it good?"

"I don't think you'll find out," I said. "It's all gone."

The man looked at my tray. "There seems to be more than enough. Do I buy it from you?"

"No, the cashier, but you're out of luck, it's all sold." I pointed to the line of people.

"Do you do this for a living?" the man said.

"Volunteer work. Raising money for the Helping Hands," I said.

"Are you Indian then?"

A hundred stupid answers came to my head but like I said, bullshit is work. "Haisla. And you?"

He blinked. "Is that a tribe?"

"Excuse me," I said, taking the fry bread out of the pan and passing it down to the cashier.

The man slapped a twenty-dollar bill on the table. "Make another batch."

"I'm tired," I said.

He put down another twenty.

"You don't understand. I've been doing this since this morning. You could put a million bucks on the table and I wouldn't change my mind."

He put five twenty-dollar bills on the table.

It was all for the Helping Hands, I figured, and he wasn't going to budge. I emptied the flour bag into the bowl. I measured out a handful of baking powder, a few fingers of salt, a thumb of lard. Sweat dribbled over my face, down the tip of my nose, and into the mix as I kneaded the dough until it was very soft but hard to shape. For a hundred bucks I made sure the pieces of fry bread were roughly the same shape.

"You have strong hands," the man said.

"I'm selling fry bread."

"Of course."

I could feel him watching me, was suddenly aware of how far my shirt dipped and how short my cutoffs were. In the heat, they were necessary. I was sweating too much to wear anything more.

"My name is Arnold," he said.

"Pleased to meet you, Arnold," I said. "'Scuse me if I don't shake hands. You with the convention?"

"No. I'm here on vacation."

He had teeth so perfect I wondered if they were dentures. No, probably caps. I bet he took exquisite care of his teeth.

We said nothing more until I'd fried the last piece of bread. I handed him the plate and bowed. I expected him to leave then, but he bowed back and said, "Thank you."

"No," I said. "Thank you. The money's going to a good cause. It'll—"

"How should I eat these?" he interrupted me.

With your mouth, asshole. "Put some syrup on them, or jam, or honey. Anything you want."

"Anything?" he said, staring deep into my eyes.

Oh, barf. "Whatever."

I wiped sweat off my forehead with the back of my hand, reached down and unplugged the frying pan. I began to clean up, knowing that he was still standing there, watching.

"What's your name?" he said.

"Suzy," I lied.

"Why're you so pale?"

I didn't answer. He blushed suddenly and cleared his throat. "Would you do me a favour?"

"Depends."

"Would you—" he blushed harder, "shake your hair out of that baseball cap?"

I shrugged, pulled the cap off, and let my hair loose. It hung limply down to my waist. My scalp felt like it was oozing enough oil to cause environmental damage.

"You should keep it down at all times," he said.

"Good-bye, Arnold," I said, picking up the money and starting toward the cashiers. He said something else but I kept on walking until I reached Pepsi.

I heard the buzz of an electric razor. Aunt Erma hated it when Pepsi shaved her head in the bedroom. She came out of her room, crossed the landing, and banged on the door. "In the bathroom!" she shouted. "You want to get hair all over the rug?"

The razor stopped. Pepsi ripped the door open and stomped down the hall. She kicked the bathroom door shut and the buzz started again.

I went into the kitchen and popped myself another Jolt. Sweat trickled down my pits, down my back, ran along my jaw and dripped off my chin.

"Karaoke?" Pepsi said. Then louder. "Hey! Are you deaf?"

"What?" I said.

"Get me my cell phone."

"Why don't you get it?"

"I'm on the can."

"So?" Personally, I hate it when you're talking on the phone with someone and then you hear the toilet flush.

Pepsi banged about in the bathroom and came out with her

freshly coiffed Mohawk and her backpack slung over her shoulder. "What's up your butt?" she said.

"Do you want me to leave? Is that it?"

"Do what you want. This place is like an oven," Pepsi said. "Who can deal with this bullshit?" She slammed the front door behind her.

The apartment was quiet now, except for the chirpy weatherman on the TV promising another week of record highs. I moved out to the balcony. The headlights from the traffic cut into my eyes, bright and painful. Cola and Aunt Erma bumped around upstairs, then their bedroom doors squeaked shut and I was alone. I had a severe caffeine buzz. Shaky hands, fluttery heart, mild headache. It was still warm outside, heat rising from the concrete, stored up during the last four weeks of weather straight from hell. I could feel my eyes itching. This was the third night I was having trouble getting to sleep.

Tired and wired. I used to be able to party for days and days. You start to hallucinate badly after the fifth day without sleep. I don't know why, but I used to see leprechauns. These waist-high men would come and sit beside me, smiling with their brown wrinkled faces, brown eyes, brown teeth. When I tried to shoo them away, they'd leap straight up into the air, ten or twelve feet, their green clothes and long red hair flapping around them.

A low, grey haze hung over Vancouver, fuzzing the street lights. Air-quality bulletins on the TV were warning the elderly and those with breathing problems to stay indoors. There were mostly semis on the roads this late. Their engines rumbled down the street, creating minor earthquakes. Pictures trembled on the wall. I took a sip of warm, flat Jolt, let it slide over my tongue, sweet and harsh. It had a metallic twang, which meant I'd drunk too much, my stomach wanted to heave.

I went back inside and started to pack.

Home Again, Home Again, Jiggity-Jig

Jimmy and I lay in the graveyard, on one of my cousin's graves. We should have been creeped out, but we were both tipsy.

"I'm never going to leave the village," Jimmy said. His voice buzzed in my ears.

"Mmm."

"Did you hear me?" Jimmy said.

"Mmm."

"Don't you care?" Jimmy said, sounding like I should.

"This is what we've got, and it's not that bad."

He closed his eyes. "No, it's not bad."

I poured myself some cereal. Mom turned the radio up. She glared at me as if it were my fault the Rice Krispies were loud. I opened my mouth and kept chewing.

The radio announcer had a thick Nisga'a accent. Most of the news was about the latest soccer tournament. I thought, that's northern native broadcasting: sports or bingo.

"Who's this?" I said to Mom. I'd been rummaging through the drawer, hunting for spare change.

"What?"

It was the first thing she'd said to me since I'd come back. I'd heard that she'd cried to practically everyone in the village, saying I'd gone to Vancouver to become a hooker.

I held up a picture of a priest with his hand on a little boy's shoulder. The boy looked happy.

"Oh, that," Mom said. "I forgot I had it. He was Uncle Josh's teacher."

I turned it over. *Dear Joshua*, it read. *How are you? I miss you terribly. Please write. Your friend in Christ, Archibald.*

"Looks like he taught him more than just prayers."

"What are you talking about? Your Uncle Josh was a bright student. They were fond of each other."

"I bet," I said, vaguely remembering that famous priest who got eleven years in jail. He'd molested twenty-three boys while they were in residential school.

Uncle Josh was home from fishing for only two more days. As he was opening my bedroom door, I said, "Father Archibald?"

He stopped. I couldn't see his face because of the way the light was shining through the door. He stayed there a long time.

"I've said my prayers," I said.

He backed away and closed the door.

In the kitchen the next morning he wouldn't look at me. I felt light and giddy, not believing it could end so easily. Before I ate breakfast I closed my eyes and said grace out loud. I had hardly begun when I heard Uncle Josh's chair scrape the floor as he pushed it back.

I opened my eyes. Mom was staring at me. From her expression I knew that she knew. I thought she'd say something then, but we ate breakfast in silence.

"Don't forget your lunch," she said.

She handed me my lunch bag and went up to her bedroom.

I use a recent picture of Uncle Josh that I raided from Mom's album. I paste his face onto the body of Father Archibald and my face onto the boy. The montage looks real enough. Uncle Josh is smiling down at a younger version of me.

My period is vicious this month. I've got clots the size and texture of liver. I put one of them in a Ziploc bag. I put the picture and the bag in a hatbox. I tie it up with a bright red ribbon. I place it on the kitchen table and go upstairs to get a jacket. I think nothing of leaving it there because there's no one else at home. The note inside the box reads, "It was yours so I killed it."

"Yowtz!" Jimmy called out as he opened the front door. He came to my house while I was upstairs getting my jacket. He was going to surprise me and take me to the hot springs. I stopped at the top of the landing. Jimmy was sitting at the kitchen table with the present that I'd meant for Uncle Josh, looking at the note. Without seeing me, he closed the box, neatly folded the note, and walked out the door.

He wouldn't take my calls. After two days, I went over to Jimmy's house, my heart hammering so hard I could feel it in my temples. Michelle answered the door.

"Karaoke!" she said, smiling. Then she frowned. "He's not here. Didn't he tell you?"

"Tell me what?"

"He got the job," Michelle said.

My relief was so strong I almost passed out. "A job."

"I know. I couldn't believe it either. It's hard to believe he's going fishing, he's so spoiled. I think he'll last a week. Thanks for putting in a good word, anyways." She kept talking, kept saying things about the boat.

My tongue stuck in my mouth. My feet felt like two slabs of stone. "So he's on *Queen of the North*?"

"Of course, silly," Michelle said. "We know you pulled strings. How else could Jimmy get on with your uncle?"

The lunchtime buzzer rings as I smash this girl's face. Her front teeth crack. She screams, holding her mouth as blood spurts from her split lips. The other two twist my arms back and hold me still while the fourth one starts smacking my face, girl hits, movie hits. I aim a kick at her crotch. The kids around us cheer enthusiastically. She rams into me and I go down as someone else boots me in the kidneys.

I hide in the bushes near the docks and wait all night. Near sunrise, the crew starts to make their way to the boat. Uncle Josh arrives first, throwing his gear onto the deck, then dragging it inside the cabin. I see Jimmy carrying two heavy bags. As he walks down the gangplank, his footsteps make hollow thumping noises that echo off the mountains. The docks creak, seagulls circle overhead in the soft morning light, and the smell of the beach at low tide is carried on the breeze that ruffles the water. When the seiner's engines start, Jimmy passes his bags to Uncle Josh, then unties the rope and casts off. Uncle Josh holds out his hand, Jimmy takes it and is pulled on board. The boat chugs out of the bay and rounds the point. I come out of the bushes and stand on the dock, watching the *Queen of the North* disappear.

Shani Mootoo

A Garden of Her Own

A north-facing balcony meant that no sunlight would enter there. A deep-in-the-heart-of-the-forest green pine tree, over-fertilized opulence extending its midriff, filled the view from the balcony.

There was no window, only a glass sliding door which might have let fresh air in and released second- or third-hand air and the kinds of odours that build phantoms in stuffy apartments. But it remained shut. Not locked, but stuck shut from decades of other renters' black, oily grit and grime which had collected in the grooves of the sliding door's frame.

Vijai knew that it would not budge up, down or sideways. For the amount of rent the husband paid for this bachelor apartment, the landlord could not be bothered. She opened the hallway door to let the cooking lamb fat and garlic smells drift out into the hallway. She did not want them to burrow into the bed sheets, into towels and clothes crammed into the dented cream-coloured metal space-saver cupboard that she had to share with the husband. It was what all the other renters did too; everyone's years of oil—sticky, burnt, over-used, rancid oil—and of garlic, onions and spices formed themselves into an impenetrable nose-singeing, skin-stinging presence that lurked menacingly in the hall. Instead of releasing the lamb from the husband's apartment, opening the door allowed this larger phantom to barge its way in.

Vijai, engulfed, slammed the door shut. She tilted her head to face the ceiling and breathed in hard, searching for air that had no smell, no weight. The husband was already an hour late for dinner. She paced the twelve strides, back and forth, from the balcony door to the hall door, glancing occasionally at the two table settings, stopping to straighten his knife, his fork, the napkin, the flowers, his knife, his fork, the napkin, the flowers. Her arms and legs tingled weakly and her intestines filled up with beads of acid formed out of unease and fear. Seeing a smear of her fingerprint on the husband's knife, she picked it up and polished it on her T-shirt until it gleamed brilliantly, and she saw in it her mother's eyes looking back at her.

* * *

Sunlight. I miss the sunlight—yellow light and a sky ceiling miles high. Here the sky sits on my head, heavy grey with snow and freezing rain. I miss being able to have doors and windows opened wide, never shut except sometimes in the rainy season. Rain, rain, pinging on, winging off the galvanized tin roof. But always warm rain. No matter how much it rained, it was always warm.

And what about the birds? Flying in through the windows how often? Two, three times a week? Sometimes even twice in a single day. In the shimmering heat you could see them flying slowly, their mouths wide open as if crying out soundlessly. They would actually be flicking their tongues at the still air, gulping and panting, looking for a window to enter and a curtain rod to land on to cool off. But once they had cooled off and were ready to fly off again, they could never seem to focus on the window to fly through and they would bang themselves against the walls and the light shade until they fell, panicked and stunned. I was the one who would get the broom and push it gently up toward one of these birds after it looked like it had cooled off, and prod, prod, prod until it hopped onto the broom and then I would lower it and reach from behind and cup the trembling in my hand. I can, right now, feel the life, the heat in the palm of my hand from the little body, and the fright in its tremble. I would want to hold on to it, even think of placing it in a cage and looking after it, but something always held me back. I would put my mouth close to its ears and whisper calming shh shh shhhhs, and then take it, pressed to my chest, out the back door and open my hand and wait for it to take its time fluffing out right there in my open hand before flying away.

But here? There are hardly any birds here, only that raucous, aggressive old crow that behaves as if it owns the scraggly pine tree it sits in across the street. This street is so noisy! Every day, all day and all night long, even on Sundays, cars whiz by, ambulances and fire trucks pass screaming, and I think to myself thank goodness it couldn't be going for anyone I know. I don't know anyone nearby.

Too much quiet here, too shut off. Not even the sound of children playing in the street, or the sound of neighbours talking to each other over fences, conversations floating in through open windows, open bricks. Here even when doors are open people walk down hallways with their noses straight ahead, making a point of not glancing to even nod hello.

Oh! This brings all kinds of images to my mind: the coconut tree outside my bedroom brushing, scraping, swishing against the wall. Green-blue iridescent lizards clinging, upside down, to the ceiling above my bed.

And dinner time. Mama's voice would find me wherever I was. "Vijai, go and tell Cheryl to put food on the table, yuh father comin home just now." Standing in one place, at the top of her meagre voice she would call us one by one: "Bindra, is dinner time. Bindra, why you so harden, boy? Dinner gettin cold. Turn off that TV right now! Shanti, come girl, leave what you doin and come and eat. Vashti, go and tell Papa dinner ready, and then you come and sit down." Sitting down, eating together. Talking together. Conversations with no boundaries, no false politeness, no need to impress Mama or Papa.

But that's not how it was always. Sometimes Papa didn't come home till long after suppertime. Mama would make us eat but she would wait for him. Sometimes he wouldn't come for days, and she would wait for him then too.

But there were always flowers from the garden on the table. Pink and yellow gerberas, ferns, ginger lilies. That was your happiness, eh Mama? the garden, eh? And when there were blossoms you and I would go outside together. You showed me how to angle the garden scissors so that the plant wouldn't hurt for too long. We would bring in the bundle of flowers and greenery with their fresh-cut garden smell and little flying bugs and spiders, and you would show me how to arrange them for a centrepiece or a corner table or a floor piece. The place would look so pretty! Thanks for showing that to me, Mama.

Mama, he's never brought me any flowers. Not even a dandelion.

I don't want him to ask how much these cost. Don't ask me who sent them. No one sent them; I bought them myself. With my own money. My own money.

He's never given me anything. Only money for groceries.

Late. Again.

I jabbed this lamb with a trillion little gashes and stuffed a clove of garlic in each one with your tongue, your taste buds in mind. I spent half the day cooking this meal and you will come late and eat it after the juices have hardened to a candle-wax finish, as if it were nothing but a microwave dinner.

I want a microwave oven.

Mama, why did you wait to eat? If I were to eat now would you, Papa, he think I am a bad wife? Why did you show me this, Mama?

I must not nag.

* * *

Vijai remained sleeping until the fan in the bathroom woke her. It sputtered raucously, like an airplane engine starting up, escalating in time to fine whizzing, lifting off into the distance.

Five-thirty, Saturday morning.

She had fretted through most of the night, twisting, arching her body, drawing her legs up to her chest, to the husband's chest, rolling, and nudging him, hoping that he would awaken to pull her body into his and hold her there. She wanted to feel the heat of his body along the length of hers, his arms pressing her to him. Or his palm placed flat on her lower belly, massaging, touching her. He responded to her fidgeting once and she moved closer to him to encourage him, but he turned his naked back to her and continued his guttural exhaling, inhaling, sounding exactly like her father.

Eventually Vijai's eyes, burning from salty tears that had spilled and dampened the pillow under her cheek, fluttered shut and she slept, deep and dreamless, until the fan awakened her.

When the sound of the shower water snapping at the enamel

tub was muffled against his body, she pulled herself over to lie in and smell his indentation in the tired foam mattress. She inhaled, instead, the history of the mattress: unwashed hair, dying skin, old and rancid sweat—not the smell she wanted to nestle in. Neither would the indentation cradle her; she could feel the protruding shape of the box-spring beneath the foam.

She debated whether to get up and thanklessly make his toast and tea, or pretend not to have awakened, the potential for blame nagging at her. She slid back to her side of his bed, the other side of the line that he had drawn down the middle with the cutting edge of his outstretched hand. Vijai pulled her knees to her chest and hugged them. When the shower stopped she hastily straightened herself out and put her face inside the crack between the bed and the rough wall. Cold from the wall trans-ferred itself onto her cheek, and layers upon layers of human smells trapped behind cream-coloured paint pierced her nostrils.

Vijai was aware of the husband's every move as she lay in his bed. Water from the kitchen tap pounded the sink basin, then attacked the metal floor of the kettle, gradually becoming muffled and high-pitched as the kettle filled up. He always filled it much more than was necessary for one cup of tea, which he seldom drank. The blow dryer. First on the highest setting, then dropped two notches to the lowest, and off. The electric razor. Whizzing up and down his cheek, circling his chin, the other cheek, grazing his neck. Snip, snip and little dark half-moon hair from his nostrils and his sideburns cling to the rim of the white sink basin. Wiping up, scrubbing, making spotless these areas, and others, before he returns, are her evidence that she is diligent, that she is, indeed, her mother's daughter.

At this point in the routine she always expects a handsome aftershave cologne to fill the little bachelor apartment, to bring a moment of frivolity and romance into the room. In one favourite version of her memories, this is what normally happened in her parents' bedroom at precisely this point. But the husband would only pat on his face a stinging watery liquid with the faintest smell of lime, a smell that evaporated into nothingness the instant it touched his skin.

She held herself tensely, still in the crack between the bed and the wall, as he made his way into the dark corner that he called the bedroom. The folding doors of the closet squeaked open. A shirt slid off a hanger, leaving it dangling and tinkling against the metal rod. Vijai heard the shirt that she had ironed (stretched mercilessly tight across the ironing board, the tip of the iron with staccato spurts of steam sniffing out the crevice of every seam, mimicking the importance with which her mother had treated this task) being pulled against his body and his hands sliding down the stiff front as he buttoned it.

Then there was a space empty of his sounds. The silence made the walls of her stomach contract like a closed-up accordion. Her body remained rigid. Her heart sounded as if it had moved right up into her ears, thundering methodically, and that was all that she could hear. She struggled with herself to be calm so that she could know where he was and what he was doing. Not knowing made her scalp want to unpeel itself. Then, the bed sagged as he kneeled on it, leaned across and brushed his mouth on the back of her head. His full voice had no regard for her sleep or the time of morning. He said, "Happy Birthday. I left twenty dollars on the table for you. Buy yourself a present."

The thundering subsided and her heart rolled and slid, rolled and slid, down, low down, and came to rest between her thighs. She turned over with lethargic elegance, as if she were just waking up, stretching out her back like a cat, but the apartment door was already being shut and locked from the outside.

The streets here are so wide! I hold my breath as I walk across them, six lanes wide. What if the light changes before I get to the other side? You have to walk so briskly, not only when you're crossing a wide street but even on the sidewalk. Otherwise people pass you and then turn back and stare at you, shaking their heads. And yet I remember Mama telling us that fast walking, hurrying, was very unladylike.

I yearn for friends. My own friends, not his, but I'm afraid to smile at strangers. So often we huddled up in Mama's big bed and read the newspapers about things that happened to women up here—we read about women who suddenly disappeared and months later their corpses would be found, having been raped and dumped. And we also read about serial murders. The victims were almost always women who had been abducted from the street by strangers in some big North American city. Mama and Papa warned me, when I was leaving to come up here, not to make eye contact with strangers because I wouldn't know whose eyes I might be looking into or what I was encouraging, unknowingly. It's not like home, they said, where everybody knows everybody.

No bird sounds—there are not quite so many different kinds of birds here. Yes, Papa, yes, I can just hear you saying to stop this nonsense, all this thinking about home, that I must think of here as my home now, but I haven't yet left you and Mama. I know now that I will never fully leave, nor will I ever truly be here. You felt so close, Papa, when you phoned this morning and asked like you have every past year, how was the birthday girl. You said that in your office you often look at the calendar pictures of autumn fields of bales of hay, lazy rivers meandering near brick-red farmhouses, and country roads with quaint white wooden churches with red steeples, and you think that that's what my eyes have already enjoyed.

"It's all so beautiful, Papa," I said, and knowing you, you probably heard what I wasn't saying. Thanks for not pushing further. I couldn't tell you that he is working night and day to "make it," to "get ahead," to live like the other men he works with. That he is always thinking about this, and everything else is frivolous right now, so we haven't yet been for that drive in the country to see the pictures in the calendars pinned on the wall above your desk. He doesn't have time for dreaming, but I must dream or else I find it difficult to breathe.

At home the fence around our house and the garden was the furthest point that I ever went to on my own. From the house, winding in and out of the dracaenas and the philodendrons that I planted with Mama many Julys ago, feeling the full, firm limbs of the poui, going as far as the hibiscus and jasmine fence, and back into the house again. Any further away from the house than that and the chauffeur would be driving us! And now? Just look at me! I am out in a big city on my own. I wish you all could see me. I wish we could be doing this together.

Papa, you remember, don't you, when you used to bring home magazines from your office and I would flip through them quickly looking for full-page pictures of dense black-green tropical mountains, or snow-covered bluish-white ones? Ever since those first pictures I have dreamt of mountains, of touching them with the palms of my hands, of bicycling in them, and of hiking. Even though I never canoed on a river or a big lake with no shores, I know what it must feel like! I can feel what it is to ride rapids like they do in *National Geographic* magazines. Cold river spray and drenchings, sliding, tossing, crashing! I still dream of bicycling across a huge continent. I used to think, if only I lived in North America! But here I am, in this place where these things are supposed to happen, in the midst of so much possibility, and for some reason my dreams seem even further away, just out of reach. It's just not quite as simple as being here.

This land stretches on in front of me, behind me and forever. My back feels exposed, naked, so much land behind, and no fence ahead.

Except that I must cook dinner tonight.

What if I just kept walking and never returned! I could walk far away, to another province, change my name, cut my hair. After a while I would see my face on a poster in a grocery store, along with all the other missing persons. The problem is that then I wouldn't even be able to phone home and speak with Mama or Papa or Bindra and Vashti without being tracked and caught, and then who knows what.

Well, this is the first birthday I've ever spent alone. But next time we speak on the phone I will be able to tell you that I went for a very long walk. Alone.

I think I will do this every day—well, maybe every other day, and each time I will go a new route and a little further. I will know this place in order to own it, but still I will never really leave you.

Mama, Papa, Vashti, Bindra, Shanti,
Mama, Papa, Vashti, Bindra, Shanti.
Mama. Papa. Vashti. Bindra. Shanti.

* * *

Twenty-four years of Sundays, of eating three delightfully noisy, lengthy meals together, going to the beach or for long drives with big pots of rice, chicken and peas, and chocolate cake, singing "Michael Row Your Boat Ashore," and "You Are My

Sunshine," doing everything in tandem with her brother and sisters and Mama and Papa. This particular characteristic of Sundays was etched deeply in her veins. (Not all Sundays were happy ones but recently she seems to have forgotten that.)

It would be her twenty-fourth Sunday here, the twenty-fourth week of marriage.

The only Sunday since the marriage that the husband had taken off and spent in his apartment was six weeks ago, and since he needed to spend that day alone Vijai agreed to go to the library for at least three hours. Before she left the house she thought she would use the opportunity to take down recipes for desserts, but once she began walking down the street she found herself thinking about rivers and mountains. She bypassed the shelves with all the cooking books and home-making magazines and found herself racing toward valleys, glaciers, canoeing, rapids and the like. She picked up a magazine about hiking and mountaineering, looked at the equipment advertisements, read incomprehensible jargon about techniques for climbing.

After about forty minutes, not seeing herself in any of the magazines, she became less enthusiastic, and eventually frustrated and bored. She looked at her watch every fifteen minutes or so and then she started watching the second hand go around and counting each and every second in her head. When three hours had passed she remembered that she had said at least three hours, and she walked home slowly, stopping to window-shop and checking her watch until an extra twenty minutes had passed.

The strength of her determination that they not spend this Sunday apart warded off even a hint of such a suggestion from the husband. What she really wanted to do was to go for the long drive up to a glacier in the nearby mountains. That way she would have him to herself for at least five hours. But he had worked several twelve-hour shifts that week and needed to rest in his apartment.

She went to the grocery store, to the gardening section, and bought half a dozen packages of flower seeds, half a dozen packages of vegetable seeds, bags of soil, fertilizer, a fork and spade, a purple plastic watering can, and a score of nursery trays. She brought it all home in a taxi. Enough to keep her busy and in his apartment for an entire Sunday. She was becoming adept at finding ways to get what she wanted.

He never asked and Vijai did not tell that from her allowance she had paid a man from the hardware store to come over and fix the balcony sliding door. She stooped on the balcony floor scooping earth into nursery trays. He sat reading the newspaper, facing the balcony in his big sagging gold armchair that he had bought next-door at a church basement sale for five dollars. She was aware that he was stealing glances at her as she bent over her garden-in-the-making.

* * *

I wore this shirt, no bra, am stooping, bending over here to reveal my breasts to you. *Look at them! Feel something!*

I might as well be sharing this apartment with a brother, or a roommate.

* * *

She feels his hands on her waist, leading her from behind to the edge of his bed. Her body is crushed under his as he slams himself against her, from behind, grunting. She holds her breath, taut against his weight and the pain, but she will not disturb his moment. She hopes that the next moment will be hers. She waits with the bed sheet pulled up to her chin. The toilet flushes and, shortly after, she hears newspaper pages being turned in the sagging five-dollar gold armchair.

Later, deep-sleep breathing and low snoring from the bedroom fills the apartment, dictating her movements. She sits on the green-and-yellow shag carpet, leaning against the foot of the husband's armchair, in front of the snowy black-and-white television watching a French station turned down low enough not to awaken him. Something about listening to a language that she does not understand comforts her, gives her companionship in a place where she feels like a foreigner. She is beginning to be able to repeat advertisements in French.

Monique Proulx

Leah and Paul, for Example

February 1991. Afternoon.

There were the sheets, the pink and mauve towels, the pile of embroidered tablecloths, the green-apple bath oil, the Scandinavian dinnerware, the fluted champagne glasses, the genuine clay casserole dishes. Now it's all over, split in two as though hacked by a maniac cleaver; the apartment is like an oilfield ripe for speculators. Now they are in the kitchen. She has opened a cupboard. He is following each of her actions as though through a magnifying glass, like a disbelieving detective.

"Surely we're not going to divide the herbs."

"I'm taking them."

Which is what she does. The sage, fennel, basil, all the jars he has taken the trouble to label in Letraset on silvered vinyl are balanced precariously in her arms. He doesn't protest immediately, for the sake of the jars he waits until she has deigned to put them down somewhere, she has always been a bit slow.

"There's no way you're taking all that."

"They're MY herbs. It's always been me who takes care of them."

"I'm the one who dried them. The jars are mine!"

"Fine. I'll put them into plastic bags."

"I don't have any plastic bags."

Bastard. Fucking bastard. She turns the words over in her mind, touches them from inside, they have a texture, a smoothness that would make them so satisfying to spit out. She keeps quiet for the moment.

"I'll bring the jars back later," she says.

"No. At least leave me the basil. The basil and the tarragon."

"You know they're the ones I like best!"

"Okay. I'll keep the fennel. And the basil."

"Why the basil? I'm not leaving you the basil."

The light surprises them from the side and forces them to blink. Their faces seem dragged down by something acrid and purulent, hate makes them tremble like crippled animals.

August 1988. Evening.

He touches her arm. Lightly, with the fat part of his thumb, a spider's touch she could let pass without noticing. She responds to him immediately, she has radar sleeping beneath her skin which wakes only when he makes contact—that's what she often tells him, anyway, with a big throaty laugh so it doesn't sound too softhearted. He increases the pressure on her arm. Beneath the tissue he can sense the stammer of an infinitely disturbing heat, he slides his fingers along her collarbone and comes to rest at the tips of her breasts, that part of her which electrifies both of them. She always wears her breasts like jewels, provocative and erect at the slightest excuse. It might seem her smile is for herself, she lets the scissors, the sprigs of parsley, the thyme, the marjoram fall to the grass, she takes off her sweater. He goes for her breasts right away, his hands hurry to knead her, to force her sharp wild cries. She looks him in the eyes, then reaches down to his zipper, she rubs his crotch and goes right to the place where it's swollen and warm, then caresses his sex admiringly, as though running her fingers along velvet.

They collapse to their knees, felled by a surge that is beyond them, into the dizzying odours of basil, tarragon, they tear off their clothes. She's so wet and writhing that her vulva keeps slipping in and out of his fingers, she swallows his sex up to the hilt, they are everywhere and nowhere, struggling nobly to ensure that life will never leave them.

"Wait," she says suddenly.

She holds him off for several seconds, yes, it's infinitely good, this moment before orgasm is worth stretching out, extreme tension, the frenzy of desire that rattles every particle of the body, we will never be more alive, more intense, always remember this. He comes in her from behind, she's the first to explode and their cries roll through the darkness to the cores of the stars.

March 1990. Night.

Through the window, above Mont Royal, she sees a star quivering. Perhaps it's Vega or the North Star, she can't be sure, the sky is diluted by the city lights. She looks away, just across from the bed, for example. On the wall is a silkscreen print, a serene seascape from which she sees, in the darkness, just a hint of light. She no longer knows where to look for reassurance; at night the familiar world slips away, cannot be counted on.

She is waiting for him. She keeps herself from thinking that she is waiting for him, instead she tells herself she has insomnia. He must have run into someone, an old pal he hasn't seen since he was a teenager, in their euphoria they will have eaten together, had two three four liqueurs, he just forgot to phone, these things happen. Or a car. She sees a long red car coming out of an intersection, she tries to make herself think about something else but the car calmly drives into her head and then, swift and gleaming, carries out various complicated manoeuvres before crashing into him, he who always crosses the street without looking. She closes her eyes, she's unable to shake these images of crushed bodies emptying their blood into hospital corridors, she'll never get back to sleep. It's three o'clock in the morning.

The telephone rings. Her hands go right to the receiver. She waits.

"It's me," he says.

It's him. He's alive. He doesn't sound drunk. In the end there's a rational explanation for everything.

"Weren't you asleep yet?"

His voice trembles, the way it does when he's uneasy. She knows his voice by heart. Suddenly, her worry about him dying gives way to another worry, infinitely more complex.

"Listen," he says. "Listen…" He blurts it all out at once, for fear of being interrupted or losing his place in the speech he's rehearsed—"I'm not coming home tonight, I don't feel like coming home, don't get upset, we've already talked about it, it's nothing serious, it's just one night, go to sleep, it's nothing."

It's true they have already talked about it. These things happen. Above all, never lie, don't live in fear of a little incidental lust. We're all adults. Occasional straying can make a couple stronger. She goes back to bed and curls up in a ball. She feels stunned, numb. To tame the howling demons, she keeps repeating to herself, over and over, it's nothing, go to sleep, it's nothing, nothing.

November 1989. Late afternoon.
He has bought flowers. Heather, Chinese lilies, mimosa, a couple of red anthuriums; he is very proud of the irregular harmony they make in the centre of the table. He has put the bottle of

vintage Roederer in the refrigerator, beside the scallop conserve and the lobsters. Nothing is too beautiful, some days, when his heart gurgles with joy and he sees indigo in even the blackest cloud.

But there's no special occasion, no spectacular event to celebrate, nothing that wasn't already there in the daily routine. It came over him this afternoon at work, he started thinking about her, about them. Especially the other one, who was galloping towards them, splitting apart the universe: theoretically they hadn't wanted any, they hadn't done it on purpose. That's how children happen most of the time, when people are in their usual state of inattention. At the beginning he concealed his hesitation, he accepted the fact that she accepted it. The feedings, the inevitable squalling, the unavoidable overwork and exhaustion, the disrupted intimacy, their whole life to be reconstructed from the bottom up, the idiocies to be recommenced by proxy, Father Stork watching horrified over his brat's escapades; it was enough to keep him from sleeping. Then he got used to the idea. Today, for almost no reason at all, a little kid swearing loudly as he walked under his window, the wonderful news struck home, he became wildly and appallingly happy about his future paternity.

Lovesick, he waits for her; patiently and laughing all alone he waits for THEM. On a candlelit evening when he's an old man, his daughter will tell him naughty interplanetary stories, and in a stentorian voice his son will sing computer hymns.

He hears her coming. She opens the door, she seems amazed to find him there. She sees the flowers. She walks up to him, frail and limping, she takes his two hands.

"I just had an abortion," she murmurs.

He finds nothing to say. She seems overcome by such great pain that there is nothing to say.

"Suddenly I was afraid," she says. "I'm afraid of children."

She presses against him, inundated by an immense fatigue. Giving something up has never been so cruel, but in the end, surrounded by his warmth, she grows calm, he rocks her in his arms for hours, sobbing to himself like an imbecile.

April 1987. Morning.

She is tall for a woman. It should be said that she stands very straight, with a hint of arrogance, and she looks at him without blinking, as one does while sizing up an opponent.

"I want unemployment insurance," she says.

"Of course. Why not?"

He is sitting behind a desk that doesn't seem to match him: some files, aseptic plants, a small glaring light that's very twentieth-century Inquisition. He's wearing a soft flannel shirt, and the corners of his mouth are turned up in a way that makes it seem he's laughing inside every time he speaks.

"How much would you like?" he asks.

"Uh … the maximum, obviously."

"Obviously."

He begins to fill out a form. She watches him as he works, his brow slightly wrinkled.

"What are you writing?"

"The usual things. You should get your first cheque within a few weeks."

"Aren't you supposed to ask me a bunch of questions first?"

"That's right." He excuses himself and stops writing. "What would you like me to ask you?"

She starts to laugh; he tries to keep a straight face but, as already noted, the corners of his mouth keep lifting.

"I don't know." She smiles. "Why I left my job. What time I get up. How many thousand cvs I've sent out and to whom and prove it."

"All right. What time do you get up?"

"Very early. Not to look for work but because I have insomnia."

"Well. Me too."

"You're not much of a bureaucrat," she notes mildly.

"I know," he admits. "I handed in my resignation today."

"Is that true?"

"It's true."

He closes the file, he has finished writing. She should get up, but she doesn't right away.

"I'm having dinner at the Funambule," she suggests.

"Okay. Me too."

"My name is Leah."

"I know. It's written in your file. I'm Paul."

"I know. It's written on your desk."

They look at each other, they smile at each other, very satisfied with themselves and the turn the day is taking.

May 1988. Late afternoon.

The old Renault coughs, hacks, stops. They exchange a tragic look.

"Oh Christ," he says, upset.

"Yeah," she sighs.

They have broken down a few kilometres from Anavissos. They are surrounded by cypress trees, climbing pistachios, the odours of eucalyptus and wild olive trees, a dry and pleasantly savage beauty but nothing much like—or in any way like—a garage. They could stop a passing car, but no cars are passing, which seemed the height of perfection a few minutes ago. With nothing else to do, they start walking. They are on what's called the Apollonian coast, the ocean splashing in their face as though they were on a postcard. Suddenly a peasant in his field, beside his donkey and a hundred tomato plants. She runs towards him. With Socratic impassivity the peasant watches her throw herself at him. She brings out her Sunday Greek.

"*Kalimera*," she begins, "can you tell me, *boreite na mou deite…*"

She returns, very proud, with a rusty Vespa. The peasant has agreed to rent it to her for a few hours in exchange for an astronomical sum plus all her credit cards as a guarantee—alas, the simple, unsophisticated rustic is a species threatened with extinction. But never mind, it's still not impossible for them to make Cape Sounion before twilight. She is absolutely determined to see the sixteen Doric columns of Poseidon's temple aflame in the rays of the setting sun—she has read fantastic descriptions of this phenomenon.

They jolt along the winding road. With every bump they howl in pain; the Vespa is endowed with all the suspension and braking power of a swallow's turd in free fall. Suddenly they spot the celebrated columns perched on the celebrated promontory. White lace, vulnerable and eternal, looking out to sea. It leaves them breathless.

They climb up to the marble terrace. The site is astoundingly beautiful and, above all, totally deserted: just cats, cats all over the place, and a dozing guard who sells them two tickets. They sit amidst the poppies, above the Gulf of Saronica, beside the white temple. Gripped by Homeric bliss, they wait for the sun to set. He inspects the sky.

"Looks like black clouds, there…"

"No," she says decisively, "in Greece it never rains."

At a quarter after five, twenty-two buses appear on the highway and, in less time than it takes to say it, they vomit a million Germans onto the white marble. The Germans wave, they call to each other, they take pictures, they jump around on the sacred stones, they are obviously waiting for the setting sun to set fire to the sixteen columns of Poseidon's temple. To avoid being trampled, Leah and Paul move aside. At twenty-five minutes after five a torrential rain begins.

They climb back onto their Vespa, so choking with laughter that even the cats, seeing them pass, condescend to give them an amused wink.

December 1989. Night.

Of course, it began with something insignificant. Even world wars spring, it's said, from something insignificant. A fateful supper, at her family's. He laughed, that was his mistake. He laughed at an untoward joke—in her opinion nasty—that someone made about her. She is wounded, she feels betrayed by him. He blames the alcohol—and what about politeness, I kill myself trying to be civilized with your family. She as much as calls him a coward. That he does not accept. He swells up, like the frog in the fable. They belabour each other with their families as though they were shameful diseases, they blurt out spiteful words that they're a thousand miles from believing.

And now they're lying side by side as though they were in a huge frozen dormitory. They are sulking. Everything would be so easy if one of them would admit to being vulnerable; I was wrong, forgive me. But they are trapped in their pride; for the first time they are refusing to give ground—and besides, they've forgotten what started it. All that's left is an undefined rancour that leaves them gasping, and a terrible feeling of being alone. He is the first to make an opening move: he puts his hand on her back. She is instantly relieved and grateful, she is dying to roll against him, but inside a small voice sneers: it's easy, it's really too easy, and she becomes stiff and hostile again. He doesn't insist.

He goes to sleep. Bitterly she watches him sleep—why didn't he persevere? What is this egotistical calm that takes him so far away from her?—she watches him sleeping the way we watch the sinking of the boat containing all our hopes.

July 1990. Noon.

He sees her—she is standing between two cars, carrying on some sort of argument. He finds this funny because neither one of them is where they're supposed to be: he ought to be working at the chalet, and officially she is imprisoned on location, filming. As always, interesting things happen by chance. He waves his arms at her, is about to call out her name. That's when he sees the blond guy. The blond guy was there before, he's the one she was arguing with, but now she's leaning forward, now she's kissing him, now she's suddenly making him blindingly real.

They walk together on the sidewalk, a meaningless stroll except for the motion of his hand on her upper arm. Far behind, he follows, he can't take his eyes off that hand, their matching stride, the shoulders that keep bumping into each other. They go into a restaurant. This time, he saw it clearly, she leaned against him in the entrance, an instinctive thrusting of her chest against him before she brushed his lips with hers, he would swear it, their heads are concealed by a partition but he imagines them moving towards each other in slow motion, and this fictional vision is more unbearable than the rest.

He has positioned himself on the other side of the street, like in a bad thriller, astounded to find himself the third party in an ordinary affair. He doesn't have a pistol in his pocket, just an old shrivelled wallet to knead in his distress. A fat woman bumps into him without stopping. "Excuse me, sir," he murmurs, he no longer knows what he's saying, or what he's doing there, taking root in the sidewalk, or how much of all this he's making up. He leaves.

Later he calls her. He pretends to be talking to her from a telephone booth far away in the Laurentians. Her voice is cool and candid, he feels reality blurring, becoming comfortable again. He asks her how the filming is going. She's got too much to do, she says, another insane day—not even time to eat. She keeps talking but he doesn't hear any more, he is wondering, amazed, where this weird pain cutting him in two is coming from.

October 1987. Evening.

It's a great party. The guests munch, drink, chatter, snort high-quality coke, smoke Quebec and Colombian grass, dance in perfectly unrestrained ecstasy. These are all the right people, they seem to have been poured from a single set of moulds. It was her idea, an irrepressible desire to celebrate, a way of saying: look, here's my past and my parallel lives, do you still want me? They have brought together their respective friends, their old lovers, their faded loves, in fact, without telling anyone, they are celebrating the beginning of an eternal epoch, the Leah–Paul cohabitation.

They flit from one guest to the next, reveal themselves as impeccable hosts. The evening advances and they only have time to brush against each other in passing, a faraway wink across the room, an impromptu kiss on the neck. But through the others and the distance that separates them they can feel their extreme complicity, their unwavering magnetic attraction, like an animal feigning sleep.

She is in full flight when he suddenly grabs her and whispers, "I want to talk to you, come here for a few minutes." His tone is emphatic, she pretends to be worried. They look through the crowded apartment for a quiet corner, they end up among the coats in the vestibule.

"Here it is," he says, "a surprise, a present for you."

He holds out something white, Keith Jarrett's *The Köln Concert* album. She starts to laugh so hard that she chokes.

"What is it?" he asks, annoyed.

She holds them, him and the album, tightly against her, she nibbles traitorously at his nose.

"I bought the same thing for you."

The evening continues and people begin to wonder where they are. Someone comes across them unexpectedly and goes back to broadcast the news to the others, with nostalgic indulgence. They are lying down in the midst of the coats, burrowed into kilometres of rain-gear, kissing and hugging as though they were all alone in the world.

January 1991. Evening.

The knives are flying. They are equally skilled in this cruel little game that consists of firing poisoned arrows at each other's most vulnerable spots, and they aren't holding back. It must have been ripe to burst, but the abscess isn't draining, they are up to their necks in the purulence and bad faith of a dying grand passion. Liar, you lied to me, he screams, it's your fault, you pushed me to the limit, she spits back, they've forgotten that words are anything but rocks to be thrown in each other's faces. They go over their life together scene by scene and they dissect it until it's unrecognizable—there, and there, look what you did to me, but remember that and that, you sneaky ingrate lowdown con artist bitch.

The accusations pile up and neutralize each other, oh how can I get to you and hurt you as much as I myself am hurt? They pass from words to deeds. She breaks a flowerpot, throws the pieces in his face. He shakes her and pushes her violently against the wall. And then they stop, halt, silence, cut.

They stare at each other, frightened, in an end-of-the-world silence. What have we done, what have you done with your heart, where did it go?

They begin to blubber, each as ridiculous as the other. They are blubbering because of these few steps too close to the irreparable, they blubber because it's snowing outside, because it's a new year and they can't even find consolation in each other's arms.

June 1992. Evening.

The theatre empties quietly. Near the exit they suddenly find themselves face to face: impossible to pretend distraction or convenient myopia. It was bound to happen one day. He's with a girl, a tall, stylish redhead who's holding him victoriously by the elbow. She is alone.

For a moment they stand there bewildered, incapable of mastering the surprise and consternation spreading across their faces. Then they begin returning to normal, gradually finding the comfortable words that pass for communication.

"How's it going?"

"Well. And you?"

Fortunately, after a brief improvisation on the weather, they have the film to talk about. She notices that his eyes are shadowed, he is working too hard or maybe the tall redhead is lasciviously consuming his nights. She doesn't really want to know. He notices that she is faintly rounded, as though the sharpest angles have been smoothed out, perhaps she's pregnant. He doesn't really want to find out. They talk long enough to save face. The tall redhead casually eyes the exit.

They say goodbye, using the same words as those who have never loved each other.

Nonetheless, they were on the verge of really talking to each other when the crowd pushed them together, but the moment passed, there are too many spectators and the play is over. They leave and go off in opposite directions. They don't turn back, no confused looks across the emptiness, they leave very quickly, carried on the wings of fear.

September 1989. Night.

She's the one who keeps the fire, like the vestals of ancient times. Knowingly she intersperses the damp birch with the cherry-wood logs, she keeps the air moving through with her magic wand, she tops it all off with a big armful of red pine that sends the flames leaping towards the sky.

"It's hell," he says, pulling back his chair.

The night is redolent of resin and the lake. They don't speak. As soon as they're out of Montreal and into this place, the wild heart of their forest, they become someone else, a new species, half animal, half human, welcomed into the grand movements of the cosmos. A raccoon has come to visit them. Before that two skunks, crafty and lame, snuck between their legs to steal potato chips. In the old spruce tree across from them, three flying squirrels have been performing reckless aerial leaps, just for them. It's endless, the actors play on and on, and they didn't even have to buy a ticket.

Now it's the moon. Red-tinged, almost round, it emerges from behind the mountain and hangs above the water.

"Come on," he whispers, "let's go out in the canoe."

They slip into the boat, glide along Indian-style, the water silent on their paddles. In front of them the moon traces a phosphorescent path; if they take it to the end they'll lose themselves in the stars, drown what's left of their fears, pierce the enigmas of the universe the way you prick a balloon. Suddenly the call of a loon. They stop in the middle of the lake.

It's a plaintive cry, a psalm, a supernatural chant. They are there in the midst of all that, the fire dancing on the shore, the moon, the night-calm lake, the song of the loon, their fingers find each other without looking, they wish they could cry— this love is such a state of grace, it's impossible that it won't last forever.

translated by Matt Cohen

Audrey Thomas

Harry and Violet

He had been sulky all day—like the summer weather back East, she thought, when you looked at the sky and brought in the garden chairs, rolled up the windows on the car. It was understandable. Now, he was going to have to share her. There were hours to go before the ferry arrived, and yet, already, she could feel herself being pulled in two directions.

"Come for a swim?" he said.

"No thanks, I have—" (no, don't do that, be honest) "I want to clean out her room."

"Couldn't you do that later?"

"Yes, but I'd rather finish all the dirty work before I go swimming, not after."

So he went down the path, towel over his shoulders, whistling loudly, without her. "Men," she thought, tipping the dustpan into the wood stove, and then, she stopped still, remembering him sitting up in bed this morning, teasing her, smiling. "I love him," she thought, and then, "Goddammit" and then (with a sigh), "Well, there's no law that says *they* have to love one another." Later, when she ran down to the store for some marshmallows—they'd have a wiener roast tomorrow, maybe drive to the park at the south end of the island, make it a real treat; the child liked it down there, because there were old logs that she could ride on, like horses, out into the bay—she saw him over on the rocks, sitting with his hands around his knees, thinking. She waved, but he didn't see her.

"Oh well," she thought, "let him sulk." (But she went back up the path discouraged.)

There were fresh sheets on the child's bed and a posy of wildflowers in a green bottle on the dresser. Also, a little tin candlestick that she herself had used, twenty-five years before, at her grandfather's summer place. She could still read the faded lettering:

Jack be Nimble
Jack be Quick

There had been no electricity, at first, at her grandfather's place, and her mother would accompany her, carrying the candlestick, into the back room where she slept. It was one of the few things from her childhood that she still owned, that candlestick. Now, she regretted lost teddybears, a certain little tea set and a doll with a china head named Miss Nanoo. She would like to have given all those things to her little girl. And the whistling tea kettle, a pop-up book about a family named the Jolly Jump-Ups; all the high-heeled shoes, and hats with polka-dot veils, for playing ladies. (But not the rabbits that died, or the stairs that creaked, or her parents' low-pitched furious arguments coming up the hot-air registers.)

"Sometimes, in town, I feel like I ought to make an appointment to see you," he said, "in order to get any real, undivided attention. Maybe that's what—"

"What's what?" she asked, sitting up.

"Nothing," he said, and pulled her down again. "Nothing."

He had such beautiful skin; she loved to run her hands down his long back and over his buttocks.

"I'll bet that you were a really naughty little boy," she said indulgently. "I'll bet that your mother had a lot of trouble with you."

"With all of us."

"With you, especially."

He laughed and rolled over on his back. "I guess so." He imitated a mother's voice. "You get into that house right now or I'll really give you something to cry about."

"God," she said, "I bet that I sound like that sometimes. I hear women in supermarkets or on the street and I wish they could hear themselves—so angry and irritated."

"No, you don't sound like that. You're far too soft with that kid. That's what's wrong with her."

"She's had a very hard time; she's very insecure."

"I think that you make it harder."

"How?" she said. "How?" Sitting up again. "I do the best that I can."

"Listen, that kid runs you. She's fucking spoiled, that's what she is."

"You don't like kids."

"That's not true."

"It is true and you know it."

Where had their closeness gone? Lying in her secret sunbathing place, beyond the apple trees, tasting each other, touching, exploring. Now, it was as if the sun had suddenly disappeared behind a cloud.

But most of the time, it had been lovely—just the two of them, for a change. "Our honeymoon," she said to him, laughing. They got up late and had special breakfasts on the porch, talking and drinking coffee, and watching the boats in the channel. Once, a big freighter went by and they spent a while daydreaming out loud and saying to each other, "Let's chuck it all and the three of us just go away some place. A hut on a beach in Pago Pago. Bread-fruit and pineapples. No need for clothes or cars. Climb up and pick your breakfast; swim out and spear your dinner. Ah yes." The freighter seemed enormous in the narrow channel; the sound of its engines throbbed long after the boat disappeared. Her eyes weren't good enough, but he made out the name: "*Tana Maru*. Oh well, Japan! Why not?"

"We could fly dragon kites and live in a paper house."

"How could we make love in a paper house?"

"Quietly," she said.

"Not you," and laughed when she blushed.

"Anyway," she said, "freighters don't take children under twelve."

"How do you know?"

"Oh, I know. I know. It's one of my big fantasies. I've got a book. What do you want to know? 'Best Buys in Freighters to the South Seas and Australia'? 'To the Orient, Far East, West-bound from Pacific Coast Ports'? 'Best Buys in Freighters Between Japan and Australia'? They don't recommend container vessels."

"You really have a book?"

"Sure. I ordered it once, when I was feeling low. Something to dream about."

He told her about his first day in Paris, walking clear across the city and hardly stopping, all day long, drunk on the beauty and romance, feeling Europe soak in through his feet. Getting stuck with his backpack in a *pissoir*. He had been with his wife in Paris. They had walked the city together. She imagined them finding a small, perfect room on a sidestreet, making love behind wooden shutters, laughing at their swollen feet.

"It would be fun to go away," he said, "just the two of us."

"How can he be expected to understand?" she thought.

"What does he really know about it?" *They* hadn't wanted children, he and his wife, or so he said.

"I can't understand why you're attracted to me," she said. She said it often.

"Because you're you."

And yet, he got upset, in town, if she couldn't drop everything and come for a walk, right then. He went by himself with his old black umbrella—a solitary figure in the rain. Sometimes, her heart ached for him, really ached, like a sore tooth, an ache that never completely went away. And yet, at other times, infuriated because he would not, *could* not understand, she saw his ego as a very large dog, which he took with him everywhere and which expected to be constantly fed. A Saint Bernard of an ego. No. Something a little more vicious, a German shepherd perhaps.

"Why are you attracted to me?" he said. He said it often. "What is it about me that attracts you?"

And she would list all the things that she loved about him— and the list was long—as they sat over their wine in the June twilight. It was a sort of game between them.

They fought too—they both had terrible tempers. But here, there hadn't been any small worried voice to suddenly pipe in with, "Hey, are you guys having a fight?"

Sunday mornings, for example. Sunday mornings had always been her special time. Particularly over here, on holiday, but also, somewhat modified, in town. She liked to lie in bed, with a book and a pot of coffee. He wanted to make love, and then, be up and doing, have a half-decent breakfast, not just sixteen cups of coffee. "Well," he would say, rolling over, "I don't know about you, but I'm getting hungry." It was hard. She found herself reading the same page two or three times. But she forced herself to look at him sweetly, from over the top of the book, and turn the page. He was not used to such treatment; he was hurt and angered by it. She was no longer used to sharing her Sunday mornings with a man. (And, of course, to make matters worse, it was the morning that the child was allowed in bed, allowed a special cup of coffee and to bring a book.)

"But here in the cabin?" he remonstrated. "Look what a lovely day it is!" It was hard, but she would not give in. Could not. And yet, she could almost hear her mother's voice, haranguing her: "You let one get away! This one, too?" As though they were a fish or some big game animal.

"We have to learn to take each other as we are," she said, fighting an urge to get up and make him a cheese omelette, with some of the fresh parsley from under the shed, buttered toast and crisp bacon, a new pot of steaming coffee.

"It seems to me that what you really mean is that you won't change, that I have to do all the changing."

"No," she said, "that's not what I mean at all."

Or was it? He had two shirts that he couldn't wear any more because so many buttons had come off. What was she trying to prove? Was she really just a bitch? She had insisted that he learn to cook and share the cooking.

He liked things spare and neat and organized. She covered surfaces with a clutter of books and papers and jugs of flowers. Pictures drawn by her little girl. Old things from secondhand stores. In her bedroom (their bedroom now), she had a large framed sepia photograph of a nurses' graduating class, in old-fashioned uniforms.

"Is one of those your grandmother?" he said, bending his head close to the picture, searching for a family likeness.

"Oh no," she said. "I saw it in a secondhand shop and thought that it was nice. On the back, it says 'Grace Harriett, 1916, second row from left in the back row.' See, that's her."

"You're nuts," he said. "You know that, don't you? Absolutely bananas."

But she refused to take the photograph down. She gave him one of the two bureaus and found herself doing it grudgingly. She admitted it, embarrassed and ashamed. The sight of his wallet and keys and loose change on the old bureau that she had so bravely painted a bright defiant red, the tears rolling down her cheeks (after changing the colour of the walls, changing the bedroom, actually, and even the side of the bed that she slept on)—it irritated her.

"You don't really want me in your life," he said.

"Oh, that's not it!" She went to him and put her arms around him. "I guess that I've learned my lesson a little too well. Give me time to get used to you. I haven't had a room of my own in ten years. I hated it at first, and then—and then I liked it. I'm sorry, I know that it's a little silly, but I wish we had space for separate bedrooms."

"And sleep separately? I can move out, you know. Maybe that would be the answer."

"Not sleep separately," she said. "Or only sometimes. I've got used to my own private space, that's all."

And he repeated again, "You just don't want me in your life."

He put a stop to the child crawling in bed with her. He wouldn't hear of it.

"She's jealous; she needs to know that she's wanted."

"This is our *bedroom*. She's not wanted in our bedroom. This is our *bed*." Then he added, sulking, "It's you she wants to crawl in bed with anyway, not me."

"She needs to feel that I still love her. She needs cuddles, just as much as you and I do."

"What am I supposed to do, shove over?"

"Would that be so hard?"

"I'd have to start wearing underpants."

She began to laugh, and although he smiled, she could see that his mind was made up.

"Sometimes," he said, "I think that I can really understand why Tom left."

"How do you know that he felt the way you do? She's his child, after all."

"Yes, she makes that abundantly clear."

So, there they were again. Stalemate. She took to going down and crawling in with the child.

Sometimes, they asked each other if maybe it was only the sex.

"Our adult lives have been so different," she said. "You are used to so much personal freedom. I've never actually lived alone with a man for more than a few months. Maybe I like children because I've had to like them, who knows? But I do like them and I *love* my child—I *love* her. She's part of me, part of my life. She and I help each other grow."

"You're ruining her," he said.

She repeated, "What do you know about it?"

One winter, he and his wife had packed up and gone to North Africa. One winter, they had lived in a small cabin in Québec. They walked all night with a lantern, bundled up against the cold, running and laughing and making angels in the snow. They had been across the whole length of the country, stopping when it took their fancy, hitchhiking, delivering drive-away cars, washing dishes in resort hotels.

(Walking all day in the streets of Paris, their arms around each other.)

Sometimes, she wondered why, after all, he left. He never spoke against his wife; indeed, he loved her still and often saw her.

"She asked me if I was happy?" he said one night, weeping, with her arms around him tight.

"What did you say?" she whispered.

"I told her that happiness wasn't the point."

Oh, how she loved him for his honesty, even when his words flew into her like arrows! He buried his face in her neck.

"I love you," she whispered, her mouth against his cheek. "I love you. It's going to be all right." She saw his wife lying alone and weeping. His ex-wife. His X.

His car was clean and tidy. Nothing out of place. Hers contained old ferry tickets, the rubber leg off a doll, a scarf that somebody left behind a year ago and might return to claim, an empty apple juice carton, a brown glove left over from last winter.

"Why do we go on with this?" they sometimes cried to one another. "It's ridiculous!"

But the last four days had been, if not paradise, something very close to it. The weather held and they lay naked in the sun.

"We are each other's Africas," she said. "Like an astronaut." And she stuck an early rose behind her ear.

They sat on the wharf and watched extravagant sunsets, then they came back up the path into the cool and private darkness. They fell deep into one another's secret places, and then, lay on the double bed, their arms around one another, while the moon stared at their silvered bodies, with its single silver eye.

Once, they woke up and they both admitted that they had to pee, so they went outside together, still naked, into the soft June night, laughing. Everything simple and easy and understood between them. No secrets. (And no little voice to say, "Hey, what are you guys doing?")

"We shouldn't really sleep with the moonlight on us," she said. "It could drive us crazy."

"Impossible, in your case," he said, kissing her. But she stayed awake a long time after that, propped on her elbow, watching his dark head on the pillow.

The child called him Harry to tease him. Because of all his dark hair and rabbinical beard. She had a doll named Harry as well, a girl doll with a mop of red wool hair. She wondered if they would have been friends, the man and the child, in some other situation. It was she who came between them. They both wanted to possess her. No. Each wanted her to say that each was number one. What did *she* want? Both of them, but not so much pulling and tugging. And, if it ever came to a choice, there was none. Always, the child was first. In that, at least, he was right.

"It's easier without a man," she thought. "But is it better?" So many broken marriages and separated children. Now, her ex-husband was with a woman who didn't want any children—or not yet. They had been to Mexico and Guatemala. Driving. Stopping wherever it took their fancy. Postcards of beaches along the Oregon coast, Sausalito, Aztec ruins, the balloon sellers in Chapultepec Park in Mexico City. They brought back a *piñata* and lovely clothes for her and her daughter. A papier-mâché bird. A wooden children's game. An armload of paper flowers. The child was with them now. In a few hours, they would put her on the ferry with some friends who were coming across. They never came when she was here, and yet, her husband's presence was all around her. His old plaid shirt hung on a hook by the door. Even his pipe lay on the mantelpiece.

As she rolled out the pastry for a pie, she wondered how her—what? lover? new old man? boyfriend?—was affected by being surrounded by so much of her past. It was her house, her cabin—or hers and her ex-husband's. He owned half of a secondhand Volkswagen, his typewriter, his books, his knapsack and tent, a few clothes. He liked it that way, he said. It was easier to move about.

She had enjoyed these four days. Loved them. Wanted more. And yet she looked forward eagerly to the coming of the child, who reached some deep place in her, where no man could ever go, a place that could never be entered by any man, not even the father, no matter how much she had loved him.

Still, she wished that the solitary man on the rocks would come up the path right now and take her, floury hands and all, and lay her down on the big bed in the other room. And no need to keep quiet. No ears to listen. Letting go.

She opened a jar of blackberry and apple and spooned it into the pie shell. "He wants me to come and get him," she thought. "I want him to come and get me."

She had not realized how lonely she was; indeed, that she was lonely at all, until she fell in love with him. When he first met her, he had not known about her child. She was alone in a café. They were reading the same book, only different volumes. Sometimes, she wondered if he felt that he had been led into her world under false pretences. The way one person will stand by the road—usually the woman—and stick out her thumb. Then, after the driver stops and is agreeable, she signals to her friend behind the bushes. What can the driver do? But it was not that she deliberately set out to deceive him, nothing like that. There they were in the café, reading the same book. Who noticed first? Who spoke first? They debated this sometimes. Talking and talking and talking. And then, they walked down to the beach and sat on a log and talked some more.

So that, by the time she said that she really had to go home now, she knew that he had never broken a bone in his life, that he liked Yeats and Bukowski, but not Eliot, that he had come for the very first time that afternoon to that café, that he was married and had no children. She mentioned the child, she must have. She always mentioned the child. But there she'd been, in a café, reading a book by herself, free to spend the afternoon sitting on a log and talking to a stranger. How was he to know that it was her one free afternoon a week? How was he to know what she meant when she said, "*I* have a child, a little girl." How was she to know that this stranger would fall in love with her?

They were both verbalizers. They turned their relationship (and everything else) over and over, looking for cracks, or even incipient cracks, giving little taps to test for clarity or weakness. (Only some things were never said, of course. How tall he was compared to ... How round she was compared to ... Being consciously careful, at first, to make no comparisons at all.) Laughing, then, at each other's irritating mannerisms. He sighed and groaned a lot; it did not mean that he was unhappy, he said, it was simply a habit. She snored if she slept on her left side. "Just wake me or turn me over if it bothers you."

He had been in the city before, five years ago, in the West End. They might have met then. Would they have liked one another? They spent whole afternoons trying to trace where each had been on some particular day.

After their second meeting, they knew that they must never see each other, alone, again.

He told her that sometimes he felt very lonely when he was with her, especially when he visited her in the communal house where she was living, even late at night, in the privacy of her own little bedroom (*her* bedroom). He felt the other people in the house; felt her ready to swing instantly from lover to mother at the sound of a distant cry.

"What would you have me do?" she said. "There are some things that I can't change."

"There are some things that you *won't* change."

"Perhaps. I don't know."

"I know it."

Often, they admitted that they weren't suited to one another. They laughed about it painfully—or cried. "Like two prisoners on a chain gang," she thought. "One tall; one short, whom Fate has manacled together."

The child was rude to him. "Why does he put ketchup on his eggs?" she said, the three of them sitting at the breakfast table. "Why does he, Mommy?"

"Ask him."

"She always turns to *you* to find out about *me*," he said.

"That's natural."

"She's rude."

And it was true. She was rude—at least to him. One day, she asked, "If you and Harry had a big fight, could you tell him to get out?"

"No," she said, "not really. He lives here now."

"But it's *your* house," said the little girl.

Sometimes she felt such anger towards that other man, the child's father, who had put her in this position. Sometimes she thought that the whole thing really wasn't worth the trouble. She had been happy that afternoon in the little café, reading her book, sipping her tea, enjoying her solitude. She hadn't been looking for anyone. All that sort of thing was behind her. He noticed her when she came in, he said, because, wherever he went, he always sat so that he could look at people. Had he been looking for someone? Had the business of the books seemed, to him, somehow a password? She had been tired that day—there were questions of mortgages and plumbing, a pregnant cat. She was waiting her turn to spend a weekend in the country. Yet, she saw this man who was reading the same book as she was. How long had he been watching her? Who smiled first? Who spoke? Later, he quoted Balthazar, when he asked if they could meet again: "'And morality is nothing if it is merely a form of good behaviour.'"

And she replied (Pursewarden): "'I know that the key I am trying to turn is in myself.'"

And now, here she was, making pies and putting lavender between the sheets. And a special pile of secondhand comic books, a miniature of the expensive, utterly worthless, but much-coveted cornflakes, so the little girl would have an easy and special breakfast in the morning, and not come in to wake her mother early. Or try to crawl in bed and be rebuffed. ("This is her first time over here with you," she cried to the invisible figure on the rocks. "She was allowed to do it! Right or wrong, she was allowed to do it. You're the adult, why can't you give a little?" But, why should he really? It was not his problem.)

After supper, they sat on the porch together, talking but not talking, really listening for the first cars as they came up from the ferry at the other end of the island.

"Already, it's not the same," he said. "I can feel it."

"I know." She put her small hand on top of his large one. "I've enjoyed these past four days. I've loved them. I guess that they seemed quite ordinary to you. I guess that this is the way you've always lived."

"Yes," he said. "With a woman, it's more or less the way that I've always lived. I'm not used to any other way."

"I love you," she said.

"In your way."

He let her go down the path alone when they heard the car stop. She was always surprised when her child had been away for a few days. How big she was! How badly her long hair needed cutting!

"Hello," she said, holding the child's face against her. "We've been waiting for you."

"I want to go and see if Connie's up," the child said. "I want to play with her tomorrow."

They went hand in hand across the road to her friend's house and arranged a picnic. The mother began to relax. Maybe it was she who caused the tension? The child wasn't going to be with them all the time; didn't want to be, in fact. She had been looking forward to seeing Connie, not them. What was she worrying about? Crossing the road again, they noticed a nest of tent caterpillars, just visible in the growing darkness.

"Can I have some, Mommy? Can I have some of those caterpillars in a jar?"

"Tomorrow," she said. "I'll fix you a jar with some holes in the lid for air."

"I'll just get two," the child said, giving a little skip. "I'm gonna name them Harry and Violet."

"We'll get them tomorrow," she promised.

(And who was Violet? It must be somebody over there. She realized with a start that her child had a whole other world "over there," that there were things which she wasn't told about, friends even. "And what do *they* do," she wondered, "about the crawling into bed?")

The child was tired and went to bed quite readily. She acknowledged the man's hug, even if she didn't exactly return it. And she called him by his right name for a change. Her mother relaxed even more. It would work out. Perhaps all three of them had been too impatient, too hostile to the idea of change. The man and woman went back out on the porch for a while, just enjoying the night and the quiet, and then, they, too, went inside to sleep. They lay in the big bed with their arms around each other.

And they woke early, smiling, as they heard the child tiptoe-ing around the kitchen, fixing her special breakfast, as she'd been told to do. Important. Respectful of them, yet anxious to get going. Her mother fought down the impulse to run out and give her a good morning kiss. She was proud of her daughter, open-ing and closing the refrigerator door so quietly, rummaging in the cupboard so carefully. (What had been forgotten? Would she remember about the mousetraps? Again, the urge to run out and take her in her arms, pin her unruly hair out of her eyes, make sure she had a cardigan.)

But she made herself lie still, smiling into the eyes of the man, feeling him move close to her, feeling him stiffen against her naked thigh. She smiled when she heard the door of the cabin close.

"Come here you," he whispered, his eyes dark, his body hard and smooth against hers. "Come here."

She shook her head and pulled him over on top of her, felt him filling up all the empty spaces, clung to him, opened to him. She shut her eyes and with a great, almost child-like sigh, gave herself up to the lovely, wet, slippery union between them. Oh God, yes, she needed this too, and from this man who loved her, heaven alone knew why. She felt all the empty and sore places fill up, expand, smooth out. Oh God, it was so nice with his dark head in the hollow of her shoulder, the songbirds outside, she couldn't stand it much longer, and neither, she knew, could he. They were always urgent in the morning. Why? She could tell that he was coming and it excited her terribly, something about the way he—

"Harder," she whispered, "harder."

And the child said, from the foot of the bed, "Hey, you guys, d'you want to meet Harry and Violet?"

Hélène Rioux

Opening Night

One day in July the opera lover with whom I was almost having an affair invited me for supper. I remember the heat of that day, forty in the shade. The opera lover had just moved into a lovely air-conditioned apartment on the twenty-fourth floor of a high-rise. He said to me: "We are going to have a housewarming party together." But what he meant was, "Just the two of us, a little romantic meal. You will see what you will see." He loved to cook.

When I arrived, I was confused by the different smells. I sniffed without distinguishing them. He said, "Don't ask what we're having, it's a surprise." Then, "Make yourself at home, I'll bring you a drink." I sat down on the leather couch. He offered me a Tequila Sunrise decorated with a carcinogenic mara-schino cherry; it was in a long-stemmed glass of Bohemian crystal. In an identical glass he served himself a Perrier water on the rocks with a slice of lemon gorged with vitamin C. "I don't drink," he said, "but I'll have a little wine when we eat, just to keep you company." On the lacquered table, he set out a plate of sturgeon caviar on toast and bite-size pastries stuffed with asparagus. "Are you pleased?" he asked. "Is it good?" His eyes were shining. He had been cooking all day when he could have been swimming in the pool or suntanning on the balcony. He must have liked me. Or at least he was very determined to win me over.

He went to the kitchen to check on the food, to stir the sauces, add a dash of salt, a sprig of rosemary, a few drops of spice oils. "It's ready. Are you hungry?" I was hungry. But the meal was a disaster. It began with quail stuffed with green grapes and flambéed with port. I had to look away. "Poor little sparrows." He flamed them at the table, a fate medieval and spectacular, the little birds held in the hollow of his hand, the flame licking the carcasses curled up there so tenderly, plump and round, the little innocent bodies. He was proud of himself. I made excuses, saying, "Sparrows, really, I couldn't." I tried a grape, which although still a grape, having been cooked with quails, no longer tasted the same. Disappointed expression on his face...

He took the plates away, he didn't dare swallow a mouthful in front of me. "It doesn't matter, I'll bring you the next course." The next course was frogs' legs in basilic butter. "Taste it at least, it's delicious, I promise; it is more tender than chicken. The sauce is a masterpiece, with fresh basil, butter, reduced with white burgundy... All right, I understand. And do you also dislike cheese?" I'd lost my appetite but all the same I murmured, "Cheese, that's fine. As long as it's not Roquefort." It was Roquefort.

For the rest of the evening he was sullen. I was also unhappy but I was determined to drag a smile out of him. I felt guilty, I had spoiled the party. Trying to get him to smile I suggested, "Next time, you can make me tofu, a cucumber sandwich"—oh no, his smiles, he would not waste them—"And poutine, a millet pie." He remained cold.

To cheer him up I told him of the time when this character,

you know, he'd just come back from India, I've already told you about that, we went to school together, and he came to my house late one afternoon with a white plastic bag full of food dangling at the end of his skinny arms, you know, he was always dressed in orange, a linen tunic, rope sandals, he'd gone to a guru in India where he was given a name meaning "sun" or something like that, I forget the Hindu word, on this occasion he had decreed that he would make the supper, my eating habits were horrible, it was shameful. He was busy in the kitchen for three hours before finally serving an entrée of raw corn on the cob, and in order to eat it, he took out his dentures. Then came a murky gruel which he called oats and turnips au gratin. He assured me it was very good for one's health, the minerals, the proteins, very balanced, very zen.

I was finally successful in extracting a smile. It was a slight one, fleeting, forced. He said I was making fun of him, going over his head, and I replied that his head was well above my means.

He cleared the table, the dishes and the glasses clinking in the kitchen. I was exhausted, ravenous and nauseous at the same time. Not a breath of air came through the open French windows. The air conditioning was clearly defective. It is always this way. Always a cold spell when the furnace breaks down. Always rain for a holiday week. The toast only falls on the buttered side. It's Murphy's Law.

Total immobility, very heavy. Covered with sweat, we listened to *La Bohême*, then *Aïda* and *Madame Butterfly*. He still did not have a compact disc player but a very sophisticated stereo system to regulate the flats and sharps, it's a long story, he wanted the pure sound, the perfect balance, he had a fine ear, the most imperceptible distortion caused a grimace of grief to bloom across his face. Then he suggested a game of chess and I lost. I don't have the head for it, I'm hopeless at chess. Besides I had such a horror of losing that I intentionally speeded up my defeat and this triumph without glory humiliated him even more.

I had finished the bottle of Alsatian wine, I felt sick, I ran to the bathroom. He followed me, he knocked on the door, "My flower, you don't feel good? Come here and stretch out." He placed a wet washcloth wrapped around ice cubes on my forehead, he made me drink some mouthfuls of an infusion, held my hand, spoke those soothing words one whispers to the dying or to children who cry. "It's all right, you didn't do it, it's all my fault, I should have asked you before making all this ... but I wanted to surprise you, serves me right ... here, drink a little more verbena ..." And the verbena would not go down. He was holding a cut-glass salad bowl, he was really in love with me, nothing was too good for me, he wouldn't want me to vomit into a plastic bucket or a saucepan, he held the salad bowl in front of me while I unloaded everything inside me: the tequila and the cherry, the green grape, the bread crusts and the fish eggs in a suspension of white wine. He patted me gently on the back while repeating with a contrite air that he should have known better, that he had seen how in a restaurant I always ordered salads, fish, a steak if need be, and between two hiccups I tried to drag forth one of his precious smiles. "It looks rather like oats with turnips, you know," I commented, casting an eye into the salad bowl.

With an uncertain air, he asked, "You made up that story, didn't you?"

"Dear friend, don't you know that truth is stranger than fiction? ... I would never have enough imagination to make that up."

"I hate it when you call me 'dear friend.'"

"Dear friend ... quickly ... the salad bowl."

He held out the salad bowl. He went to rinse it and returned with cold compresses for my forehead. Meanwhile I had vomit in my hair but he said, "It's nothing serious, I'm going to run you a bath." I was so limp that he had to take off my clothes. I was so limp he had to lead me to the bathroom. "Do you want me to help you?" I stammered yes, otherwise I would certainly drown myself. The water was lukewarm. I was shivering. I demanded, "More hot, please ... dear friend." He poured the shampoo on my hair, he massaged my head which was rattling, my head was so heavy, my head was so sick, then with one hand he held it, while with the other he ran a stream from the shower. "More cold now ... very cold ... hot now ..."

"Is it a hot and cold shower that you want?"

"I want my spirits to return ... they are returning ... I feel them returning ..."

And after three or four of these brutal transitions from boiling to freezing, they had returned very well. I was still staggering a little coming out of the bath, but only a little, and it was from weakness. He gave me a very effective pill for my headache, and a toothbrush, of which he kept some in reserve. I chose the yellow with hard bristles, I brushed vigorously and gargled with mouthwash. My haggard features peered out at me from the mirror. He dried me with a big Turkish towel, a chaste kiss on my belly, my knees, my feet. "And what would you like now? Would you like to lie down?"

He carried me as far as his bed. I was a little drowsy, nearly swaying. I sensed him at regular intervals entering the room, approaching me, leaning over me with solicitude. At one point I turned on the bedside lamp. He came at once and said, "You must be starving, my poor flower."

"I am ravenous."

"If you would like to go out ..."

"I have nothing to wear."

"True ... And if I ordered Chinese, would that bother you?"

"Go for Chinese."

"Egg noodles."

"Go for the noodles."

"With vegetables only."

"Go for the vegetables."

"We'll eat on the balcony."

We ate on the balcony by the glimmer of two candles under the crescent moon and a garden of stars. It looked like a hanging garden, an upside-down garden. We tilted our heads, hoping to see a shooting star, a meteorite streaking through space. He asked, "Now how's it going? Things are improving?" "Yes, yes." "The bouillon is light, isn't it?" "Very light." We drank weak green tea. He had loaned me one of his t-shirts. The blue night streaked to burgundy or vice versa. I put my feet beside his thigh on his cushioned chair. He caressed them absentmindedly, then with more eagerness. He said, "The feet, what a neglected part of the body, unappreciated, sometimes even despised." He said, "Me, feet, they turn me on. They look solid but they are vulnerable. Full of hollows and bumps, like valleys, a foot, it is like a landscape." I raised the stakes, saying, "And then, it is sympathetic. Without pretension." He passed his finger between my toes, saying, "Here, between the toes, it is secret, sensitive, it is fluttering." Under the influence of this light caress, I felt myself becoming euphoric little by little. He massaged the sole of my foot. He remarked, "You have soft soles. Sometimes the sole is rough."

"In winter it is rough."

"Yes, the heating."

"Nylon stockings, boots."

"It stirs me up when it's rough, it stirs me up when it's soft. You have a silky sole."

He put my feet on his knees. He took them one by one in his hands as if they were birds, quivering quails. He approached them with his lips. He said, "By the way, this character…"

"What character?"

"The comical person you were talking about a few minutes ago ..."

"Oats with turnips?"

"Yes."

He kissed my toes one at a time, holding my heel in the palm of his hand, he caressed my arch with his thumb, I began to feel suggestive tickles all the length of my legs, rising up the inner sides, microscopic ants climbing single file up a mountain path.

"What puzzles you?"

"Well, I don't know ... who he was, how you became friends with him. It's so very strange to imagine you with that kind of man."

"We met in school, we were in grade twelve. Then he had a brush cut, heavy black-rimmed glasses, the kind with Coke bottle bottoms, he wore a steel grey suit, his father's ties. The laughing stock of the class, I'll tell you. He was always like that. The butt of their jokes, the scapegoat."

"The whipping boy."

"The bogeyman."

"First in the class?"

"No, not so. Below average. No good in math, no good in physical education, strong in history. Crazy about overly elaborate philosophy, deadly boring. His speech was slow and hesitant ... I like that, your tongue under my toes ..."

"They remind me of little pillows ... In short, you took pity on him, right?"

"No, at that time I never said a word to him. I was content to laugh at him, like everybody else. It was only some years later, I frequently visited a man, you know, I told you about him, who was into transcendental meditation."

"You never told me about that."

"It's not important ... anyway, him, he knew him. He had returned from India. Oats with turnips, I'll say."

"You're easy to follow."

"A cult, over there, he'd been renamed. At first I didn't recognize him. He held immersion sessions."

"Immersion?"

"Yes, in a bath. You had to be completely under the water, a tube in the mouth, you know, like a periscope."

"A snorkel, you mean."

"All right, a snorkel, if you wish, but me, it reminded me of a periscope, a contraption which rose out of the water to spy all around ... Apparently it was like a return to the mother's womb. A very beneficial technique. The Rebirth."

"Yes, I've heard something about that. So, did you take the plunge?"

"You're kidding me ... No, the mother's womb, it didn't really inspire me. And besides, I couldn't bring myself to be naked in the bath with him all around holding the periscope. I should say the snorkel. His monastic air literally froze me. But he did calculate my biorhythm and my astrological chart."

"And then?"

"According to these calculations we were meant for each other. Our physiological clocks marked the same hour, our planets coincided very strangely. Venus in Taurus for both of us. The harmony of our libidos was supposed to be complete."

"You verified this?"

"Alas, he was not my type. When I explained this to him, he couldn't believe his ears. I had to handle it with three pairs of white gloves. It is difficult to tell a man he is unattractive. They cannot conceive that we are rejecting them because they are unattractive. A certain kind of unattractiveness, I should say. Because another kind, on the contrary, can be irresistible."

"You mean a virile unattractiveness?"

"Like yours. But he was, you could say ... too macrobiotic ... And then, I don't know, but his false teeth, his pimples."

(Just thinking of it, I nearly vomited again.)

"And then, he had to redo his calculations?"

"Calculus."

"What did you say?"

"I was joking. No, he didn't redo his calculations, he was infallible, the pope of the arcane. But he stared at me for several seconds, then declared, with grand condescension, that my aura was completely blurred."

"Me, I find your aura delicious."

I was feeling beautiful, these touches to my feet made me give in to a state of subtle enjoyment, as if the centre of sensation had been transported there, concentrated between my toes and my ankles. I leaned my head against the back of the garden chair, I contemplated the moon smiling with self-satisfaction, I dreamed of the constellations constellating and the galaxies turning. Like the stars turning around their sun, his thumb was delicately turning around my anklebone. Then I closed my eyes and I kept moaning very slowly. My breathing speeded up, I could hear a soft moaning coming from my mouth, I felt my lips forming the sound "yes" at closer and closer intervals, I had my head thrown back, my feet abandoned to his hands. When he began to suck my toes, tiny bubbles burst under my skin, my mouth went dry while elsewhere another part of my body was liquefied (is this the principle of body language?). Images filed through my head: precise, vague, vague, precise, colours, black, colours, sprays of colours, geysers which splashed through the black in my head, I never wanted to open my eyes again, never wanted to move again, I would stay there spellbound in this no-man's time, clutching the fleeting beauty of this instant which was escaping me, all of my strength holding out against its ending and refusing at the same time the idea of attaining it, holding off till infinity the culmination, the final act, one more minute, my tormentor, isn't it so, the little death is so slow in coming, then all at once a long shudder shook me, I arched under the manifold eye of the night, these wonderful stars, and I cried out, I think.

translated by Diane Schoemperlen

Margaret Atwood

Bluebeard's Egg

Sally stands at the kitchen window, waiting for the sauce she's reducing to come to a simmer, looking out. Past the garage the lot sweeps downwards, into the ravine; it's a wilderness there, of bushes and branches and what Sally thinks of as vines. It was her idea to have a kind of terrace, built of old railroad ties, with wild flowers growing between them, but Edward says he likes it the way it is. There's a playhouse down at the bottom, near the fence; from here she can just see the roof. It has nothing to do with Edward's kids, in their earlier incarnations, before Sally's time; it's more ancient than that, and falling apart. Sally would like it cleared away. She thinks drunks sleep in it, the men who live under the bridges down there, who occasionally wander over the fence (which is broken down, from where they step on it) and up the hill, to emerge squinting like moles into the light of Sally's well-kept back lawn.

Off to the left is Ed, in his windbreaker; it's officially spring. Sally's blue scylla is in flower, but it's chilly for this time of year. Ed's windbreaker is an old one he won't throw out; it still says WILDCATS, relic of some team he was on in high school, an era so prehistoric Sally can barely imagine it; though picturing Ed at high school is not all that difficult. Girls would have had crushes on him, he would have been unconscious of it; things like that don't change. He's puttering around the rock garden now; some of the rocks stick out too far and are in danger of grazing the side of Sally's Peugeot, on its way to the garage, and he's moving them around. He likes doing things like that, puttering, humming to himself. He won't wear work gloves, though she keeps telling him he could squash his fingers.

Watching his bent back with its frayed, poignant lettering, Sally dissolves; which is not infrequent with her. *My darling Edward*, she thinks. *Edward Bear, of little brain. How I love you.* At times like this she feels very protective of him.

Sally knows for a fact that dumb blondes were loved, not because they were blondes, but because they were dumb. It was their helplessness and confusion that were so sexually attractive, once; not their hair. It wasn't false, the rush of tenderness men must have felt for such women. Sally understands it.

For it must be admitted: Sally is in love with Ed because of his stupidity, his monumental and almost energetic stupidity: energetic, because Ed's stupidity is not passive. He's no mere blockhead; you'd have to be working at it to be that stupid. Does it make Sally feel smug, or smarter than he is, or even smarter than she really is herself? No; on the contrary, it makes her humble. It fills her with wonder that the world can contain such marvels as Ed's colossal and endearing thickness. He is just so *stupid*. Every time he gives her another piece of evidence, another tile that she can glue into place in the vast mosaic of his stupidity she's continually piecing together, she wants to hug him, and often does; and he is so stupid he can never figure out what for.

Because Ed is so stupid he doesn't even know he's stupid. He's a child of luck, a third son who, armed with nothing but a certain feeble-minded amiability, manages to make it through the forest with all its witches and traps and pitfalls and end up with the princess, who is Sally, of course. It helps that he's handsome.

On good days she sees his stupidity as innocence, lamb-like, shining with the light of (for instance) green daisied meadows in the sun. (When Sally starts thinking this way about Ed, in terms of the calendar art from the service-station washrooms of her childhood, dredging up images of a boy with curly golden hair, his arm thrown around the neck of an Irish setter—a notorious brainless beast, she reminds herself—she knows she is sliding over the edge, into a ghastly kind of sentimentality, and that she must stop at once, or Ed will vanish, to be replaced by a stuffed facsimile, useful for little else but an umbrella stand. Ed is a real person, with a lot more to him than these simplistic renditions allow for; which sometimes worries her.) On bad days though, she sees his stupidity as wilfulness, a stubborn determination to shut things out. His obtuseness is a wall, within which he can go about his business, humming to himself, while Sally, locked outside, must hack her way through the brambles with hardly so much as a transparent raincoat between them and her skin.

Why did she choose him (or, to be precise, as she tries to be with herself and sometimes is even out loud, *hunt him down*), when it's clear to everyone she had other options? To Marylynn, who is her best though most recent friend, she's explained it by saying she was spoiled when young by reading too many Agatha Christie murder mysteries, of the kind in which the clever and witty heroine passes over the equally clever and witty first-lead male, who's helped solve the crime, in order to marry the second-lead male, the stupid one, the one who would have been arrested and condemned and executed if it hadn't been for her cleverness. Maybe this is how she sees Ed: if it weren't for her, his blundering too-many-thumbs kindness would get him into all sorts of quagmires, all sorts of sink-holes he'd never be able to get himself out of, and then he'd be done for.

"Sink-hole" and "quagmire" are not flattering ways of speaking about other women, but this is what is at the back of Sally's mind; specifically, Ed's two previous wives. Sally didn't exactly extricate him from their clutches. She's never even met the first one, who moved to the west coast fourteen years ago and sends Christmas cards, and the second one was middle-aged and already in the act of severing herself from Ed before Sally came along. (For Sally, "middle-aged" means anyone five years older than she is. It has always meant this. She applies it only to women, however. She doesn't think of Ed as middle-aged, although the gap between them is considerably more than five years.)

Ed doesn't know what happened with these marriages, what went wrong. His protestations of ignorance, his refusal to discuss the finer points, is frustrating to Sally, because she would like to hear the whole story. But it's also cause for anxiety: if he doesn't know what happened with the other two, maybe the same thing could be happening with her and he doesn't know about that, either. Stupidity like Ed's can be a health hazard, for other people. What if he wakes up one day and decides that she isn't the true bride after all, but the false one? Then she will be put into a barrel stuck full of nails and rolled downhill, endlessly, while he is sitting in yet another bridal bed, drinking champagne. She remembers the brand name, because she bought it herself. Champagne isn't the sort of finishing touch that would occur to Ed, though he enjoyed it enough at the time.

But outwardly Sally makes a joke of all this. "He doesn't *know*," she says to Marylynn, laughing a little, and they shake their heads. If it were them, they'd know, all right. Marylynn is in fact divorced, and she can list every single thing that went wrong, item by item. After doing this, she adds that her divorce was one of the best things that ever happened to her. "I was just a nothing before," she says. "It made me pull myself together."

Sally, looking across the kitchen table at Marylynn, has to

agree that she is far from being a nothing now. She started out re-doing people's closets, and has worked that up into her own interior-design firm. She does the houses of the newly rich, those who lack ancestral furniture and the confidence to be shabby, and who wish their interiors to reflect a personal taste they do not in reality possess.

"What they want are mausoleums," Marylynn says, "or hotels," and she cheerfully supplies them. "Right down to the ash-trays. Imagine having someone else pick out your ash-trays for you."

By saying this, Marylynn lets Sally know that she's not including her in that category, though Sally did in fact hire her, at the very first, to help with a few details around the house. It was Marylynn who redesigned the wall of closets in the master bedroom and who found Sally's massive Chinese mahogany table, which cost her another seven hundred dollars to be stripped. But it turned out to be perfect, as Marylynn said it would. Now she's dug up a nineteenth-century keyhole desk, which both she and Sally know will be exactly right for the bay-windowed alcove off the living room. "Why do you need it?" Ed said in his puzzled way. "I thought you worked in your study." Sally admitted this, but said they could keep the telephone bills in it, which appeared to satisfy him. She knows exactly what she needs it for: she needs it to sit at, in something flowing, backlit by the morning sunlight, gracefully dashing off notes. She saw a 1940's advertisement for coffee like this once, and the husband was standing behind the chair, leaning over, with a worshipful expression on his face.

Marylynn is the kind of friend Sally does not have to explain any of this to, because it's assumed between them. Her intelligence is the kind Sally respects.

Marylynn is tall and elegant, and makes anything she is wearing seem fashionable. Her hair is prematurely grey and she leaves it that way. She goes in for loose blouses in cream-coloured silk, and eccentric scarves gathered from interesting shops and odd corners of the world, thrown carelessly around her neck and over one shoulder. (Sally has tried this toss in the mirror, but it doesn't work.) Marylynn has a large collection of unusual shoes; she says they're unusual because her feet are so big, but Sally knows better. Sally, who used to think of herself as pretty enough and now thinks of herself as doing quite well for her age, envies Marylynn her bone structure, which will serve her well when the inevitable happens.

Whenever Marylynn is coming to dinner, as she is today—she's bringing the desk, too—Sally takes especial care with her clothes and make-up. Marylynn, she knows, is her real audience for such things, since no changes she effects in herself seem to affect Ed one way or the other, or even to register with him. "You look fine to me," is all he says, no matter how she really looks. (But does she want him to see her more clearly, or not? Most likely not. If he did he would notice the incipient wrinkles, the small pouches of flesh that are not quite there yet, the network forming beneath her eyes. It's better as it is.)

Sally has repeated this remark of Ed's to Marylynn, adding that he said it the day the Jacuzzi overflowed because the smoke alarm went off, because an English muffin she was heating to eat in the bathtub got stuck in the toaster, and she had to spend an hour putting down newspaper and mopping up, and only had half an hour to dress for a dinner they were going to. "Really I looked like the wrath of God," said Sally. These days she finds herself repeating to Marylynn many of the things Ed says: the stupid things. Marylynn is the only one of Sally's friends she has confided in to this extent.

"Ed is cute as a button," Marylynn said. "In fact, he's just like a button: he's so bright and shiny. If he were mine, I'd get him bronzed and keep him on the mantelpiece."

Marylynn is even better than Sally at concocting formulations for Ed's particular brand of stupidity, which can irritate Sally: coming from herself, this sort of comment appears to her indulgent and loving, but from Marylynn it borders on the patronizing. So then she sticks up for Ed, who is by no means stupid about everything. When you narrow it down, there's only one area of life he's hopeless about. The rest of the time he's intelligent enough, some even say brilliant: otherwise, how could he be so successful?

Ed is a heart man, one of the best, and the irony of this is not lost on Sally: who could possibly know less about the workings of hearts, real hearts, the kind symbolized by red satin surrounded by lace and topped by pink bows, than Ed? Hearts with arrows in them. At the same time, the fact that he's a heart man is a large part of his allure. Women corner him on sofas, trap him in bay-windows at cocktail parties, mutter to him in confidential voices at dinner parties. They behave this way right in front of Sally, under her very nose, as if she's invisible, and Ed lets them do it. This would never happen if he were in banking or construction.

As it is, everywhere he goes he is beset by sirens. They want him to fix their heart. Each of them seems to have a little something wrong—a murmur, a whisper. Or they faint a lot and want him to tell them why. This is always what the conversations are about, according to Ed, and Sally believes it. Once she'd wanted it herself, that mirage. What had she invented for him, in the beginning? A heavy heart, that beat too hard after meals. And he'd been so sweet, looking at her with those stunned brown eyes of his, as if her heart were the genuine topic, listening to her gravely as if he'd never heard any of this twaddle before, advising her to drink less coffee. And she'd felt such triumph, to have carried off her imposture, pried out of him that minuscule token of concern.

Thinking back on this incident makes her uneasy, now that she's seen her own performance repeated so many times, including the hand placed lightly on the heart, to call attention of course to the breasts. Some of these women have been within inches of getting Ed to put his head down on their chests, right there in Sally's living room. Watching all this out of the corners of her eyes while serving the liqueurs, Sally feels the Aztec rise within her. *Trouble with your heart? Get it removed*, she thinks. *Then you'll have no more problems.*

Sometimes Sally worries that she's a nothing, the way Marylynn was before she got a divorce and a job. But Sally isn't a nothing; therefore, she doesn't need a divorce to stop being one. And she's always had a job of some sort; in fact she has one now. Luckily Ed has no objection; he doesn't have much of an objection to anything she does.

Her job is supposed to be full-time, but in effect it's part-time, because Sally can take a lot of the work away and do it at home, and, as she says, with one arm tied behind her back. When Sally is being ornery, when she's playing the dull wife of a fascinating heart man—she does this for people she can't be bothered with—she says she works in a bank, nothing important. Then she watches their eyes dismiss her. When, on the other hand, she's trying to impress, she says she's in P.R. In reality she runs the in-house organ for a trust company, a medium-sized one. This is a thin magazine, nicely printed, which is supposed to make the employees feel that some of the boys are doing worthwhile things out there and are human beings as well. It's still the boys, though the few women in anything resembling key positions are wheeled out regularly, bloused and suited and smiling brightly, with what they hope will come across as confidence rather than aggression.

This is the latest in a string of such jobs Sally has held over the years: comfortable enough jobs that engage only half of her cogs and wheels, and that end up leading nowhere. Technically she's second-in-command: over her is a man who wasn't working out in management, but who couldn't be fired because his wife was related to the chairman of the board. He goes out for long alcoholic lunches and plays a lot of golf, and Sally runs the show. This man gets the official credit for everything Sally does right, but the senior executives in the company take Sally aside when no one is looking and tell her what a great gal she is and what a whiz she is at holding up her end.

The real pay-off for Sally, though, is that her boss provides her with an endless supply of anecdotes. She dines out on stories about his dim-wittedness and pomposity, his lobotomized suggestions about what the two of them should cook up for the magazine; *the organ*, as she says he always calls it. "He says we need some fresh blood to perk up the organ," Sally says, and the heart men grin at her. "He actually said that?" Talking like this about her boss would be reckless—you never know what might get back to him, with the world as small as it is—if Sally were afraid of losing her job, but she isn't. There's an unspoken agreement between her and this man: they both know that if she goes, he goes, because who else would put up with him? Sally might angle for his job, if she were stupid enough to disregard his family connections, if she coveted the trappings of power. But she's just fine where she is. Jokingly, she says she's reached her level of incompetence. She says she suffers from fear of success.

Her boss is white-haired, slender, and tanned, and looks like an English gin ad. Despite his vapidity he's outwardly distinguished, she allows him that. In truth she pampers him outrageously, indulges him, covers up for him at every turn, though she stops short of behaving like a secretary: she doesn't bring him coffee. They both have a secretary who does that anyway.

The one time he made a pass at her, when he came in from lunch visibly reeling, Sally was kind about it.

Occasionally, though not often, Sally has to travel in connection with her job. She's sent off to places like Edmonton, where they have a branch. She interviews the boys at the middle and senior levels; they have lunch, and the boys talk about ups and downs in oil or the slump in the real-estate market. Then she gets taken on tours of shopping plazas under construction. It's always windy, and grit blows into her face. She comes back to home base and writes a piece on the youthfulness and vitality of the West.

She teases Ed, while she packs, saying she's going off for a rendezvous with a dashing financier or two. Ed isn't threatened; he tells her to enjoy herself, and she hugs him and tells him how much she will miss him. He's so dumb it doesn't occur to him she might not be joking. In point of fact, it would have been quite possible for Sally to have had an affair, or at least a one- or two-night stand, on several of these occasions: she knows when those chalk lines are being drawn, when she's being dared to step over them. But she isn't interested in having an affair with anyone but Ed.

She doesn't eat much on the planes; she doesn't like the food. But on the return trip, she invariably saves the pre-packaged parts of the meal, the cheese in its plastic wrap, the miniature chocolate bar, the bag of pretzels. She ferrets them away in her purse. She thinks of them as supplies that she may need if she gets stuck in a strange airport, if they have to change course because of snow or fog, for instance. All kinds of things could happen, although they never have. When she gets home she takes the things from her purse and throws them out.

Outside the window Ed straightens up and wipes his earth-smeared hands down the sides of his pants. He begins to turn, and Sally moves back from the window so he won't see that she's watching. She doesn't like it to be too obvious. She shifts her attention to the sauce: it's in the second stage of a *sauce suprême*, which will make all the difference to the chicken. When Sally was learning this sauce, her cooking instructor quoted one of the great chefs, to the effect that the chicken was merely a canvas. He meant as in painting, but Sally, in an undertone to the woman next to her, turned it around. "Mine's canvas anyway, sauce or no sauce," or words to that effect.

Gourmet cooking was the third night course Sally has taken. At the moment she's on her fifth, which is called *Forms of Narrative Fiction*. It's half reading and half writing assignments—the instructor doesn't believe you can understand an art form without at least trying it yourself—and Sally purports to be enjoying it. She tells her friends she takes night courses to keep her brain from atrophying, and her friends find this amusing: whatever else may become of Sally's brain, they say, they don't see atrophying as an option. Sally knows better, but in any case there's always room for improvement. She may have begun taking the courses in the belief that this would make her more interesting to Ed, but she soon gave up on that idea: she appears to be neither more nor less interesting to Ed now than she was before.

Most of the food for tonight is already made. Sally tried to be well organized: the overflowing Jacuzzi was an aberration. The cold watercress soup with walnuts is chilling in the refrigerator, the chocolate mousse ditto. Ed, being Ed, prefers meatloaf to sweetbreads with pine nuts, butterscotch pudding made from a package to chestnut purée topped with whipped cream. (Sally burnt her fingers peeling the chestnuts. She couldn't do it the easy way and buy it tinned.) Sally says Ed's preference for this type of food comes from being pre-programmed by hospital cafeterias when he was younger: show him a burned sausage and a scoop of instant mashed potatoes and he salivates. So it's only for company that she can unfurl her *boeuf en daube* and her *salmon en papillote*, spread them forth to be savoured and praised.

What she likes best about these dinners though is setting the table, deciding who will sit where and, when she's feeling mischievous, even what they are likely to say. Then she can sit and listen to them say it. Occasionally she prompts a little.

Tonight will not be very challenging, since it's only the heart men and their wives, and Marylynn, whom Sally hopes will dilute them. The heart men are forbidden to talk shop at Sally's dinner table, but they do it anyway. "Not what you really want to listen to while you're eating," says Sally. "All those tubes and valves." Privately she thinks they're a conceited lot, all except Ed. She can't resist needling them from time to time.

"I mean," she said to one of the leading surgeons, "basically it's just an exalted form of dress-making, don't you think?"

"Come again?" said the surgeon, smiling. The heart men think Sally is one hell of a tease.

"It's really just cutting and sewing, isn't it?" Sally murmured. The surgeon laughed.

"There's more to it than that," Ed said, unexpectedly, solemnly.

"What more, Ed?" said the surgeon. "You could say there's a lot of embroidery, but that's in the billing." He chuckled at himself.

Sally held her breath. She could hear Ed's verbal thought processes lurching into gear. He was delectable.

"Good judgement," Ed said. His earnestness hit the table like a wet fish. The surgeon hastily downed his wine.

Sally smiled. This was supposed to be a reprimand to her, she knew, for not taking things seriously enough. *Oh, come on, Ed,* she could say. But she knows also, most of the time, when to keep her trap shut. She should have a light-up *joke* sign on her forehead, so Ed would be able to tell the difference.

The heart men do well. Most of them appear to be doing better than Ed, but that's only because they have, on the whole, more expensive tastes and fewer wives. Sally can calculate these things and she figures Ed is about par.

These days there's much talk about advanced technologies, which Sally tries to keep up on, since they interest Ed. A few years ago the heart men got themselves a new facility. Ed was so revved up that he told Sally about it, which was unusual for him. A week later Sally said she would drop by the hospital at the end of the day and pick Ed up and take him out for dinner; she didn't feel like cooking, she said. Really she wanted to check out the facility; she likes to check out anything that causes the line on Ed's excitement chart to move above level.

At first Ed said he was tired, that when the day came to an end he didn't want to prolong it. But Sally wheedled and was respectful, and finally Ed took her to see his new gizmo. It was in a cramped, darkened room with an examining table in it. The thing itself looked like a television screen hooked up to some complicated hardware. Ed said that they could wire a patient up and bounce sound waves off the heart and pick up the echoes, and they would get a picture on the screen, an actual picture, of the heart in motion. It was a thousand times better than an electrocardiogram, he said: they could see the faults, the thickenings and cloggings, much more clearly.

"Colour?" said Sally.

"Black and white," said Ed.

Then Sally was possessed by a desire to see her own heart, in motion, in black and white, on the screen. At the dentist's she always wants to see the X-rays of her teeth, too, solid and glittering in her cloudy head. "Do it," she said, "I want to see how it works," and though this was the kind of thing Ed would ordinarily evade or tell her she was being silly about, he didn't need much persuading. He was fascinated by the thing himself, and he wanted to show it off.

He checked to make sure there was nobody real booked for the room. Then he told Sally to slip out of her clothes, the top half, brassière and all. He gave her a paper gown and turned his back modestly while she slipped it on, as if he didn't see her body every night of the week. He attached electrodes to her, the ankles and one wrist, and turned a switch and fiddled with the dials. Really a technician was supposed to do this, he told her, but he knew how to run the machine himself. He was good with small appliances.

Sally lay prone on the table, feeling strangely naked. "What do I do?" she said.

"Just lie there," said Ed. He came over to her and tore a hole in the paper gown, above her left breast. Then he started running a probe over her skin. It was wet and slippery and cold, and felt like the roller on a roll-on deodorant.

"There," he said, and Sally turned her head. On the screen was a large grey object, like a giant fig, paler in the middle, a dark line running down the centre. The sides moved in and out; two wings fluttered in it, like an uncertain moth's.

"That's it?" said Sally dubiously. Her heart looked so insubstantial, like a bag of gelatin, something that would melt, fade, disintegrate, if you squeezed it even a little.

Ed moved the probe, and they looked at the heart from the bottom, then the top. Then he stopped the frame, then changed it from a positive to a negative image. Sally began to shiver.

"That's wonderful," she said. He seemed so distant, absorbed in his machine, taking the measure of her heart, which was beating over there all by itself, detached from her, exposed and under his control.

Ed unwired her and she put on her clothes again, neutrally, as if he were actually a doctor. Nevertheless this transaction, this whole room, was sexual in a way she didn't quite understand; it was clearly a dangerous place. It was like a massage parlour, only for women. Put a batch of women in there with Ed and they would never want to come out. They'd want to stay in there while he ran his probe over their wet skins and pointed out to them the defects of their beating hearts.

"Thank you," said Sally.

Sally hears the back door open and close. She feels Ed approaching, coming through the passages of the house towards her, like a small wind or a ball of static electricity. The hair stands up on her arms. Sometimes he makes her so happy she thinks she's about to burst; other times she thinks she's about to burst anyway.

He comes into the kitchen, and she pretends not to notice. He puts his arms around her from behind, kisses her on the neck. She leans back, pressing herself into him. What they should do now is go into the bedroom (or even the living room, even the den) and make love, but it wouldn't occur to Ed to make love in the middle of the day. Sally often comes across articles in magazines about how to improve your sex life, which leave her feeling disappointed, or reminiscent: Ed is not Sally's first and only man. But she knows she shouldn't expect too much of Ed. If Ed were more experimental, more interested in variety, he would be a different kind of man altogether: slyer, more devious, more observant, harder to deal with.

As it is, Ed makes love in the same way, time after time, each movement following the others in an exact order. But it seems to satisfy him. Of course it satisfies him: you can always tell when men are satisfied. It's Sally who lies awake, afterwards, watching the pictures unroll across her closed eyes.

Sally steps away from Ed, smiles at him. "How did you make out with the women today?" she says.

"What women?" says Ed absently, going towards the sink. He knows what women.

"The ones out there, hiding in the forsythia," says Sally. "I counted at least ten. They were just waiting for a chance."

She teases him frequently about these troops of women, which follow him around everywhere, which are invisible to Ed but which she can see as plain as day.

"I bet they hang around outside the front door of the hospital," she will say, "just waiting till you come out. I bet they hide in the linen closets and jump out at you from behind, and then pretend to be lost so you'll take them by the short cut. It's the white coat that does it. None of those women can resist the white coats. They've been conditioned by Young Doctor Kildare."

"Don't be silly," says Ed today, with equanimity. Is he blushing, is he embarrassed? Sally examines his face closely, like a geologist with an aerial photograph, looking for telltale signs of mineral treasure: markings, bumps, hollows. Everything about Ed means something, though it's difficult at times to say what.

Now he's washing his hands at the sink, to get the earth off. In a minute he'll wipe them on the dish towel instead of using the hand towel the way he's supposed to. Is that complacency, in the back turned to her? Maybe there really are these hordes of women, even though she's made them up. Maybe they really do behave that way. His shoulders are slightly drawn up: is he shutting her out?

"I know what they want," she goes on. "They want to get into that little dark room of yours and climb up onto your table. They think you're delicious. They'll gobble you up. They'll chew you into tiny pieces. There won't be anything left of you at all, only a stethoscope and a couple of shoelaces."

Once Ed would have laughed at this, but today he doesn't. Maybe she's said it, or something like it, a few times too often. He smiles though, wipes his hands on the dish towel, peers into the fridge. He likes to snack.

"There's some cold roast beef," Sally says, baffled.

Sally takes the sauce off the stove and sets it aside for later: she'll do the last steps just before serving. It's only two-thirty. Ed has disappeared into the cellar, where Sally knows he will be safe for a while. She goes into her study, which used to be one of the kids' bedrooms, and sits down at her desk. The room has never been completely redecorated: there's still a bed in it, and a dressing table with a blue flowered flounce Sally helped pick out, long before the kids went off to university: "flew the coop," as Ed puts it.

Sally doesn't comment on the expression, though she would like to say that it wasn't the first coop they flew. Her house isn't even the real coop, since neither of the kids is hers. She'd hoped for a baby of her own when she married Ed, but she didn't want to force the issue. Ed didn't object to the idea, exactly, but he was neutral about it, and Sally got the feeling he'd had enough babies already. Anyway, the other two wives had babies, and look what happened to them. Since their actual fates have always been vague to Sally, she's free to imagine all kinds of things, from drug addiction to madness. Whatever it was resulted in Sally having to bring up their kids, at least from puberty onwards. The way it was presented by the first wife was that it was Ed's turn now. The second wife was more oblique: she said that the child wanted to spend some time with her father. Sally was left out of both these equations, as if the house wasn't a place she lived in, not really, so she couldn't be expected to have any opinion.

Considering everything, she hasn't done badly. She likes the kids and tries to be a friend to them, since she can hardly pretend to be a mother. She describes the three of them as having an easy relationship. Ed wasn't around much for the kids, but it's him they want approval from, not Sally; it's him they respect. Sally is more like a confederate, helping them get what they want from Ed.

When the kids were younger, Sally used to play Monopoly with them, up at the summer place in Muskoka Ed owned then but has since sold. Ed would play too, on his vacations and on the weekends when he could make it up. These games would all proceed along the same lines. Sally would have an initial run of luck and would buy up everything she had a chance at. She didn't care whether it was classy real estate, like Boardwalk or Park Place, or those dingy little houses on the other side of the tracks; she would even buy train stations, which the kids would pass over, preferring to save their cash reserves for better investments. Ed, on the other hand, would plod along, getting a little here, a little there. Then, when Sally was feeling flush, she would blow her money on next-to-useless luxuries such as the electric light company; and when the kids started to lose, as they invariably did, Sally would lend them money at cheap rates or trade them things of her own, at a loss. Why not? She could afford it.

Ed meanwhile would be hedging his bets, building up blocks of property, sticking houses and hotels on them. He preferred the middle range, respectable streets but not flashy. Sally would land on his spaces and have to shell out hard cash. Ed never offered deals, and never accepted them. He played a lone game, and won more often than not. Then Sally would feel thwarted. She would say she guessed she lacked the killer instinct; or she would say that for herself she didn't care, because after all it was only a game, but he ought to allow the kids to win, once in a while. Ed couldn't grasp the concept of allowing other people to win. He said it would be condescending towards the children, and anyway you couldn't arrange to have a dice game turn out the way you wanted it to, since it was partly a matter of chance. If it was chance, Sally would think, why were the games so similar to one another? At the end, there would be Ed, counting up his paper cash, sorting it out into piles of bills of varying denominations, and Sally, her vast holdings dwindled to a few shoddy blocks on Baltic Avenue, doomed to foreclosure: extravagant, generous, bankrupt.

On these nights, after the kids were asleep, Sally would have two or three more rye-and-gingers than were good for her. Ed would go to bed early—winning made him satisfied and drowsy—and Sally would ramble about the house or read the endings of murder mysteries she had already read once before, and finally she would slip into bed and wake Ed up and stroke him into arousal, seeking comfort.

Sally has almost forgotten these games. Right now the kids are receding, fading like old ink; Ed on the contrary looms larger and larger, the outlines around him darkening. He's constantly developing, like a Polaroid print, new colours emerging, but the result remains the same: Ed is a surface, one she has trouble getting beneath.

"Explore your inner world," said Sally's instructor in *Forms of Narrative Fiction*, a middle-aged woman of scant fame who goes in for astrology and the Tarot pack and writes short stories, which are not published in any of the magazines Sally reads. "Then there's your outer one," Sally said afterwards, to her friends. "For instance, she should really get something done about her hair." She made this trivial and mean remark because she's fed up with her inner world; she doesn't need to explore it. In her inner world is Ed, like a doll within a Russian wooden doll, and in Ed is Ed's inner world, which she can't get at.

She takes a crack at it anyway: Ed's inner world is a forest, which looks something like the bottom part of their ravine lot, but without the fence. He wanders around in there, among the trees, not heading in any special direction. Every once in a while he comes upon a strange-looking plant, a sickly plant choked with weeds and briars. Ed kneels, clears a space around it, does some pruning, a little skilful snipping and cutting, props it up. The plant revives, flushes with health, sends out a grateful red blossom. Ed continues on his way. Or it may be a conked-out squirrel, which he restores with a drop from his flask of magic elixir. At set intervals an angel appears, bringing him food. It's always meatloaf. That's fine with Ed, who hardly notices what he eats, but the angel is getting tired of being an angel. Now Sally begins thinking about the angel: why are its wings frayed and dingy grey around the edges, why is it looking so withered and frantic? This is where all Sally's attempts to explore Ed's inner world end up.

She knows she thinks about Ed too much. She knows she should stop. She knows she shouldn't ask, "Do you still love me?" in the plaintive tone that sets even her own teeth on edge. All it achieves is that Ed shakes his head, as if not understanding why she would ask this, and pats her hand. "Sally, Sally," he says, and everything proceeds as usual; except for the dread that seeps into things, the most ordinary things, such as rearranging the chairs and changing the burnt-out lightbulbs. But what is it she's afraid of? She has what they call everything: Ed, their wonderful house on a ravine lot, something she's always wanted. (But the hill is jungly, and the house is made of ice. It's held together only by Sally, who sits in the middle of it, working on a puzzle. The puzzle is Ed. If she should ever solve it, if she should ever fit the last cold splinter into place, the house will melt and flow away down the hill, and then ...) It's a bad habit, fooling around with her head this way. It does no good. She knows that if she could quit she'd be happier. She ought to be able to: she's given up smoking.

She needs to concentrate her attention on other things. This is the real reason for the night courses, which she picks almost at random, to coincide with the evenings Ed isn't in. He has meetings, he's on the boards of charities, he has trouble saying no. She runs the courses past herself, mediaeval history, cooking, anthropology, hoping her mind will snag on something; she's even taken a course in geology, which was fascinating, she told her friends, all that magma. That's just it: everything is fascinating, but nothing enters her. She's always a star pupil, she does well on the exams and impresses the teachers, for which she despises them. She is familiar with her brightness, her techniques; she's surprised other people are still taken in by them.

Forms of Narrative Fiction started out the same way. Sally was full of good ideas, brimming with helpful suggestions. The workshop part of it was anyway just like a committee meeting, and Sally knew how to run those, from behind, without seeming to run them: she'd done it lots of times at work. Bertha, the instructor, told Sally she had a vivid imagination and a lot of untapped creative energy. "No wonder she never gets anywhere, with a name like Bertha," Sally said, while having coffee afterwards with two of the other night-coursers. "It goes with her outfits, though." (Bertha sports the macramé look, with health-food sandals and bulky-knit sweaters and hand-weave skirts that don't do a thing for her square figure, and too many Mexican rings on her hands, which she doesn't wash often enough.) Bertha goes in for assignments, which she calls learning by doing. Sally likes assignments: she likes things that can be completed and then discarded, and for which she gets marks.

The first thing Bertha assigned was The Epic. They read *The Odyssey* (selected passages, in translation, with a plot summary of the rest); then they poked around in James Joyce's *Ulysses*, to see how Joyce had adapted the epic form to the modern-day novel. Bertha had them keep a Toronto notebook, in which they had to pick out various spots around town as the ports of call in *The Odyssey*, and say why they had chosen them. The notebooks were read out loud in class, and it was a scream to see who had chosen what for Hades. (The Mount Pleasant Cemetery, McDonald's, where, if you eat the forbidden food, you never get back to the land of the living, the University Club with its dead ancestral souls, and so forth.) Sally's was the hospital, of course; she had no difficulty with the trench filled with blood, and she put the ghosts in wheelchairs.

After that they did The Ballad, and read gruesome accounts of murders and betrayed love. Bertha played them tapes of wheezy old men singing traditionally, in the Doric mode, and assigned a newspaper scrapbook, in which you had to clip and paste up-to-the-minute equivalents. *The Sun* was the best newspaper for these. The fiction that turned out to go with this kind of plot was the kind Sally liked anyway, and she had no difficulty concocting a five-page murder mystery, complete with revenge.

But now they are on Folk Tales and the Oral Tradition, and Sally is having trouble. This time, Bertha wouldn't let them read anything. Instead she read to them, in a voice, Sally said, that was like a gravel truck and was not conducive to reverie. Since it was the Oral Tradition, they weren't even allowed to take notes; Bertha said the original hearers of these stories couldn't read, so the stories were memorized. "To recreate the atmosphere," said Bertha, "I should turn out the lights. These stories were always told at night." "To make them creepier?" someone offered. "No," said Bertha. "In the days, they worked." She didn't do that, though she did make them sit in a circle.

"You should have seen us," Sally said afterwards to Ed, "sitting in a circle, listening to fairy stories. It was just like kindergarten. Some of them even had their mouths open. I kept expecting her to say, 'If you need to go, put up your hand.'" She was meaning to be funny, to amuse Ed with this account of Bertha's eccentricity and the foolish appearance of the students, most of them middle-aged, sitting in a circle as if they had never grown up at all. She was also intending to belittle the course, just slightly. She always did this with her night courses, so Ed wouldn't get the idea there was anything in her life that was even remotely as important as he was. But Ed didn't seem to need this amusement or this belittlement. He took her information earnestly, gravely, as if Bertha's behaviour was, after all, only the procedure of a specialist. No one knew better than he did that the procedures of specialists often looked bizarre or incomprehensible to onlookers. "She probably has her reasons," was all he would say.

The first stories Bertha read them, for warm-ups ("No memorizing for *her*," said Sally), were about princes who got amnesia and forgot about their true loves and married girls their mothers had picked out for them. Then they had to be rescued, with the aid of magic. The stories didn't say what happened to the women the princes had already married, though Sally wondered about it. Then Bertha read them another story, and this time they were supposed to remember the features that stood out for them and write a five-page transposition, set in the present and cast in the realistic mode. ("In other words," said Bertha, "no real magic.") They couldn't use the Universal Narrator, however: they had done that in their Ballad assignment. This time they had to choose a point of view. It could be the point of view of anyone or anything in the story, but they were limited to one only. The story she was about to read, she said, was a variant of the Bluebeard motif, much earlier than

Perrault's sentimental rewriting of it. In Perrault, said Bertha, the girl has to be rescued by her brothers; but in the earlier version things were quite otherwise.

This is what Bertha read, as far as Sally can remember:

There were once three young sisters. One day a beggar with a large basket on his back came to the door and asked for some bread. The eldest sister brought him some, but no sooner had she touched him than she was compelled to jump into his basket, for the beggar was really a wizard in disguise. ("So much for United Appeal," Sally murmured. "She should have said, 'I gave at the office.'") The wizard carried her away to his house in the forest, which was large and richly furnished. "Here you will be happy with me, my darling," said the wizard, "for you will have everything your heart could desire."

This lasted for a few days. Then the wizard gave the girl an egg and a bunch of keys. "I must go away on a journey," he said, "and I am leaving the house in your charge. Preserve this egg for me, and carry it about with you everywhere; for a great misfortune will follow from its loss. The keys open every room in the house. You may go into each of them and enjoy what you find there, but do not go into the small room at the top of the house, on pain of death." The girl promised, and the wizard disappeared.

At first the girl contented herself with exploring the rooms, which contained many treasures. But finally her curiosity would not let her alone. She sought out the smallest key, and, with beating heart, opened the little door at the top of the house. Inside it was a large basin full of blood, within which were the bodies of many women, which had been cut to pieces; nearby were a chopping block and an axe. In her horror, she let go of the egg, which fell into the basin of blood. In vain did she try to wipe away the stain: every time she succeeded in removing it, back it would come.

The wizard returned, and in a stern voice asked for the egg and the keys. When he saw the egg, he knew at once she had disobeyed him and gone into the forbidden room. "Since you have gone into the room against my will," he said, "you shall go back into it against your own." Despite her pleas he threw her down, dragged her by the hair into the little room, hacked her into pieces and threw her body into the basin with the others.

Then he went for the second girl, who fared no better than her sister. But the third was clever and wily. As soon as the wizard had gone, she set the egg on a shelf, out of harm's way, and then went immediately and opened the forbidden door. Imagine her distress when she saw the cut-up bodies of her two beloved sisters; but she set the parts in order, and they joined together and her sisters stood up and moved, and were living and well. They embraced each other, and the third sister hid the other two in a cupboard.

When the wizard returned he at once asked for the egg. This time it was spotless. "You have passed the test," he said to the third sister. "You shall be my bride." ("And second prize," said Sally, to herself this time, "is two weeks in Niagara Falls.") The wizard no longer had any power over her, and had to do whatever she asked. There was more, about how the wizard met his comeuppance and was burned to death, but Sally already knew which features stood out for her.

At first she thought the most important thing in the story was the forbidden room. What would she put in the forbidden room, in her present-day realistic version? Certainly not chopped-up women. It wasn't that they were too unrealistic, but they were certainly too sick, as well as being too obvious. She wanted to do something more clever. She thought it might be a good idea to have the curious woman open the door and find nothing there at all, but after mulling it over she set this notion aside. It would leave her with the problem of why the wizard would have a forbidden room in which he kept nothing.

That was the way she was thinking right after she got the assignment, which was a full two weeks ago. So far she's written nothing. The great temptation is to cast herself in the role of the cunning heroine, but again it's too predictable. And Ed certainly isn't the wizard; he's nowhere near sinister enough. If Ed were the wizard, the room would contain a forest, some ailing plants and feeble squirrels, and Ed himself, fixing them up; but then, if it were Ed the room wouldn't even be locked, and there would be no story.

Now, as she sits at her desk, fiddling with her felt-tip pen, it comes to Sally that the intriguing thing about the story, the thing she should fasten on, is the egg. Why an egg? From the night course in Comparative Folklore she took four years ago, she remembers that the egg can be a fertility symbol, or a necessary object in African spells, or something the world hatched out of. Maybe in this story it's a symbol of virginity, and that is why the wizard requires it unbloodied. Women with dirty eggs get murdered, those with clean ones get married.

But this isn't useful either. The concept is so outmoded. Sally doesn't see how she can transpose it into real life without making it ridiculous, unless she sets the story in, for instance, an immigrant Portuguese family, and what would she know about that?

Sally opens the drawer of her desk and hunts around in it for her nail file. As she's doing this, she gets the brilliant idea of writing the story from the point of view of the egg. Other people will do the other things: the clever girl, the wizard, the two blundering sisters, who weren't smart enough to lie, and who will have problems afterwards, because of the thin red lines running all over their bodies, from where their parts joined together. But no one will think of the egg. How does it feel, to be the innocent and passive cause of so much misfortune?

(Ed isn't the Bluebeard: Ed is the egg. Ed Egg, blank and pristine and lovely. Stupid, too. Boiled, probably. Sally smiles fondly.)

But how can there be a story from the egg's point of view, if the egg is so closed and unaware? Sally ponders this, doodling on her pad of lined paper. Then she resumes the search for her nail file. Already it's time to begin getting ready for her dinner party. She can sleep on the problem of the egg and finish the assignment tomorrow, which is Sunday. It's due on Monday, but Sally's mother used to say she was a whiz at getting things done at the last minute.

After painting her nails with *Nuit Magique*, Sally takes a bath, eating her habitual toasted English muffin while she lies in the tub. She begins to dress, dawdling; she has plenty of time. She hears Ed coming up out of the cellar; then she hears him in the bathroom, which he has entered from the hall door. Sally goes in through the other door, still in her slip. Ed is standing at the sink with his shirt off, shaving. On the weekends he leaves it until necessary, or until Sally tells him he's too scratchy.

Sally slides her hands around his waist, nuzzling against his naked back. He has very smooth skin, for a man. Sally smiles to herself: she can't stop thinking of him as an egg.

"Mmm," says Ed. It could be appreciation, or the answer to a question Sally hasn't asked and he hasn't heard, or just an acknowledgement that she's there.

"Don't you ever wonder what I think about?" Sally says. She's said this more than once, in bed or at the dinner table, after dessert. She stands behind him, watching the swaths the razor cuts in the white of his face, looking at her own face reflected in the mirror, just the eyes visible above his naked shoulder. Ed, lathered, is Assyrian, sterner than usual; or a frost-covered Arctic explorer; or demi-human, a white-bearded forest mutant. He scrapes away at himself, methodically destroying the illusion.

"But I already know what you think about," says Ed.

"How?" Sally says, taken aback.

"You're always telling me," Ed says, with what might be resignation or sadness; or maybe this is only a simple statement of fact.

Sally is relieved. If that's all he's going on, she's safe.

Marylynn arrives half an hour early, her pearl-coloured Porsche leading two men in a delivery truck up the driveway. The men install the keyhole desk, while Marylynn supervises; it looks, in the alcove, exactly as Marylynn has said it would, and Sally is delighted. She sits at it to write the cheque. Then she and Marylynn go into the kitchen, where Sally is finishing up her sauce, and Sally pours them each a Kir. She's glad Marylynn is here: it will keep her from dithering, as she tends to do just before people arrive. Though it's only the heart men, she's still a bit nervous. Ed is more likely to notice when things are wrong than when they're exactly right.

Marylynn sits at the kitchen table, one arm draped over the chairback, her chin on the other hand; she's in soft grey, which makes her hair look silver, and Sally feels once again how banal it is to have ordinary dark hair like her own, however well-cut, however shiny. It's the confidence she envies, the negligence. Marylynn doesn't seem to be trying at all, ever.

"Guess what Ed said today?" Sally says.

Marylynn leans further forward. "What?" she says, with the eagerness of one joining in a familiar game.

"He said, 'Some of these femininists go too far,'" Sally reports. "'*Femininists.*' Isn't that sweet?"

Marylynn holds the pause too long, and Sally has a sudden awful thought: maybe Marylynn thinks she's showing off, about Ed. Marylynn has always said she's not ready for another marriage yet; still, Sally should watch herself, not rub her nose in it. But then Marylynn laughs indulgently, and Sally, relieved, joins in.

"Ed is unbelievable," says Marylynn. "You should pin his mittens to his sleeves when he goes out in the morning."

"He shouldn't be let out alone," says Sally.

"You should get him a seeing-eye dog," says Marylynn, "to bark at women."

"Why?" says Sally, still laughing but alert now, the cold beginning at the ends of her fingers. Maybe Marylynn knows something she doesn't; maybe the house is beginning to crumble, after all.

"Because he can't see them coming," says Marylynn. "That's what you're always telling me."

She sips her Kir; Sally stirs the sauce. "I bet he thinks I'm a femininist," says Marylynn.

"You?" says Sally. "Never." She would like to add that Ed has given no indication of thinking anything at all about Marylynn, but she doesn't. She doesn't want to take the risk of hurting her feelings.

The wives of the heart men admire Sally's sauce; the heart men talk shop, all except Walter Morly, who is good at by-passes. He's sitting beside Marylynn, and paying far too much attention to her for Sally's comfort. Mrs. Morly is at the other end of the table, not saying much of anything, which Marylynn appears not to notice. She keeps on talking to Walter about St. Lucia, where they've both been.

So after dinner, when Sally has herded them all into the living room for coffee and liqueurs, she takes Marylynn by the elbow. "Ed hasn't seen our desk yet," she says, "not up close. Take him away and give him your lecture on nineteenth-century antiques. Show him all the pigeon-holes. Ed loves pigeon-holes." Ed appears not to get this.

Marylynn knows exactly what Sally is up to. "Don't worry," she says, "I won't rape Dr. Morly; the poor creature would never survive the shock," but she allows herself to be shunted off to the side with Ed.

Sally moves from guest to guest, smiling, making sure everything is in order. Although she never looks directly, she's always conscious of Ed's presence in the room, any room; she perceives him as a shadow, a shape seen dimly at the edge of her field of vision, recognizable by the outline. She likes to know where he is, that's all. Some people are on their second cup of coffee. She walks towards the alcove: they must have finished with the desk by now.

But they haven't, they're still in there. Marylynn is bending forward, one hand on the veneer. Ed is standing too close to her, and as Sally comes up behind them she sees his left arm, held close to his side, the back of it pressed against Marylynn, her shimmering upper thigh, her ass to be exact. Marylynn does not move away.

It's a split second, and then Ed sees Sally and the hand is gone; there it is, on top of the desk, reaching for a liqueur glass.

"Marylynn needs more Tia Maria," he says. "I just told her that people who drink a little now and again live longer." His voice is even, his face as level as ever, a flat plain with no sign-posts.

Marylynn laughs. "I once had a dentist who I swear drilled tiny holes in my teeth, so he could fix them later," she says.

Sally sees Ed's hand outstretched towards her, holding the empty glass. She takes it, smiling, and turns away. There's a roaring sound at the back of her head; blackness appears around the edges of the picture she is seeing, like a television screen going dead. She walks into the kitchen and puts her cheek against the refrigerator and her arms around it, as far as they will go. She remains that way, hugging it; it hums steadily, with a sound like comfort. After a while she lets go of it and touches her hair, and walks back into the living room with the filled glass.

Marylynn is over by the french doors, talking with Walter Morly. Ed is standing by himself, in front of the fireplace, one arm on the mantelpiece, his left hand out of sight in his pocket.

Sally goes to Marylynn, hands her the glass. "Is that enough?" she says.

Marylynn is unchanged. "Thanks, Sally," she says, and goes on listening to Walter, who has dragged out his usual piece of mischief: some day, when they've perfected it, he says, all hearts will be plastic, and this will be a vast improvement on the current model. It's an obscure form of flirtation. Marylynn winks at Sally, to show that she knows he's tedious. Sally, after a pause, winks back.

She looks over at Ed, who is staring off into space, like a robot which has been parked and switched off. Now she isn't sure whether she really saw what she thought she saw. Even if she did, what does it mean? Maybe it's just that Ed, in a wayward intoxicated moment, put his hand on the nearest buttock, and Marylynn refrained from a shriek or a flinch out of good breeding or the desire not to offend him. Things like this have happened to Sally.

Or it could mean something more sinister: a familiarity between them, an understanding. If this is it, Sally has been wrong about Ed, for years, forever. Her version of Ed is not something she's perceived but something that's been perpetrated on her, by Ed himself, for reasons of his own. Possibly Ed is not stupid. Possibly he's enormously clever. She thinks of moment after moment when this cleverness, this cunning, would have shown itself if it were there, but didn't. She has watched him so carefully. She remembers playing Pick Up Sticks, with the kids, Ed's kids, years ago: how if you moved one stick in the tangle, even slightly, everything else moved also.

She won't say anything to him. She can't say anything: she can't afford to be wrong, or to be right either. She goes back into the kitchen and begins to scrape the plates. This is unlike her—usually she sticks right with the party until it's over—and after a while Ed wanders out. He stands silently, watching her. Sally concentrates on the scraping: dollops of *sauce suprême* slide into the plastic bag, shreds of lettuce, rice, congealed and lumpy. What is left of her afternoon.

"What are you doing out here?" Ed asks at last.

"Scraping the plates," Sally says, cheerful, neutral. "I just thought I'd get a head start on tidying up."

"Leave it," says Ed. "The woman can do that in the morning." That's how he refers to Mrs. Rudge, although she's been with them for three years now: *the woman*. And Mrs. Bird before her, as though they are interchangeable. This has never bothered Sally before. "Go on out there and have a good time."

Sally puts down the spatula, wipes her hands on the hand towel, puts her arms around him, holds on tighter than she should. Ed pats her shoulder. "What's up?" he says; then, "Sally, Sally." If she looks up, she will see him shaking his head a little, as if he doesn't know what to do about her. She doesn't look up.

Ed has gone to bed. Sally roams the house, fidgeting with the debris left by the party. She collects empty glasses, picks up peanuts from the rug. After a while she realizes that she's down on her knees, looking under a chair, and she's forgotten what for. She goes upstairs, creams off her make-up, does her teeth, undresses in the darkened bedroom and slides into bed beside Ed, who is breathing deeply as if asleep. *As if.*

Sally lies in bed with her eyes closed. What she sees is her own heart, in black and white, beating with that insubstantial moth-like flutter, a ghostly heart, torn out of her and floating in space, an animated valentine with no colour. It will go on and on for-ever; she has no control over it. But now she's seeing the egg, which is not small and cold and white and inert but larger than a real egg and golden pink, resting in a nest of brambles, glowing softly as though there's something red and hot inside it. It's almost pulsing; Sally is afraid of it. As she looks it darkens: rose-red, crimson. This is something the story left out, Sally thinks: the egg is alive, and one day it will hatch. But what will come out of it?

Dionne Brand

No Rinsed Blue Sky,
No Red Flower Fences

The apartment had tried to kill her again. She painted the walls as fast as she felt threatened. The city, she had been all through it in her searching, was dotted with bachelor apartments which she could not afford and hated anyway. As she moved from one to the other, she painted the walls. First yellow, to be bright and then white to be alone. She told her friends that it was so that she could fill the rooms with her own self, so that she could breathe and put up her own paintings, her own landscapes on the walls. She had to live there but she didn't have to lose all sense of beauty, with their tatty walls and nothing in them as if no one ever lived there. Out of embarrassment she never said, but it was also because somehow she thought that the creditors, the mornings full of bills, would go away or she could feel them gone in the blinding white. Even with the walls so clean she never had money and when she didn't have it most, the apartment scared her.

It was an old building, four storeys (she hated high rises), wooden floors and old stucco walls. It creaked everytime someone passed in the corridors. When she had money the creaking sounded homely, like living with family. But when she was flat broke and depressed, the sound of footsteps outside the door made her jumpy. A queasy feeling appeared in her chest, as if a passage opened up between her throat and her heart and a fine and awful sound passed through, hurting the columns of arteries and the empty food cavity. The pain and the sound collapsed in her diaphragm. Her hand would reach to her soft stomach to assure the queasiness. But even her hands, as tender as they would have liked to have been, were frightened and upset the order of things, inciting her face and head to sadness and then reproach for such weakness and then pity for her blackness and her woman's body, and hopelessness at how foolish she was in not even being able to pay the rent, or fix her teeth, which she dreamt nightly fell out in her hands, bloodless.

Some mornings she woke up hearing the tree not far from her window sighing as an unexpected wind blew through it. Then she thought that she missed her children who were growing up far away without her. She wanted to gather up children and take them outside. They would like the sound, the island, the ferry. She could see their legs, bony and shine black, trembling to catch dirt and bruises.

The city could be so nasty when she had no money. Money was so important. If you had none, it made you feel as if you'd never done a thing in your life.

She'd worked "illegal" for six years. Taking care of children, holding their hands across busy streets, standing with them at corners which were incongruous to her colour, she herself incongruous to the little hands, held as if they were more precious than she, made of gold, and she just the black earth around. She was always uncomfortable under the passing gazes, muttering to herself that she knew, they didn't have to tell her that she was out of place here. But there was no other place to be right now. The little money fed her sometimes, fed her children back home, no matter the stark scene which she created on the corners of the street. She, black, silent and unsmiling; the child, white, tugging and laughing, or whining.

The city was claustrophobic. She felt land-locked. Particularly on humid days in the summer. She wanted to rush to the beach. But not the lake. It lay stagnant and saltless at the bottom of the city. She needed a piece of water which led out, the vast ocean, salty and burning on the eyes. The feel of the salt, blue and moving water, rushing past her ears and jostling her body, cleaning it, coming up a different person each time as she dove through a curling wave. Not knowing how it would turn out. A feeling of touching something quite big. She always imagined and tasted that plunge into the sea, that collision with the ocean. Suddenly every two years she felt like leaving, going to dive into the ocean just once. Scratch the money up, beg for it, borrow, work back-breaking weeks scrubbing floors; but leave.

Some mornings she woke up looking up through the blind, the building, cloud, sky, surface. If the rain had fallen, rinsed blue, she hoped that the sea would be outside the apartment. Just there, just a few steps away. Some mornings she'd hear a small plane in the sky, a plane that would only fly over water, grass and red-wrung flower fences. The sea must be outside if all the sounds, plane tree, 11 o'clock and rinsed blue sky were there. She lay on the floor loving the sound, making ready to see the sea a few steps from her window.

The threat of being evicted hung over her head. She thought that when she walked in the street, people noticed. They must've. If there was anything that tipped them off, it was the sign she wore in her eyes. She kept them lowered or at courageous times she stared until they removed their own eyes. On the bus, when she had the fare, she always stood, trying to appear thinner than she was, bent, staring out the window. She did not ask for apologies when people jostled her; she pretended that it did not happen. She did try sometimes. Sitting in two seats and ignoring people coming in but by the time two or three stops had passed she would ring the bell, get off the bus and walk quickly home.

Returning home her imagination tightened the walls of the apartment giving them a cavernous, gloomy look. She would lie on the floor and listen for footsteps in the corridor outside. The phone would ring and startle her. The sound would blast around in her chest and she would pray for it to stop, never thinking to answer it. It would course its way through her arms so that when she looked at her fingers they would seem odd, not hers or she, not theirs. Frightened until it stopped, then anxious at perhaps having missed a friend listening to the ringing on the other side. Some of her friends knew that she never answered the phone and so would let it ring; but even though she knew the signal, she worried that perhaps other people, other than friends, had caught on. So when the ringing continued she was more afraid, thinking how persistent her enemies were.

The apartment had two rooms. She needed a place with two rooms. Each so that she could leave the other. The large room, when it was painted and when she threw out the bed seemed like someone else's place.

After she had sent the baby home, she had thrown the bed out. It was only a reminder of the long nine months and the hospital staff's cold eyes. When she'd left with the new baby she had pretended that someone was coming for her, waiting for her outside. But no one was there, no one knew and the name she had used was not hers. Nor did the baby exist. No papers. She would be found out if she registered the little girl. So small and wiry and no papers.

In the smaller room she kept a desk with a light to one corner. Two short black shelves were stuffed with books and papers which she could not throw out because she might need them as evidence that she tried to pay this bill or that one. She wrote anonymous letters to the immigration department asking if maybe she gave up would they still send her home... would they please have pity for her children.

A peacock rattan chair sat under the poster of home. A girl in a wet T-shirt, the sea in back, the sun on her body, represented home. Home had never been like that, but she kept the poster. Its glamour shielded her from the cold outside and the dry hills back home at the same time. The chair creaked everytime the humidity in the room changed.

In the days after she had read *Siddhartha*, someone had given it to her saying she would find peace, she lay for hours chanting "om." She attributed the creaking chair to the spirit of her great grandmother coming to visit. And for at least two months chanting "om" helped to calm her now chronic worrying. She sat cross-legged, her back vertical to the floor of her room, her hands, thumb and index finger softly clasped. So she buried the sound of the footsteps outside her door in a long breathy "om," hoping that this one syllable expressed the universe. She actually saw the deep blue softing shape of "om," approached its glowing dark, telling herself that this would save her from the thin sharp voices on the phone, the girl in the wet T-shirt, the child with the white hand, the lewd traffic whirling in the middle of the street.

Once when she was nine, a long time ago, she'd seen a woman, old, bathing herself on the edge of the sand and water, dipping a cup, lifting it to her head, rubbing the shade of her long flaccid breasts. How bold, she thought, then walked past and turned slightly to see her again, still there, her face sucked to her bones, her eyes watery from age, unblinking. The woman, the gesture had stayed with her, marked her own breasts, her eyes. She willed herself not to feel hungry but to stay alive, present. She would lessen the number of her movements, she would design efficient strokes, nothing wasted. She would become the old woman. But how could she, so far from there.

There was a fireplace in the large room. Not a real one. One of those with two electric ranges strung across. It should have been real for its ornate facade. It may have been copper underneath the crude layers of paint. After two years of living in the apartment, she discovered that the fireplace worked. She found this out through the woman across the hall who invited her to a Christmas party. The woman was Jamaican, she had a fifteen year old daughter coming to meet her soon and a man friend who came every two weeks to sleep in the daytime on Sundays. He was tall, round, with a prickly thick moustache. The woman short, round, pulled her hair tightly back on these occasions. The rest of the time she wore it wild. All this she learnt by looking through the peep-hole at her neighbour when she was not afraid to look in the hallway.

Still, of all the places she had lived, she felt the strongest here. After years of dodging the authorities and the bill collectors, she had acquired some skill in putting them off. She realized that rudeness and sometimes a frank "I don't have any money," would do. She consoled herself that there was no debtors prison and often, when she could bring up the nerve, told them, "Take me to court." But creditors had more stamina than she and they would keep calling and threatening and she would break down and promise them her life. One had told her to go and sell her body if she had to and why were you people coming to this country, if you couldn't pay your bills, he had yelled into her ear. Her days then were heady. Each ring of the phone, each footstep in the hall, each knock on the door threatened to blow everything to hell. Those days the white walls came alive, glaring at her, watching her as she slept fitfully.

Mostly she did not remember her dreams. And mostly they were full of her watching herself as a guest at some occasion. She played all the parts in her dreams. Dreamer, dreamed. She was female and male, neutral. She never dreamed of anything that she was not. When she practised to fly in her dreams, it was she who flew. Swooping down like a pelican into the water and changing course upward before touching. She had rehearsed that swooping since she was three, noticing the pelican's clumsy transforming glide into the sea at Point Fortin by the sea, its wet, full exit, its throat expanding fishlike. And she had practised never reaching things too. One day a grove of orange balisier growing not far from the house caught her eye. After what seemed like hours of walking she never arrived at the grove and cried loudly until someone came to get her sitting in the dirt road.

Dreamer remained the same and often less than dreamed. It would surprise her to awaken to her thin, unvoluptuous body, limited to the corner of the floor on which she slept. Dreamed would return to limitlessness and the dreamer, to the acute clarity of the real—the orange juice, the telephone, the white Toronto street in winter.

Her sleeping was worse in the winter. There was an urgency to sleep at any hour. Especially when she had not seen the sun for days. A kind of pressure brought on by the grey sky, which she opened her eyes to on winter mornings, packed itself around her temples. It made her eyelids feel swollen and she spent half the day trying to recover herself. Each morning she would have to convince herself to get up from her half sleep which would make her sick. This half sleep did not belong to the dreamer or the dreamed. The avoided telephone calls recurred, answer no, ring no, answer, cupped to her mouth; the empty stomach; looking for a job, four hundred University eighth, no tenth floor, the immigration department, the smell of the lobby, it rose from the carpet, mixed with the air conditioner and the thud of the elevators. People hunched their shoulders, all the women, she included, perfumed to sickness, nylon encasing their legs, stood stiffly in the elevator ... pleading with someone there ... would they send her home, would they pity her children please ...

She fled. She could only perfect this flight in her dream. Rushing outside to the street, she plunged into the sea of snow, wrapped bodies, snorting cars making clouds of smoked ice. Reaching the subway, she rode to the end, where the work crowd thinned out—High Park, Runnymede, Old Mill. Coming up, the train reached a bare sky, scarred trees, gully, apartment building, stopping. She came out, let the train pass, sat looking through the glass of the station. She sat there for hours, getting back on the train, changing stations, only to find herself sometimes back in the elevator trying not to breathe the perfume, the smell of whiteness around her, a dull choking smell.

Wrestling to wake up, she tried to pull herself out of this half sleep which belonged to things out of her control. Movements rushed against each other. Shorter distances, more brusque, inhabited this sleep. Jumping to her feet, she realized that she was asleep. For the act of jumping found her lying, still on the floor, now surrounded by her body and her heavy face, with a film of flesh and thought to remove before rising and trying to decide what to do next.

The room becoming clearer than its uncharted corners. The tree over the next apartment building in the shadow of her thoughts, spread out its meagre twigs to form a shield against the cold, heavy air. Rushing to the window she looked at the street below, empty of people, still dark.

... this day if the sky could not move, if the heavy angle of the air would not shift to some other colour, at the corner she would knead a headache from her brow, walk to the middle of the street, the glowing centre of the wide lewd road and kneel down ...

Rushing to the window she looked at the street below, empty of people, still dark. Not sea and blue, no red flower fence and high sky.

Midday found her on the street corner, a little white hand in hers, her other hand kneading a headache from her brow.

Diane Schoemperlen

She Wants to Tell Me

*Y*ou're sitting there like a bouquet of flowers, pastel, perfumed and conspicuous. You want to tell me your whole life story. You also *want another drink. How can I refuse you either? How can I refuse you anything?*

You say, "Your geraniums are lovely."

It's that special single hour on a late summer's evening when the light has gone all sentimental, the birds are singing dementedly, and way out in suburbia, some beautiful virgin boy is mowing his mother's lawn, flexing his thighs, and dreaming he's the singer in a rock and roll band.

"I've never had much luck with flowers myself," you tell me. "I find it easier just to let some man buy them for me."

Here our downtown birds are ratty old pigeons, circling aimlessly, preening and cooing at nothing. Our downtown boys in their black leather jackets are always playing video games, flexing their fingers, hooked, and I can't imagine what they might be dreaming. Most of them will survive.

"They always die on me."

You sniff the breeze, which is supposed to smell like berries or white sand, but in this neighbourhood is mostly exhaust. You massage it into your bare arms anyway, stretching your legs, kicking off your shoes (which are perfect) and settling in. The soles of your feet are dirty and smooth, like a child's.

"The flowers, I mean."

Our ice cubes are melting. I'll go in and get some more. I wish I had an ice bucket, a silver one. You do. You must.

"Expensive feet, I've always had expensive feet. I can only wear Italian shoes. It gets to be like a curse. I had to search the whole city to find such marvellous shoes."

And here I sit, me with my plain old peasant feet, domestic feet propped up on a flower pot, swelling and smelling in the heat.

Get more wine. Also domestic. But you are, I imagine, too well-bred to notice.

"It hardly smells like summer any more," you observe. "The nights are getting cooler, longer. Where does the time go? It seems to pass so slowly but always carries on, and then in the end, it's nothing but gone. This wine is delicious."

You think you're in Italy, Paris, on the Riviera or the Virgin Islands, anywhere but here, examining your fingernails, tucking your hair behind one ear, pulling up your lacy white skirt to catch the last of the sun. You think that I'm just like you—which is flattering but nerve-racking. I'd hate like hell to disillusion you.

"In the beginning I just loved this building. Being up in the air like this, I thought I was on top of the world."

The balconies on either side, above and below us, are like blinkers. They are cluttered with various junky but revealing accumulations: gas barbecues, an exercise bike, water skis, a baby carriage, underwear and pantyhose draped over the side, red geraniums and a sleeping bag—these last being mine. I like to sleep out here when it's hot. The bugs don't bother me much.

"But sometimes now I feel like a little girl up in the attic playing dress-up, clomping around in my mother's high-heels."

There's a siren in the street. I can almost hear the crowd converg-

ing. But we're up high enough here to be immune. At least we like to think so.

"All dressed up and no place to go."

Directly across is another high-rise, higher, with offices inside—doctors, lawyers, psychiatrists, I suppose. The windows are all copper-coloured, like those expensive pots and pans you always see hanging around magazine kitchens.

"Other times I get to thinking about all those people below me, layers and layers of them, doing whatever it is that normal people do—watching TV, making popcorn or love, putting their babies to bed. They don't know that I'm walking around on their heads. They don't care. But sometimes," you tell me, "sometimes, I can feel their hard little skulls under my bare feet like pebbles."

You were out on your balcony, right next door, when I came out here onto mine. Leaning against the railing, you were shielding your eyes with one hand and peering up at the sky. No, more like into it, deeply. Watching for something, a flock of fabulous birds, an alien invasion by air, or maybe a sign from God. Your balcony is empty, tells me nothing.

"Hunter says I'm starting to sound crazy again. He says, 'Marguerite, you're losing it.' But maybe I'm just fooling around."

Finally you turned toward me and, ordinarily enough, waved across. I beckoned you over with my frosted glass, wanting to share the wine so I could dispense with feeling guilty about drinking alone.

"I met Hunter in a tavern in Toronto. He was there with his buddies for a beer after work, watching the strippers and pumping the pinball machine full of quarters. I have no idea now what I was doing there. Hiding. Finding him in a dump like that made him seem more real than the rest. I still thought falling in love was an acceptable practice. For a few months anyway, I took Hunter to be an ordinary man, normal, decent and dependable. Which was what I thought I wanted. That was then."

Next to you, Marguerite, Hunter is ordinary (lots of men these days wear earrings—*I know that), so ordinary that he could be almost any-thing to you: lover, husband, best friend, second cousin twice-removed. It's hard to tell. He's too dark to be your brother. There is about the two of you none of that aggressive self-insistent happiness which marks new-lyweds and people who are together when they shouldn't be.*

"We came here by accident, more of an experiment than a decision, the transplant of something vital into something else."

I was glad when you moved in. That apartment had been vacant for months and I'd pretty well given up on the people on the other side. They're an old foreign couple with a pack of little rat dogs over-running their apartment. Their grown-up children come over on Sundays with casseroles, pies and flowers done up like wreaths—as if they've already died and gone to heaven. Maybe they think they have.

"I never dream about him any more. Mostly now I dream about babies, having them, losing them, buying them. I also dream about trains, catching them, missing them. Sometimes they're coming right into the bedroom. If you dream about a dead cat, what do you think that means?" you ask me. "Hunter holds me when I wake up crying but it doesn't help any more."

I've been listening to the sounds from your apartment but all I get is the usual: vacuum cleaner, sometimes rock and roll records turned up too loud, the bed banging against the wall, the occasional argument in the middle of the night but I can never make out the words and there are no dishes breaking.

"You know what I mean."

Somewhere over the years, I have become the kind of woman other people feel compelled to confide in. Time and again I've kept my big mouth shut on all sorts of serpents and secrets, justifying their faith in me.

"You're so easy to talk to."

But other times too, I've come home from an evening with friends, half-drunk, tender and sobbing with the sheer weight of knowing so many things about so many people. They give me too much credit, they forget that I'm a person, not just a receptacle. I can spill things too. The beans. My guts. The wine. I can be dangerous too, not always just vicarious.

"My first husband's name was Frederick."

I've always hated that name. Makes me think of a beagle with slippers in its mouth.

"We met on a Mexican beach where we had both gone to recuperate—from different things, of course. I was just out of the hospital and he was just out of a miserable marriage in Vancouver. He'd lived there all his life, brilliant and crazy, always wanting to dive off a high-rise into the sea. I wanted to meet a genius. I wanted to meet a maniac. Frederick was the man of my dreams. In that warm water we were like swordfish, supple and salty and tasty. We were young. Six months later we flew back to Mexico and were married on that very same beach. My bridal bouquet burned up in the sun. More wine please."

We're well into our second bottle now. It's a good thing I keep a supply in. You just never know when you'll need another drink.

Now that I've got you here, I don't want to think of you jumping up and running away.

"Back home, marriage was nothing like Mexico or swimming, nothing at all. I told him what I wanted but he wasn't listening, or maybe he was down by the sea."

You're talking in code and assuming, in the way of unhappy young women, that I know much more or much less than I do. You're right either way.

"I want them to know I'm a person, not just a place."

I'm wanting to believe everything you're telling me. I'm willing to listen to anything. Nothing about you can surprise me now.

"I nearly drowned once when I was a child, but I got over it. I'm a superb swimmer now, so they tell me."

There is no way of knowing if what you tell me is true. But that, I suppose, can be said of most people. The truth, like old wooden houses in the winter, is always shifting, cracking, settling back down in some other season, some other place. Nobody wants to admit that truth, like time, can never stand still. It is always a becoming, always a changing, always a staying-the-same.

"I was already sick by that time and was supposed to stay in bed all day. I was happier then than I've ever been since. I always kept the curtains closed. One wall was filled with floor-to-ceiling bookshelves. I read with a flashlight so I didn't have to open the drapes. The other wall was covered with dolls and stuffed animals, hung from little hooks by little strings around their little necks. Their bulging faces only frightened me when I was delirious from the drugs or the pain. The rest of the time they were quite friendly. But I still can't sleep if there's any part of me, even one toe, hanging off the edge of the bed."

I can't sleep in the bed at all. In the summer I sleep out here. In the winter I sleep on the couch. Nobody knows this about me. I sleep alone.

"There was one doctor who said there was nothing wrong with me. He said it was all in my head."

You know what they say: Two heads are better than one.

"We got rid of him."

It was all in his head.

"Everything I wanted came to me before I even had to ask for it. Silent nurses relayed tray after tray up the stairs. They would slide into my room, sighing and patting my hair, spoon-feeding me sometimes, bringing me whatever I cried for: icing sugar, jelly beans, lemonade, pink mints."

More wine.

"My tutors were all handsome young men who seemed to be hiding from something. My favourite was the one who taught me how to play the banjo and five-card stud. About everything else, he couldn't care less."

Me neither.

"I just naturally assumed this was how all little girls were treated. And if they weren't, they should be. I thought everyone was just like me. Or wanted to be."

Some things never change.

"Once I saw a man beating a little dog in the gutter with a baseball bat. When I tried to stop him, he swung at me too. This was either in Mexico or Toronto, I forget which. This was later."

It's as if you're wrapped in something. Valium or some vague aura, mysterious but convincing. The sunset, the wine, your slack voice, all are equally potent, and I am captured by the puzzle, the pieces you offer me, one at a time, like grapes. Everything is going wine-coloured around me, especially your hair, with the sun going down all through it.

"My father was a diplomat, whatever that means. It was never really explained to me and I never thought to ask. It was enough to know that he was someone important, always dressed in a three-piece suit, talking on the telephone, bringing home presents, buying black cars, always going away again."

My father was an alcoholic, whatever that means.

"Most of the time he ignored me, which was comforting."

Comforting enough.

"He's retired now, my old man, still handsome and lolling around exclusive hotels, sending me postcards that I stick on the bathroom wall. He never interested me much anyway."

I picture the old man lounging in a hot tub, sucking on crab legs, white grapes, the succulent oiled shoulder of some ripe debutante. He drinks dry martinis all day long. He beckons for a pen, dashes off something slightly witty, slumps back into the water, his fatherly impulses stifled or satisfied for now. Having a wonderful time. Glad you're not here. You never interested him much anyway.

"My mother's funeral was a discreetly grand affair. Nobody asked the uncomfortable questions and only her old black maid, Maisie, was primitive or generous enough to cry. There were thousands of flowers, white lilies mostly, her favourite, like snow-banks on the altar. I wore the most gorgeous blue silk, raw silk—everyone loved it."

The more you drink, the more your accent goes southern. Imagining you in front of a white pillared mansion becomes irresistible. In ten starched crinolines, you're waving and weeping till your eyes are like bruised peaches and the tops of your breasts swell and pulse. Two blue peacocks, dazzling and heartless, strut stiffly around you. An old yellow dog lies on the lawn, sleeping or dead. Your man is going off to war (Civil) and we all know he'll never come back. Sad, so sad, this scene is so sad it should be on the cover of a romance novel. Somewhere in it there are also magnolia blossoms, in your hair or scattered around your feet.

Oh shit. Frankly Scarlett, I don't give a damn.

"My mother had no influence on me, none at all."

This cannot, is not, will never be true.

"Once I thought she never really wanted me."

Once I thought I could see the future but it was only a coincidence.

"But then she left me a fortune."

Fortunes. I collect them, the kind that come in cookies: You will have good luck and overcome many hardships. For better luck you have to wait till autumn. You will receive a gift from a friend. Good news will come to you from far away.

I figure if I keep them long enough, they're bound to come true.

"When I was a little girl, I wanted to be a fortune teller."

And what are you now? Don't you dare start reading my mind.

"My second husband, Max, was killed six months after the wedding. It was his own damn fault. That was when I decided I would never get married again. There's nothing sure in this world."

I'll drink to that.

"Hit by a bus."

The nerve of some people.

"Just that morning, we'd bought tickets to Spain. I went by myself but it wasn't the same. I'd forgotten about the bulls."

I'm afraid to imagine the sound.

"Once I saw a chicken with its head cut off running by the side of the road. That was in Spain too."

Once I chopped a chicken's head off with an axe. The axe was dull and it took a long time. That was on the farm. Then we made soup for supper.

"The thing about travelling is you're always thinking that the next restaurant, hotel room, city or country will be the perfect one, the one thing you've been searching for all your little life. I could have been a gypsy if I'd wanted to."

Even your purse is like a suitcase, lumpy with eccentric items, I imagine—a hammer, a box of sugar cubes, and a syringe.

"In a hotel room in Paris, I found a photo album stashed behind the bed. Everyone in it looked happy and French, black and white. There were all combinations, young and old, men and women, with statues, horses, dogs, hugging each other. Everywhere there were trees, flowers, windows, rocking chairs, lace. There was a whole series of women clowning in white face for Hallowe'en or a play, doing mime in the street. Every little thing looked French. This is my favourite."

In the photograph you hand me, four young women are lounging around a fountain with flowerbeds. They're dressed in loose long skirts and sandals, resting their heads and hands on each other, lovingly. They're carrying things, paper bags, purses, a sweater. They're going somewhere, shopping, home, or out of the country. They look quite beautiful and intense, yes, very French. If they could talk, I wouldn't know what they were saying.

Why are you carrying these handsome anonymous women around in your purse as if they were good old friends?

"I want to be just like them. I want to be in the picture."

What you tell me is like marbles, those clear glass ones, green that you can see through if you hold one up to your eyeball. Marbles, the big ones, hard and flawless, no avenue in. They hit off each other in the dirt, spin away in tangents, out of reach altogether.

"When we moved into this place, I found a hundred dollar bill behind the stove."

What are you doing always looking behind things, beds and stoves, looking for other people's treasures or castoffs, finding them too? I found a diamond ring once but I sold it.

"I thought it was a lucky omen."

I thought you were perfect.

"Sometimes, just to cheer myself up, I use some of the money to send myself flowers. And then I pretend I don't know who they're from."

I thought you were going to teach me something, maybe how to swim.

"All I want to do is sleep."

You're no longer emotionally charming.

"The worst thing about being in jail that time was having to phone home and explain why I wouldn't be there for Christmas."

You're too young to know so much.

"I've never liked Christmas much anyway."

Too bad.

"I thought it would be different."

It is.

"Everything, I mean."

Are we drunk yet?

"It wasn't my fault."

I'm just feeling bitchy.

"You'll see what I mean when I tell you."

I'll try.

"All my lies are white ones."

There he is now, just in time, Hunter on the next balcony, waving "Hello" and "Come home" in one simple gesture. He's so graceful for a man. You gulp down your wine, gather up your purse, your perfect shoes, rush off barefoot and unsteady. Why are we looking so guilty? He's so powerful for a man.

You're off to your apartment which, I imagine, is laid out just like mine and furnished finely but starkly. Vivid white walls, old wicker painted black, pink vases and pillows scattered around strategically. These are called accents. No plants—they would die. No dirt—of course not. There may be a red stain somewhere on the white rug but it could be anything. It could have been there when you moved in. There is also an aquarium, full of flowers instead of fish.

You're off now to perform unimaginable acts: making filet mignon, juicy and rare; overseas phone calls; love.

I'm just going to sit here awhile and finish my wine. As soon as I lie down in the dark, I'll be trying not to listen. You're not quite a stranger any more, an intimate one if you are. I know too much now to invent you.

I want to tell you my whole life story.

Bronwen Wallace

An Easy Life

Right now, Marion is giving her kitchen its once-a-year major cleaning, right down to that little crack where the gunk builds up between the counter and the metal edge of the sink. She's going at it with Comet and an old toothbrush, singing along to the Talking Heads on her Walkman, having a great time. She smoked a joint with her coffee before she started this morning. It helps. She's already done the fridge, the stove *and* the oven, wiped down the walls. Just the counters and drawers to go, really. Then the floor. Marion does a little dance over to the cupboard for the Lysol.

It's a beautiful day. The patio door is half open and the air that blows in is real spring air without that underscent of snow. Crocuses glow in creamy pools of purple and gold, all along the stone path to the garden. Soon, there'll be daffodils, tulips. And hyacinths, Marion's favourite, their sweet, heavy scent filling the kitchen, outrageous, it always seems to Marion, like the smell of sex.

Marion has thick auburn hair and the fine, almost translucent complexion that often goes with it. These days, she's got it cut short with longer wisps over her forehead and at the back of her neck. She has always been beautiful, not in any regular, classic way, certainly, but because she has the kind of bone structure that can give a face movement. At forty-two, her beauty seems deeper, more complex than it ever was, as if it's just beginning to discover all its possibilities. Everyone who knows Marion acknowledges how beautiful she is. The other thing they say is that she seems to have a very easy life.

She was born Marion Patterson, the youngest of three, the only daughter of a Home Economics teacher and a high school principal. Her health was always excellent, her teeth straight. She watched "Howdy Doody" and "Father Knows Best" and saw the first-time appearances on "The Ed Sullivan Show" of both Elvis Presley and The Beatles. In school she was one of those people who manage to get high marks without being a browner and at the same time is pretty, popular and good at sports.

All of this had its predictable effect when she entered university. After her first class, English 101, Marion walked directly to the centre of the campus where a long-haired boy with deep-set, deep-brown eyes was handing out leaflets. END CANADIAN COMPLICITY IN VIETNAM, they said. Below that was the time and place of a meeting. Marion took a leaflet. She also went to the meeting.

By Christmas she was spending most of her time in the coffee shop reading *Ramparts* and *I.F. Stone's Biweekly*, and talking to anyone who would listen about what she read. She wore short skirts, fishnet stockings and turtleneck sweaters in dark colours. Her hair was long then, straight down her back, almost to her waist, and her face was sharper than it is now, vibrant in an almost aggressive way that some men found intimidating.

One man who was not intimidated was Carl Walker, a second-year art student who spent his afternoons in the coffee shop smoking and sketching. Marion had one of the strongest profiles he'd ever seen. In April, Carl and Marion were arrested at a demonstration outside the U.S. Embassy in Toronto.

That summer they were married. Marion wore a long, red Indian cotton skirt, a tie-dyed T-shirt and a crown of daisies and black-eyed Susans. Carl wore blue jeans, a loose white shirt and a button that said, L.B.J., L.B.J. HOW MANY KIDS DID YOU KILL TODAY? Back at school, their tiny apartment was the favourite hangout of campus politicos. Carl made huge pots of chili, Marion rolled the joints and everyone argued with their mouths full. Over the stereo was a poster showing the profiles of Karl Marx, Mao Tse Tung and Ho Chi Minh. SOME PEOPLE TALK ABOUT THE WEATHER, it said above the profiles. And below, in larger letters, WE DON'T.

When Marion got pregnant, she and Carl decided to quit university and find a place in the country. They could grow their own food, Carl would continue painting, Marion would read.

"Who needs a degree?" Marion said.

"Just you wait," replied Marion's women friends, among whom feminism (or Women's Lib as it was then called) was making rapid advances. "Wait'll you have a colicky baby and it's thirty below outside. Carl'll go on painting the great male masterpiece and you'll be up to your elbows in shit."

Not so, however. Jason Dylan Walker was rapidly followed by Benjamin Joplin and Joshua Guthrie. All of Marion's labours were short, the boys were born undrugged, screaming red and perfectly formed. Carl was always there. He was—and still is—an enthusiastic parent, willing to do his share. He also kept on painting and managed to mount two highly acclaimed shows in six years. His paintings began to sell for very respectable prices.

Both Marion and Carl took pride in their organic vegetable garden and were keenly involved in a protest that stopped Ontario Hydro from building transmitter towers through a strip of choice farmland in their community. Marion raised chickens,

Carl baked bread and they both spent hours taking the boys for walks in the woods around their farm. When Josh was five, Marion decided to go back to school. Carl's growing reputation got him an excellent faculty position in the art department of a small community college, they moved into the city and Marion got her Masters in Psychology and Education. For the last five years, she has been a guidance counsellor at Centennial Secondary School. She is good at what she does. Not only do most of the kids like her, they sometimes listen to some of what she has to say. What's more, some of what she has to say is actually relevant to their lives as they see them.

Of course, Marion and Carl argue, who doesn't. And sometimes they both wonder what it would have been like if they'd waited a while, met other people, maybe travelled a little, if they hadn't been, well, so young. On the other hand, they also believe you have to go with what's happening at the time. Surprising as it may seem, this attitude still works for them.

Or so Marion says.

"Oh, Marion," her friends reply, only half-laughing. "Wake up. Look around. The sixties are over."

Marion knows what they're getting at, of course. For every Marion Walker, married at eighteen and having three kids bang, bang, bang, who ends up cleaning her spacious kitchen in her tasteful house on her tasteful street, a little stoned and more beautiful than she was twenty years ago, there are thousands of others with their teeth rotted and their bodies gone to flab on Kraft Dinner and Wonder Bread, up to their eyeballs in shit. Women whose husbands left them (as, in fact, Marion's own brother, Jeff, left his first wife, Sandra, with a three year old and a set of twins, with no degree because she'd worked to put him through med school and with support payments based on his last year as a resident rather than his present salary as a pediatrician), or, worse yet, women whose husbands are still around, taking it out on them, women who are beaten, whose kids end up in jail or ruined by drugs or...

Or take Tracey Harper, for example. She's just come home from her Saturday afternoon shift at Harvey's. The kitchen is scrupulously clean, as it always is, and on the table, in exactly the same spot as last Saturday and the Saturday before and every day after school for as long as she can remember, is a note in her mother's thick, wavery writing: "*Your supper's in the fridge. Just heat and eat. Love, Leslie.*"

In the living room, the television is on full-blast, as always, "Wheel of Fortune" is half over and Leslie is sprawled on the couch, sound asleep, mouth open, snoring. On the table beside her, in a row, is a bottle of Maalox, a bottle of Coke, a bottle of rum, an empty glass and an empty package of Export "A"s. If Leslie were still awake, which would be unusual, she would light a cigarette, take two drags, put it in the ashtray, take two sips of rum and Coke, a sip of Maalox, two more drags of her cigarette and so on, never breaking her pattern until she ran out or passed out, whichever came first. It's by the same rigorous adherence to a system that she manages to keep her kitchen clean and food on the table for her daughter.

In so doing, she has done one helluva lot better—and she would be the first to tell you this—than her own mother. Like Tracey, Leslie came home to her mother passed out on the couch and the television blaring. Where Tracey stands in the doorway and watches men and women win glamorous merchandise and large sums of money on "Wheel of Fortune," Leslie would stand and watch women's wildest dreams come true, right there, on "Queen for a Day." What's changed (besides the television shows, of course) is that Tracey comes home to a clean kitchen and a meal, whereas Leslie came home to a shithole and nothing to eat. The other thing that's changed is that she, Leslie, has managed to keep her boyfriends out of Tracey's bed, which is more than her mother ever did for her.

What hasn't changed (besides the idea that winning something will improve your life): Tracey's eyes and her way of standing in the doorway, both of which are exactly like her mother's. Already she has the look and posture of someone whose parents abandoned her early. It doesn't matter to what—drugs, alcohol, violence, madness or death—she has that look. That particular sadness which starts in the eyes and goes bone deep, displacing all traces of the child she was, leaving the shoulders stiff and thin, all their suppleness and softness gone for good. The softness that some of us are allowed to carry (that Marion Walker carries, for example) a good distance into our lives.

So Tracey is standing in the doorway of the living room, waiting for her supper to heat up, watching her mother sleep. Her mother is only seventeen years older than she is, which makes her thirty-four, but she looks about sixty. Her belly bloats out over the waistband of her jeans and the skin that shows, in the space between her jeans and her T-shirt, is grey and puckered. If statistics are anything to live by (and surely they're as reliable as game shows), Leslie will be dead in five to ten years. *How* is still being decided by her cells. Will it be her stomach, where the ulcer has already made its presence known? Her heart or her lungs, whose complaints she hears but manages to ignore? Right now, her cells are deciding her future.

As indeed Tracey's cells are deciding hers. If she goes back to her boyfriend Kevin's tonight after the movies, as she usually does, she will get pregnant. Everything in her body (the delicate balance of hormones controlled by her pituitary gland, the ripened ovum swimming in her right fallopian tube) is ready. In one sense, her pregnancy has already been decided. Statistically, it's almost inevitable. If it actually occurs, then, given that course of events which are so usual as to seem almost natural, Tracey may replace Leslie in a few years, exactly as she is—passed out, bloated on the couch.

Lately, though, Tracey is beginning to think that maybe it isn't such a great idea after all, dropping out of school and living together, which is what she and Kevin are planning to do as soon as he gets on at Petro-Can.

What she is hearing, under the chatter of the TV and her mother's snoring and the sausages hissing in the pan behind her and her own confused thoughts, is the voice of her guidance counsellor at school, Mrs. Walker, who is one of the weirdest people Tracey has ever met. Sometimes they don't even *talk*, for fuck sake, they go to the mall and try on clothes. Seriously.

But what Mrs. Walker is saying now inside Tracey's head is: *Well, really, Tracey, your marks aren't that bad, you know. And you've got more experience of life than most kids your age. What you've gotta decide is how you're going to use that to your advantage. Any ideas?*

And then Tracey is amazed to hear her own voice, there, inside her head. As amazed as she was last Wednesday, when she heard herself say: *Well, I always thought I might like to be a physiotherapist.*

Physiotherapist. Yeah, right. She'd just read it on one of those stupid pamphlets they have outside the guidance office.

That's not a bad idea, Tracey, Mrs. Walker is saying now, *I think you'd be really good at that. In some ways working with people who've been injured might be a little like helping your mom. Now you'd have to go to university, so we're going to have to figure out some money schemes but I...*

And then she goes on, laying it all out like it's possible, and now Tracey sometimes thinks that maybe it just is. She walks over to the TV, turns it off, goes to the couch and picks up the empty glass and the cigarette pack, butts the last cigarette, which is stinking up the ashtray. She takes the glass, the full ashtray and the empty pack to the kitchen counter, comes back and eases her mother's body gently along the couch a little ways so that her neck isn't cramped over the arm like that. Then she gets her sausages and macaroni from the stove and heads for her room.

Already, she's thinking she might tell Kevin she doesn't want to go out tonight, though it's hard to imagine having the nerve to actually say that to him. Right now, it's just sort of there, like a buzzy place, inside her head. Right now, she's just going to eat her supper and study for her math exam. Then she'll see.

Marion fills the sink with hot water, adds detergent and a few drops of Javex and dumps in the contents of the left-hand middle drawer, the one where she keeps all the stuff she hardly ever uses. Tea strainers, pie servers, cookie cutters, two ice picks and a couple of those things you use to make little scoops of melon for fruit salads.

"Melon ballers," the boys call them.

Outside, she can see Ben and Josh sorting stuff for a garage sale tomorrow, hauling everything into the driveway and organizing it into piles. Hockey sticks and skates, a huge box of Lego, Jason's old ten-speed, a bunch of flippers and some diving masks, tennis racquets, a badminton set, ski poles. They lift and carry the awkward bundles with ease, competent and serious. Even Josh is almost past the gangly stage, almost completely at home in the body he'll live in for the rest of his life.

A body that seems so much like a stranger's to Marion these days, even as she watches him, his every movement familiar. It's hard to believe she used to take it so for granted. All of it. The rooting motions their mouths made when she picked them up to nurse. The ease with which she oiled and powdered their bums, handling their penises as casually as she'd handle her own breasts, pushing back their foreskins to check for redness, helping them aim over the potty when she was training them. It doesn't seem possible.

Marion wipes out the drawer with a damp cloth, empties the sink, starts drying the stuff and putting it back, automatically, still watching the boys. Sometimes she doesn't know and it scares her. She can feel it, inside, what she doesn't know. It's like when she miscarried between Jason and Ben and how, even before the blood came, from the very beginning, she knew something was wrong, terribly wrong and there was nothing she could do about it even though it was there, right there, inside her own body. She can feel the cold sweat of it, the way she felt it then, all over her.

And no one else seems to notice, that's what really gets to her, they seem to see her as, well, *finished*, somehow. Carl and the boys. Or the kids she sees at work, other people's kids, as precious and impossible as her own. That she should be expected, should get *paid*, to sit in an office and tell other people's kids what to do with their lives seems crazy to her sometimes. Crazier that they listen.

Ben and Josh turn suddenly and see her in the window. They wave vigorously and Ben gets onto his old skateboard, mouthing something Marion can't hear with the Walkman on and the window between them. She shakes her head, but he keeps on, tilting the skateboard wildly, his arms waving a crazy semaphore, insisting on her attention. It reminds her of when they were little, all crowded around her, and she'd send them outside, just long enough for a coffee or to talk to Carl for a few minutes. How every two seconds they'd be at the door, wanting her to watch something or do something.

It used to drive her crazy sometimes. Still does. Even now as she waves, shaking her head again, vigorously this time, she can feel that familiar pulse of irritation at her temples, quick and absolute as the swell of love that comes with it.

Anger and tenderness. That she can feel so many conflicting

things, that she can know so little about anything she feels and still manage to appear a competent adult. Sometimes it scares her. Knowing there's no end to feeling like this, ever.

The best Tracey Harper can do right now is to crouch behind the chest of drawers in her bedroom and listen as Kevin bangs and bangs and bangs on the door to the apartment. Before, it was the phone ringing and ringing and ringing. Her mother has slept through it all, which, even for her, is amazing.

"All right, bitch. I know you're in there." Kevin gives the door a kick.

Silence.

Then Tracey hears him stomp down the stairs, she hears the outer door bang shut. In a few minutes his car squeals off down the street. Tracey can see it perfectly, the dark blue, rusted-out '78 Firebird and Kevin inside, his knuckles white around the steering wheel, really fuckin' pissed off.

For a minute she thinks of getting up, going out, trying to find him. It would be a lot easier than this is. She wishes she'd never met that fucking bitch Walker. Now she's going to have to spend her time avoiding Kevin, who will be on her ass every goddamn minute. Phoning her at all hours, following her to and from school. All she'll be able to do is ignore him and keep on walking.

Even when he grabs her arm, hard, next Friday afternoon and pulls her towards him. Even when she has to kick him, she won't speak, she'll just get the fuck out of there and keep on going. It's all she can do.

And it isn't Kevin's fault, either. Though he's acting like a jerk right now, he's an okay guy. Next week he'll get on at Petro-Can, and had he and Tracey gone through with their plan, everything might have worked out fine for them, statistics be damned.

As it is, Tracey will spend the next three weeks sitting silent in Marion Walker's office, not even looking at her, arms clamped around her chest as if it takes her whole strength to hold its contents in.

She will look a lot the way she looks now, crouching against the wall of her bedroom, hugging her knees to her chest as if the effort of keeping them from jumping up, running into the hallway and never stopping till she finds Kevin, wherever he is, takes everything she's got.

Which it does.

Drawers and counters done, Marion goes to the cupboard for the pail and sponge mop, but before she starts the floor, she fills the coffeemaker and turns it on so that it will be ready when she is. She puts a new tape—*Patsy Cline's Greatest Hits*—into the Walkman and gets down on her knees to do the tough spots near the sink and under the edge of the stove. A whiff of Lysol stings her nose. Once the hard stuff's loosened, she does the rest with the mop, singing again, having a great time.

Sometimes what Marion thinks is simply that she's lucky to have such an easy life. "Karma" some of their friends used to call it, hanging out at the farm, smoking black hash, letting the boys run naked through the fields.

Other times she knows damn well it's because of Carl and their double income, her education, her parents' double income even, everything that's made her luck possible. Political, not spiritual, and she should damn well face up to what that means. Whatever that means.

Sometimes she just doesn't know, and it scares her.

Besides, who knows what will happen next, even in an easy life. In five minutes, for example, Jason will be driving in from the mall where he works part-time as a clerk at Music World, speeding, already late to pick up his girlfriend, Karen. While in an apartment nearby, someone else knocks back his last beer and climbs into his car to go get more before his friends show up. Two cars, both driven by teenage boys, hurtle towards each other, like sonar blips on a great map of possibilities, like cells gone haywire. Marion's own death ticks in her cells as it does in anybody's. Anything can happen, any time.

Still crouching behind her dresser, Tracey Harper has fallen asleep. She is dreaming. In the dream she is in a red Corvette convertible, moving very fast along a highway which is like a highway in a cartoon show, with flowers springing up on all sides, and birds and rainbows filling the sky. Mrs. Walker is driving and the two of them are laughing and eating triple-scoop French chocolate ice-cream cones from Baskin-Robbins. The dream is so vivid that Tracey can taste the cold chocolate on her tongue and feel the wind in her hair. She can hear herself laughing and laughing, and in the dream she reaches over and puts her hand, just there, for a moment, on Mrs. Walker's arm. In the dream, she has no idea where they are going.

Meanwhile, a few blocks away, Jason pulls up in front of Karen's place, gets out of the car and goes around to the back porch where she is waiting for him in brand-new, acid-washed jeans and a yellow sweatshirt, one of her mother's daffodils stuck behind her ear.

Meanwhile, Marion's kitchen gleams, the sun shines through the window, the crocuses pulse and shimmer as the afternoon wanes. Marion pushes the mop and pail into the corner and tiptoes around the edge of the floor to the coffeemaker, pours herself a cup and tiptoes back towards the patio door.

The breeze feels wonderful on her hot face. She wipes the sweat off her forehead with the back of her hand as she steps out, and that for some reason makes her think of the day she took Tracey Harper to the mall because she couldn't think of anything else to do and how they'd tried on clothes and makeup in The Bay. Tracey wanted to do Marion's face and she let her though she never wears makeup. Now, she can feel Tracey's fingertips again on her eyelids and her cheeks. They stick slightly, pulling at her skin, as if Tracey is pressing too hard, exasperated with something she sees there, something she can't erase or alter. And at the same time, they flutter and soothe, almost as a lover's would.

Anger and tenderness. From nowhere, Marion feels the tears start. On the Walkman Patsy Cline is singing one of those songs that someone sings when they've been ditched, trying to cram a lifetime of pain into every note.

And so Marion just stands there, on her patio, with a cup of coffee in her hand, crying like an idiot. Partly because it's finally spring and she's a little stoned. Because of her kids and her job. Because she's like that, Marion, soft and open, in her easy life.

But not only because.

Linda Svendsen

White Shoulders

My oldest sister's name is Irene de Haan and she has never hurt anybody. She lives with cancer, in remission, and she has stayed married to the same undemonstrative Belgian Canadian, a brake specialist, going on thirty years. In the family's crumbling domestic empire, Irene and Peter's union has been, quietly, and despite tragedy, what our mother calls the lone success.

Back in the late summer of 1984, before Irene was admitted to hospital for removal of her left breast, I flew home from New York to Vancouver to be with her. We hadn't seen each other for four years, and since I didn't start teaching ESL night classes until mid-September, I was free, at loose ends, unlike the rest of her family. Over the past months, Peter had used up vacation and personal days shuttling her to numerous tests, but finally had to get back to work. He still had a mortgage. Their only child, Jill, who'd just turned seventeen, was entering her last year of high school. Until junior high, she'd been one of those unnaturally well-rounded kids—taking classes in the high dive, water ballet, drawing, and drama, and boy-hunting in the mall on Saturdays with a posse of dizzy friends. Then, Irene said, overnight she became unathletic, withdrawn, and bookish: an academic drone. At any rate, for Jill and Pete's sake, Irene didn't intend to allow her illness to interfere with their life. She wanted everything to proceed as normally as possible. As who wouldn't.

In a way, and this will sound callous, the timing had worked out. Earlier that summer, my ex-husband had been offered a temporary teaching position across the country, and after a long dinner at our old Szechuan dive, I'd agreed to temporarily revise our custody arrangement. With his newfound bounty, Bill would rent a California town house for nine months and royally support the kids. "Dine and Disney," he'd said.

I'd blessed this, but then missed them. I found myself dead asleep in the middle of the day in Jane's lower bunk, or tuning in late afternoon to my six-year-old son's, and Bill's, obsession, *People's Court*. My arms ached when I saw other women holding sticky hands, pulling frenzied children along behind them in the August dog days. So I flew west. To be a mother again, I'd jokingly told Irene over the phone. To serve that very need.

Peter was late meeting me at the airport. We gave each other a minimal hug, and then he shouldered my bags and walked ahead out into the rain. The Datsun was double-parked, hazards flashing, with a homemade sign taped on the rear window that said STUD DRIVER. "Jill," he said, loading the trunk. "Irene's been teaching her so she can pick up the groceries. Help out for a change." I got in, he turned on easy-listening, and we headed north towards the grey mountains.

Irene had been in love with him since I was a child; he'd been orphaned in Belgium during World War II, which moved both Irene and our mother. He'd also reminded us of Emile, the Frenchman in *South Pacific*, because he was greying, autocratic, and seemed misunderstood. But the European charm had gradually worn thin, over the years; I'd been startled by Peter's racism and petty tyranny. I'd often wished that the young Irene had been fondled off her two feet by a breadwinner more tender, more local. Nobody else in the family agreed and Mum even hinted that I'd become bitter since the demise of my own marriage.

"So how is she?" I finally asked Peter.

"She's got a cold," he said, "worrying herself sick. And other than that, it's hard to say." His tone was markedly guarded. He said prospects were poor; the lump was large and she had the fast-growing, speedy sort of cancer. "But she thinks the Paki quack will get it when he cuts," he said.

I sat with that. "And how's Jill?"

"Grouchy," he said. "Bitchy." This gave me pause, and it seemed to have the same effect on him.

We pulled into the garage of the brick house they'd lived in since Jill's birth, and he waved me on while he handled the luggage. The house seemed smaller now, tucked under tall Douglas firs and fringed with baskets of acutely pink geraniums and baby's breath. The back door was open, so I walked in; the master bedroom door was ajar, but I knocked first. She wasn't there. Jill called, "Aunt Adele?" and I headed back down the hall to the guestroom, and stuck my head in.

A wan version of my sister rested on a water bed in the dark. When I plunked down I made a tiny wave. Irene almost smiled. She was thin as a fine chain; in my embrace, her flesh barely did the favour of keeping her bones company. Her blondish hair was quite short, and she looked ordinary, like a middle-aged matron who probably worked at a bank and kept a no-fail punch recipe filed away. I had to hold her, barely, close again. Behind us, the closet was full of her conservative garments—flannel, floral— and I understood that this was her room now. She slept here alone. She didn't frolic with Peter any more, have sex.

"Don't cling," Irene said slowly, but with her old warmth. "Don't get melodramatic. I'm not dying. It's just a cold."

"Aunt Adele," Jill said.

I turned around; I'd forgotten my niece was even there, and she was sitting right on the bed, wedged against a bolster. We kissed hello with loud smooch effects—our ritual—and while she kept a hand on Irene's shoulder, she stuttered answers to my questions about school and her summer. Irene kept an eye on a mute TV—the U.S. Open—although she didn't have much interest in tennis; I sensed, really, that she didn't have any extra energy available for banter. This was conservation, not rudeness.

Jill looked different. In fact, the change in her appearance and demeanour exceeded the ordinary drama of puberty; she seemed to be another girl—sly, unsure, and unable to look in the eye. She wore silver wire glasses, no makeup, jeans with an over-size kelly-green sweatshirt, and many extra pounds. Her soft straw-coloured hair was pulled back with a swan barrette, the swan's eye downcast. When she passed Irene a glass of water and a pill, Irene managed to swallow, then passed it back, and Jill drank, too. To me, it seemed she took great care, twisting the glass in her hand, to sip from the very spot her mother's lips had touched.

Peter came in, sat down on Jill's side of the bed, and stretched both arms around to raise the back of his shirt. He bared red, hairless skin, and said, "Scratch."

"But I'm watching tennis," Jill said softly.

"But you're my daughter," he said. "And I have an itch."

Peter looked at Irene and she gave Jill a sharp nudge. "Do your poor dad," she said. "You don't even have to get up."

"But aren't I watching something?" Jill said. She glanced around, searching for an ally.

"*Vrouw*," Peter spoke up. "This girl, she doesn't do anything except mope, eat, mope, eat."

Jill's shoulders sagged slightly, as if all air had suddenly abandoned her body, and then she slowly got up. "I'll see you after,

Aunt Adele," she whispered, and I said, "Yes, sure," and then she walked out.

Irene looked dismally at Peter; he made a perverse sort of face—skewing his lips south. Then she reached over and started to scratch his bare back. It was an effort. "Be patient with her, Peter," she said. "She's worried about the surgery."

"She's worried you won't be around to wait on her," Peter said, then instructed, "Go a little higher." Irene's fingers crept obediently up. "Tell Adele what Jill said."

Irene shook her head. "I don't remember."

Peter turned to me. "When Irene told her about the cancer, she said, 'Don't die on me, Mum, or I'll kill you.' And she said this so serious. Can you imagine?" Peter laughed uninhibitedly, and then Irene joined in, too, although her quiet accompaniment was forced. There wasn't any recollected pleasure in her eyes at all; rather, it seemed as if she didn't want Peter to laugh alone, to appear as odd as he did. "Don't die or I'll kill you," Peter said.

Irene had always been private about her marriage. If there were disagreements with Peter, and there had been—I'd once dropped in unannounced and witnessed a string of Christmas lights whip against the fireplace and shatter—they were never rebroadcast to the rest of the family; if she was ever discouraged or lonely, she didn't confide in anyone, unless she kept a journal or spoke to her God. She had never said a word against the man.

The night before Irene's surgery, after many earnest wishes and ugly flowers had been delivered, she asked me to stay late with her at Lion's Gate Hospital. The room had emptied. Peter had absconded with Jill—and she'd gone reluctantly, asking to stay until I left—and our mother, who'd been so nervous and sad that an intern had fed her Valium from his pocket. "Why is this happening to her?" Mum said to him. "To my only happy child."

Irene, leashed to an IV, raised herself to the edge of the bed and looked out at the parking lot and that kind Pacific twilight. "That Jill," Irene said. She allowed her head to fall, arms crossed in front of her. "She should lift a finger for her father."

"Well," I said, watching my step, aware she needed peace, "Peter's not exactly the most easygoing."

"No," she said weakly.

We sat for a long time, Irene in her white gown, me beside her in my orange-and-avocado track suit, until I began to think I'd been too tough on Peter and had distressed her. Then she spoke. "Sometimes I wish I'd learned more Dutch," she said neutrally. "When I met Peter, we married not speaking the same language, really. And that made a difference."

She didn't expect a comment—she raised her head and stared out the half-open window—but I was too shocked to respond anyway. I'd never heard her remotely suggest that her and Peter's marriage had been less than a living storybook. "You don't like him, do you?" she said. "You don't care for his Belgian manner."

I didn't answer; it didn't need to be said aloud. I turned away. "I'm probably not the woman who can best judge these things," I said.

Out in the hall, a female patient talked on the phone. Irene and I both listened. "I left it in the top drawer," she said wearily. "No. The *bedroom*." There was a pause. "The desk in the hall, try that." Another pause. "Then ask Susan where she put it, because I'm tired of this and I need it." I turned as she hung the phone up and saw her check to see if money had tumbled back. The hospital was quiet again. Irene did not move, but she was shaking; I found it difficult to watch this and reached out and took her hand. "What is it?" I said. "Irene."

She told me she was scared. Not for herself, but for Peter. That when she had first explained to him about the cancer, he hadn't spoken to her for three weeks. Or touched her. Or kissed her. He'd slept in the guestroom, until she'd offered to move there. And he'd been after Jill to butter his toast, change the sheets, iron his pants. Irene had speculated about this, she said, until she'd realized he was acting this way because of what had happened to him when he was little. In Belgium. Bruges, the war. He had only confided in her once. He'd said all the women he'd ever loved had left him. His mother killed, his sister. "And now me," Irene said. "The big C which leads to the big D. If I move on, I leave two children. And I've told Jill they have to stick together."

I got off the bed. "But, Irene," I said, "she's not on earth to please her father. Who can be unreasonable. In my opinion."

By this time, a medical team was touring the room. The junior member paused by Irene and said, "Give me your vein."

"In a minute," she said to him, "please," and he left. There were dark areas, the colour of new bruises, under her eyes. "I want you to promise me something."

"Yes."

"If I die," she said, "and I'm not going to, but if I do, I don't want Jill to live with you in New York. Because that's what she wants to do. I want her to stay with Peter. Even if she runs to you, send her back."

"I can't promise that," I said. "Because you're not going to go anywhere."

She looked at me. Pale, fragile. She was my oldest sister, who'd always been zealous about the silver lining in that cloud; and now it seemed she might be dying, in her forties—too soon— and she needed to believe I could relieve her of this burden. So I nodded, *Yes*.

When I got back, by cab, to Irene and Peter's that night, the house was dark. I groped up the back steps, ascending through a hovering scent of honeysuckle, stepped inside, and turned on the kitchen light. The TV was going—some ultra-loud camera commercial—in the living room. Nobody was watching. "Jill?" I said. "Peter?"

I wandered down the long hall, snapping on switches: Irene's sickroom, the upstairs bathroom, the master bedroom, Peter's domain. I did a double-take; he was there. Naked, lying on top of the bed, his still hand holding his penis—as if to keep it warm and safe—the head shining. The blades of the ceiling fan cut in slow circles above him. His eyes were vague and didn't turn my way; he was staring up. "Oh sorry," I whispered, "God, sorry," and flicked the light off again.

I headed back to the living room and sat, for a few seconds. When I'd collected myself, I went to find Jill. She wasn't in her downstairs room, which seemed typically adolescent in decor—Boy George poster, socks multiplying in a corner—until I spotted a quote from Rilke, in careful purple handwriting, taped to her long mirror: "Beauty is only the first touch of terror we can still bear."

I finally spotted the light under the basement bathroom door.

"Jill," I said. "It's me."

"I'm in the bathroom," she said.

"I know," I said. "I want to talk."

She unlocked the door and let me in. She looked tense and peculiar; it looked as if she'd just thrown water on her face. She was still dressed in her clothes from the hospital—from the day before, the kelly-green sweat job—and she'd obviously been sitting on the edge of the tub, writing. There was a Papermate, a pad of yellow legal paper. The top sheet was covered with verses of tiny backward-slanting words. There was also last night's pot of Kraft Dinner on the sink.

"You're all locked in," I said.

She didn't comment, and when the silence stretched on too long I said, "Homework?" and pointed to the legal pad.

"No," she said. Then she gave me a look and said, "Poem."

"Oh," I said, and I was surprised. "Do you ever show them? Or it?"

"No," she said. "They're not very good." She sat back down on the tub. "But maybe I'd show you, Aunt Adele."

"Good," I said. "Not that I'm a judge." I told her Irene was tucked in and that she was in a better, more positive frame of mind. More like herself. This seemed to relax Jill so much, I marched the lie a step further. "Once your mum is out of the woods," I said, "your father may lighten up."

"That day will never come," she said.

"Never say never," I said. I gave her a hug—she was so much bigger than my daughter, but I embraced her the same way I had Jane since she was born: a hand and a held kiss on the top of the head.

She hugged me back. "Maybe I'll come live with you, Auntie A."

"Maybe," I said, mindful of Irene's wishes. "You and everybody," and saw the disappointment on her streaked face. So I added, "Everything will be all right. Wait and see. She'll be all right."

And Irene was. They claimed they'd got it, and ten days later she came home, earlier than expected. When Peter, Jill, and I were gathered around her in the sickroom, Irene started cracking jokes about her future prosthetic fitting. "How about the Dolly Parton, hon?" she said to Peter. "Then I'd be a handful."

I was surprised to see Peter envelop her in his arm; I hadn't ever seen him offer an affectionate gesture. He told her he didn't care what size boob she bought, because breasts were for the hungry babies—not so much for the husband. "I have these," he said. "These are mine. These big white shoulders." And he rested his head against her shoulder and looked placidly at Jill; he was heavy, but Irene used her other arm to bolster herself, hold him up, and she closed her eyes in what seemed to be joy. Jill came and sat by me.

Irene took it easy the next few days; I stuck by, as did Jill, when she ventured in after school. I was shocked that there weren't more calls, or cards, or visitors except for Mum, and I realized my sister's life was actually very narrow, or extremely focused: family came first. Even Jill didn't seem to have any friends at all; the phone never rang for her.

Then Irene suddenly started to push herself—she prepared a complicated deep-fried Belgian dish; in the afternoon, she sat with Jill, in the Datsun, while Jill practised parallel parking in front of the house and lobbied for a mother–daughter trip to lovely downtown Brooklyn for Christmas. And then, after a long nap and little dinner, Irene insisted on attending the open house at Jill's school.

We were sitting listening to the band rehearse, a *Flashdance* medley, when I became aware of Irene's body heat—she was on my right—and asked if she might not want to head home. She was burning up. "Let me get through this," she said. Then Jill, on my other side, suddenly said in a small tight voice, "Mum." She was staring at her mother's blouse, where a bright stitch of scarlet had shown up. Irene had bled through her dressing. Irene looked down. "Oh," she said. "Peter."

On the tear to the hospital, Peter said he'd sue Irene's stupid "Paki bugger" doctor. He also said he should take his stupid wife to court for loss of sex. He should get a divorce for no-nookie. For supporting a one-tit wonder. And on and on.

Irene wasn't in shape to respond; I doubt she would have anyway.

Beside me in the back seat, Jill turned to stare out the window; she was white, sitting on her hands.

I found my voice. "I don't think we need to hear this right now, Peter," I said.

"Oh, Adele," Irene said warningly. Disappointed.

He pulled over, smoothly, into a bus zone. Some of the people waiting for the bus weren't pleased. Peter turned and faced me, his finger punctuating. "This is my wife, my daughter, my Datsun." He paused. "I can say what the hell I want. And you're welcome to walk." He reached over and opened my door.

The two women at the bus shelter hurried away, correctly sensing an incident.

"I'm going with Aunt—" Jill was barely audible.

"No," said Irene. "You stay here."

I sat there, paralysed. I wanted to get out, but didn't want to leave Irene and Jill alone with him; Irene was very ill, Jill seemed defenceless. "Look," I said to Peter, "forget I said anything. Let's just get Irene there, okay?"

He pulled the door shut, then turned front, checked me in the rear-view one last time—cold, intimidating—and headed off again. Jill was crying silently. The insides of her glasses were smeared; I shifted over beside her and she linked her arm through mine tight, tight. Up front, Irene did not move.

They said it was an infection which had spread to the chest wall, requiring antibiotics and hospital admission. They were also going to perform more tests.

Peter took off with Jill, saying that they both had to get up in the morning.

Before I left Irene, she spoke to me privately, in a curtained cubicle in Emergency, and asked if I could stay at our mother's for the last few days of my visit; Irene didn't want to hurt me, but she thought it would be better, for all concerned, if I cleared out.

And then she went on; her fever was high, but she was lucid and fighting hard to stay that way. Could I keep quiet about this to our mother? And stop gushing about the East to Jill, going on about the Statue of Liberty and the view of the water from the window in the crown? And worry a little more about my own lost children and less about her daughter? And try to be more understanding of her husband, who sometimes wasn't able to exercise control over his emotions? Irene said Peter needed more love, more time; more of her, God willing. After that, she couldn't speak. And, frankly, neither could I.

I gave in to everything she asked. Jill and Peter dropped in together during the evening to see her; I visited Irene, with Mum, during the day when Peter was at work. Our conversations were banal and strained—they didn't seem to do either of us much good. After I left her one afternoon, I didn't know where I was going and ended up at my father's grave. I just sat there, on top of it, on the lap of the stone.

The day before my New York flight, I borrowed my mother's car to pick up a prescription for her at the mall. I was window-shopping my way back to the parking lot, when I saw somebody resembling my niece sitting on a bench outside a sporting goods store. At first, the girl seemed too dishevelled, too dirty-looking, actually, to be Jill, but as I approached, it became clear it was her. She wasn't doing anything. She sat there, draped in her mother's London Fog raincoat, her hands resting on her thickish thighs, clicking a barrette open, closed, open, closed. It was ten in the morning; she should have been in school. In English. For a moment, it crossed my mind that she might be on drugs: this was a relief; it would explain everything. But I didn't think she was. I was going to go over and simply say, *Yo, Jill, let's do tea,* and then I remembered my sister's frightening talk with me at the hospital and thought, *Fuck it. Butt out, Adele,* and walked the long way round. I turned my back.

One sultry Saturday morning, in late September—after I'd been back in Brooklyn for a few weeks—I was up on the roof preparing the first lessons for classes, when the super brought a handful of mail up. He'd been delivering it personally to tenants since the box had been ripped out of the entrance wall. It was the usual stuff and a thin white business envelope from Canada. From Jill. I opened it: *Dearlingest* (sic) *Aunt Adele, These are my only copies. Love, your only niece, Jill. P.S. I'm going to get a job and come see you at Easter.*

There were two. The poems were carefully written, each neat on their single page, with the script leaning left, as if blown by a stiff breeze. "Black Milk" was about three deaths: before her beloved husband leaves for war, a nursing mother shares a bottle of old wine with him, saved from their wedding day, and unknowingly poisons her child and then herself. Dying, she rocks her dying child in her arms, but her last conscious thought is for her husband at the front. Jill had misspelled wedding; she'd put *weeding.*

"Belgium" described a young girl ice skating across a frozen lake—Jill had been to Belgium with her parents two times—fleeing an unnamed pursuer. During each quick, desperate glide, the ice melts beneath her until, at the end, she is underwater: "In the deep cold / Face to face / Look, he comes now / My Father / My Maker." The girl wakes up; it was a bad dream. And then her earthly father appears in her bed and, "He makes night /

Come again / All night," by covering her eyes with his large, heavy hand.

I read these, and read them again, and I wept. I looked out, past the steeples and the tar roofs, where I thought I saw the heat rising, toward the green of Prospect Park, and held the poems in my lap, flat under my two hands. I didn't know what to do; I didn't know what to do right away; I thought I should wait until I knew clearly what to say and whom to say it to.

In late October, Mum phoned, crying, and said that Irene's cancer had not been caught by the mastectomy. Stray cells had been detected in other areas of her body. Chemotherapy was advised. Irene had switched doctors; she was seeing a naturopath. She was paying big money for an American miracle gum, among other things.

Mum also said that Jill had disappeared for thirty-two hours. Irene claimed that Jill had been upset because of a grade—a C in Phys Ed. Mum didn't believe it was really that; she thought Irene's condition was disturbing Jill, but hadn't said that to Irene.

She didn't volunteer any information about the other member of Irene's family and I did not ask.

In November, Bill came east for a visit and brought the children, as scheduled; he also brought a woman named Cheryl Oak. The day before Thanksgiving, the two of them were invited to a dinner party, and I took Graham and Jane, taller and both painfully shy with me, to Central Park. It was a crisp, windy night. We watched the gi-normous balloons being blown up for the Macy's parade and bought roasted chestnuts, not to eat, but to warm the palms of our hands. I walked them back to their hotel and delivered them to the quiet, intelligent person who would probably become their stepmother, and be good to them, as she'd obviously been for Bill. Later, back in Brooklyn, I was still awake—wondering how another woman had succeeded with my husband and, now, my own little ones—when Irene phoned at 3 a.m. She told me Jill was dead. "There's been an accident," she said.

A few days later, my mother and stepfather picked me up at the Vancouver airport on a warm, cloudy morning. On the way to the funeral, they tried to tell me, between them—between breakdowns—what had happened. She had died of hypothermia; the impact of hitting the water had most likely rendered her unconscious. She probably hadn't been aware of drowning, but she'd done that, too. She'd driven the Datsun to Stanley Park—she'd told Irene she was going to the library—left the key in the ignition, walked not quite to the middle of the bridge, and hoisted herself over the railing. There was one eye-witness: a guy who worked in a video store. He'd kept saying, "It was like a movie, I saw this little dumpling girl just throw herself off."

The chapel was half-empty, and the director mumbled that that was unusual when a teenager passed on. Irene had not known, and neither had Mum, where to reach Joyce, our middle sister, who was missing as usual; Ray, our older brother, gave a short eulogy. He stated that he didn't believe in any God, but Irene did, and he was glad for that this day. He also guessed that when any child takes her own life, the whole family must wonder why, and probably do that forever. The face of my sister was not to be borne. Then we all sang "The Water Is Wide," which Jill had once performed in an elementary-school talent show. She'd won Honourable Mention.

After the congregation dispersed, Peter remained on his knees, his head in his hands, while Irene approached the casket. Jill wore a pale pink dress and her other glasses, and her hair was pinned back, as usual, with a barrette—this time, a dove. Irene bent and kissed her on the mouth, on the forehead, then tugged at Jill's lace collar, adjusting it just so. It was the eternal mother's gesture, that finishing touch, before your daughter sails out the door on her big date.

I drank to excess at the reception; we all did, and needed to. Irene and I did not exchange a word; we'd just held each other for a long minute. From a distance, and that distance was necessary, I heard Peter talking about Belgium and memories of his childhood. On his fifth birthday, his sister, Kristin, had sent him a pencil from Paris, a new one, unsharpened, and he had used it until the lead was gone and it was so short he could barely hold it between his fingers. On the morning his mother was shot, in cold blood, he'd been dressing in the dark. The last thing she had said, to the Germans, was "Don't hurt my little boy." This was when Mum and I saw Irene go to him and take his hand. She led him down the hall to his bedroom and closed the door behind them. "Thank God," Mum said. "Thank God, they have each other. Thank God, she has him."

And for that moment, I forgot about the despair that had prompted Jill to do what she did, and my own responsibility and silence, because I was alive and full of needs, sickness, and dreams myself. I thought, *No, I will never tell my sister what I suspect, because life is short and very hard*, and I thought, *Yes, a bad marriage is better than none*, and I thought, *Adele, let the sun go down on your anger, because it will not bring her back*, and I turned to my mother. "Yes," I said. "Thank God."

Holley Rubinsky

Rapid Transits

My da isn't that old, but he has a tremor of the hands that shivers up to his neck and gives his head a quick snap once in a while. So small a movement that you'd hardly notice, but I've been watching him my whole life. "I thought it would of come, Harriet," he says of the baby and my belly sticking halfway out to here, but I can only shrug. Some creatures have more sense than others; they stay where the staying's good.

"Fine hotel, maybe," I say, but he doesn't get it and frowns. His eyebrows are so sparse and light, you can hardly see them. "Good room," I say, tapping my belly. "Pool and all. Cheap."

He grins then and shows his missing front tooth that used to scare me. All a man needs is to let a little stubble grow and have a front tooth missing and it doesn't matter who he is, he looks bad. One day the tooth was just gone, fell out over meatloaf in a cafeteria downtown he said. It took my mother some doing to make him wear a false one, and then he took to flicking it when you least expected it.

I have him in the kitchen, sitting on a straight-back chair, facing me. I know he's not comfortable, you can see how his elbows on the table are holding up his weight, but Bill doesn't have much furniture, he never needed it. "Did you like the bus?"

"I dislike buses," he says, sounding grand like something he's rehearsed in front of a mirror. "I am so used now to travelling by air." Anyone can see from his shiny suit and thin cheeks that this fellow couldn't afford a plane from one side of Timbuktu (the one in California) to the other, but it doesn't stop him lying. He needs to do it.

I offer him an apple, but he shakes his head sadly. He tilts his chin back and opens up and I see he hasn't got much left, maybe enough for chomping Gerbers Junior dinners. He shrugs, though, and looks at me and smiles. When he smiles, his eyes water as though he might cry. Eyes like my da's, ripe and juicy, slightly past prime like good stewing fruit, usually mean a person doesn't have a grip on things. Once he said to my auntie: How does a baby come out such a small hole?

My da has come all this way to see his grandbaby, but there is none, yet.

Before I spied him down the road at the bottom of the hill and my heart started to sink, I was sitting happy and round as a pumpkin under an apple tree. The apples are Gravensteins and Bill says they're having an on-year; they're big and tart and crispy. Foam was gathering at the corners of my mouth as I chewed. I have big horse-like teeth, but it doesn't bother me. When you're born funny-looking or have a speech defect or epilepsy, after a while you realize you don't have too much to worry about, because the worst has already happened. I don't know whether I read this somewhere or made it up.

It's my fault he's here. The time not to write a letter to someone you haven't seen in a blue moon is when you're suddenly feeling a little lonely for them and sorry for them, both feelings together. Having found this little town and a job in the hardware store where I met Bill, maybe in the dither of my own good fortune, I wrote my da at his last address, a boarding house in Eureka CA.

"So you're settled down," he says, racking his brain for conversation. When you're as pregnant as I am, you don't mind just sitting and seeing what happens next.

"You might say."

"Is this feller the father?"

I'd laugh if it wasn't so sad. I have to turn my face away quick. I've been telling people it's a lover who died of leukemia. That kind of thing.

He's staring at my tits that have got even bigger. "Wisht it was mine," he says and that opens a whole new kettle of fish.

In my teens, I expected a dwarf would rape me. It was the worst thing I could think of, I was young then, and all the other girls wanted to date the tall, good-looking fellows on the basketball or football teams, but I didn't stand a chance. Even if I were to take off my clothes and fall into a helpless swoon, they would've just laughed, because my body isn't an attractive one. It doesn't have smooth tits with rosebud tips or a slender wasp-like waist or curved hips. My hips are up too high, like somebody who has fallen from a tall building and landed feet first, what would happen then. Your heels would push leg bones which would push the hip bones, which would tuck up too near the bottom of the rib cage. In this way, except for being normal height, I look a bit like a dwarf myself, that squat, solid sort of hunched look, like you couldn't knock them over with a feather and better not try.

I have the kind of tits that never were young. Not creamy or perky, certainly no tidy handful. When they started to grow I was eleven and built chunky and they just took off. While other girls were whining about training bras I was wrapping gauze tightly around my chest, which just made me look even more barrel-chested. The tits came in veined and droopy, full and big. They looked like those of a full-grown woman who had given birth to seven babies and nursed them all. I didn't think they were exactly ugly, there was something remarkable about them, I saw kinds like mine on fertility goddesses in books, for example, but other people did. Think them ugly. But I suspect too much of a good thing just scared the shit out of them.

I offer him more coffee. He nods yes, yes and then I go ahead and put out some shortbreads I made just yesterday. He drops crumbs when he eats because his tongue does a lot of work, mashing the bits on the roof of his mouth. He's hungry, though, and like any woman, I begin cataloguing what's in the fridge, and imagine dishes: spaghetti, piping hot with tons of Parmesan on top, or the corn-and-hamburger casserole flavoured with chili that Bill likes. Seeing my da is like being in a dream; it was my dreaming brought him here, to this unlikely place.

In one dream, I'm looking down at him while he is thumping me on the head like he used to do, for fun I guess; he said his da did that to him and I should know what it felt like. That time, I was outside playing in the dirt with some captured caterpillars (the black furry kind, their insides the brightest yellow and green), when he came along and raised me up by my arm until I was standing, and then he put his hand under my little green and white checkered dress and pinched my tummy and then he started thumping me on the head, with his thumb and middle finger, like you do tiddlywinks, still holding me and saying something, I don't recall what. He smelled like what later I knew was Old Spice and whiskey. His nose was red, he was starting to cry. Meanwhile, thump thump on the crown of my head and me writhing and wiggling and squirming. Just then a swallowtail butterfly fluttered through the garden and in my mind I ran after its red-with-the-black-dot targeted tail until I caught up and then I fluttered away, and my da was left thumping on an abandoned body, though the bruise on my arm lasted.

Probably he didn't thump me often. I remember it, but that's kids, if they have a certain turn of mind, they remember all the bad things. I was proud, like most kids are. Mess with them once, they never forget.

Just then the outside door swings open, the latches make rattly sounds, and Bill comes onto the service porch that's just off the kitchen, thumps mud off his boots. He's been over the way working gardens all day. When he stamps his feet, the whole kitchen shakes a bit, because the house is wood, and old, and has a very comforting smell of wood stove, grease, and rust. Bill has tools he's collected from other old-timers slung on great big nails. My da wipes his face on his sleeve, reminding me I have forgot to put out napkins, and then brushes his lips with his smooth fingers to be extra sure. I see by this behaviour that he wants to impress Bill. I see by the way he squares back his shoulders and sets his face kind of proud yet humble that he wants something. I also see he's going to be mighty surprised, as Bill puts it.

When Bill opens the door to the kitchen, I stay sat for the introductions. It's part of getting away with a lot when you're pregnant. My da's transparent eyebrows raise up and he can't disguise that he thought Bill was going to be a young fellow. My da tries to stand up but I guess he's too taken aback, he starts shivering more than usual and sits down again. "Bill," I say, "this here's my father, who I don't think I told you about." Bill is seventy-one with a few teeth missing himself, so they make quite a pair.

The man is standing outside a bedroom door in a hall lit by the overhead light from the kitchen that's throwing shadows up the stairs. In front of his bedroom, in the puddle of dingy light, he slumps, shirtless. He's small, no taller than I am, has a thin kind of body, but not wiry; his shoulders are curved and soft as a woman's and his skin is very white. He has some long brown hairs on his belly and his lower arms. He has been drinking, which he usually does in the evenings, only tonight he's in worse shape; he started to barbecue us some hamburgers, wearing his chef's hat, the white puffy kind, and singing and not paying enough attention. The fire leapt out of the barrel barbecue and he had to step all over the flying shreds of unburnt papers on the flagstone patio (the flagstones are new), which blackened a few of them and my mother was very angry. Although just to look at her you wouldn't have known it, exactly. You might have felt it. Anger comes rolling off her in waves.

It's chilly out in the hall, and to get into his bedroom he has to beg. "Mommy?" he says, rubbing a hand over his little pot-belly. His belly looks like a growth above his thin legs, pooching out, pooching out we used to say, over his belt and under the slight concavity of his chest. He is trying again. Scratch, scratch he goes with his fingernails, trying to be cute by doing like our pussycat, Midnight, does. Then he sniffles, loud enough so she has to hear. "Mommy?"

Somebody's watching him. He knows it, raises his face a bit, catching the little light there is, and covers his face with his arm. It's dramatic and pitiful and I hate her. He makes me want to cry.

I feel sorry for him and with my mind climb inside him and look out through his eyes. I am him, so drunk I don't feel ashamed of myself, just goosebumpy on my upper arms that I start rubbing briskly, which upsets my balance and I teeter, hit the door with my forehead and stay there. "Crud," I say. "Come on, Mommy, come on for Moses' sake." I'm dizzy behind my eyes which is a sure sign it's working, all that booze; as long as the dizziness stays and doesn't move down to my belly and make me sick, I don't mind. I can lie awake on a propped-up pillow, eyes open in the dark, and still snore so she thinks I've passed out. (She likes that, I think. She'll say, Oh, you passed out again last night; say it with that look, a snake spitting venom into the coffee she's pouring from the automatic pot I bought her for her birthday. Oh, you'll need lots of this, she says, pushing the cup and saucer my way. Don't slurp, she'll say, reminding me of when I poured coffee into the saucer when we were at a restaurant which we don't do very often, and so what happened was a big disappointment to her. I was telling a story about people I come from in the South, how they do things, but Mommy didn't hear that part, she only saw me slurping and she rose from the table and called for her coat. I had to stumble along behind, my tie soaked with coffee which happened when I shoved back the chair fast so as not to lose her, and then I really was a mess, which is what she said, You-are-a-mess, through clenched teeth, when we got out on the street. I could have sweet-talked my way out of it, but unfortunately I was having trouble with my words.) I don't pass out, though. Something in me wakes up when the rest of me needs to sleep, and although I look asleep, inside I am on the ball and keeping watch.

A squeak from my door that I've been leaning against sets me back to myself, looking at my da across the hall, my heart whammering in my ears like after running fast a long way. He kicks once against his own door and whispers something I don't hear. Then he's quiet. I start back to bed and realize he's in my room. My feet stick to the floor in a cold sweat. He smells. His eyes are red-rimmed and sad. He says, "Go get in bed, now, Harriet, and get under the covers. Do what your da tells you."

And I do, I'm ten years old.

It went on for a few years. He'd come in and lay himself down beside me and use me as a post, pretty much like some dogs do on a person's leg, or even I've seen them use legs of a chair. He never did anything nasty, never touched skin. He just put his hand on the mound that was my groin, and later on my tits, and then told me to lay still, lay still, don't move, don't move and he would rub up and down on my thigh through the covers. Now, knowing more about these things, I realize his underpants must have been goopy but he would just get up and leave quietly; he never showed me his thing.

Tonight we eat in the kitchen, as Bill and me are accustomed to doing, and my da eats more than his share; you can see he was hungry. We have zucchini bread with fresh whipped cream and honey on it for dessert. At half-past eight Bill leads him upstairs, using the kerosene lamp, a habit for no reason; there's plenty of electricity here, we're not so far off the beaten track. But he's been doing it that way, lights out at seven, for umpteen years and it's his business. We go to our rooms early and in the beginning, if I'd turn on the reading light beside my bed, Bill'd not say a thing, but gradually I came to respect his ways and he mine and so if I have reading to do, I do it by kerosene lamp and let the neighbours think what they will. He settles him in the guest room, although Bill never has guests, his folks and sisters have passed on. Like the other upstairs rooms, there's linoleum on the floor and vinyl draped at the window and the bedding is a thin sheet and an Army blanket and a pillow about the size of a healthy cabbage. There's a chest to put your clothes in, if you can get the drawers to pull out straight, and they're lined with news-papers, old ones, some from WWII and delicate as old lace.

I hear Bill telling my da how to do the lamp, while I wash the dishes in the old tin tub, using a candle or two; I know my way around now. Then I scrub my hands with Lava soap and a brush and go up for the night. Bill says, "Goodnight, Harriet," and I answer, "'Night, Bill," and he says, "Call me now," and I say, "I will," like we've been doing ever since it was apparent my time was coming. It's like that TV family, the Waltons, that everybody was watching so intently for a time, and it's goofy, that calling back-and-forth from room to room but it's so peaceful, too, your heart could lurch. My da says nothing, but I hear him anyway, listening.

Maybe it was having my da in the house that makes me not fall asleep, maybe it was the baby kicking, shifting inside me, and about time, turning head downwards, readying to make an entrance. I hope so, there's something so lonely inside me for that baby it's hard to breathe sometimes, if I let my thoughts go with it. I wanted something to hold and my arms ached in the night. I figured it was Nature's way of helping you let go of the comfort of that padded pa-whumpity-thump deep inside you, because after a time, you want it to quit, you'd go through anything to rid yourself of the burden and its secrets; you want whatever it is in the light, so you can see it and get your hands on it.

Through the pink curtain, there's not much moon, hardly a sliver across my cold floor. I have a throw-rug, one of those homey braided things, that I ordered through Sears and it helps, that first shock when you're sitting on the edge of the bed on an icy morning. It's got so I wear socks to bed now, thick ones like the road crews wear, cotton and wool blend with a red band across the top. My circulation seems to have slowed down all through me, except for my belly where the baby feels warm, a mix of earth and fire.

The clock ticking on the bedside table says three when I hear the padded footfalls in the hall. I listen for Bill—he pees in the night and you can always hear it hit the water with a splash, he's been a bachelor all his life—but it isn't Bill, and the creepy feeling on my neck says I'm right. Then I remember my da and it's him, in a strange house, up roaming. Since my mother remarried, he's not been able to get a grip on himself; he slid from head caretaker in a high school to a part-time night watchman, if he's working at all.

He says something, but I can't hear it and before I think to stop myself, I start across to the door. An odd whispering comes through, like something you'd see in a Jack Nicholson movie, as if the door itself is talking to me. My heart is thumping through the big blue vein I've seen pictures of, that carries blood to the little one; the thumping moves my belly. I can't open my mouth and say anything, nothing comes to my brain. My mind dashes out, into the cold hall, edges of linoleum lifting from the old pine floor, to where my da stands barefoot, but I can't do it, can't get inside; instead, I glimpse us, my da and me, foreheads pressed either side of my door. Like listening to the past so still and deep, no words at all, except the one he's saying. "Mommy," he says. I hear it this time. I brace my hip and shoulder against the door, because Bill and me have no need for locks. My belly lies sideways so that if my da decides to stoop and listen, he can hear his grandbaby's heartbeats. Other than the racket inside my head, there's no sound; it's so quiet you can hear the new fridge, a self-defroster, click on. I know his forehead is pushing on my door, I feel it, and his hand is on the knob, throbbing to turn it. I've seen it before, that exact scene, him on my mother's door, afraid to discover it locked. He would wait and breathe and breathe and turn and cross the hall, to me.

At breakfast my da cocks his head sideways and gives me a little wink. Then he raises his arms up slow like someone about to receive a blessing, you see them on TV, and his wrist bones come out of his sleeves. His hands are thin, the skin stretched smooth and oddly hairless, slightly reddened, like maybe psoriasis healed up. He raises his arms to me and something in me rushes out to him, bawling like a baby.

But there's something niggling in the back of my brain, something I can't quite get my finger on, and then I think of it. When I was twelve and just becoming sexy in the naïve way girls have and my da was in, rubbing on me, his hand on a tit but not massaging it, just holding, he always was polite, I pulled down the elastic on my summer nightgown and handed him one. I don't know what I thought would happen, I didn't consider. He opened his mouth automatically, I could see his face turning, glancing up at me from where he was settled against me, head at armpit level, left leg sprawled over my legs under the covers; face turning toward the flashes of headlights passing outside, his eyes dark, and he opened his mouth and took in my nipple and began sucking. Then he shifted his body and held my tit in both hands, kneading it like a kitten without claws, and used his tongue in a way that later I would know to be like a baby does, that whole-jaw sucking movement, tongue curling around the nipple. It felt good, that warm, wet tugging, the few times it went on.

Remembering makes me blush and I open the door of the wood stove to check the morning muffins. I fuss with coffee and mugs and get the fresh cream we trade with a neighbour for, while I sort myself out. It becomes clear in me I don't want him around when my baby is born, I don't want him even in the same county. I take a breath. "I know how it looks, big house and all," and shake my head no.

His eyes water up, but I've seen it before.

Not that old or that young, either, I've done my share of moving around. I knew my da had come up on the bus because he smelled like it. Buses smell like green disinfectant and sometimes, if the bus has come a distance, like dried urine that the cleaners always miss. Buses smell cloudy, the air thick with breath from body-insides and worn-down ideas stroking around inside heads; and all it takes is one smoker to get the rest of them going and then it gets in the air conditioner system and stays. That's what he smelled like, and slightly fishy, too, like somebody wearing his clothes too many days.

I used to get on a bus and go, get off, eat in the café attached to the station and climb on again. A bus breathes with people, usually poor, going where they've been called to: a dying, a funeral, a surgery, a sickness, sometimes a wedding; or looking for a job, a town to live in where you belong, a man, a woman; sometimes looking for a lost child. When it rains and the bus is moving smoothly down the road in the dark, lights from a city or houses darting in and out through streaked windows and the windshield wipers going slop, slop, it's soothing, cars passing fast and furious, horns going, like in another world, so far away on the other side of the thick walls of the bus, while inside you listen, picking up pieces of quiet conversation and having one of your own with the old lady beside you who is afraid of dying alone in her house with no one to find her. She says she picks flowers between watching game shows, playing bridge, and listening to all the Yankee games on the radio. She can tell you the players and their batting averages; she's a fan, sitting in her house having trouble sleeping, afraid she'll have a heart attack in bed and not make it to the living-room phone and wondering if she will fall and not be able to get up and wondering how long she could be there before anybody finds her. She has a theory that perhaps sleeplessness has to do with body temperature. Once while visiting overnight her hostess gave her some booties and when her feet were warm, she fell asleep. But probably she fell asleep easily because she was in someone else's house and not alone in her own where she has to stay awake, I think, in order to make sure she can get to the phone if she starts to die. In her own house she has to stay a bit on the alert.

Long distance travel by bus has its own rhythm and thoughts

go deep, vibrate to the bus's vibration as it cruises along, beating its scheduled trail around the country. After days and days of deciding which greasy food to eat, of keeping track of your suitcase and tickets and keeping your bottom off of toilet seats and avoiding drunks and other men, your self becomes very compact and floats in and out.

Once drifting on a bus at midnight with lightning off in the distance, voices murmuring, a radio clicking on, the crinkly flipping of a magazine page and me snuggled in with two seats to myself, the driver wheezes into a small town rest stop and speaks over the microphone very politely so as not to wake sleepers. He says not to forget the number of your bus and don't be late getting back and be careful going down the steps and watch your step outside because it's raining cats and dogs. As it turned out, he was from that small town and I stayed. Not for him, personally, but for the kind of place that would raise a man up to be so kind.

I stand in the yard beside the old house that needs paint with the old man who is like my guardian, whose house it is. After supper we came out to watch things and listen, to the birds, the rustling of a cat, the cozy chit-chat of chickens; we look at the clouds and notice the changes in shape. We smell the air full of dying green from the hills, slopes cooling as the season shifts gears into what we hope will be Indian summer. We look at the garden and notice the winter squash blossoms that are new since yesterday. Bill's not had a family, not even been married, but he's game and says it's never too late. Last year he bought a whole side of beef for the freezer, thought he was just foolish and not foresighted.

I stand in the yard that's big and flat and thick with grass and watch the sky. I would like to remember my da like people do in the TV commercials for the phone company: a soft-focus old fellow, white of hair and bright of spirit, who would fill you full of sweet memories, that you would want to phone right now. With my da, though, I tried to ignore him drunk and avoid him sober and all the time I was busy doing that, I was watching him and letting him into me; like seepage in a basement, he got in.

Already my tits are oozing. It's going to be an affair to beat all when I've got my little suckling and I know things now and I'm not budging from this town, this land, this spot. If you were looking down from the big house further up the hill, or were a tourist driving by, you might see us just standing here for a time, looking at the sky and hills, but mostly standing, holding down this corner of the earth, holding tight, keeping it quiet and calm, so that you'd be free to move into the fast lane with your headlights on and horn blaring.

Katherine Govier

Home for Good

When the affair broke off for good, Suzanne went back to Calgary to live. It was a transfer, in fact a promotion. Everyone in the city was rich. The skyline had sprung up like pistons and houses in the old neighbourhood were being bought up by millionaires. Only the river was the same. Lyall and Bonnie lived along it, their back yard rose from the shallow banks and spread up the hill between willow trees to the glass doors of the dining room. There were two cars in front and three children downstairs somewhere.

The broadloom looked like an extension of the lawn. It flowed silver green under Suzanne's feet and seemed to buzz with static. She sat listening to talk of the boys' tennis and a house boat in the Kootenays feeling that their childhood had been one long trick. Perhaps it had not happened with these people at all, perhaps not in this place. Memory, at any rate, provided no environment, and she had little to say to them.

As Suzanne stood to leave, she leaned over and poured the dregs of her tea into a plant pot. It was a habit she had from living alone; someone had told her once that cold tea was good for plants. Lyall jumped. His face crumpled oddly, like a ball with a puncture in it. "She's going to kill our plants," he complained to Bonnie. It was an awkward moment. He sounded like a fearful child who believed others had the power of life or death. He sounded as if he saw Suzanne as a stranger, a dangerous viper who could poison this, his carefully built refuge.

In a sulk, she went back to the apartment she had yet to furnish and headed straight for the kitchen sink. She was going to wash every one of her white dishes before she put them in the cupboards where they would stand in racks in order or size, irreproachable. She had come home for help, really, yet her reappearance seemed to be a threat. Thanks to their mothers, everyone knew about the married man. In this town, Suzanne was a marked woman, one who had ventured off the ordained path, a bad person, even. She banged the plates into the drainer. Lyall of all people ought to understand, being a bad boy himself.

She turned the hot water tap hotter. Just as she dipped her hands back into the painful, bubbling bath the telephone rang. She let it go four times, so that the caller would know it was an inconvenience, and then dried her hands and set out to find the phone. It was on the floor behind a crate of books.

"Hello mother."

Her mother called several times a day to find out how she was feeling. Someone who had been jilted by a married man may deserve what she got, but none the less a daughter's grief must not be ignored.

"I'd rather do it myself," Suzanne said, "honest. I know where I want the stuff to go."

At first Suzanne had resisted coming home. Finally it was a decision less to come here than to leave the other place. The job would be good, and being near her parents a comfort, she had supposed.

"No Mom, I haven't called Gemma."

She had no intention of calling Gemma. She was out of touch with nearly everyone. They had gone to school together, but in their twenties they had so energetically taken up the things called lifestyles. Great barriers had been raised by the kind of music one listened to, by how much money one had, or wanted to have, by whether one lived downtown or in a suburb. On visits home Suzanne had felt superior to her friends even though they had houses and cars and she lived on the third floor of what one of the few of them who travelled east had called a boarding house.

It wasn't a boarding house, it was a townhouse cut into apartments, and it was an apartment much envied by her Toronto friends. It galled Suzanne that her sophistication, her interesting job, the artists and homosexuals she knew only made the old crowd feel sorry for her. And it galled her more that their pity affected her, that she *minded* if in their eyes she was not making a success of her life.

But now they were over thirty and surely the self-consciousness had gone. Moving home, living here had put Suzanne in a sentimental frame of mind; she wanted to find those old friendships. Not Gemma, however. Gemma was the only other one who had not married, Gemma had various scandalous liaisons with other people's husbands. People would try to team her up with Gemma. Exactly for that reason she had no interest in Gemma.

"She'd love to hear from you."

"Maybe I'll get a chance when I've finished unpacking," she said. She'd been close to her mother, always, but since she'd arrived home she was constantly irritated by her. "Look," she said angrily, "I tried the only person I cared about and it didn't work." She put down the phone, her stomach churning.

She walked over to the dormer window which made an alcove in her living room. She was a tenant in the attic of the kind of old house she had grown up in. The house had been painted and papered and divided into "heritage" apartments, although only fifteen years had passed since she left. Surely things happened too quickly in this town. Everything was a mistake, including the apartment. It had reminded her of a Toronto apartment, that was why she had taken it. But in Calgary it didn't seem so choice; it made her feel as if she couldn't afford anything better.

From the window she could see over to the riverside park where she and Lyall and Joey had played kick the can on long summer evenings. The light lasted until ten o'clock, sometimes later, and their voices had carried in the twilight with what seemed even then to be a sorrowful timbre. They had hated having to go in after dark. One night they arranged to sneak out and come back to the park at two in the morning.

It had been her idea, more daring than she understood, at fourteen or fifteen. Joey had come into the yard and knocked softly on the window of her room, which was off the rumpus room. She had met him in the side alley, and they had walked in the middle of the empty road all the way there. The park was gloriously dark, the dew forming. They set out across the damp grass; they could see a red light over by the trees. As they came closer they could make out Lyall, his bicycle upside down, spinning the wheels, and the reflector glowing.

They came together breathless, uncertain of what to do. Away from the houses and the street the dark settled around them and became transparent, like a day from which all else had fled. They had never seen the middle of the night, outside, before. Their parents would kill them if they found out they were gone. It became necessary to do something to make this meeting worthy of its attendant risks.

They walked in single file between birches which looked a painted white, and found a picnic table, the kind made of heavy planks with benches attached. They'd spent an hour moving it twenty feet over to the bank. Then they had pushed it over so that it splashed into the water. They watched it bob up on an angle, like a bottle, and float away, and then they went home.

It was for such pranks that Lyall and Joey got the name of the bad boys. Lyall whined and had asthma attacks and endless enthusiasm for crime; Joey was blond and chubby and could carry anything off. In their grade five class Suzanne had laughed when he threw wads at the teacher but when he went to the principal's office to get the strap she remained demurely in her front seat. From shame, she had not dared look at him when he swaggered back down the aisle, after. "Twenty times," he whispered. "She drew blood, but I never even winced. I told her it hurt her more than it hurt me. Then she cried."

You couldn't get Joey by punishing him; he'd been punished so often, bearing it had become a badge of courage. What Joey did for Suzanne was to tell her about the things he did, the things she didn't dare do. He stole and he drank and he spied on the adults. He knew whose father had dirty books and whose mother was drunk in the afternoon and who gave the black eye to the woman who worked in the corner store. Suzanne relied on him to explain these things.

By high school, Joey had turned out fat and aggressive. In grade ten his parents gave him an Italian motorbike, blue. The next year he had a car. After the graduation dance he was speeding along Elbow Drive at four in the morning; neither Lyall or Suzanne was with him then, they had new friends. The car went out of control and crashed into a telephone pole, and he was dead.

Dead, just like that. Even for a bad boy, death seemed an extreme punishment. Word got around the neighbourhood by noon the day after. Suzanne was sent across the lane to express condolences to Joey's mother. It was a brilliant sunny noon. The woman was lying on the sofa in the den with the drapes closed, eating chocolates from a box. When Suzanne said she was sorry, Joey's mother just looked at her. "What do you think you're doing," she said, "walking around here alive?"

Suzanne left the house and walked home through the back lane. There was the place where the bad boys had tied her to the fencepost, back in grade six. She leaned on the post and cried. She didn't see Joey these days, but she still felt as if he explained the world to her. She wanted to know what he would have said about the pain, this time. "The glass stuck into my neck, my guts went all over the wheel, God reached in the window and took away my licence?"

That was how he might describe it, but how would he explain it? When he first got his scooter, Joey had sat in this very lane, his short, fat legs in khaki trousers spread over the egg-shaped motor. "I can drive faster than anyone else," he said, "because I don't care what happens to me. That makes it easy."

"But I care what happens to you," Suzanne had said.

He nodded, but she could see it didn't make any difference. She had not understood him; then she had not wanted to be his friend. But now, when he was gone, she saw. He was doing what the characters did in short stories, their teacher said, he was giving out clues which only the ending would explain. Suzanne went home then and told her mother that Joey had warned her ahead of time that he was going to die. Her mother had taken her in her arms.

"People often seem to do that," her mother had said, "especially those who die young."

Die young? Suzanne had thought. But youth was not the issue. She had not yet accepted that they would all die sometime; she was shocked that Joey had died at all, that he had left the world rather than his boyhood.

Suzanne turned away from the view. The dishes were still in the sink, but she bent and began to unpack books. Starting one thing before finishing another had become a problem. She picked up a copy of *The Sun Also Rises*. English 383, 1968. On other campuses there were fee strikes and computer burnings but in Calgary it was still raccoon coats and team pennants, Jumping Jack Flash at the beer bashes. At a basketball game the cheerleaders were pushed off the floor by a gang of scraggy girls wearing gas masks and yelling about insults to women. It was during a discussion of this very book that Suzanne's professor had invited his students to lie down on the floor and touch each other.

She did it, wanting to giggle, at first. But from that prone position, and hands crisscrossed over her body, she had looked into the ceiling, and through it, and had realized that everything, everything was going to be very different than what she expected.

Suzanne dropped Hemingway, and pawed through the box, coming upon old Norton anthologies, editions of Shakespeare's plays, her frosh beanie, the gift spoon from a fraternity formal. She had walked out of the classroom that day, telling the professor that encounter was not for her. How did it happen then that the rest of them turned out normal, and she had gone away? Should she have lain down and let them touch her?

Anyway it did no good to carry all this stuff around with her. All the way east, and in and out of those third floors. Now she'd brought it all home again and she couldn't throw it out. Anyway she might reread things, and catch what she seemed to have missed the first time.

In 1968 Suzanne had been living with three other girls in a rented bungalow across from Motel Village, ten minutes from the campus. That fall there was a sudden frost while the leaves were still green and the birches had turned a full, fantastic orange. Lyall came up beside her one day and drew a marijuana cigarette out of his pocket. Suzanne remembered distinctly that she was annoyed; she was wearing knee socks and penny loafers and thought she would be immune to this. But Lyall was insistent. He drew long experienced breaths and didn't talk in between. "Something to tell you," he gasped.

They walked along the highway passing the cigarette back and forth. Suzanne felt nothing, and figured he was acting. He came into her house. One of her roommates had hung a poster of a maharishi on the living room wall. Lyall put his face up to the paper and began to count the tiny dots that made the colour. "I got my guitar run over in Banff," he said. "I threw it in front of a truck and the splinters flew out like arrows." He began to cry. Suzanne understood that he was missing Joey, and she comforted him. Perhaps he was trying to be Joey.

It was nearly a year later that her mother called to say that Lyall had come back from California very sick. She said they had found him in the park by the river, digging a hole. He had said he was trying to bury the bad Lyall. Suzanne's mother thought that was a crazy thing, she repeated it, a crazy thing. "We never called him bad," she said.

Suzanne went to visit him in the psychiatric ward. He entertained her rather grandly, bringing out his beadwork, and some poems. His face was fat because he was being treated with drugs. As far as Suzanne knew, none of it did him any good. Two things happened to him there; he met Bonnie, and he lost control of his mind. Bonnie was a nurse. She kept telling him he was going to be fine, and the more she told him, the more he told terrible stories. Boundaries seemed to have broken down in his mind; he bled words, awful words, private words. Suzanne particularly hated it when he told her how sexy Bonnie was and how she let him do this and that but not the other.

When he got out he took other drugs. He told Suzanne he could see the curvature of the earth, when he looked into the distance, and that once, in a public washroom on Banff Avenue he had seen his own dead face. He went back into the hospital. The shock treatments were an unusual choice, but the family was impatient; they wanted him cured, quickly. Shocks, Bonnie told Suzanne brightly, were meant to eradicate certain bad memories that were depressing him. When he came out he was soggy, like a log which had begun to burn but had been doused with water.

When Bonnie and Lyall were married there were three bridesmaids, each with a different floral print in her dress. After the ceremony, the guests danced on the patio of Lyall's family's house, in front of the tennis court. All of the old neighbours were there. Even Joey's mother was there, healed up, sealed up, drinking a lot of champagne. You'd never have known that anything had changed since the children were really children.

Suzanne stacked the books neatly on the floor beside the boxes. None of them had taught her what she needed to know. She was not giving up on them, but she wasn't sure if she wanted them in the room. There must be a book somewhere that said how you were supposed to feel when you were no longer young, but you were not yet dead; when something illegitimate, something you were never meant to have in the first place, like endless youth, or another woman's man, was taken away from you. She had never found such a book. She went back to the kitchen sink. The water was murky and cool.

She had seen Lyall only twice between his wedding day and today. The first time was when she came home to visit after she tried telling the married man she wouldn't see him again. Bonnie and Lyall had lived further out then, near Chinook Mall. The two women, never friends, walked on a frozen patch of grass by the children's skating rink. Suzanne fought disdain for Bonnie; it was not the decade for being a housewife. Bonnie sensed it. "The children need me, Lyall needs me," she said defensively. "But I always know I can do fine on my own if anything happens to him."

Suzanne resented that. The implication was that Lyall was fragile, or spoiling, and she would not betray him by believing it. But later he came to her city, alone. She had gone back to seeing the married man then, and was in love. Lyall talked about racing a motorcycle. He talked about going back to the land, about making films. Suzanne was mystified by these urges: what was it he so desperately needed to express? She couldn't remember anything original in him, even before his treatments.

In a hotel bar done up to resemble a library, Lyall drank a good deal. The stories began to come, as she had known they would. Once, he claimed, he had made Bonnie drive him miles over back roads, forcing her to get out every few miles so he could hit her. The way he got her to do it was by telling her he would kill her if she didn't, he confessed with a giggle.

Like a lot of things Lyall had said, the boast seemed only half true, but the truth and the lie mixed became doubly depressing. Suzanne sat there wondering what Joey would have done, if he'd lived. Joey might have become a middle-aged wife beater, and she would have hated him. But he was too smart for that, he had understood all of this from the beginning, and that was why he said he hadn't cared. He had cared, only his caring had taken the form of recklessness inviting death.

It was frightening, how she longed for Joey all these years. Lyall was a poor substitute. Back in her apartment she stared at the wall where the old plaster cracked in a jagged line between the windows. If Lyall wasn't crazy then he must be sane. First she pitied Bonnie and then she blamed her. Then she decided she'd never see either of them again.

But now she had come home. She put the last of the dishes up and let the water run out of the sink. She paced the apartment from one side to the other. There seemed to be nowhere to sit. She'd never bothered much with furniture. Maybe now that she was home for good she would start buying things.

She began kicking the empty cartons toward the stairs. She kicked them hard, and liked the noise. So much of her had been kept in, waiting. The affair was over. Her twenties were over, her escape was over. She had come home and she had been reduced to needing Lyall, Lyall who had always needed her and Joey so much more.

What she thought about then was Lyall's drugs, Lyall's shock treatments, Lyall's rushed cure. She had never dared to ask him how much he had forgotten. What she wanted to ask him today was if he remembered the night they stole the park bench, the way it looked, bobbing silently eastward in the river. The carpet, the kids, and Bonnie had stopped her. And then the look on his face, when she poured her tea in the plant. He had forgotten it, at least forgotten the wonder of it. Forgotten all but some vestige. She was with the bad boy in his memory in some small way, a rustle under the bushes, a flicker in deep darkness, just enough to bring that twitch of fear to his face.

Suzanne was standing at the window, crying. Please let me have a friend here, let me have a life here, she thought. How had the past been taken away? Had the shocks done it, or the drugs administered later; perhaps the sweetness of Bonnie had done it. It could have been nothing more sinister than time, the natural death of brain cells. There were deaths and more deaths. This memory died fifteen years ago with Joey, and then again, later, in Lyall. That meant she was the only person who kept it. And that would be all right, she decided, wiping her eyes. She had a feeling she was going to live a long, long time.

Elisabeth Harvor

How Will I Know You?

W
hen she stood in the doorway to his cubicle one cold
and sunny Monday morning in early spring, feeling
newly shiny and slim and reading him some of the winning
entries from a *Globe and Mail* contest for invented mistakes that
drunken or incompetent sign-painters might make—HAZ-
ARDOUS FOOTBATH, SMALL APARTMENT FOR RUNT, HOSPITAL
NOT RESPONSIBLE FOR YOUR LONGINGS—he laughed, looking
with surprised alertness into her eyes, and then just before noon,
on his way past her desk, he dropped a note on her letter tray
while she was talking on the phone to a friend who worked in a
bookstore two blocks south of the park. She kept trying to read
the note while she was listening to her friend go on and on about
a mad customer—mad as in deluded—and finally felt she had no
choice but to interrupt her to say that someone from down the
hall had just stopped by to dump an incredibly complex-looking
document on her desk and she was going to have to hang up so
she could try to deal with the damn thing before lunchtime. And
feeling a little guilty but excited—no, no, no, not feeling guilty at

all *and* excited—she said a rushed goodbye to her friend and picked up the note to at last give it her passionate attention:

Memo to Marianne,

On my way through the park this morning I spotted a hazardous footbath (it has a fountain in the middle of it, which has very sensibly decided to spout wine, not water) and it occurred to me that we might give it a try one of these balmy spring noontimes, and then after we've been to the hospital for emergency treatment for intoxication we might catch sight of a sign saying HOSPITAL NOT RESPONSIBLE FOR YOUR LONGINGS and at this point we might stop to ask ourselves: If the *hospital* is not responsible for our longings, then who *is*? Am I? Are you?

                                                                                Farley

P.S. Please meet me for lunch today, twelve sharp, so that we can discuss this matter.

She noticed that he'd erased a word before writing "intoxication" over it. The erased word was "alcoholism." It made her feel happy that he was using the sign-makers' jokes to escalate the already intoxicated feelings between them. It was as if the sign-makers had, without knowing it, become matchmakers. Personal matchmakers to two people they didn't even know and would never know. She was also relieved that he hadn't mentioned the apartment for runt, partly because while reading the runt sign to him she had all at once heard it as "apartment for rut," but also because she had felt embarrassed for his sake since he happened to be really quite extraordinarily short.

On the way to the restaurant, though, sitting on one of those pelts of wooden beads that drivers throw over the driver's seat to ward off back pain, he looked tall. He had the chest and the powerful neck of a much bigger man. Seated, he was majestic, protectively attentive. But then she had never been one to look down on men who were short—she was tiny herself—and had often even preferred them; had in fact often found them to be braver and more scrappy than the men who towered.

At the restaurant she drank five glasses of wine to his one (but he was driving) and on the way back to the office he played her a tape of "So Long, Marianne"—she was touched that he owned it and even dared to wonder if he had bought it because of her—and then he sang along with "You're really such a pretty one, I see you've gone and changed your name again ..." which made them both smile because she really *had* gone and changed her name, but only the spelling of it, from the prim Mary Ann to the more sexually sweet Marianne, and after they'd pushed their way through the revolving doors of their building—PLEASE USE REVOLTING DOORS, one of the *Globe* contestants had written—he said goodbye to her at the door to her office and then whispered, "So long, Marianne," in a way that really seemed to be saying "Hello, Marianne, hello, hello, hello, hello...." But it really and truly was goodbye, as it turned out, because he called in sick every day the rest of the week and then the following week went on vacation with his wife and sixteen-year-old daughter, and on his return it was clear that he had spent at least part of his holiday perfecting a heartbreakingly friendly smile with no emotion at all in it. It was at this same time that insomnia moved permanently into her bed, to spend all of the hot summer nights with her. But why? When almost nothing had happened, or had had time to happen? The answer, to Marianne at least, was perfectly clear: because it took no time at all to have everything happen in the heart—ways they would touch each other, a whole life together.

But then she told herself that she didn't really want to have to go to all the trouble of arranging her life to allow another person to come into it. Why squander, she would think, her sweet evenings of solitude? And once her children were safely asleep in their beds, she would sink into a deep chair with a magazine or a novel, having already reached over to the phone to take its receiver off the hook. She would only lift it up now and then to check to see if there was a message for her on her call-answer service. The times she got a dial tone would be almost hilariously humbling—that she was going to such extreme lengths not to be reached when in fact no one in the whole world was trying to reach her.

But she continued to have trouble sleeping, and one hot day in August she walked over to the Sunshine Trading Company to buy a box of Sleepytime Tea and a tall bottle of tablets made from hops and valerian. She also picked up a copy of a local holistic newspaper called *Vital Signs*. The signs, she saw, leafing quickly through its pages while waiting in line for her turn to pay for her pills, were both astrological and medical. It also just so happened that in this particular issue a man named Ray Fennimore, the paper's resident herbalist, had devoted his entire column to sleeplessness. According to Ray, the causes and cures were complex and varied. He used a wide variety of herbs in his treatments, but had also incorporated into his medical game plan "several other modalities." *If you would like to see Ray for a private consultation*, said the italics at the bottom of his column, *call Gandee Falls 613-762-8903.*

From the phone in her office, Marianne called Gandee Falls

and Ray answered. He had a fine voice, musical and thoughtful. They talked for nearly fifteen minutes, mainly about herbs for sedation. "I think I'd really have to see you, though, to sift through all the possibilities of your case."

She asked him what the charge would be.

"Sixty-five dollars per consult. But you have to bear in mind that we'd be talking on the generous side of an hour."

She asked about buses, how long it would take to get out to Gandee Falls.

"A little over an hour." And then a shorter local bus trip out into the country. About twenty minutes. "But listen, if we can settle on a date right now, I can arrange to drive in to the depot to meet you."

She thanked him for his kindness. "I could get time off work a little after two on Friday afternoon."

He said good, there was a bus in at three-forty-five. "How will I know you?"

She said she would carry a copy of *Vital Signs*.

Friday was a perfect clear day, ruffled by hopeful breezes, and Marianne, in spite of the weeks of almost no sleep, took pleasure in the trip to Gandee Falls as the bus passed through all the green and surreal country towns. Travelling by public transportation was also superbly relaxing—back in the days when she was still married to Gary they used to get into terrible fights in the car, and one Sunday morning when they were on their way to have lunch with friends who lived north of Kleinburg, Gary had flown into a rage because she had brought along a small picnic of carrot sticks and almonds wrapped up in foil. Also a banana. Which he had knocked out of her hand as she was beginning to peel it, with the consequence that when it had started rolling around down on the floor of the car she'd used an angry sandalled foot to mash it into a gritty purée and then scooped it up to paw on the front of his shirt. While he'd been craning away from her, trying to ward off the purée, the car had drifted across the median line and he'd had to fight it back to the right side again—the whole careen a desperate episode in which they had just narrowly managed to miss getting themselves killed.

There was no one waiting for her at the bus depot in Gandee Falls.

She looked at her watch. "Are we in early?" she asked the driver.

On the contrary. Five minutes late.

Had Ray Fennimore already been and gone? Marianne pulled *Vital Signs* out of her bag to glance at his picture again and saw for the first time that he looked a little unreliable and moody. His long black hair looked lankly dull and unkempt. But she told herself to keep calm. In all likelihood he would arrive any minute. She pictured him wearing a Peruvian poncho and Gandhi glasses. Gandhi glasses in Gandee Falls. The studious herbalist. She walked past a row of men sitting on a bench, taking in the scene, then made her way out to the front of the depot.

She stood waiting in the hot sun and tried to hold her face in an attitude of attractive repose. She could see several churches: a nearby yellow one with black trim, and three modest white ones—country churches that had somehow found their way into town—and several blocks to the left of the depot a tan clapboard cathedral dwarfed by a massive greystone real cathedral perched on a high hill of parks and organized gardens. As for the air, it was clear, almost country air, but at the same time it seemed sad—seemed to smell of ice cream and controlled sorrow. And the town's children, in their laundered pastel overalls and perfectly pressed pale little shirts, also somehow managed to give off an air of having been raised in an atmosphere of criminal neglect. The town didn't even seem to be a town in Ontario, it was too dry and church-dominated and hilly and sad, and wherever the falls of Gandee Falls were falling, they were falling nowhere nearby.

After fifteen minutes of waiting and of not daring to go inside to look for a phone in case she should miss him, Marianne found a pay phone beside the Ladies Room and phoned Fennimore's number.

But the line was busy.

She went outside again, into the hot wind, and this time she looked to the right, toward a used-car lot and back again toward the yellow church whose square steeple gave it a lonely and squat Baptist look.

Three minutes later she was back inside the depot again, back at the phone.

This time she got him.

"Oh Christ," he said. "I just totally forgot." And then he told her that he was expecting company for a sit-down dinner at six o'clock and that he'd have to somehow work in the consultation with her before the company came.

"How long do you think it'll take you to get into town?"

But he must have forgotten this part of the arrangement as well because after a startled pause he said he would come right away. "Be there in twenty minutes. Wait out at the front."

While Marianne was standing out on the sidewalk with the hot wind blowing in her hair, a car pulled in beside her. "Need a lift somewhere?"

The driver was young, with long shining black hair and dark wire-rimmed glasses, and so for a confused moment she mistook him for Fennimore, concluding that it was out of apology that the herbalist was now making a lighthearted joke. "Mr. Ray Fennimore?" she asked him, opening the door and peering in.

The man grinned up at her, uneasy but jaunty.

"Sorry," she whispered, flustered. "I was expecting someone else."

Five minutes later another car. Another stranger. A ruined anxious boy's face on a man of forty. "Want a drive, sweetheart?"

She backed up and stood against the wall of the station. She lifted the copy of *Vital Signs* in front of her breasts and held it there tightly. People would think she was trying to convert them to some old-time religion. She was by this time feeling irritably morose, and in an embittered way even relieved to be alone, as if she had been stood up on a blind date by someone she'd already decided must be bizarrely unappealing. She thought of her children, and wondered if they'd got home from school yet. She had taped a note to the door of the fridge, telling them that she'd gone to Gandee Falls for an appointment and would be home no later than seven. Now she wished that she had also given them Fennimore's name and number. In case she was late getting back. In case they needed to reach her for some reason. She could go inside the station right now and go back to the pay phone and put in a call to them. But what if Fennimore arrived while she was away from her post? She didn't want to miss him, by now all she was wanting was to get out to his place and have the consultation in a hurry, get it over and done with.

Forty-five minutes had now passed and she was beginning to wish that she'd asked him to pick her up at a restaurant, she was nearly dying of hunger, she could have been eating an early supper while she was waiting for him to decide whether or not he was going to show up.

Or he won't come at all, she thought. Never planned to. By now putting nothing past him.

At a quarter past five, a battered station wagon pulled in

against the curb on the far side of the street and a big man with a grey brush cut got stiffly out. He looked straight at her. "Marianne?" he called over to her.

She crossed the street to him. She asked doubtfully, "Are you Ray Fennimore?"

"I guess I must look older than the picture in *Vital Signs*."

She was trying to hear if his voice still sounded musical and thoughtful. Not very, but she got into the car with him anyway, even though anxiety gripped her. Her mind was filled with only one thought: How could this person, at any time in his life, have been the dark young man in the photo? She saw that above his right ear he had a scar with an elongated halo of hairless skin around it. A war wound? But perhaps she only thought it was a war wound because it was shaped like a torpedo. And below his military haircut and scar, a face that suggested a well-groomed ruddy fury. She had also taken note of the fact that he'd said "the picture," not "*my* picture." There was also the puzzle of the car to unravel: it smelled so poisonous—of diesel oil and paint remover and spilled kerosene. Of ancient cigarette smoke too, and of old paint-spattered rags. Three lumpy sacks had been thrown onto the back seat. Beans, she thought. Or bodies! But it was no joke, the car was truly noxious, a toxic ruin. What kind of car was this for a herbalist?

But they were already driving south through Gandee Falls on their way out of the town. Very soon they would be coming to bungalows, woodlots, open country. She said in a voice that she tried to keep from sounding squeaky and small, "Do you sell food out at your herb place?"

He said no, only herbs.

She told him that she was going to be needing some food very soon, that she hadn't eaten a thing since early morning. But then a happy thought occurred to her. "Why don't we find a place to talk right here in Gandee Falls? You can talk and I'll eat, and that way we can save you the twenty minutes you'd waste driving me back into town again."

She saw by the perplexed look he threw her that he'd had no intention of driving her back into town. He said that eating in Gandee Falls was totally out of the question. "My wife and I are expecting six guests for a sit-down dinner at six o'clock and I promised to help out."

She wondered why he kept speaking, in tones of such solemn respect, of the sit-down dinner. Didn't people the whole world over sit down to eat? And at this, a mad (or possibly sane) thought occurred to her: the sit-down dinner was an invention. There was no wife, no dinner table, no casserole keeping warm on the back of the stove. There was no stove. Fennimore lived all alone in a shack out in the Ontario bush. Nothing in it but a phone and a typewriter and a few medieval bunches of dried herbs (looking like switches) and a collection of knives. She pictured the terrifying décor of the even deeper wilderness that would lie a mile or two behind his ill-equipped (or dangerously equipped) cabin: a clearing, and in the middle of it an old mattress and two or three discarded car seats uprooted like pulled teeth. This man, in all likelihood, wasn't even Fennimore at all, but Fennimore's deranged uncle or older brother. She began to feel a dread which was both a fear of circumstances and a fear that she would not properly defend herself in fearful circumstances. Which she knew meant that her terror was taking on a social dimension and so was managing to convert itself, with no help from her, into the kind of humiliation that made her feel she almost had no right to ask, "Would there be a market or a little store nearby where I could perhaps just quickly pick up some fresh fruit or something?"

He said no. Everything closed, closed down at five.

Hysteria rose in her. Hunger was making her feel lightheaded, deranged. She cried out in desperate (but small-voiced) outrage, "But I have to eat something! Isn't there a health food store somewhere around here that's still open? How can everything just shut down at five?"

Fennimore seemed to implode at this, wrenched the wheel hard left, then took off at a much greater clip through a series of streets and sidestreets that were curved or crooked. What was he doing? Heading even faster out of town, and by a confusing back way that she'd later never remember? They would get smashed up, and this was the very least of the bad things that would happen. "Where are we going?" she called out to him, trying to call out in a way that would not sound like crying out.

He shouted that they were going to a health food store—he did know of one place that might still be open. And very soon after this he did indeed make a violent turn into an alley where he had to slam on the brakes in order not to crash into a long collection of sheds not much bigger than cupboards.

He had parked behind what looked like the back of an old warehouse. He was furiously flushed and talking and breathing fast, his voice sour but urgent. "It's in there—it's called The Good Earth. Just walk down the plank between those two sheds and then hang a left. But make it snappy, we're working with an extremely tight schedule here."

She followed his directions and was surprised and above all intensely relieved to discover that the back of the shack she came into really was The Good Earth. She hurried along a dim aisle of vats and barrels to ask a girl down at the front for roasted sunflower seeds.

But the girl said that they were fresh out of the roasted. "We've got the raw, though."

But Marianne said she absolutely must have the roasted.

"You might try Herbie's Herbs, across the street and down that way just a wee bit. See the hanging sign with the tree on it?"

Marianne, out of breath, stood waiting for a chance to cross over to Herbie's Herbs. Cars drove by her with calm-looking people inside them. At last she was able to make her way through a clear space in the traffic and once she was inside Herbie's Herbs she shovelled a scoop of roasted sunflower seeds into a clear plastic sack. She was by now trembling with hunger, nearly tearful. She was also feeling frantic at the thought of keeping Fennimore waiting. If I don't hurry right back he'll be mad, she thought. She was feeling a bit dizzy, the armholes of her sleeveless blouse were limp with the damp of nervous perspiration. She pictured Fennimore drumming his fingers on his steering wheel, his face morbidly florid. He had lied to her too, telling her that everything closed down at five, and now she wasn't even able to find things, out of panic. The twist ties! She must be staring straight at them. Oh *there*, to the left of the spice jars. She reached one of them down and while she was twisting it around the neck of her little sack of seeds she remembered a story a friend had once told her, about a woman who'd accepted a drive from a man she had met at a picnic, and how when the driver refused to let her off at the corner of her street and had instead taken off at high speed for the highway, she'd opened his glove compartment and had methodically begun to float his bills and credit cards and postcards out the window—such a damning trail of identification that he'd had to skid to a stop, then throw himself out of his car at a run. And while he was running and stumbling along a deep ditch, cursing and searching like a bad giant in a fable for his lost possessions, the inventively methodical woman had fled. It occurred to Marianne that she must have been subconsciously recalling the clever-woman story while she was still in Fennimore's car because she now remembered that she'd noted that the door to his glove compartment had been removed, exposing a view of a roll of silver masking tape (wide enough to tape a mouth or a pair of eyes shut) and a heavy pair of pliers. Would she be able to make Fennimore slam on his brakes by tossing his pliers out the window? She didn't think so. But she simply must stop trying to frighten herself, the man was only unpleasant, after all, he was hardly a psychotic. And so she tried to think only practical thoughts. For instance, what else did she need? Yogurt! She hurried down to the wall of refrigerators at the back of the store, picked out a blueberry one, half-quart size, squinted up at the wall for plastic spoons. They'd be up at the front, but knowing this didn't keep her from peeking into each of the side aisles, just in case the spoons should magically appear. But no. And she should go to the organic fruit counter too, get herself an orange.

But the oranges looked battered and mouldy, and she instead picked out two nectarines. Her stomach was swarming with panic at the thought of how Fennimore's rage must be building out in the hot smelly car and so she said in a quick worried voice to the clerk up at the cash register, "Do you have any spoons?"

"Right here," said the young woman. Her eyes were shrewdly kind and she had poked what looked like ebony chopsticks into a chignon at the top of her springy fair hair. She reached to her left to extract a plastic spoon from a clutch of spoons that had been shoved into a pink pottery mug.

"Oh good," said Marianne. But she was feeling swimmy and damp up in the top of her own head, as if she might need to faint or throw up. "I'm in a bit of a hurry, actually, so I guess I'd better pay for these things quickly."

Her hands shook as she pulled the money out of her wallet, and when she glanced up she saw that the cashier was looking truly concerned for her. What a lovely kind face the young woman had! As if a life spent living in a small town had made her clairvoyant. Marianne felt a mad desire to say to her, "I think I might be in some kind of trouble, I wonder if you could advise me—"

But that's perfectly silly, said the prim voice of her upbringing.

This Ray Fennimore writes a fine column on herbs for a health magazine, he's merely a bit cross with his wife because of the (much) aforementioned sit-down dinner, he's merely a bit of a passive aggressive, and she started to go toward the front door of the store so that she could cross the street to make her return to the other store and walk through its dim length to hurry back to the dusty back alley and Fennimore's car.

She had almost reached the big bins at the front when she turned back to the young woman. The thought struck her that God had arranged for her to be given a second chance, that God had arranged for The Good Earth to be strategically out of what she was wanting in order to get her beyond the magnetic field of Ray Fennimore and his toxic car and a darker fate. At this revelation, she spoke imploringly to the cashier. "I just realized something: I have to get to the bus station right away. Do you know where I could pick up a cab in a hurry?"

And the young woman called to her with a voice that seemed to sing out with pure rescue, "Turn left, run eight blocks, bus leaves at five-twenty! But it's sometimes a bit late! And there's usually two or three cabs at the front of the Embassy Hotel! A tall brick building! Painted red!"

Marianne breathlessly thanked her, then ran with a pain in her side all the way to the tall red hotel.

There was a black cab lying in wait there, long gleaming black panther, engine idling. Marianne pulled its door open and flung herself into the back seat. "The bus station!"

But the cabby, who had the calm flaxen fairness she had always associated with farm boys, seemed disoriented, sleep-deprived himself. And the early evening traffic was by this time barely moving. He shook his head, as if trying to clear it. And as he nosed the car out into the street he said, "This has not been my week."

Marianne was still feeling frantic, and even kept turning to look over her shoulder in paranoid terror, she was so afraid that Ray Fennimore's green station wagon might now be tailing the cab. Still, she felt compelled to ask the driver in a dry social voice, "What was so bad about it?"

The cabby said that he came from a good Christian family, and that he wasn't a bigot, or at least not to the extent that his daddy was. "He hates people who are gay. Me, I try to be tolerant. But these last few days, ninety per cent of my trade has been individuals of an alternative sexual persuasion."

Now they were trapped behind an army truck whose tied-on brown canvas roof made Marianne think of an evil prairie schooner. Why doesn't he try to pass it, she thought. And then: Is he gay himself? Is this what he's working his way up to confessing? Or maybe he thinks I am.

"So then last night this guy gets into my cab and I say to him, 'So how are you this fine evening?' And he—"

Now the military truck was moving very slowly ahead, almost asphyxiating them with its military fumes.

"Could we maybe try to get past these guys?"

"Got his blinkers on, but we should be able to shake him in a minute or two. Anyway, then this guy says to me, 'Totally shitty,' and so I go, 'Anything I can do to make you feel better?' And he goes, 'Thanks for the offer, buddy, but you just haven't got the sum of the parts,' and so then I decide that's *it*"—he slapped the steering wheel for effect as he said this—"I've *had* it, and I slam on the brakes and I go, 'Get outta my cab,' and he goes, 'Why? Because I'm *gay*?' and I go, 'No, because you're an *asshole.*'"

Gandee Falls, thought Marianne—town of short fuses, but now she could at last see the square-steepled yellow church with its four tiny black spires pointing up like four petrified wicks and so knew that they must be getting close to the depot.

And now she could see worse: the bus she'd arrived on was just taking off, backing in its bland and stone-deaf way out of the station. She whimpered at the cabby, crying, "Please please please please *please* let me catch that bus," and tossing a ten-dollar bill at him, she pushed open the door and half fell onto the hard ground, but then right away stumbled up to run to the backing-up bus, banging with her crying fists on the doors until the driver let her in.

As the bus was moving out of town, Marianne dumped the sunflower seeds into the yogurt and then began to feed herself rapidly, wolfing down her food with the miniature spoon. In a rage beyond rage, Fennimore might manage to smash up all on his own, on the way home to his dinner. Was possibly even already dead or dying. She leaned back against the bristly plush of the bus seat and tried to feel guilt but couldn't seem to manage it. But then she also imagined a quite different scenario: she was driving out into the country with Fennimore and the trip was uneventful, but the evening at his house was a social embarrassment because he was barely bothering to take the time to talk to her about herbs, being too busy pouring glasses of wine for his friends. Then she pictured herself alone once again and standing on a deserted strip of highway just within sight of Fennimore's place (by now a Victorian stone mansion on a grim rise in a grove of dark trees) and this time she was waiting for the local bus into Gandee Falls but she kept having to step back whenever a car with a man wearing dark glasses would swerve in, its driver rolling down his window to call out and ask her if she was wanting a lift. But then another possibility occurred to her: Fennimore hadn't bothered to wait for her at all. Within five seconds of her disappearing into The Good Earth he was off.

That, she decided, is the real story. And she imagined herself telling it to a friend or to some of the people at work, a cautionary tale about her trip out into the deranged country, the short wild ride with the psychotic herbalist. She even had a punch line for it. A punch line that could double as a premonition. But it was a premonition that would come true only if she didn't allow herself to believe in it: That night she slept.

And in fact that night, after the children were in bed and she had taken the phone off the hook so that Fennimore couldn't call her up and accuse her, she did sleep, and with nothing to help her but a cup of Sleepytime Tea. She lay awake only long enough to recall the first few moments following her return home and how she had gone to the living-room doorway to ask her children if they'd been worried about her and how after a very long pause—the pause that it seemed to her all adolescent children must reserve for their parents (the pause in which they seem forever to be deciding that they might not have the strength to answer at all)—her oldest daughter, dressed all in black and sitting with one long booted black leg hanging over the arm of the big cane chair by the far window, had called out in an amused voice, "No! *Should* we have been?"

Toward morning Marianne dreamed that she was driving at a great clip through sunlit mountains on a crowded bus with no driver. Then she was in a car with a man who was an expert driver even though he seemed to be in a coma, he was so deeply asleep. A puffy calm sleeping man in a grey raincoat. She felt she must get him to wake up and so pulled at his sleeve until he opened his eyes. But once he was awake, he began to weave drunkenly, still infected by sleep—for a moment he was even Farley, but then she wasn't even with him any more, she was living in a tower with her three children, and then she was opening her bedroom window to see that there was a telephone hooked outside in the bright sunlight, on the outside brick wall of her neighbour's fifth-floor corner apartment. A phone that only a fireman could use. A fireman or an angel. "But how convenient," she said to herself, still lulled as she was by the impenetrable logic of the country of dreams.

Joyce Marshall

Blood & Bone

Because Fran's new job, as executive director of a small avant-garde filmmaker's guild, was reported briefly in several newspapers, her daughter, unnamed by Fran, called (and this was the first jolt) Shirlene by her adoptive parents, was able to get in touch with her. Luckily Fran was alone in her office when the call came through. With an extraordinary sense of lightness and disconnection, as if her new desk, the still unassimilated view of scabbed warehouse walls and perfunctory trees, even the chair she sat on, were falling away from her and she was floating, Fran listened to that first question. "Does 22 May, 1963, mean anything to you?" then a rattle of half-coherent speech in the same odd, scraped little voice, about how the girl (Shirlene) had obtained Fran's surname, McDiarmid (which she mispronounced), from the Children's Aid Society, had been calling people, talking to Parent Finders, for six months. And would catch the next bus from Ottawa, had she explained that part, she was up there studying at Carleton, and would be in Toronto by—

"I have a better idea," Fran said, her first utterance, it occurred to her, since she'd admitted (in words she could no longer remember) her connection with that day in 1963. As Shirlene must realize, things were a bit hectic at the moment, there'd be only odds and ends of time. But as it happened, she had to be in Ottawa herself next Monday, she'd fly up Friday night, Shirlene should come round for breakfast Saturday, call her from the lobby of the Lord Elgin at half past eight.

But she'd just spoken her name to the desk clerk Friday night when the hand touched her. She turned, met eyes—blue, level with her own, behind glasses—a wide smile.

"Yes," said the telephone voice, "it's me. I couldn't wait till tomorrow. I just couldn't. I've been standing here," the smile broadened, "since seven o'clock."

"Fine. I don't know about you but I could use a drink. The bar here's fairly pleasant. A bit mixed as to clientele but a shade less cheerless than the rooms. Suppose you grab us a table while I—"

"Oh, I don't drink," the girl said, and Fran realized what gave the voice its queer, pinched sound. It was strained through that smile.

"Coffee then? Because I'm afraid that if you're a herb-tea freak—"

The girl said that she could drink ordinary tea. "When I have to," she added.

"We'll go down to the restaurant then. It's Murray's, isn't it? Well, *faute de mieux*." The smile made no response. Fran was about to say more about the rooms, the clattery air-conditioning that, as she recalled, couldn't be turned off, then realized that there was no way to explain that what she wanted, needed even, was padding, at least for the first while.

She finished registering, conscious of those eyes upon her back, left the girl, who'd trailed her to the elevator, in the hallway, still smiling that set but excited smile.

The room was as dingy as she'd expected. There was no time

to arrange her thoughts, as she'd planned to do tonight in the strange room, or even redo her face, though it too, she thought, could use padding. The girl was so clearly impatient. Why do I keep calling her the girl? she wondered. Because my daughter was airy, light; whenever I could let myself think of her she was running. And the girl waiting downstairs was bulky, big, rosy and freckled, with sand-textured, sand-coloured hair in lumpy curls.

All week since the call had come, she'd found herself examining the young women filmmakers who came into the office—an anorexic crew, their hair lank or spiky around pinched little faces. Like that one? she'd ask herself. Like that one? And last night, lying beside Terence, the radio talk-show host with whom she shared occasional nights, she'd felt so apprehensive (of that light, flitting creature, her abandoned daughter) that she'd almost confided in him. Terence knew about the child. She'd told him one night when they were both a little drunk. She wasn't sure why; he had been in one of his analytic moods and had ways of making her talk. She'd felt depressed about the collapse of her latest job with no substitute in sight. He'd said very little but since then she'd often noticed him examining her, deciding something, she thought, or perhaps just acknowledging something already decided.

She drew a comb through her newly cut, raggedy hair, yanked at her match-thin skirt. It hadn't occurred to her to dress in any special way but now she felt herself too tight, too stylish, trivial even. Well, *faute de mieux*, she thought, picked up her bag, and went down.

"I should warn you I may not be good at this." There were only half a dozen others in Murray's—so much for padding—and three waitresses loitering near the coffee station. "You'll make allowances?" She smiled nervously, meeting the girl's smile, forgot what she'd meant to say, was relieved when a waitress wandered over and she could order tea for Shirlene (who declined food), coffee and a sandwich she didn't want for herself. "You don't mind if I smoke while we wait? Though I'm afraid that even if you do mind—" Another attempt at lightness died against that smile. "How much do you know about me?" The smile, which seemed not to have changed unless to stretch wider, gave her no help.

"Then suppose I fill in the gaps. I'm 40 years old. Less a month. I was—am—an only child. I grew up in Toronto and, except for a few months in Sault Ste. Marie, for a purpose you know, I've always lived there. I was married briefly in my twenties but I didn't have any—any more children. So if you were hoping for swarms of new relatives—perhaps it's just as well— I've noticed those mammoth reunion scenes in the papers, people one wouldn't want to have anything to do with. True, there's my mother—my father died five or six years ago—but she's old, I think on the whole—" She thought of her mother's face, pouched and draggy now, beginning to be less the face of the abrupt, nervous woman who'd always been able to find cracks in her, becoming simply the face of an old person. But still able to hurt.

"So what else?" Fran said. "I have a fairly useless BA, artistic inclinations but no corresponding talents, so I've worked at various jobs on the fringes of the arts, organized film festivals and arts conferences, been executive director of this and that. I seem to enjoy helping groups get on their feet. But they're usually sickly and can't walk very well or far; the present one's limping already, I'm afraid. And if they can walk I lose interest. But apart from that tendency to chop and change I don't think there are any serious—" She was afraid to look up, in case the smile had become fixed again and she'd smile inanely in return. "Isn't that what you wanted? To find out about—" While I've sat here being myself—deprecating, rueful—the self, let's face it, that I put on when I'm trying to charm someone. "Or do you want me to explain why I gave you up? I hadn't any choice. Honestly, I hadn't."

"Oh, I forgave you for that," the girl said. "I forgave you ages ago."

"Did you? Then I'm glad." Surprised too by something, almost an indulgence in the flat, rather blurred voice. "Well, I'm curious even though you don't seem to be. Do you still live in the Soo? When you're not at Carleton?"

"I don't even remember the Soo," the girl said. "The folks moved to Toronto when I was two. We have our own home in East York."

"And do you have a good relationship with—your folks?"

"Yes. I was lucky. They're good Christian people. They gave me a good Christian upbringing in a good Christian home."

Fran waited but there was no more. And she had no right to prod. "Do they know about this?" she asked and, when the girl shook her head, "Shouldn't you have told them?"

"They've always said I shouldn't intrude on your life, that forgiveness was between you and the Lord Jesus, so as long as I prayed for you and they prayed for you—"

"I see." She used to make them up in various ways, especially at the beginning, because, though she couldn't risk imagining the child too clearly, she'd needed a picture of them—the Madonna mother, slow, gentle-moving, the strong father swinging the child onto his shoulder. Far away in a city of which she'd seen little except that church-sponsored refuge and the hospital. And now she didn't have to imagine them. The "home" in East York is a tacky little bungalow, she thought, the man sells shoes in Eaton's, they feel threatened by the "Pakis" they see on the subway (but nowhere else), their speech is flat and loose, they drop their g's, they'd despise women like me if they had any notion that we existed. And they hadn't even known what to feed her. The flush on the girl's cheeks wasn't from health, as she'd believed; the skin was scaly, chapped. And her teeth, though white, were thin-looking, fluted.

The girl, she saw, was watching her. Her eyes, of so light a blue they seemed flat, intent above the smile. "I guess I must look like him," she said. "My father."

So that's what it was, a simple search for resemblance, anchoring. "I've been thinking about that too," Fran said. "I can't see that you look much like either of us." Like Chat's other daughters perhaps, she thought. There'd been a picture on his office desk—two not-quite-blonde girls with doughy faces, clumsy mouths. Lumps, she'd thought, and blamed his wife.

"I hope you'll tell me his name," the girl said. "Though I can understand that you might not want even to think of him after he deserted you and all. But I'd like to—well, tell him—"

"That you forgive him too. Is that the whole point of this—?" She steadied her voice. "You're too late. By about six years. He's dead." She stirred the coffee that seemed to have appeared (and begun to cool) in front of her. "Hasn't it occurred to you that if either of us had felt a need for forgiveness we might have preferred to ask for it ourselves?"

"Oh, I hope you did. Often when I was praying for you I used to imagine you and him praying too."

"Well, I wasn't. And out of my knowledge of your father," words she'd never used, even in her mind the child had been wholly hers, "I'm ready to swear he wasn't either." The smile was so extended now it showed paleness inside the lips. "Tell me," Fran said, "what made you decide to go against your folks and forgive me in person?"

The girl looked down, flushed. When her eyes came up, they were brilliant. With tears. A few actual, slipping tears. "You see, a wonderful thing happened. I've been saved. You know, born again. Me and my three girlfriends, we were in my room, wondering how we could give our lives more meaning, when suddenly Our Lord spoke."

"In words? Never having had such an experience myself—"

"Well, we heard him. We all heard him. And vowed there and then to devote our lives to his service." The words tumbled now. "One of my three girlfriends writes these really great gospel songs and we all play guitar. So this summer after we graduate, we're going to go forth and preach the Word."

"Isn't that a bit presumptuous?" Fran said. "If you want to help people, aren't there other needs—hunger, injustice?"

"Oh, that's just social work. You don't have to be a Christian to do that. What we feel is we've been given a very precious thing and we must share it. So as soon as we've made everything right in our own lives, we're going to go out onto the street. Wherever two or three are gathered together." The smile was suddenly smug. "That's a prayer," she said.

"Yes, it's an Anglican prayer. 'There am I in the midst of them.' That's how it goes. I had a good Anglican upbringing. Not good enough for you and your folks perhaps or you and your friends. Damn it," for she'd identified the smile. She'd seen it on street corners, on the television screen. Anyone not lost beyond recall, it said, would be bound to agree with me. "How dare you forgive me and your—your father for something you know nothing about? I didn't see you after you were born. I heard you give a single, disconsolate wail. Then they took you away. The Children's Aid Society thought that was best. So did your father. He did as much for me, for us, as he could. He had other commitments. Children. So I had to go away to have you alone. I won't load it on you, the physical things, having my breasts bound to stifle the milk. I'd tell myself I'd done the right thing. Then I'd hear that crying, getting fainter as they carried you away. It went on for years. I'd hear it and ask myself how much of the crying was anger, how much grief." All through that first hungry, promiscuous time. Worse after she married Keith. She didn't tell him but he was far enough into his medical studies, he knew about women's bodies. And they were young, they couldn't handle it. Poor Keith, she thought, of whom I tried to ask too much. Another child. A life. Something to still the crying. Well, Keith was a prosperous urologist now, an unrepentant extra-biller; she sometimes ran into his wife on arts committees. "So that's what your sinful mother was doing," Fran said, "while you and your folks were praying for her. She was listening to her daughter crying."

Shirlene had neglected to take away her smile. Tears were sliding down her cheeks. "Oh, I didn't know," she said.

"No, of course you didn't. How could you?" Fran said. "But, please. Don't cry. I didn't mean to—"

"Fornication was bad enough but now you tell me it was adultery." She sobbed.

"Damn those people! They made you feel guilty."

"No. No, they didn't. You're wrong. They're not like that. They said it wasn't my fault. They said it and said it." She sniffed weakly, groped for her bag. "I think I'll just go now."

To her born-again friends. People who used words like fornication and adultery and make an important distinction between them. They'll know how to console her.

Half turned away now, the girl was trying to reach round her glasses to mop at her eyes.

"You'll be back tomorrow, though?" Fran said. "For breakfast? As we arranged?"

"What's the use? You laugh at me and then you tell me things that make it all worse. It wasn't suppose to be like this."

"I'm sorry. I have a bad habit of levity. I warned you I mightn't be good at this. So please. Meet me in the lobby at 8.30. I may not know much about your Lord Jesus but I can't believe he'd want you to walk out on me just when I've found you."

Not that smile again, she begged. Not that wide, excluding, infinitely complacent stretching of the rather pulpy lips. But her daughter's face was sober as she said with a little catch, "Okay."

"She's not just yours," Chat said and snatched the child from her arms. All night she ran and couldn't run, at times light, a wisp she couldn't control, then heavy, rooted, listening to their laughter, always just ahead of her in brightness she could sense but couldn't see, would never see, she knew. It isn't fair, she thought, even said aloud, cried out, because no matter how hard she tried she would remain behind in shadow, empty.

"I'm going to tell you about your father." They'd had a cautious breakfast and taken the elevator to Fran's room. The rain that had been falling in silent streaks when Fran awoke at six o'clock was falling still. Fran had tried without success to turn off the noisy air-conditioning. The room smelled of regurgitated cigar smoke. "I didn't think I would but I've changed my mind," she said. Because you said, "It wasn't supposed to be like this?" Because Chat told me in a dream that it was all my fault, I'd let you be given to terrible people, placed an intolerable burden on his child? Or was that what he'd told her? She'd wakened, aware for the first time in years of the crying child. And of Chat's face and presence, which so seldom came back to her now; even on that drunken foolish night when she'd confided in Terence she'd had no real sense of him.

Perhaps if I tell it very simply, she thought, no irony, no words meaning more than they say, she'll realize there's no guilt she must assume. Or was it all more selfish? Having suffered for this girl, she must prove her worthy of the suffering.

"Can we leave the Lord Jesus out of it?" she said. "When I'm through, you can go off and pray or sing hymns on the street, anything you like."

"Okay." The girl was sprawled in the big chair, her jeans stretched to whiteness over her heavy thighs.

"I was eighteen," Fran said, "and had just finished high school. Your father was sixteen years older. His wife had taken their children to England and he was holed up in a friend's cottage on Georgian Bay, near where my parents had a summer place, working on a new course for the autumn; he taught at U of T. We met one day in a little cove near his place. My mother and I had reached the point with each other where I could scarcely breathe without enraging her, and as there weren't any young people my age, things were pretty tense except weekends when my father came up. So I'd take off after breakfast and spend all day at the cove. It was a marvellous place, half-hidden by an upthrust of rock with more rock in folds all around it—you know, that pinky grey granite, sprinkled with mica flecks—" though perhaps she didn't know; vacations to her folks probably meant two weeks at Wasaga Beach. What a snob I am, she thought. That's part of the trouble, the sense that she doesn't know any of the things, even the words I know.

"I'd dragged my canoe up into one of the folds," she said, "and was swimming around without my bathing-suit when your father came clambering down, stripped, anchored his clothes with a rock, tucked his glasses beneath them—that's one thing you got from him, you're shortsighted too, aren't you?—and waded in." The first man's body she'd seen—thick at belly and waist, ferned so surprisingly with hair—sharp against rock and astringent sky, then shimmering toward her in the water.

"He didn't see me till he was almost on top of me," she said. "I don't know which of us was more embarrassed. We swam around for ages, talking vaguely to show we weren't feeling awkward, looking firmly at each other's faces. The sun left the cove.

I was freezing so I said, 'Look, turn away so I can get out and when I'm dressed, I'll holler and turn away.'" Was that how it was? Idyllic, a bit simpleminded? I felt foolish. Outraged because he'd invaded my private place and wouldn't do anything to help me. Powerful in a strange way. Or is that true? How much do I remember? Oh, why did I start this? she thought. Speaking to myself as much as to her, not sure what I remember or don't remember.

"This part you must try very hard to understand." She glanced at the girl. Behind her the rain still plunged, darkening the room. The smile, which had flickered on and off during breakfast, was absent now. "He didn't seduce me," she said. "We were fifties people. I was a virgin. He'd married young." ("And one day there was this terrible thunderstorm," she heard her voice going drunkenly on to Terence. "We grabbed our clothes and ran and at some point—in the doorway, I think—we collided and it was thunder and lightning all over again.")

"It just seemed to come naturally," she said now. "Out of the place. Out of being together day after day. If anyone was at fault, it was me. I played the role of mystery girl from the deep. I wouldn't tell him my name or where I lived, and I pretended to be older. He couldn't see too well without his glasses. He was upset when he discovered I wasn't really 24." Appalled that what he must have thought of as a pleasant summer diversion had turned into a poor little ex-virgin weeping and snuffling in his borrowed bed. And I hated him, hated sex, hated everything about it. And two days later I was back at the cove, terrified that he wouldn't want to make love to me again. I felt obsessed, half-crazed by my changing moods of wanting and not wanting, dreading and longing. He must have been as obsessed as I was because he never sent me away.

"We used to spend hours in the water together," she said. Laughing as we dove round and over each other. And the cold shock of his penis the time he swam over me and took me while we were swimming. We did have our bold, lovely times. He said he'd remember that till he died—did you, Chat?—and I clung to him gulping, half drowned and laughing. "I used to feel beautiful," Fran said, "as I never did before or since." Because I never again had an academic lover with quotations for every occasion. Shakespeare, Marvell, Donne. It all spilled down on me.

"So that's what you came from." The girl's face and body were dim as if she too were underwater. "Though I didn't find out," Fran said, "till I was back at Toronto and starting my first year at university. I was still seeing your father." Rushed, humbling couplings—in his car, twice in a sleazy unsoundproof room at the Selby Hotel, once on his office desk. Through it all the sound of her own voice—fussing, railing, demanding more time than he could give her. But he wanted me too, I swear. He couldn't break away from me.

"He did everything he could," Fran said, "found a place for me to go, gave me money, coached me in the story I was to tell my parents." After those two awful nights in the motel when he fed me gin and quinine till my ears rang, while I half-scalded myself in hot baths. I cried and cried, knowing that if I didn't miscarry I'd lose him forever. "I was supposed to be working in the Soo," she said. "Taking time off to find myself as people were beginning to do in those days. We still saw each other for about a year afterwards. Till he got another job and left town." Poor Chat. He must have been afraid he'd never be rid of me. Always running into me on the campus. They had a rule that they didn't speak on those occasions, but when she felt too miserable she'd place herself in his way so he'd have to look at her. Or she'd rush uninvited to his office. And sob. Talking talking talking. Wanting him so badly but only once—the day he told her he was going away—he locked his office door and made love to her on the floor.

"He was the only person I could talk to," Fran said. And he let me. Sitting there, looking down. The one time he used the words "my daughter" I screamed, "How dare you call her yours when you wouldn't even come and visit me in that terrible place?" "I felt so false," she said, "having to chatter with my friends about dates and parties, act like an ordinary rebellious teenager with my parents." I still live like that, she thought, within limits set by what people think they know of me, even in my thoughts, most of the time. Only Terence knows (and Keith if he remembers), and Terence, I think, is using the knowledge for purposes of his own. It isn't fair, she thought. Shirlene can live openly. Chat could show who he was. I've had to run behind in shadows, the scapegoat for them both.

"It may not be much of a story," she said. "But it wasn't just cheap and nasty—or a seduction." The girl's face still had that underwater look. A big girl melting away. A big, silent girl. "It's cost me a lot telling you this," Fran said.

The girl hesitated. Her lips moved as if she were trying to smile. "You haven't told anything important, though. Like did he repent? Did he confess to his wife?" and when Fran simply stared at her, "Well, did he?"

"I doubt it," Fran said.

"Then how could he live?"

"With difficulty, probably, as most of us live. Is that all you got out of it?"

"No, it wasn't all." The smile was beginning to come back—flat, indulgent, vaguely pitying. "Perhaps I shouldn't say it though. You don't like it when I say things."

"Of course you can say—whatever it is. Who has a better right than you? But try to understand. Your Lord Jesus doesn't rule out understanding—or compassion. In fact, it's his trade—his *métier* Heine called it."

"Oh, why are you so snobby, always talking French?" The girl was no longer lolling. She was sitting upright. "I listened like you told me. I noticed how you kept stopping, then trying to make excuses for yourself. Because you realize you had it coming, you deserved to be left. Swimming around naked with a strange man. Telling lies. He must have despised you," and before Fran could interrupt, "You weren't completely bad, though. You accepted the consequences of your sin. You let me be born. But now, instead of atoning, you live a useless life working for those artsy groups. I was telling my three girlfriends. They couldn't get over it."

"You mean you let those kids paw over my life?"

"It's not too late, though." The smile was bland. "Because I can see that whether you admit it to yourself or not—"

"How in hell would you know what I admit to myself or don't admit? A silly little girl who can't open her mouth without showing how little comprehension, how little sense of what other people—. Try to remember that next time you think of telling someone she isn't completely bad. And proposing to go out and preach to the heathen. People won't even be offended; they'll laugh. They will," for Shirlene was trying to speak. "They may listen if the songs are as great as you say, but the minute you open your mouth looking the way you do, they'll laugh."

"What's wrong with the way I look? You're just jealous because you haven't found what I found."

"I don't believe you heard anything that day," Fran said. "You just talked yourselves into thinking you did. And now it's become an ego trip—an excuse for not looking at the real world, which is a bit more complex than you and your silly gang of little—" The girl was leaning forward, fists on her knees, her face white except for the scaly patches on her cheeks. They could go on like this, Fran knew, as mothers and daughters do, finding cracks, spots that could hurt. (Though she's never said the word. I wonder why.) "But we're not," Fran said, "I gave you away. I can't get you back. I don't even want to get you back. Not now. So late. So go, will you?" To her surprise the girl had begun to rise to her feet, seemed to rise very slowly, perhaps because she was so bulky and so tall. "I've upset you in all sorts of ways," Fran said. "I'm sorry. Try to forget these last two days. And me. Pray. Pity me. Sing your great gospel songs on the Yonge Street strip. Anything. Anywhere. Just go. Please, Shirlene." Speaking the name, she realized, for the first time.

The girl wasn't quite smiling and she was still pale, but her eyes were bright. "See you," she said. "In Toronto. After term ends."

"No," Fran said. "I won't." Learn all I'd have to learn, so late, starting back at the beginning. Hurt and go on hurting, while inside I'm saying (though this part I won't have to learn, I seem to know it already): this child must not suffer, even at my hands. "Surely you don't want it either," she said.

The smile came out on her daughter's face, wide and benevolent, showing the undersides of the lips. "Oh, I want it all right," Shirlene said.

Jane Rule

Lilian

Like the pages of a pop-up book, the scenes of love remain, three-dimensional, the furniture asking more attention than the flat doll who is more like wallpaper, a bedspread, a detail rather than the focus of memory. It might have been a way of dealing with pain but instead is the source of it, flat loss in so many really remembered rooms. Like a book, too, it can be shut and stored on a shelf with only the spine exposed, *Lilian*, without author or publishing house, but there is a prominent date, 1952. The twinge of pain is like the ache of a bone broken twenty-five years ago; you tend to think of the present weather rather than the old accident. Until someone asks, "How did it happen? Why does it still hurt?" A lover's question. Then there is the furniture again and the flat figure, and you, like a huge, old child, poke a finger as large as your old self once was into the flimsy trap of a very old beginning.

"There," you say, "are the twin beds pushed together. That's my desk at the foot of them. You can see the photographs I kept under the glass, the list of letters owing, a pair of gloves with the tips cut out of the fingers. It was very cold. That little gas fire didn't work very well, and it was expensive. We hadn't any money. That's the door to the kitchen, and that one went into the hall."

"But where is she?"

"Out, probably ... no, she's in the kitchen. She's just come in from work and is putting on a kettle for tea."

"I want to see her."

There she is, simply a woman standing by a small gas stove, her back turned.

"Her face!" she insists.

But none of her faces is properly filled in. One has only the trace of a cheekbone, another simply a pair of glasses, and the hair's not real, put on carelessly by a crayon the wrong colour. Her clothes, like those of a paper doll, are more important: a suede jacket, a grey skirt with two pleats down the front nearly to the ankles. She has a purple and grey scarf, a pale lavender twin set. She can be undressed. How long has it been since anyone wore that sort of bra? You'd forgotten about the peach-coloured underwear. The body itself is an exaggeration of breasts and pubic hair, done in black and white.

"She looks very ... English," she says, charmingly daunted.

You laugh, touch the very real red-gold hair, turn a face to you which you don't have to struggle to remember or forget, never sure which it is, and kiss a mouth which will never taste of tea. Her breasts are freely available to you under the pale green shirt. Trousers the same colour are on an elastic waistband. You have made love with her often enough to know that she likes to come first, quickly, in disarray, one exposed breast at your mouth, your hand beneath trousers pulled down only low enough to reveal the mound of curly red-gold hair. To feel compromised excites her aggression, and you have learned not to be surprised at the swiftness of her retaliation, fake-coming to her assault so that you can both finally lie naked in a long feasting pleasure, where she can make no comparisons because her husband never does that, because you and Lilian had never even heard of it. When you came upon it in a novel written by a man, she was long since gone, but your need to taste her was as sharp as your simpler desire had been on those dark, English afternoons when she came in, her hair smelling of the tube, her face and hands cold, wanting a bath first to get warm, wanting her tea, before the ten minutes of touching which was all it ever occurred to either of you to do.

"Was she very good?" her voice asks, breath against your thigh.

Your tongue lies into her what is not a lie. The first woman is perfect, being a woman, even if everyone after that is far, far better, as has certainly been the case. Nearly without exception.

"Look at me."

You do. She is the age Lilian was, thirty. Nearly all of them have been, though you've grown twenty-five years older, will be forty-five in a few days' time. Her mouth from so much love-making is dark and swollen, her chin chafed, as if by winter weather. You are glad it is very cold outside, an excuse for her if she needs one.

"She's the only one you ever lived with?"

You nod.

"Why?"

"She was free."

She begins to cry, tears of a sort you had not seen until after Lilian. You wonder if that's one of the ways you've set Lilian apart, being able to remember that she never cried like that for herself or you. They are tears you have watched on a dozen faces since. You don't really want her to begin to talk about her children, but you don't stop her as you do if she mentions her husband, even to abuse him. You have not asked her to leave any of them. It is she, not you, who is unhappy about spending only a rare night in your bed. Most meetings have to be timed as if they were evenings at the PTA. She tries not to share her guilt about how she is neglecting her children's teachers. The guilt she feels about neglecting you is confused by the fact that you are never neglected in her thoughts. You are her private obsession. She leaves behind a toothbrush, a comb, a shirt to encourage the same state of mind in you.

"I must go. It's time to go," she is saying, wiping her eyes on the clothes she is gathering up.

You admire her fully realized body as she walks across the room. She pauses and turns to you.

"Why did she leave you?"

"Because I am not a man," you answer, as you have answered the same question a dozen times before.

"She married then?"

"No. Eventually she found a woman to live with."

She turns away again, puzzled. You would not have tried to explain further even if she'd stayed to ask. Once you did try. The anger that had obliterated Lilian's face and left her body grossly exposed in black and white, like a cheap Polaroid picture, obliterated and stripped the questioner, who should have known then she was being raped and did not, flattered by the force of it.

The water is running in the shower now. She must go home, smelling as if she'd been to the PTA. On a better night, you would shower with her, mark her with quick pleasures. You might even joke about putting a little chalk dust in her hair. Tonight you put on a kimono, tidy your own clothes away, open the door to your study and turn the light on over your desk. You are sorting papers when she comes to the doorway, dressed and ready to leave.

"Are you angry with me?"

"Of course not."

You are never angry now. You go to her, kiss her throat, smile.

"God, she must regret it. Every time she reads about you ..."

You shake your head, wearing your expression of tolerant indulgence for her admiration of your work, your success. The fantasy she is calling up is one you've tried to nourish for years but even the most outlandish fantasy needs some shred of evidence to feed on. You have none. Lilian always believed in your work. Success wouldn't increase or diminish that, and it would never bring her back.

"Don't shake your head. You're too modest ... well, you are, about your work." But you have made her laugh now at the immodesties she enjoys. "You're so beautifully unlike a man."

Usually you help her to leave, but now you cannot because you so much want her to go.

"I want to be with you on your birthday. Why does it have to be on a Sunday night?"

"It isn't. It's on any night you can get away."

"You don't let yourself mind about anything, do you? I wish I could be like that. I'll be horrible to the children and to him all evening, knowing you're alone, wanting to be with you. Will you be alone?"

"Actually, I like to be alone on my birthday. It's my one anti-social day of the year. Well, that and New Year's Eve."

"Just the same, miss me a little."

You agree to. You know you will miss her ... a little. Inflicting a little pain is necessary to her as a way of sharing it. When she can't, she won't come back; and you are slower now to encourage the break, though you know that to extend the strain on her for too long is a matter of diminishing returns. It's not that you'd have any difficulty replacing her. There is an understudy in the wings right now, who is free on your birthday, but you won't see her. She seems young, though she's thirty. Lilian at that age had none of the vestiges of childishness you notice increasingly now. She had not been raising children, of course, and was not absorbed, as all the others have been, with the ways of children and therefore inclined to tip into baby talk or take delight in small surprises. She had been as absorbed in her work as you were in yours.

"You're tired," she says.

"I'm getting old."

Again she laughs, as you intend her to, and now you must help her leave even though you want her to go. It takes only a gesture, a quick fingering into her still wet centre.

"Oh, don't love, don't. I've got to go."

"Then go ... quickly."

So beautifully unlike a man? So unbeautifully like one, and you've got so good at it that you manage this sort of thing very well by now. Then, as you turn back from seeing her out, there before you again, instead of your carefully tidied living room, is that pop-up book interior, the desk with its comic gloves at the foot of the shoved-together twin beds. You try to stay as large as the years have made you, as invulnerable to that anger and pain, suffered by a person twenty-five years ago, no bigger than your fucking finger, but your hand is on the desk chair. You pull it out and sit down. The gloves fit. The notes you are taking are for a book written so long ago you have almost forgotten it. The kitchen door opens, and there in it is Lilian, not a cardboard caricature, but Lilian herself. You keep on working. You do not want her to speak.

"Look at me," she says, and you do, surprised by the clarity of her face, afraid.

"You don't want a lover and a friend; you want a wife or a mistress."

"What's the difference?" you ask.

"You're not a man. You have to grow up to be a woman, caring as much about my work as I care about yours."

"I can't."

As she begins to change, fade, flattens to the cardboard figure you are now so familiar with, you grow into that huge, old child again, alone again as you have been at every beginning since, whether birthday, New Year's Eve, or love affair, closing the cover of the one book you will never write, *Lilian*.

Ethel Wilson

Till Death Us Do Part

I have a friend, well I should say an acquaintance, well anyway someone who works with me in the wool shop that is, and she is a very interesting girl not because she says anything, oh no. She is very silent and I don't know whether she is bad tempered or just silent. I think she is proud. Her name is Kate and she is very efficient in the wool shop. If her expression was happier I would say she is beautiful. She is small with a natural golden coiffure or is it coiffeur, well what I mean hair-do and a very clear complexion but I wish she would respond a bit. She silences me. We never laugh and I am used to laughing when I feel like it.

Kate seems to have got a queer defensive thing, I can't imagine why. Perhaps she *has* to defend herself in some way. Me being older than she is although I am junior in the shop, I've had to knock about a bit and I know things happen sometimes so you *have* to defend yourself but she doesn't need to defend herself against me, I'm not going to do her any harm, or is she jealous? oh surely no. I'd like to like her but as it is she won't let me. I think she's scared of intimacy but heavens I don't want to be intimate. Probably she just doesn't like me. Oh well, you can't like everyone.

If I say, Good morning isn't it a lovely day, she says it's going to rain. And if I say, Did you see that warship come into harbour this morning, she says, That wasn't a warship. At first I used to argue a little but that was silly and got nowhere. She'd be better to say just Yes and No. It would save argument and be pleasanter. And better still I'd be wiser not to make a remark of any kind. However.

The result is that neither of speaks because it is no fun speaking, except to the customers and we are both lovely to the customers. The owner and manager is away sick and I sure hope she comes back soon and sweetens the atmosphere a little. Perhaps Kate has a secret sorrow. Well so have I.

I began to go home at night pretty ruffled. I knew I was being put in my place and supposed to stay there but couldn't see why this should be. I'm a human being too, aren't I.

Today I was very pleased at a good order of wool to a new customer for bed jackets and I thought why not say so.

Yes, said Kate, I saw you. You didn't sell her enough wool for those bed jackets. I could of told you. Then we'll be out of wool when she wants it.

I was really annoyed and said, I always sell that amount for bed jackets and in my experience—and then I thought, This isn't intelligent, and I said no more.

Then I thought What shall I do about this. Shall I

Sit on a stile and continue to smile
That should soften the heart of this cow

but it did not soften the heart. However I had to speak to Kate because the telephone rang and someone asked if Mrs. Physick was there. I said I was sorry but Mrs. Physick was away ill and could I take a message. And the lady said, Oh dear, well I'll get in touch, but say her aunty called.

I said to Kate, That was Mrs. Physick's aunty and I was to say she called.

Kate said, Mrs. Physick hasn't got an aunty.

Well really that attitude made me mad if people have to feed their ego that much, so when I got home at night I rang up Mrs. Physick's place although I didn't really know her and I said to the person who came to the phone, Oh it's Muriel Brown from the shop, and please would you kindly tell Mrs. Physick that her aunty rang up today.

And the person said, Her aunty? Mrs. Physick hasn't got an aunty. Oh you must mean Mrs. Bonaventure, she always calls her aunty. Was there any message?

I felt very small and said, Oh no, she only rang up and will get in touch, and the lady said, Yes she did.

I sat still on the telephone stool and thought So she's right and there isn't any aunty and I can't win.

I had begun to be very introspective because there were ever so many more silly little things like that and I started not sleeping at night. I've got troubles of my own.

One morning Kate came in late to the shop with her right hand bandaged and began to fumble among the boxes. She didn't seem to want to speak about her hand nor about being so late but turned her face away from me and then she dropped a box because she only had her left hand, and the balls of wool rolled all over the floor.

Oh I said, don't try to pick them up! and I began to pick them up. I looked up at her from where I was on my knees and I saw that her face was scarlet and I knew that Kate's pride was hurt to an absurd degree that she should have to be indebted to me, picking up the balls of wool off the floor.

When I had finished I straightened up and looked right at

her. I said with authority (a trembling sort of authority I'll tell you, because I had become frightened of Kate and what snub might lie in wait for me), I said, You are not used to letting people do things for you or letting them co-operate with you, but you must let me help you all I can with the boxes and things. It will be a pleasure I assure you except I'm sorry about your hand. Oh what is wrong with your hand?

My hand ... said Kate turning deathly white, and she had been so scarlet, my hand ... my hand ... and a customer came in.

July 7.

I began writing this about Kate's hand and her strangeness and then I was much busier for some days and I hadn't time to write down about it. A story has to end and this story hasn't ended yet and I don't know what the end will be.

Kate tried to ignore her hand as much as possible and went back again into her silent way and I went back into my silent way except that I did watch to make things easier if possible, lifting, and boiling the kettle for tea and so on. I do think the shop had the unpleasantest feeling that ever I knew in a place but I decided to go on with it. There's always something.

I got a letter from my sister in Portage la Prairie and she said that when their busy season was over she and Frank would put the boys at his mother's and they might drive to the coast and see how I was getting along, and oh how my heart warmed up under these circumstances. She wrote about Peterborough Edwards too and that was the first time she had mentioned Peterborough Edwards and I found that I didn't mind at all because although it was all on account of Peterborough I had left Portage la Prairie and at first I had felt really badly about it, I found that by this time I was relieved about Peterborough rather than feeling badly. You can go on and on and on with a person till you get past the disappointment point, and then they begin to bore you. I was really just a habit with Peterborough although to my surprise he was awfully shocked when I decided to go off. You never can tell. I like it here in Vancouver except for Kate, it's a change but then I might like to go back to Portage la Prairie some time but no more Peterborough unless he can make up his mind. It seems that he had rung up my sister to see was there any news from me but she was very airy fairy with him she said and she said I was having a wonderful time in Vancouver.

Ha ha.

After a week Kate had the bandage off her hand and it was really very nasty looking. There were still plasters on it as if there were cuts and it was evidently painful, so I helped all I could but not what you'd call ostentatious. There was once that Kate turned to me with such lovely sweetness and gratitude and her pretty customer smile and oh how my heart warmed as it does, foolishly I expect.

That sweetness did not last only long enough for me to think how lovely it would be, because then Mrs. Physick rang me up.

All my arrangements with Mrs. Physick had been made by mail and so I had not seen her because the doctor said she must have this operation.

But now Mrs. Physick asked me to go and see her in the evening if convenient and take the order book and the old order book too, to compare stocks for ordering. She sounded quite young, I was surprised.

After I hung up I said to Kate, Is Mrs. Physick old or young? She sounds quite young to me.

Kate said coldly, It all depends on what you call young.

Kate was uneasy. At last she said, Why did she ring you not me? Why did she tell *you* to take the order books?

Well really how silly! Mrs. Physick probably wanted to give

me the once-over but it was no good entering on a silly argument so I said snappishly Better ask her yourself, and we were quits but the atmosphere was nearly unbearable again.

July 10.

I took the order books to Mrs. Physick's flat where she lived with a woman friend who Mrs. Physick told me had a hat shop. Mrs. Physick was lying on a couch and said she was still taking it easy after the operation. She was pleasant looking, youngish but her hair going grey. She had the nice kind of face with some lines on. We went through the order books and she told me to leave them and she'd run through them again and then Kate or I could come and get them. She looked at me and said, How do you get along with Kate?

I said, Oh I get along. And then I said, But I don't think she likes me.

Mrs. Physick looked worried and she put out her hand. I know, she said, it's not easy. Don't take it personally.

I was afraid of beginning to discuss Kate which would be a disloyal thing to do and anyway I did not think Mrs. Physick would do such a thing, Kate being the senior employee.

Just the same I said, Oh yes it is personal. It would be impossible not to feel that—but I don't take it too seriously. I'll be going now Mrs. Physick, is there anything else?

Mrs. Physick did not speak for a moment and then she looked down and almost whispered, Kate is a very unhappy young woman.

I was standing up to go. I wondered whether I ought to tell her about Kate's right hand or was even that talking too much. However, I blurted out, She hurt her right hand, I think she had an accident, she didn't say, the bandage is off now and it looks nasty but she can manage more easily.

Mrs. Physick stared at me. An accident? she said, an accident to her right hand? It seems to me people always have accidents to their left hand! What kind of accident?

I said, I don't know. She didn't say. It looked to me as if something had hit it.

Mrs. Physick was silent and then spoke sort of unhappily, Oh do be good to her, she said, and I said I'll try. I began to think that Mrs. Physick might be the whole world to Kate and she couldn't bear to have her friendly to any new person.

July 17.

It must have been a few days after I wrote last time and I had been doing what Mrs. Physick said, making every allowance and paying no attention and I thought that perhaps Kate seemed happier and I remember feeling happier myself, and easier, when one day I saw a woman in black standing very still outside the door of the shop. Kate was serving a customer at the back of the shop where the new stock of children's small foreign toys are and I was in the front with a customer who wanted to make some baby outfits. There was the wool and there was the pattern book. The customer was taking a long time looking and making little remarks to herself, and in between I happened to look at the glass front door.

The woman began to peer closely this way and that through the glass as though she was looking for someone. She saw me but paid me no attention. I had to attend to my customer and so I could not keep looking at the woman as I wanted to. But I did see that now she was bending down and gazing in and then it seemed to me that she saw what she was looking for. She looked fixedly and with a very unpleasant expression deep into the shop. Between pleasing my customer and advising with her and looking at the woman and looking to see if Kate had seen her, it was all difficult, but the woman (I could see) remained bent down nearly double and peering in.

Next time I could look away from my customer I saw the woman had gone, and I saw that Kate was moving up the shop with her customer who had in her hand one of those little music boxes that seem so funny in a wool shop.

Oh the woman wore a shabby black coat and had her head tied up like an old peasant woman. Her face was sallow, almost yellow, but although I did not know her, there was something familiar about her face and then I knew that if you can have someone ugly look like someone pretty, this woman looked like Kate.

I was very horrified because I thought could this ever be the mother of Kate who is so pretty and so clean and proud and refined and tension-full and—as Mrs. Physick said—so unhappy. And I thought Oh how terrible, Kate going home every night to perhaps such a mother in a small place and coming back in the morning full of the feeling of it. How terrible! Next day the woman came again and I found myself watching each day for her and each day she came and bent down to peer through the glass but if Kate was in full view, or on the approach of Kate, she always vanished.

I began to make up stories in my head and I think that Kate had forbidden the mother ever to come near the shop, and so shame her who was so proud, but that in order to annoy her the woman came every day and watched, and that was the kind of woman she was.

Sometimes either Kate or I go into the little back place and get out new stock or paper bags or something, and one of these times when Kate was in the back, the woman came to the door. This time she was bolder. She put her hand on the latch and pushed the door open and stood and I saw more clearly her yellow face which seemed to me terrible and without, well, without humanity. I went up to her (and I felt ready to defend Kate) and said, Can I do anything for you? and the sour smell of cheap whiskey came strong right at me. I did not know what to do. She gave me a look only, and then with a kind of derision she looked slowly round the shop, up and down the shelves, as if to fix in her mind the kind of heaven her daughter came to every day.

I said again, Can I do anything for you? and I wondered Is she foreign or what because she doesn't answer, and all the time the reek of whiskey was on her, when Kate came out from the back and suddenly stopped. The peculiar bright scarlet came up her neck and over her face and then the whiteness and she looked like a frozen woman.

I did not know what was the best thing to do. Everything rushed through my mind in a turmoil about Kate's pride and tension and the hurt right hand and Mrs. Physick saying She is unhappy and there was a kind of yawning terribleness of how unhappy she must be to act like she does. There was also this at the same moment, that I must do something at once and that I must not let Kate think in all her pride that I knew that this woman (a hag if ever I saw one) could be her mother, or the sight of me would always be unbearable to her. So I stepped between them and took the evil-smelling woman gently but firmly by the shoulder and said Let's ... let's go outside, and I walked her out of the door and shut it.

She was surprised at my action and looked angrily into my face and tried to shake me off.

I got a perfect right, she said, to go into your old shop, and I said, Oh no, you've been drinking, we can't have you in our shop, and she said, I have not so been drinking, and she looked very vicious. Then she spat at me and that made me really mad, a little short and sharp spit.

So I said, You certainly have been drinking and I'll have to get a policeman if you try to come into our shop, there's a policeman at the Bank at the corner, and the woman looked at me like a snake and slipped out of my hand and was gone. There's nothing like the word policeman.

I stood outside in the fresh air for a minute. I felt awful, not just because of this woman but because of Kate. Then I went into the shop but I left the door wide open because it seemed to me the whole place smelled of the stench of that woman. It was lucky there was no customer there, but it would have been just the same if there had been a customer.

Kate was not in the shop. So I wondered What do I do now? It isn't natural for me ever to go to the back and talk to Kate about anything but I'd better do it, casual like, and now. So I went into the back and I think Kate had had her head on the desk but she straightened up and looked at me quite wild.

I didn't seem to notice, I hope, and said, Did you see that woman in the store? She'd been drinking so I took her out and told her not to come in. She said she'd come in if she liked but I said No, not when she'd been drinking, in fact I'd have to call a constable if she came in again and she beat it. I kind of hated to speak to an old wom... an old lady like that but what could I do. I hope that was all right? I said, anxious like.

Kate nodded her head, still looking at me in that wild way, and I went back into the shop. When the time came to close up I could not bear to think of Kate going home to what she was going home to, but what can you do?

July 25.

This has been an uncomfortable week. If it weren't for the fact that business is good and us busy (I think those little foreign dolls and houses and things in the window attract people) I don't think I could stick it. Things seem out of control. Kate is the silentest person I ever did see, but more than that she is so unhappy. It would be no good trying to horn in with a little comfort and what's more she looks ill, in herself, I mean. Her hand was very inflamed this morning and she had it bandaged all over again, but badly. Could I help you fix that, I said, and she said, Well just a bit tighter here, and pin it, and then she actually said Thank you.

I'm not one to tell tales but I just felt that it was too much responsibility and I must go and talk to Mrs. Physick after supper. Mrs. Physick came to the door herself and she looked better but she moved slowly and we went into the room and sat down.

I said I'm very worried Mrs. Physick about Kate, and I told her about the woman and about Kate's reaction to the woman (all out of proportion, I thought, though it sure was bad enough) and how her hand was infected and red and swollen up her arm and what could we do. I said, I am very willing to go and do things up for her at her home but I don't know where she lives.

No no, said Mrs. Physick. That would never never do. Kate is very very proud (I said, I'll say she's proud) and it would spoil your relations together for always if you went into that house and saw it—she'd never forget it. I know it. I'll go. I can drive the car now. You go home. I'll phone later. So I went home.

It was midnight before Mrs. Physick phoned and she didn't waste words.

She said, Can you carry on alone tomorrow? Maybe I'll be down for a bit some time. I got Kate into hospital. She's running a fever. When I got there the mother let me in but Kate's bedroom door was closed. Yes it was locked and I had to knock and knock and call but she was suspicious and it was some time before she'd let me in. To think of her barricaded against that woman! I don't blame her. The place was a dirty shambles. Well goodnight Muriel. Do you know my belief? My belief is that bitch hit her on the hand with a bottle.

July 29.

I'm carrying on at the shop with Mrs. Physick down half days. Kate's been up to the O.R. and they've taken splinters of glass out of her hand. I don't know how I can bear it when Kate comes back, and she will come back, to think of her and that mother going on for ever and ever together and no escape till death comes for one of them, whatever way it comes, but some way death will part them.

There was a letter from Peterborough Edwards tonight when I got home, addressed care of my sister. Peterborough wants to come down to Vancouver on his holiday. He seems upset. I won't answer right away. Do him good to be upset. But my mind turns to Peterborough Edwards as a comfort when I think of Kate and her mother going on until death parts them. I don't say I'd really choose Peterborough Edwards and I never thought I'd turn to Peterborough on account of these circumstances but he might be a comfort and anyway, what can you do?

Isabel Huggan

Secrets

My mother and her friends had secret lives. Growing up in Garten I learned that duplicity was as necessary, as natural to their existence as breathing. Their lives were made up of layers, like the parfait desserts they took to church suppers, and at some level or another they all shared different secrets with each other. I sometimes wondered how my mother kept it all straight, who knew what about whom. I always seemed to be making mistakes, divulging Linda's secrets to Amy or Sharon's to Joyce, not with any malicious intent but from forgetfulness. Mavis had no such difficulty. Entrusted with her friends' secrets, she gave back in kind.

Here is a secret. My mother and her friends Beverly Mutch and Nelly Tabor all slipped into the city regularly to have electrolysis treatments on their chins and upper lips. That was *their* secret; if you didn't keep it hush-hush, then it was money wasted, wasn't it? I wasn't officially admitted to that secret until I was seventeen, when one day Mavis made me stand by the bathroom window while she examined my face.

"Oh dear, I'm afraid you've inherited my skin in more ways

than one," she said, and her voice was regretful yet filled with something like enthusiasm. Here was a fault we both shared and it would be plucked out. We could be made perfect together. "Rena Louise said I should check your facial hair for darkening. You come along in with me this week and we'll let her have a look."

In this way I was initiated into the secret rites of little jabbing needles and quick searing pain and women with perfumy hands and peppermint breath leaning over me, grotesque through the underside of the magnifying glass with which they would study my face. Rena Louise had smooth, waxy skin that made me think of pale pink tulips, and she wore a deep pink smock with a large floppy bow at the neck. She said she could fix me up in no time and I wouldn't have "so much as a shadow on that pretty face." In fact, the treatments often left little red welts that made me as self-conscious as hair would have, but she had told the truth and my secret was safe. Only my mother and Rena Louise and Mrs. Mutch and Mrs. Tabor knew that God had meant me to have a moustache. I suppose my father must have known, since it was his money that paid for the treatments, but like all matters of a female nature it was never mentioned between us.

My mother is teaching me how to dance. I am already taller than she is but she is playing the role of the man, leading. We are dancing first in the living-room but the rug interferes with my mother's sliding turns so we move to the smooth hardwood floor of the dining-room where we circle around the table. We do the foxtrot and the waltz, we spin past the china-cabinet and the sideboard, we dance until my arms ache from this strange, formal position, one hand on my mother's shoulder and the other clenching hers in mid-air. She is flushed and her eyes are bright. "Oh Elizabeth," she says when we stop. "I do love to dance."

Men were generally excluded from secrets, as if there were a conspiracy among the women to keep things from the husbands. In fact, those men were often involved in the secrets themselves—they simply weren't part of the intricate network of telling and not telling. For example: Beverly Mutch wasn't really a widow; her husband had gone to Montreal a long time ago and sent her a postcard from the LaSalle Hotel that said "Goodbye, Bev." Only Mrs. Mutch's most intimate friends (Mavis being one) knew that. Just as none of Peggy Bonnet's friends would have dreamed of telling her *their* secret, that her husband fondled their breasts whenever he got the chance.

Here's another. Vera, who played the organ at church, kept a bottle of sherry right out on her kitchen counter where she could get at it during the day, which is why she sometimes played so badly at choir rehearsals on Thursday nights. Sometimes the entire soprano section, which sat near the organ, could smell it on her breath but they never let on because our minister, Reverend Hartwell, was absolute death on drinking and everybody liked Vera. Since she was always sober on Sunday mornings, the sopranos agreed among themselves, they'd do their part too. It was a secret for years. As was the information that when Mrs. Hartwell went off to visit her relatives in Halifax she was really over in the sanatorium having one of her bad spells.

A lot of women in Garten had bad spells of one kind or another. I didn't really think of it at the time, it seemed to be part of being a woman—they kept secrets and had bad spells. With my mother it took the form of tension headaches, certainly more acceptable than Mrs. Hartwell's nervous breakdowns but still not to be mentioned. That was because to ease her pain she visited a chiropractor in the city for manipulation treatments, a fact that had to be kept quiet so that Dr. Waddell didn't find out. "If I ever hear of you or *any* of my patients going to one of those quacks I won't have you in my office again!" he had said when she asked him what he thought about chiropractors.

"It just burns me up," she'd say to her best friend June on the phone, "the way Bob Waddell thinks those pills he prescribes are the reason my headaches are better when I know full well it's the treatments." But she could never bring herself to tell him, to risk losing the pills or incurring his wrath. In case someday she really needed him if I were sick or Frank keeled over. In case it made things awkward in the bridge club they belonged to. It was easier to keep it all secret—and if that made her tense, well, there was June to talk to, and there were always the pills.

My mother is teaching me how to dance. There's going to be a dance after the Grade 8 graduation on the weekend and she is preparing me. I don't expect anyone to ask me except in the Paul Jones and the Snowball, but I go along with her cheerful delusion that I will be dancing my feet off. "It isn't the steps you need worry about, Elizabeth," she says. "A good dancer just follows gracefully. There now, don't pull like that. You can't go your own direction, you must flow with your partner. Flow. That's it. Don't look at your feet, look at me. There now, see?" Embarrassed, I look directly at my mother, into her blue eyes. I feel she is forcing me to love her. I cannot resist the insistent rhythm of the waltz. I let myself relax and think that she will take care of me if I love her, that I will float above the ground and never trip or fall. "There now," she says again with satisfaction. "You're getting it. You're dancing like a dream."

The cause of my mother's headaches, and a host of other tension-related illnesses she suffered, was no secret. Over the years I heard her on the phone talking about what a difficult, unmanageable child I was and I knew it was all my fault, all her disappointment and frustration. The phone-calls themselves were part of a secret life she led with June and Nelly and Gladys and Wilma as soon as my father was out the door in the mornings. I was often home from school with ear infections in the winter months, and lay on my stomach at the top of the stairs listening to my mother's voice down in the kitchen. She and her friends reviewed their lives in such elaborate detail that although I only heard my mother's end of these conversations, I learned to piece together, from her comments, what the other women were saying. Sometimes there was laughter, but what I seem to remember best are the endless exchanges of daily events delivered in a weary, resigned sort of way. They knew each other's menus ("I think I'll heat up that roast beef with the gravy and add a few potatoes, maybe a chopped onion for supper tonight") and financial matters ("Frank says $2.95 a yard is madness but I just told him you have to pay if you want quality that will *last*"), they told each other about their ailments ("Well, Wilma says she's found that taking a little lemon juice in warm water right when she gets up makes a world of difference, it's worth a try, I think") and their heartaches.

"I simply don't know which way to turn, June," Mavis would say, her voice rising with anxiety, and I'd be wondering if she *meant* me to hear, if she knew I was there at the top of the stairs. "That child gets more headstrong by the day and nothing I do does any good. I don't know, I simply don't know." Silence then, while June would offer advice or solace, possibly in the form of some complaint about her daughter Trudy, my classmate. I would get up quietly and tiptoe back to bed, huddle under the covers and hate her for talking about me. There was no privacy, no protection; all my mother's friends knew how impossibly bad I was. My life was not my own when it was being told about that way, and I thought my mother was wicked and disloyal.

Now, of course, I can see how useful those telephone conversations were, and how much more I would have suffered without them. Women like Mavis, married to men like Frank, with children like me... women like that needed each other. Without that receiver into which to pour their troubles, there would have been little comfort or release. Their secret phone life provided them with an escape from the realities of Garten they'd not have had otherwise. Although some of the younger and more adventurous women she knew took jobs in the city selling cosmetics or working as receptionists, Mavis mainly had friends whose husbands preferred them to stay at home. After a certain time, a married woman had a responsibility to stop work and raise her family—none of the tellers in my father's bank, for example, was over 25. There were rare exceptions—Mrs. Mutch who ran her own lingerie store but of course she didn't have a family—but it would still be fair to say that in Garten women were expected to be housewives. "Keeping the home fires burning," my father called it.

Mavis and June decided one year—as a lark, they said—to apply for the seasonal staff Moodies took on during the Christmas rush, to make themselves some extra money for presents. Moodies was a genteel department store in the city, with extremely refined salesladies waiting on customers from behind glass cases filled with kid gloves, cashmere scarves, hosiery, lingerie, handbags. It was so genteel that these women didn't have to handle cash—they sent their customers' money up pneumatic tubes in small brass cylinders to a department that dealt with the harsher aspects of commerce such as making change. Mavis and June, being exactly the kind of women that Moodies catered to, found themselves hired on the day they applied. But the next day, right after breakfast, my mother got on the phone.

"He says absolutely no, June," she said. Her voice quavered with a peculiar whiney note, the way I knew I sounded when my parents prevented me from doing something. "I talked myself blue in the face but he wouldn't listen. He just kept on at the same old thing, no wife of mine, no matter what…" Silence, and here June must have come in with her own sad tale. Her husband Arthur was thought to be more easygoing than Frank but he must have put his foot down too, since in the end neither woman ever worked at Moodies. "I'm not telling a soul about this, are you?" Mavis said near the close of their conversation. "It's too upsetting. Well, it'll be our little secret now, won't it June?" As far as I know, that was the last time they tried to earn money.

What Mavis and June and the others did with their time and energy was to throw themselves into church work. If the church hadn't already been there, they would have invented it, or some similar structure that would have collapsed without their support. They made it seem, with their fervour, that the word of God was dependent for survival on their tubs of potato salad, their bales of cast-off clothing, their rummage sales and socials, their countless projects. The division of labour within the church was reflective of the way that marriages worked in Garten: the elders of the church, the husbands and fathers, were its brain, figuring out the finances, hiring the right kind of preachers for what we wanted to hear; and the body of the church, including its heart, were the wives and daughters, who arranged the flowers on the altar and took turns cutting Weston's white bread into little Communion cubes. The first time I was allowed to help Mavis with this job down in the church kitchen I stuffed myself with cut-off crusts and said I wished there was some jam to go with them. She turned on me with an angry, stricken face.

"This is a sacred task," she said. "You must take it seriously."

"It's just dumb old bread," I said, knowing that was heresy and not caring. I hated it when Mavis took that tone about churchy things, making them far more important than I knew they really were. She was so angry at me that if we'd been alone she might have slapped me, but there were other women in the kitchen and so she held herself in check. She told me to get my coat and wait for her outside after I'd apologized to her and the others. I stood in the doorway in what I meant to be a defiant pose and looked at the bunch of them, flushed and busy in their flowered aprons, looking back at me with charitable faces. I wanted to say the most awful, mean things I could, to somehow make Mavis stop cutting up bread like it mattered, to free us all from the rules for believing in all this dumb stuff. But instead, of course, I mumbled that I was sorry and ran upstairs.

We belonged to Bethel United Church, whose congregation had changed from Methodist to United in 1925, and in which Mavis always said she felt right at home. Her family had been Methodist until union, and she liked the plain interior of the church that reminded her of her childhood. The white walls, varnished oak pews and pulpit, the panes of pebbled glass in the windows—there was nothing in Bethel to distract from the word of God. She liked it too, I think, because it represented a minor victory in her life with Frank. He had been raised a Lutheran, and in the first years of their marriage in Toronto they had gone back and forth to one another's churches, neither one giving way. But the transfer to Garten meant starting afresh; and here Frank found that the United was a real up-and-coming church, attracting the new people in town, the young couples with growing families, the very people he wanted to put money in his bank. As for the Lutherans, he had all the connections he needed there because of his German name and heritage; he could make himself at home in this predominantly German community with a well-chosen German phrase or two. By going to the United Church he was covering more bases for the Imperial, he said. We still, when we visited my Nana or she visited us, went to the Lutheran church—but I grew up believing that after centuries of dithering mankind had found the true way in the amalgam of the Uniteds.

Religious affiliation was an important part of Garten life, not only for the women who ran the bazaars and sang in the choirs, but as social definition. It told as much about you as where you lived or what your father did or whether you went into commercial or academic in high school. You always had to know what people "were"; it was like knowing their name or phone number, and when you met someone, it was one of the first questions you asked.

My parents always made a point of finding out early whether newcomers to Garten would be joining our congregation or not. I remember one couple, who had become quite friendly with my father while discussing loans and mortgages, who came to dinner their first week in town. The conversation turned to which church they'd be attending—there were plenty to choose from, my father said, but for his money you couldn't find better than Bethel.

"Actually, we're going to drive over to St. John's in Guelph," the wife said.

"Oh, you're Anglican, then," my mother said. (I heard her the next morning telling June she'd known all along they were, just from the snooty way the woman acted.) "Why don't you go to St. Margaret's here in town?"

"Well, what we *really* go for is the music, you see," said the husband, little suspecting he was sealing his fate with the Kesslers and would not be thought well of again. "They have a marvellous choir at St. John's, simply marvellous. And an excellent organist, as good as any I've heard. His postludes alone are worth the price of admission."

Polite laughter and the topic was swiftly changed; only after they'd gone did my parents dissect their impiety. Going to a particular church for business reasons, now that was practical, even necessary. But "Imagine!" my mother kept saying, as if to elicit from my father even stronger declarations of shock. "Imagine going for the *music*! If that doesn't beat the band!" Anglicans were prone to this kind of excess, it seemed, so likely to stray off onto wayward paths that had nothing to do with God, she ought not to have been surprised, she said.

My mother is teaching me how to dance. It is a rainy Saturday afternoon and I am listening to the radio in the kitchen as I stand by the sink polishing silver. I am helping Mavis get ready for a dessert bridge that night, for which all the pie forks must be shining. I turn up Connie Francis singing "Who's Sorry Now?" just as Mavis comes into the room. "Heavens, is that back?" she says. "That was popular when I used to go dancing with Tim, goodness, 25 years ago." She comes over and slips her arms around my waist, humming. I am startled and pull away, not used to this kind of impromptu embrace, but she is determined, and begins to turn me around the floor. "Come on now, Elizabeth, this is a good song. No wonder it's come back." "Who's Tim?" I ask. "Was he your boyfriend before Daddy?" "Oh, I suppose you could say so," she says. "He was a brother of a girl in our office and he used to take me dancing out on the Pier. Oh my, he could dance!" Her voice is reflective and I can tell she is seeing things I am not. The song ends and I want to ask her more but I can't think how to start. As if she reads my mind, she volunteers some information. "We saw each other for a few years, Elizabeth, but all we had in common, really, was the dancing. And when you decide to settle down with someone, you have to have more in common than that!" She smiles and leaves me here at the sink. I am thinking about how she and Frank never dance, how he says it's a waste of time to walk around to music. I wonder what it is that they found in common.

There were more than enough churches in Garten to keep the women busy, but no synagogue—the nearest Jews were twenty miles away in the city, evident chiefly in the clothing-stores of the business section. They were said, by my father, to own the entire street, one way or another. My mother and her friends used to entertain each other on car rides back and forth by imitating the Jewish saleswomen in the dress and hat shops they went to when Moodies didn't have what they wanted. "Liss-en, maaa-dam, it's you. Trust me!" they said to each other in heavily accented voices, affecting gestures and mannerisms I never observed in the Jewish women themselves but that brought them to mind. They *were* different, those ladies, and I liked them. They had dark hair and eyes and gypsy-like jewellery and they smelled like spice. They'd try to make you buy things by telling you lovely lies. They told me I looked wonderful in bright reds and pinks when Mavis said any fool could see my colour was navy blue.

I liked the Jewish stores for the same reason I liked going to the city—it was all proof that another world was waiting for me after Garten, a world in which the rare and exotic would be commonplace. I saw it as a beginning, a step in the right direction; for my mother I think it was like coming up against a stone wall, facing the fact that her life was limited by my father's, that she'd never get back to the real city, to Toronto, again. She did not pine for youth the way some women do, she longed only for Toronto itself where she had been a secretary on Bay Street during her twenties. Whenever she reminisced, she always interwove street names throughout the memories, like a sweet essence penetrating her present life.

"I took the Danforth car," she'd say, or "Of course, Eileen was up at Pape and Eglinton, no wonder!" or "Right at St. Clair and Yonge, I nearly died of embarrassment!" Everything, everything was anchored in *place*; everything happened at Eaton's College Street, over on Spadina, somewhere off the Kingsway, down at the foot of Bay.... She always said she could find her way blindfolded in Toronto, she knew its grid of streets by heart; oddly enough, anywhere else she had no sense of direction, and the small towns and cities around Garten confused her utterly. "Here, you follow the map," she'd say. "I don't know where we are."

After I turned sixteen and got my driving licence, I was allowed to share the driving with Mavis, an arrangement that suited us both. While she kept her various appointments in the city, I went to the library and looked up books unavailable in Garten's Carnegie, or else wandered through the art supply store across from Moodies. Sometimes I nicked down a side-street to a small Chinese restaurant where I ordered egg rolls and green tea and smoked secret Du Mauriers.

In those years after my father had left the bank and was setting up the hardware business, my mother's visits to her chiropractor became more frequent. Occasionally we'd be accompanied by June and Trudy—June was the only friend who knew about the treatments—but most often we went alone, which I much preferred, since I loved to drive and Mavis would never allow me behind the wheel ("I'd never forgive myself if anything happened") when there were other people in the car. All Trudy ever wanted to do was to shop for clothes and talk about her boyfriend Glen, and I sat in the back seat with her on those journeys in an agony of bad temper and boredom. I'd find myself listening to Mavis and June instead of us as a way of tuning out Trudy, but I had to be careful about how I listened, for my mother's eyes would flicker to the rear-view mirror every few moments to check whether or not they were being overheard and if she saw my face attentive she'd let her voice drift away to a whisper, or raise her eyebrows at June to caution her. I never grasped what their conversations were about, she need not have worried; the two women had set up a code in which little was said but much understood. "Well you know *Arthur*," June would say, and I'd be no wiser; yes, we all knew Arthur, but what, but *what*? What was the information they were passing back and forth? Their voices would have a humorous edge, but there was something else under that, a brittle, discontent, unhappy sound. "You know *Arthur*..." What did that mean? What did they know about Arthur? What did they know about Arthur and Frank and each other that could not be spoken? June's voice sounded, it seemed to me, as if she had given up on Arthur. Was that it—had Mavis and June given up on something?

Our usual routine was to leave for the city as soon as I got home from school and be back in time to get Frank's dinner on the table. One winter afternoon when we'd gone in alone, we parted as we always did in the parking-lot behind Moodies, and agreed to meet at 5.30 in the lingerie department where there was a sale. I stood for a moment by the car and watched my mother going down the street and thought how right she looked in the city, in her fur jacket and matching hat, how much more in place she appeared here than on Front Street at home. From the back, I thought, she didn't look as if she had blinding headaches; you could imagine she was happy when you couldn't see her face.

I finished making notes at the library with nearly half an hour to spare, and decided to sneak down to the tea-room in the basement of Moodies for a quick Coke and cigarette. I hurried down the marble steps to the glass doors of the tea-room and was pushing them open when I recognized the back of my mother's head. She still had on her fur hat but her jacket was draped over the back of her chair. She was leaning forward across the table and I could tell from the movements of her head that she was talking to the person facing her. I had never seen him before in my life..

He wore the black shirt and white collar of a minister or priest, and had the kind of humble, wishy-washy face I'd often seen on such men. His rimless glasses caught the light and shone at my mother in a benevolent way; what little hair he had was sandy-grey and I could see he was quite thin. I let the glass door swing shut and stood there on the other side, trying to think who he might be. I didn't want to get involved in a discussion about religion with some fanatic—it occurred to me that my mother might have heard about the fuss my essay "Science, the New Religion" had caused in Mr. Hawthorne's class, and it'd be just like her to worry that I was losing my faith and go and get help from some city church. She knew I couldn't stand Reverend Hartwell.

But it wasn't about me. It was about her. I knew that when I watched the way his hands reached over and took hers, those agitated creatures with a life of their own; the way he placed them on the table and patted them, the way he left his hands there over them. I knew when I saw how her body caved in toward him, and their heads bent forward and what they were saying was making them sad. More sad than my losing faith. More sad than I wanted to know about. I turned and ran up the steps and stood at the top, panting. Watching them through the glass I had had to consider an alarming possibility: what if my mother had *real* secrets?

Whoever that man was, he had seen me through the door without any expectation or recognition; he and I were truly strangers. But where did he fit in *her* life? Where? I went directly to the lingerie department. My heart pounded as I stood fingering rows of lacy slips and crinolines, wondering what it all meant. I thought of running back down to the tea-room, surprising them, but some other part of my brain held me back, suggested that now I still had power; I knew something and my mother didn't know that I did. Once I confronted her she would somehow turn the tables. If I wanted to know more, if I wanted to know it all, I had to hold this secret in.

Mavis appeared right on time, looking as if she'd just come in from outside. "Let's have a look at these nighties," she said. "You could do with another, Elizabeth."

"I already looked and I don't like any of them," I said, in what I hoped was a peevish tone indicating that I'd been there for some time. "Let's just go home. I'm beat." I paused, wanting my next question to be a little dangerous, but only a little. "Do you feel better?"

She looked surprised at my solicitous concern but answered easily. "Oh my yes, dear, it's a miracle what that man can do. If I could see him more often I'd never have an ache or pain."

All the way home in the car we were silent, watching the windshield wipers make their hypnotic sweeps against the oncoming snow. From time to time I would look over at her with amazement—whatever she was up to, she was a liar. A vague kind of excitement flushed through me and I sensed that my life was changing with this knowledge.

Sure enough, at the dinner table that night I couldn't look at my father without thinking of how my mother was pulling the wool over his eyes too. I saw before me the minister's hands holding hers, and wondered if he were in love with her. Oh, how awful, my mother cheating on poor Frank! A new and tender concern for my father surfaced, and with a clarity sprung from pity, I saw him for what he was … So diligent, so faithful, working so hard to give Mavis the things she loved, like her fur jacket and our new dining-room suite. Okay, he hadn't moved back to Toronto the way she'd always planned they would—was that his fault? Oh, it wasn't fair, it wasn't fair!

My mother is teaching me how to dance. We have been doing this for years now but there are always new things to learn, increasingly intricate steps. There are quick little reversals, neat crossovers and slides, and an

*exquisite balancing on the ball of the foot that is like something we do
in basketball when we pretend to pivot one way but then throw the ball
the other. All these steps, my mother says, she perfected in Toronto back
in the days when she was a working girl. "We could dance all night until
the band went home," she says, laughing. "Why, we were so good we
used to win dance contests time after time out there on the Pier. It got so
the other dancers hated to see us arrive."*

The winter pressed down on us and pushed us together for
warmth. I felt as if I couldn't breathe much of the time, questions
for my mother were clogging my throat. Yet the longer I went
without asking her who the man was, the stronger I felt within
myself.

I decided to follow her about three weeks later, a bitterly cold
and windy afternoon. In the parking-lot I turned in the other
direction as if I were going to the library, but as soon as she'd got
around the first corner I turned and ran back. Sure enough, she
wasn't going up that street to the chiropractor's office but down
the other way, across the busy main street. I edged my way
through jostling afternoon crowds, keeping close to shop windows in case she turned, but she never looked back. What I was
doing was very wrong, I thought to myself with a feeling of
pleasure. It was almost satisfying to be doing something so
unequivocally wrong, like reading someone's mail, with a real
excuse. I was only doing it for Frank.

Two blocks off the main street I saw her turn and enter a small
grey stone church. I recognized it as St. Barnabas, an Anglican
church, which at least meant it wasn't a priest. But I remembered
what Joyce had told us in CGIT group about being in St. Barnabas with her aunt last year, who said it was so high it might as
well be mick. She said there were statues and candles and incense
just like in the RC church in Garten—we all knew about that

because we'd been taken there by our CGIT leader one afternoon and Father Fultz had shown us around, tried to explain to us the stations of the cross and the intercession of the Virgin Mary and all the beauty of the Mass. All we saw was the glisten of gold and fluttering rows of cranberry glass, and our hearts turned to stone against these pagans.

I crouched behind a car and waited for a while to see if she meant to stay or whether she was just calling for that man. After a few minutes I was so cold that I turned back toward Moodies, mulling over new possibilities. Mavis hates what she called "fancy Anglicans," so she couldn't be going to St. Barnabas for anything but to see the thin little man. He wasn't nearly as attractive as my father—now that I thought of it, Frank was quite handsome for a man in his fifties. I was having to re-evaluate my parents' marriage in the light of what I knew about love and marital fidelity, all of it gleaned from movies and women's magazines. Romance, that's what Mavis was missing in her life. Romance. My father should take her out, buy her flowers, stuff like that. Hold her hand across a restaurant table, that's what he had to do.

Frank was reading the paper when I approached him in the living-room. "Daddy, I was just thinking. I don't mind staying alone if you wanted to take Mommy out on her birthday next week...like, you could go in and see a movie." He bent the paper down and looked at me oddly. "Or something," I finished lamely.

"What are you up to? Stay alone, eh? Invite your friends over and get up to Lord knows what. No sir, Elizabeth, it's not that easy!" He laughed then, and called for my mother. "You hear that, Mavis? She wants us to go out so she can have the house to herself. Wants me to take you to a movie."

My mother came in from the kitchen, untying her apron. "You know watching anything on a big screen like that gives me a headache, Elizabeth. Why are you so thoughtless?"

The next time I followed her, nearly two weeks later, it was raining, one of those wicked March days that promises spring but never delivers. Mavis held her umbrella at an angle as she walked, her head tilted forward as if in a great hurry. This time I waited until she'd been in the church a few minutes before going forward, inching behind parked cars, to have a look at the sign on the corner of the lawn. It was shaped like a church window, and under glass, white letters on a black board provided all the information St. Barnabas wished to impart.

Rector: Canon Timothy Box
Second Sunday in Lent
8.30 AM Holy Eucharist
10.30 AM Solemn High Mass
Church School and Nursery
7 PM Choral Evensong
Lenten Weekday Services
12.05 PM Holy Eucharist
4.30 PM Evensong

Of course. Timothy Box. Standing there with icy rain streaking my glasses so that the world around me blurred and ran into itself I suddenly saw, I suddenly knew. Heard music, heard Connie Francis singing, saw my mother dancing in the arms of her old love Tim. They had found each other again after all these years, destined to be together but kept apart by... here I stopped, unsure of my ground. Had he fled to the church when she chose a banker as a more suitable husband? Or was his Anglican faith what she meant when she said they had nothing in common— had she rejected the life of a canon's wife and taken up with Frank on the rebound? Infinite speculation.

I saw them as they'd been, young and whirling happily to the music out on the dance floor above Lake Ontario. I imagined them now, as they were, down in one of the Sunday-school rooms of St. Barnabas, her fur jacket hung on a chair, her hat off, yes, definitely her hat off, and he, Timothy Box, placing a record on the record-player, turning up the volume just a little so that only they could hear. "Who's sorry now, who's sorry now, whose heart is aching for breaking each vow?" Or maybe something more upbeat, there were so many old songs that Mavis liked to dance to—"Making Whoopee," that was one of her real favourites. Down there in the basement of the church, my mother and a nearly bald minister, dancing in secret. My mother, capable of deception, unfaithful and getting away with it.

The image began to fade and was replaced with a sombre realization: now that I knew, I had a responsibility. It was up to me to put a stop to this, to bring her to her senses and back home to Frank's waiting arms. Around the edges of this thought suddenly blossomed new, frightening ideas. Maybe I was too late. Maybe she could never love Frank again. Maybe, after all, I didn't blame her. Maybe I no longer knew whose side I was on. All the way back to Moodies in the rain, I wondered what I would do.

Studying for Easter exams prevented me from going into the city with my mother the next few weeks, which was fine with me; I knew I wasn't ready yet to make my move, whatever that move was. Mavis herself was easier to get along with than she'd been in some time, and although we didn't have much to do with each other except at meals, I hated to jeopardize the feeling of peace there now was in the house. She seldom lay down in her room any more, and never took Dr. Waddell's pills after meals the way she had the last couple of years. What I found hard to understand was how my father didn't seem to be noticing any of this—he seemed as distant and preoccupied with his hardware as ever.

Still, I decided that I would go into the church the next time, and find them together, and tell my mother she had to stop, no matter what. The scene played in my head along with remnants of movies and excerpts from Playhouse 90. I rehearsed my lines, the declaration of shock and grief with which I would punish that dancing pair.

A warm April afternoon, the snowdrops and crocuses on Brubacher already fading and the tulips well up; spring was here. The moment of disclosure was at hand.

As if scripted, we left the parking-lot behind Moodies agreeing to meet in an hour. Smiling at her, saying "See you, Mom," and wondering why she didn't suspect me. How could she not know that I knew? She had always said she could read me like a book.

Waiting until she turned the corner, waiting at the intersection, waiting until she went in the side door—all so familiar now, these steps of the plot. I wondered if the front doors were locked, or if the side door led right down to the basement where they met. Did he put his arms around her? Did he say "Bless you, Mavis, you've come!" Did he *kiss* her?

I noticed, as I stood hesitating on the corner, that some other women had gone in the side entrance, followed by an old man with a cane and another woman on her own. They must be going in to pray, I thought; how shocking to think of those two dancing in the basement below them. Dancing or . . . no, I couldn't let myself think anything else but dancing. That was enough, that was bad enough. I waited until another two women started up the walk to the church and then slid in the side door behind them.

I stepped into the gloom of the vestry, where I could make out display cases of pamphlets and booklets, and a table covered with a purple cloth with a brass plate on it, and a wooden money box on a stand with a black and white photograph of an Eskimo child above it. The women went ahead and pushed through

wooden doors into the body of the church. As they did so, and
the doors swung open and shut again, I heard my mother's voice.
High and clear, echoing, a half-singing sound.

And our mouths shall show forth Thy praise.

Then, a solemn male voice I was sure must be Timothy Box,
for it sounded as thin and sandy as he looked.

O God, make speed to save us.

Then my mother again, and underneath her voice I could
hear whispery, faint voices, like crumpling paper, the voices of
the other women, the old man.

O Lord, make haste to help us.

It was like a love duet the way their voices went back and
forth like that, like Kathryn Grayson and Howard Keel, or Jane
Powell and ... who? I couldn't think. I wasn't sure I'd ever felt
exactly this way in a movie, although what was happening here
seemed more like a movie than real life. Carefully, I pushed the
doors and looked in.

Directly ahead of me stretched a red carpeted aisle and to the
left of that, halfway up the row of pews, sure enough, my
mother. Her head was raised so that she was looking up to where
he stood at the front of the church, now reading verses from a
Bible held in the wings of a brass eagle. When he finished, everyone began to recite something together, and I saw that Mavis
was holding in her right hand a maroon book, open but barely
glanced at; her head never inclined toward the book, she kept
her face tilted up looking at Timothy Box. But she was speaking,
I could hear her voice. She knew all the words, I realized with a
jolt. She must have memorized all this stuff.

He hath put down the mighty from their seat,
and hath exalted the humble and meek.
He hath filled the hungry with good things;
And the rich he hath sent empty away.

Pale April light leached in through the stained-glass windows, came to rest on burnished brass and wood, was absorbed by velvet and stone. There was a musky smell I guessed must be incense, and in niches along the walls there were indeed small statues, some with little bouquets below them. The place had a festive, dressed-up air, not like a church at all; there'd be a lot of things to look at and enjoy here whether or not you were listening to the words or thinking about God. I could imagine liking a place like this myself, but I couldn't understand what Mavis saw in it—St. Barnabas was everything she said she despised. This Box person must somehow have her in his power, that was it. I knew that women would do anything for love.

With that he was chanting again and the scattering of women were saying something back in the same way, and then there was a scraping noise, a rasping shuffle and everyone was kneeling. My mother was kneeling too.

Christ have mercy upon us.

Like a Catholic, her, the one who loved the plain white walls of Bethel.

O God, make clean our hearts within us.
And take not thy Holy Spirit from us.

God, I thought, was it Timothy Box she came for or *this*? Was this the dancing? What I was planning to do ... now I was not so sure. Maybe I would be taking the holy spirit from her.

I let the door close silently and went back into the vestry, aware for a moment only of my own terrible loneliness. There was simply not a soul to turn to, no one who would make haste to help me. If that was how Mavis felt ... But it was still wrong, all her lies, all her deceiving ways. I picked up a couple of pamphlets that welcomed strangers to St. Barnabas, thinking that I might use them someday as a weapon if I needed to. I could leave one lying on my desk where she'd see it if she were snooping around my room, the way I knew she did. It would serve her right. Or I could send it in an envelope to my father and watch her face when he opened it and said, "Now what the devil is this, Mavis?"

But I knew I wouldn't, even as I was imagining it. I kept seeing her head bent forward, her forehead resting on her clasped hands on the pew ahead, kneeling and praying. This whole thing made me want to cry, to run in there and blame her for even more than I'd made up in my head these past weeks. It wasn't fair.

I let myself out the side door into the sunlight and began walking back to Moodies. I didn't want this secret, I didn't want it at all. But I knew, as I stood over a grate by the curb and ripped up the pamphlets into little pieces and let them fall through into the sewer below, that I had it now, and that I'd be keeping it.

Frances Itani

Marx & Co.

"She did ask for me?"

And Wilf said, yes, could she come first thing in the morning? Jill had an eleven o'clock appointment at the hospital, and wanted Margot, no one else, to accompany her.

The purple smudges shifted on the sea far below the slope of the field. Margot hung up the phone and stood at her kitchen window, watching the tide slide off sideways toward the Point, toward the red cliffs where she and Jill had lounged in canvas chairs, where she and Jill had run down the dunes spilling onto the beach, leaving the splay prints of mammoths behind. Jill had been her friend for 22 years. They had raised children side-by-side on these two farms. But was this surprising?—only once, years ago, had they articulated the friendship. Not planned conversation; they'd been laughing, but in a serious way. Jill was healthy then; her straw-coloured hair blown out behind her in the wind.

"If ever there comes a day," Jill had said, "if ever the day comes when I need you, you'll hear my cry all the way across the ridge. You'll hear it piggy-backed on the North wind."

But it hadn't been like that. During the past four months—eleven, since the mastectomy—a distance, a formality, had grown between them. Yes, it was during the last four that Jill had withdrawn to a place Margot was not admitted. Not Margot, not Jill's husband Wilf, not anyone. And what astonished and troubled most was that Margot could not tell Jill how she felt about her. How she loved her and valued her and how Jill had been the best friend Margot had ever had. These things didn't matter any more because Jill had turned her face toward death. She became irritated, impatient, when anyone talked to her like that. All the while, her face sucking in the pain. Even while she slept, while Margot or Wilf sat in a chair beside her, her mouth and eyes and chin twisted to the pain. How could anyone reach through that? What did love matter then?

Margot and Wilf held brief low-toned conversations in the kitchen doorway; there seemed a hushed, almost secretive air in the rooms—death circling the old farm. Wilf would continue to look after his foxes. And Margot would go back to James, to her own home, and sit quietly, and think of Jill propped against five pillows in the sickroom, Jill turned toward the window where the curtains were pulled back sharply, Jill looking out and down at a sullen ribbon of sea.

Was this, finally, the cry, piggy-backed on the North wind? *What is meaning? What is life?* she and Jill used to call out over the sand. Tears pouring down their cheeks as they laughed and cried their way through years when they had not had a moment to themselves. The third eye of each ever on the flat sand as the children below skittered sideways like the crabs they pursued, as they stamped tiny feet at waves swooshing in, sucking out. "Look, Mommy, look! See what I've made in the sand." "Look at the rope, Mommy." Holding up Medusa-like tangles. For the children wanted always to check, to know that their mothers were there, laughing crazily as they might be, but there, to nod, to wave, to call back; to say that things were right. And the treasures the children heaped at their feet: moon shells that lost their sparkles of pink and green even before they had dried in the sun, hermit crabs coiled in houses that were too large for them, chipped razor clams and mussels—rarely a perfect specimen. Dulse and twigs and brittle sea urchins and knobbed walking-sticks heaped at the feet of the two friends who called out, laughing, crying, *What is life?* And who agreed—bringing up the rear of the parade between the paths of corn as their children turned toward home, supper, bed; as the red dog pelted past the silhouette of the Point in its last frenzy before turning to the barn—agreed, that if only they knew the right questions to ask, if only, if only... *then* they might learn the answers. And after the children were in bed—brimming, it seemed, with excuses to stay awake—each of the women became aware of the other in the next farm, the ridge separating the two stretches of land. Aware of children, husbands, *friend*. In those fatigued moments, those final moments before giving over the end of day, leaning, separately now, with every one of the senses ... to the sea. To the clouds, now pink, now black, now grey and dolphin-like, heaped in a corner niche of sky; to the cool salt smell on the air. For always the sea could be smelled, even in a rising storm, even in the barnyard close to the fox-pens and clumps of dried manure; always, could they smell the sea. Gathered that last moment of day when the fields sloped through the night down to the out-line of cliffs, and waves lapped at the edge of the continent as on a map carved from memory—memory accreted from separate days, each distinct and brought into brilliant relief, but altering in so slight a way as to be unremarkable, the etchings drafted onto and making up the greater whole.

In the kitchen, now, Jill's kitchen, it had been four months since Margot's eyes had been admitted beyond the cupboard doors. Wilf spoke, again in low tones; he'd be outside, cleaning the fox pens. Jill wanted to have a shower and would need Margot's help for her dressings. The spring water was in the jug, the tea in a bowl by the stove. Wilf's hand making the gesture, the final futile gesture that summed all of life. *The tea was in the bowl.* Herbal tea. A package lay on the countertop. In the cupboard above, the door open, row upon row of bottles, labelled, arranged by colour and size. *What were these?* But Wilf lowered his head. And clomped outside in his rubber boots.

What had Jill been consuming? Powders, herbs, vitamins, extracts, every shape colour dimension; for months, it seemed, as there were hundreds, thousands of capsules and flat discs of pills. Jill had on her purple dressing-gown, was suddenly behind Margot. *What, Jill, what have you been—?* But some questions bear no scrutiny. There were no answers, only the noise of caps removed, bottles tipped, sorting and counting, a handful swallowed with three glasses of spring water. An entire handful. No, no answers, because this was grim business, the business of holding off death. Yet Margot's eyes had been admitted, beyond the cupboard doors.

In the bathroom, after her shower, Jill watched Margot's face in the mirror as she let the towel drop from her shoulders. Wilf had already set the chair before the sink. "I haven't been to my doctor," Jill said, "since May. Broke off the appointments. I've been seeing a specialist in herbal remedies." She, too, made the gesture. The tea was in the bowl. She needed Margot to apply the dressings before they drove to the hospital clinic. "The tea bags," she said, "squeeze them just until they're not dripping, put them directly on the cancer. You'll have to cover them with gauze, tape them. My arms are too weak."

Yes, Jill watched Margot's face as Margot inspected the chest wall, now dug out in craters, even where the one breast had been removed. Some craters pin-point, some as wide as two and three inches. Marching across the skin. The tea bags still warm and set into the worst of the craters. Then, layers of gauze, a piece of plastic wrap and tape—though it was not easy to find an area where tape could be stuck, everything so excoriated and raw.

They cried together as Margot did the best she could with the soggy tea. Poor body, she said, over and over to herself, poor, eaten-away body.

Margot pushed Jill in a wheelchair through right-angled halls, reported to the desk, sat with rows of patients in a room grown silent with disease. There was nothing, nothing to say. They waited 40 minutes until a nurse called Jill's name and led them to an examining-room that had three white doors. One off the waiting-room, one off an internal corridor—for the doctor's entry—one at the side leading to the nurses' station.

"The Marx brothers," Jill said, between her teeth. "Marx and Company. Are you ready for *The Act*?"

The nurse had scowled when she'd seen that Margot was staying with Jill. "I want her here," Jill had said. The nurse had left a gown, said they had only a few minutes before the doctor would be in. Patient to sit on the edge of the table; gown to be open at the *front*.

And then—Marx & Co. *The Act*. Did it really happen the way Margot's memory-etchings held it in relief? She was often to wonder as she looked out her kitchen window at a sky of raw wool, raked by a wire brush. Wondered what she had been a part of as, weeks and months later, she watched the face of the sea change from day to day and without warning; wondered until she knew she could be certain of nothing. *What is meaning? What is life?* The door to the waiting-room locked; the door to the nurses' station closed; Jill hissing, "Quick, she's gone. Get the tea bags off. Hide them. He'll think I've been to a witch doctor." Margot's fingers working at the buttons of Jill's blouse, slipping it over her thin and fragile bones, tugging at the tape, whipping off the gauze, stuffing the tea bags into the wastebasket, ramming the bandage, the plastic wrap, the twisted tape on top, the two of them doubled over, choking, dying with laughter. *The tea was in the bowl. What is life?* Marx & Co. The third white door opening suddenly, admitting Dr. Paley, his intern, his medical students. Smiling when he saw their tears of laughter, or were those—?

Margot and Jill suddenly sober. Dr. Paley took Jill's hand in his, his expression unchanged as he examined her chest, Jill's eyes never leaving his face, watching for a sign, a white flag waved, a piece of rudder cast adrift. Not a single question from him about where she'd been the past four months, why she'd broken off treatment.

"You're very sick, Jill. I'd like to admit you as an in-patient. Will you? In a day or two? Will you think it over?" Jill having left the ship to go out into the current, clinging to the rudder, yes, but already having been swept away.

Margot drove back from hospital, headed up the lane into an afternoon sky of shifting violets and blues, Jill looking straight ahead, saying, "You know the way we've talked all these years, Margot? About how we'll never find the answers till we know what the true questions are? It's taken a long time, but I finally do know some of the answers."

"Do you now?"

"You know what else?"

"What?"

Jill grinned. "I'm taking them with me."

And they ended the afternoon that way. Laughing till the tears poured out of them, until Jill began to cough and cough and went into spasm and Margot thought she'd have to pull over, but made it to the crest of the hill where Jill's house marked the descent to the other side, down, down the sloping fields to the sea. Wilf coming out when he heard the car, and when he looked at Jill and Margot and saw them laughing, he, too, smiled and followed them inside, a secret, pleased look on his face.

And Margot, her thoughts both invaded and blocked by Jill, experiencing the deepest sort of pessimism, as if the structure and bone of life were falling away. Years later, looking away from the kitchen window, from the sink, from the cupboard door, from the row of corn bowed to the yoke of the sea breeze, from the clouds, blue and whipped in the western sky, recalled herself the way she often sat by the cliffs, reading in the canvas chair, in the stillness of afternoon heat that held only the cries of gulls. *What is meaning? What is life?* Recalled herself the way she would look up at the gulls drifting across the sky, to confirm the sluggish feeling of somehow having been interrupted. A recollection as inconstant as the roar of sea that moved inside the head, the roar that came with the North wind and embedded itself as long as the North wind continued to blow. Weaving itself down through the cells of the brain until it was impossible to remember whether true silence had ever existed.

Shirley Faessler

Lucy & Minnie

Lucy is a very good-looking woman, a natural blond with teeth like little pearls and a beautiful figure size twelve. She can put on a thirteen ninety-five dress and on her it looks like a million dollars. She takes a beautiful tan and in the summer with her tan she wears a lot of white. White is white but on Lucy it looks like snow. She's not exactly a chicken, she's a good forty at least, if not more, but you wouldn't give her more than twenty-five at the outside. She's a dress buyer for a cheaper-line department store with good pay and trips out of town. She lives in a four-room apartment which she keeps like a little doll's house, so clean you could eat off the floor. She also keeps an old mother at the Jewish home, and that must cost her a good four hundred a month. The old lady is *oiverbootl*, she doesn't even know where she's at, and Lucy could of put her in a Gentile nursing home for half of what the Jewish home charges, but her conscience wouldn't let her do it. Aside from the fortune it costs her to keep her mother there with all the extras, she's a good daughter to her in every other way too. Every Sunday come rain or shine she goes to visit the old lady, who talks foolish like a child, half the time calling her own daughter Ma.

Lucy's best friend, Minnie, is what you might call a grass widow. Her husband, Archie, walked out on her fifteen years ago and hasn't been heard from since. They say he stepped out one night, told her he was going to get some cigarettes, and never came back. Matilda—that's the woman they call Blabmouth behind her back—says it didn't happen that way at all. She says if it was cigarettes Archie was after, he could of got them downstairs at his mother-in-law's grocery store.

Minnie's mother ran a grocery store. Minnie and Archie and their five-year-old boy, Sonny, lived over the store in three rooms; the old lady had her own place downstairs back of the store. Matilda says Minnie was playing cards the night it happened, that she got home around seven in the morning and her mother was just opening up the store. According to Matilda, the mother said, "What did you need to come home so early? You're a free lady now, you haven't got no husband. Archie ran away." Then the old lady began to curse her, if you can believe that of a Jewish mother. And cursed herself too for raising such a daughter.

They say Minnie was pretty wild when she was young. Her father was very strict, he used to take the strap to her for coming home late, a girl of seventeen. When he died, Minnie refused to sit *shivah* for him, and that caused a scandal on the street.

Matilda says that Sonny isn't Archie's kid. She says that Archie fell for Minnie and married her knowing she was two months pregnant. I never met the man, all I know about him is that he was some kind of *shlemiel* and had a job in a cleaning plant.

You can't believe everything Matilda says. Still and all, I can't picture a Jewish father—*shlemiel* or otherwise—walking out on his own five-year-old kid, so there must be something in what Matilda says about Sonny not being Archie's kid.

Lucy and Minnie got to know each other from living on the same street, but just to say hello. Lucy's father was still alive and Lucy was still living at home. She used to step in the store to pick up a few odds and ends, and that's how they got to know each other.

About a year after Minnie's husband skipped, Lucy's father died. Lucy already had her job as a dress buyer and had to go out of town a lot on buying trips, so she couldn't look after her mother who was already getting to be a little soft in the head. That's when she began making preparations to get the old lady in the Jewish home. Which isn't so easy as it sounds. You have to pay through the nose for a start and they've got such a long waiting list that it's practically impossible to get an old parent in without knowing somebody on the board. Being a buyer, Lucy got to know a lot of business people, so she was able to swing it.

Minnie, meantime, was having her own problems. Her mother died a couple of months after Lucy's father, and she was stuck with the grocery store, which she hated from having to slave in it as a kid. With her mother dead, there was nobody to look after Sonny, so she had to quit the part-time job at Kresge's which she took after Archie left.

The week Minnie sat *shivah*—for her mother she did sit—Lucy came around a couple of times to pay her respects. That's when they got to be real friends. Minnie was in a terrible state, she talked real wild. She told Lucy she'll burn down the store and collect the insurance. Lucy paid no attention, she figured Minnie was in a state of shock. She stepped in one night and nearly fell over when she saw Minnie in a huddle with a guy they call the Torch. He was a neighbourhood boy, a parolee fresh out of Kingston, where he'd done a two-year bit for arson—a Jewish boy at that, if you can believe it. Lucy's a smart cookie, she took everything in her own hands. She told the Torch to beat it or she'll call the cops, then gave Minnie a strict lecture. Lucky for Minnie that she listened. With Lucy's help, she put the building up for sale, sold the store lock stock and barrel, and realized a nice few thousand dollars.

It so happened there was an apartment for rent in the same building where Lucy was living, and she got Minnie to take it. That's when their real friendship began. Lucy worked, chipped in more than her share for the food, Minnie did the shopping and cooked the meals. They were like sisters, Lucy and Minnie, and Sonny was in seventh heaven. He loved Lucy, he called her Aunt Lucy. From being left alone with his grandmother, who was always busy in the store, all of a sudden he had a full-time mother and an auntie.

When Lucy had her holidays, the three of them went to Miami Beach. They took Sonny everywhere: to the movies, to Chinatown, and even to the races when the spring and fall meet was on at the Woodbine. Three, four nights a week Minnie went to play poker, and Lucy stayed home with Sonny. Lucy herself liked a gamble; she played the races, the stock market, and one night when Minnie took her to a game, she got hooked to poker. After that they went together to play and took Sonny with them. He was a good kid, you could take him anywhere. The game runner always made a place for Sonny at the table, between Minnie and Lucy. Every pot Lucy took she gave the kid a quarter. Ten o'clock she made him go to bed; she was stricter with him than his own mother. There was always a bed in any game-runner's house for Sonny to sleep, and he always went to bed ten o'clock sharp with a nice few dollars in his little purse.

I got to meet them at Helen Lieberman's Friday-night game, but that goes back a few years. Sonny's twenty-one now, and at that time he couldn't of been more than eight. That would make it thirteen years ago. My God, how time flies!

Anyway, getting back to that night at Helen's thirteen years ago ... I came early to Helen's and we sat around kibitzing, me and four other hands, waiting for Lucy and Minnie to show. I never met them till that night. All I knew about them is that they're a pair of fast players, and very good friends. Half past eight and we're still sitting, drinking coffee, waiting. The girls start getting impatient, and Helen was getting nervous. "Let's play," she says, "I'll take a hand myself till they come."

She'll take a hand, that's a very big deal. Helen's a fast player but not at her own game. All you'll get off her is the quarter edge; she'll fold every hand till she gets a pair on the wire to come in with. You won't get no gamble off a game runner, that's for sure, and Helen's no exception. Who wants to play six hands with Helen playing on a sure thing and raking half a buck a pot, but nobody has the nerve to speak up. Except me. I have a reputation for speaking my mind.

"Without me," I said. "Half a buck rake from six hands is too rich for my blood."

Helen looks hurt. "*Oy Gottinu*," she says, "since when do I take a half when we're playing short? I'll take a quarter till the game gets full."

That'll be the day. She'll take a quarter when you see her and a quarter when you don't.

All of a sudden Mrs. Cramer jumps up from the table. She's a very high-strung, nervous woman; they call her Crazy Cramer behind her back. "I have to phone Raymond," she says and steps over to the phone which Helen keeps on a small table by the kitchen door.

Raymond is Mrs. Cramer's husband. He's an insurance salesman, a real cutie, a rounder. They say that aside from treating her like dirt, he also keeps another woman. But we're not supposed to know that; Crazy Cramer pretends that everything between them is lovey-dovey. Anyway, she picks up the phone and dials her number. "Hello, dear," she says, "I'm at Helen's. What? Oh, that's right, I did tell you where I was going. I forgot."

The girls wink behind her back. She's not talking to Raymond, she's talking to an empty phone. Matilda went upstairs once and listened in on the extension and all she heard was the phone ringing at the other end and Crazy Cramer talking on the downstairs phone as if she was connected.

Crazy Cramer is still on the phone. "Oh, you're *terrible*, Raymond," she says and starts giggling like sweet sixteen talking to a date. "I won't be late. Win, lose or draw, I'll be home by two." She puckers up her mouth, gives a kiss to the mouthpiece and comes back to the table blushing like a bride. How can a woman be so foolish? Who's she kidding? Herself, nobody else.

We met him once, this wonderful Raymond of hers, and this is how it happened. One night she tapped out at Helen's game and asked Helen for money. "Can you lend me some money?" she says, and Helen comes out with, "My mother claims she didn't raise no foolish children, so the answer is no."

Crazy Cramer had been playing hard luck for weeks and was already in to her for plenty; still and all, she had no call to talk to her like that. Mrs. Cramer is slow pay but she pays up every nickel, and Helen's been running a game long enough to know that some players you can talk to like that and some you can't. Some players can take an insult, spit in their eye and they'll say it's raining; but not Mrs. Cramer, she insults very easy. She didn't say a word, just got white as a sheet and started to tremble.

I felt very sorry for the woman. I was playing lucky and I felt very tempted to take ten off the stack I had in front and loan it to her. But I didn't do it because it's hard luck to take money off the table when you're going good; you could start going bad yourself. In a game of poker you have to look out for number one.

Anyway, Helen starts to deal; everybody's quarter edge is in except Mrs. Cramer's. "In or out?" she says when Helen comes to her, thinking maybe she's still got a few hideaway bucks on her. Sometimes a loser will do that; they won't go in their poke to get case money, they'll pretend they're broke and get money off the house if they can. I've done it myself.

Mrs. Cramer picks up her handbag off the floor. "In," she says, "put me in a quarter." Helen puts the ante in for her and deals around. Cramer's high on board with a king. "Bet a dollar," says Cramer, and puts her finger in for the bet. Helen lays down the deck. "No finger bets here, Mrs. Cramer. Put your money in." Crazy Cramer opens up her purse, turns it upside down and empties everything out on the table: lipstick, compact, comb, Kleenex, Rolaids, Tums, a gas bill, keys, car tickets, a chequebook, a ballpoint—everything except money. Then she shoves everything back in her purse. "See me through this hand," she says, getting very tense, "I'm not asking for blood, Helen." By this time she looks as if she could use a transfusion.

Helen says, "Do me a favour, please, and fold your hand." Cramer says, "No. Put my bet in." Helen pays no attention; she calls for me to bet out. I'm sitting next to Cramer with a jack on board. I put a buck in for the bet, Crazy Cramer grabs it off the table and tears it up in little pieces like confetti.

You see a lot of funny things at the games, but this is something I never saw before. I took my stack off the table, who knows what she'll do next. Mrs. Cramer turns over her hole card, a king. She had a pair of kings to come in with and not a dime to bet out on them. She gets up from the table trembling like a leaf, but very calm. "How many years have I been playing here?" she says to Helen.

"Who knows?" says Helen. "Do I keep an attendance record?"

"I'm playing here seven years," says Cramer.

"So what do you want?" says Helen. "A medal?"

"I lose hundreds here, I ask for a few measly dollars and I'm insulted," says Cramer, beginning to cry.

"What is she crying?" says a player they call Auntie Dora. Nobody bothers to answer. Auntie Dora is an old hand around seventy-five and deaf as a post.

"Mrs. Cramer," says Helen, "I never said no to you before, but enough is enough. I'm running a game. Say yourself, can I stake every loser that sits at my table?"

"I'm due for a break," says Cramer. "I want to have the game at my house next Friday."

Sometimes a game runner will do that, give her night over to a loser. The rake is good for about twenty bucks an hour. The game usually goes from eight till around five, six in the morning, and it gives the loser a chance to get herself straightened away.

"With pleasure," says Helen. "Get a few hands together and I'll come to you myself."

To get rid of her we all gave our word we'll come to her game next Friday.

"Call me a cab," she says, like royalty.

Helen calls a cab and gives her two bucks for the fare.

We came to her game next Friday like we promised. I was very surprised to see what a nice house she lives in. We started to play around half past eight, Mrs. Cramer dealing and raking half a buck a pot. Half past twelve she puts a clean cloth on the table, gives everybody a linen serviette if you please, and brings out the supper, a regular banquet. Her own baked lima beans, her own corned beef, chicken livers with lung, a rice casserole with barley and mushrooms, Cokes, coffee, a banana cake and chocolate chip cookies that she made herself. She waited on everybody else but didn't eat a bite herself. She's sitting on pins and needles waiting for us to finish. She had a nice few bucks on her from the rake and wanted to get the game going again.

I was a nice winner, so I took my time; a loser always eats fast, a winner takes her time. I'm still eating and she takes my plate off the table. "Take it easy," I told her, "you'll live longer and wind up stronger."

Quarter past one we're finished and the game starts up again. Crazy Cramer deals around, and deals herself in too. We're sitting seven hands, she didn't need to play, but she couldn't keep away. She was a loser right off the bat. For a player like Cramer there's no bad cards in the deck.

Half past two, rake and all, she starts going broke at her own game. She's a very unstable woman, how can you feel sorry for a person like that?

All of a sudden her wonderful Raymond comes in, dressed like a prince. Crazy Cramer jumps up like somebody goosed her. "Oh, Raymond," she says, "I'd like you to meet the girls." He takes a fast look-see and without waiting for any introductions goes upstairs. Crazy Cramer picks up the deck; she starts excusing him, her face is on fire. A few minutes later and he's back, dressed in red-and-black-striped pajamas. "I'll give you five minutes to throw these bums out," he says to his wife, "or I'll come down and personally throw them out myself."

He goes upstairs and we start packing in. Auntie Dora doesn't know what's going on, she's still holding her hand. "What's the matter?" she says, and Matilda shouts in her ear, "He called us bums."

"That's all?" she says.

I gave her to understand that we're being kicked out. For myself it couldn't matter less, I was a nice winner. But she was a loser over eighty bucks and got very worked up. She's been playing forty years, she says, and something like this she never saw in her whole life. "Very nice," she says to Crazy Cramer, who's crying by now. "Very nice, Mrs. Cramer."

And that's how we met this wonderful Raymond of hers.

Anyway, getting back to that night at Helen's, the night I met Minnie and Lucy for the first time... Mrs. Cramer sits down after that fake call to Raymond, and Matilda—who can be real bitchy in a kind of sly way—starts singing, "Love, Your Magic Spell Is Everywhere."

Mrs. Cramer is a very restless woman who never sits still for a minute. Win or lose, she's always twisting and turning in her chair as if she's sitting on pins and needles. She weighs altogether a hundred and two pounds and has big eyes, a pointed nose and hardly any chin. Sitting still for a change and looking daggers at Matilda who's a big woman, she looks like a starved little bird sizing up a big fat worm.

Then a very unexpected thing happened. Mrs. Cramer picks up her cup of coffee which is cold by now, leans across the table and gives it to Matilda, a face full of coffee! Well, you can imagine the hey rube that followed. Matilda, with her face wet and coffee dripping off her chin on that sweater she wears all the time, stretches halfway across the table, grabs Mrs. Cramer by the hair and starts banging her head on the table. "You're crazy," she says, "no wonder they call you Crazy Cramer." Mrs. Cramer doesn't make a move. Matilda's banging her head in and Cramer's saying, "Excuse me, I didn't mean to do it."

Helen, meanwhile, is hollering, "Matilda, behave yourself!" and Auntie Dora keeps asking, "What are they fighting?" Helen's husband, Harry, comes to the door and stands there yawning and scratching himself, he's always half asleep. He doesn't know if he should interfere, he takes his orders from Helen. "What are you standing!" she hollers, so he goes behind Matilda, grabs her around the middle and lifts her off her feet. Matilda takes her handbag off the floor and goes to the bathroom to clean herself up.

Mrs. Cramer, who's white as a ghost by now, goes over to the sink, takes a drink of water, then looks at herself in the mirror.

"Look what she did to my hair," she says, half crying. She puts a comb through her hair, which she wears in a kind of pompadour style, comes back to the table and lights a cigarette; her hand is trembling. "She's jealous," she says, "that's why she keeps needling me. She can't get a man of her own, so she goes after someone else's husband." She takes a deep drag on her cigarette and says, "A home wrecker is the lowest kind of human being."

Matilda is supposed to be having an affair with Milky. When Milky goes for a poker load, Matilda's already in the car riding up front. He calls her his sweetheart and it could be that they've got something going between them. Personally, I find that very hard to picture.

Matilda finally comes out of the bathroom with her sweater sponged off. It's a good thing it had coffee spilled on it, otherwise it would never get washed. Same minute the doorbell rings. Harry goes to the door and lets in Lucy and Minnie and Sonny.

I took to Lucy right away. She was very friendly and really something gorgeous to look at. I'm not the kind of woman to be jealous of another woman's looks. My husband thinks that I'm the cat's meow, and if a woman is appreciated by her husband she can hold her own anywhere. He's an older man, I'll admit, and I can just imagine what they say behind my back. The probably say that I'm married to an old *shmendrik* and that he gives me money to play because he can't give me anything else. To your face butter wouldn't melt in their mouth, but you'd be surprised how two-faced they can be behind your back.

Minnie was something different from Lucy, very reserved and not very friendly. She was dressed in a slacks suit, too mannish for my taste but on her it looked good, she has that kind of figure, flat-chested. Her hair she wore in a kind of boyish style, too young a haircut for a woman of her age. It would suit a teenager, and Minnie at that time must of been a good thirty. Sonny, eight years old, was a living doll with a peaches-and-cream complexion and blond hair. Doesn't begin to resemble Minnie, who looks like a gypsy with her dark skin and black hair. Not that it's any of my business, but I remember hearing that Archie was dark complexioned too.

The game started off real fast. Right off the hop Lucy raised up a nice pot, took the hand, put a dollar in the kitty—she and Minnie were kittying—and gave a quarter to Sonny. Minnie, I noticed, didn't give the kid a quarter from any of her pots. Ten o'clock Lucy says to him, "Sonny, it's time." He took his little red purse off the table, said good night like a little gentleman and went to sleep in the front room on Helen's chesterfield.

That was thirteen years ago, and over the years I got to know them *pretty* well. Well, I shouldn't say I got to know them pretty well, because aside from the games, they kept to themselves. They didn't socialize around with the players. Once in a blue moon on an off night when there was no game going anywhere, you'd get an invite to Lucy's or Minnie's place for a game of gin rummy. At their own place they were wonderful hostesses; at the poker games Minnie was very bossy with Lucy. But they never had a quarrel. They were a pair of fast players, and win or lose, they never caused no disturbance. It was a pleasure to sit at the same table with them. They were an asset to the games. All a game runner had to say was, "Lucy and Minnie are coming," and the players came running.

Sonny's twenty-one now. It's hard to believe, but that kid actually grew up under my eyes. When he was thirteen, four-teen, he stopped coming to the games with Lucy and his mother; by that time he was old enough to stay home by him-self. He had three years in high school, and when he was eigh-teen he quit school and got himself a shipper's job in a dress factory. He bought a car and used to drive Lucy and his mother to the games. Sometimes he even looked in around three, four in the morning to see if they're ready to come home.

Two weeks ago on a Monday we were playing at Matilda's. Around three in the morning the doorbell rings, and it's Sonny. Minnie was losing, she wanted to play a while. "Go home, Sonny," she told him, "we'll play a while."

"Not me," says Lucy. "I have to go out of town tomorrow." She breaks out the kitty, gives Minnie her share, takes the other half for herself, and goes out with Sonny.

Friday Milky comes to take me to Helen's, and Matilda's riding up front, very excited. "Did you hear the news!" she says. "Lucy eloped with Sonny."

Naturally, I couldn't believe my ears. "Where'd you hear that?" I asked her. "Who told you?"

"Me," says Milky. "I just rode Minnie over to Helen's. I could see she was steamed up over something, so I asked her what's the matter and she opened up to me. Don't say I told you," he says and lets us off at Helen's without even coming in for the fare, he was so nervous.

We step in to Helen's, and sitting around the table is Helen, Minnie, Auntie Dora, Crazy Cramer, rich Mrs. Mintz, Rose Naftuly—that's a player they call Murder Incorporated behind her back—and Millie, who's a young player new to the games. We sit down and nobody even bothers to give us a hello, they're so busy talking.

Minnie finally looks at me and says, "What do you think of it?"

"Think of what?" I answered, pretending I don't know anything.

"Don't tell me Blabmouth here didn't tell you," she says, pointing with her thumb at Matilda who's already sitting next to her. "Have a look at this," she says and hands me a telegram. "Read it. Read it out loud," she says, "don't keep Matilda in suspense."

DEAR MA, I read out loud, LUCY AND I ARE ON OUR HONEY-MOON. WE GOT MARRIED TODAY AND ARE VERY HAPPY. SONNY. I noticed that the telegram came Tuesday, from Miami Beach.

"So what's your problem?" I said. "He's happy."

"It's easy for you to talk," she says, "you're not a mother."

Crazy Cramer puts in her two cents' worth. "It might work out better than you think. Look at Dolly and Sambo. She's a good twenty years older and they're happy."

"Don't even mention that low-life Sambo in the same breath with Sonny," says Minnie, doing a slow burn. She lights a cigarette and says, "Ever since Arch passed away, that kid's been my whole life. Anything he ever wanted off me he got, and this is how he repays me."

"I didn't know Archie passed away," I said.

She gives me a very cold look. "So far as I'm concerned, he's as good as dead."

"Do you want my advice, Minnie?" says Helen. "It's not worth getting worked up over. Your health's more important. You've got your own life to lead and life's too short."

"What did she say?" says Auntie Dora, and Millie, the new player, leans over and tells her in her ear, "She said life's too short."

Matilda speaks up. "It's funny when you come to think of it, the way she used to give Sonny a quarter from the pots for bringing her luck. She always said Sonny was her lucky piece," says Matilda, who's practically in Minnie's lap by now.

"Get off my lap, please," says Minnie. "I know this is a great picnic for you."

Millie, the new player, isn't interested in the gossip, she wants the game to get going. "Let's play," she says to Helen, then says to Minnie, "I only met Lucy the once and from what I saw of her I think she's a very nice girl."

"Girl!" says Minnie. "She's my age."

"You'd never know it," I said, "she keeps herself very youthful." Actually, she does look older than Lucy, but it's a remark I shouldn't of made. I happened to say it without thinking.

She turned on me like a snake. "Shake hands with Blabmouth," she says, "you're a good friend too.

"We were like sisters," she says to Helen. "We were closer than sisters. Now it's good-bye, Minnie, hello, Mother-in-law. We're kitty partners over fourteen years. Did you ever see me kitty with anyone except that whore?"

"Behave yourself, Minnie," says Helen, "that's no way to talk."

"That's what you know about it," says Minnie. "She's a two-timing bitch *and* a whore."

All of a sudden she starts to cry, which is very unusual for Minnie, she's a very controlled woman. "She's got Sonny now, what does she need me," she says and her eyes are running with tears.

From what I understand, she didn't feel this bad when Archie lit out. Minnie never cracks. To get a word out of her is like pulling teeth, so naturally that last remark of hers made me think.

Next few days I thought about it and thought about it. I wished I had someone to talk to, but they'd never convince me that a situation like that is possible between two Jewish women. I tried to discuss it with my husband, but he's developed an ulcer recently and couldn't care less.

Anyway, next thing you know the couple are back from their honeymoon and Minnie's at the airport to meet them.

Sonny took his clothes out of his mother's apartment and moved in to Lucy's. They still eat together and Sundays the three of them go to the Jewish home to visit Lucy's mother. Minnie calls the old lady *machetayneste*—her son after all is married to her daughter. The old lady still calls her own daughter Ma, and sometimes she thinks that Minnie is her Ma.

Lucy and Minnie are back at the games, kittying, good friends, and everything from the outside is the same as it was before. What I mean is, it is and it isn't. Things are the same and they're not the same. I still wish I had an intelligent person to discuss it with.

Sharon Butala

Act of Love

This is perhaps not a story to tell, she thinks. Then, no, this is perhaps the *only* story to tell. It's the story of how she was raped, once when she was maybe thirty-one or -two, and how all the bad things that ran wordlessly through her culture about herself and about women as a species flooded over her and she blamed herself and was ashamed and never told anybody till she felt securely beyond her youth.

Not that it helped. By then she had gone too far for rage, too far for thoughts of beatings, castration, murder, or a life lived without men. What she thinks, increasingly, glumly, since that first telling of it, is there was nothing she could have done about it then, and there's still nothing she can do about it. In fact, she's just grateful he didn't break any bones, subduing her easily with his weight and implacability, so that she acquiesced as the only way to avoid being hurt. Nor did he force her to any act of extreme perversion that would have haunted her dreams for the rest of her life. Even her children weren't in the house, but were away visiting their grandparents. Yes, she thinks, I was very lucky.

Not that she doesn't see the irony of her conclusion. As far as she knows, she was the only one he followed home that night, she was the only one he raped. But for years she didn't even call it rape. She didn't call it anything, she didn't even think about it. One night she was sitting talking about a mutual friend with a man she'd just met that day, when she heard herself say, calmly, conversationally, that was the night I was raped.

Since then she's been thinking about it a lot, has been going over all the details one by one, as far as she can remember, since it happened twenty-five years before. Stop that, she tells herself. If you doubt each detail as you remember it, you'll soon doubt that you were raped at all. And she remembers the ugly muscles of his upper arms and the way he pushed her, relentlessly, inex- orably, till he was inside the house, then in the bedroom, then lying on the bed on top of her.

She doesn't understand why she didn't feel like the woman she'd seen in a television movie who'd been raped and who went a little crazy afterward, took a dozen baths and was afraid to go out at all and then set up a trap for the man, inviting him over, planning to say, "Come in," when he knocked on her door, and then to blast him with a shotgun. And there were other stories too, in magazines and on radio and television about women reacting to rape. She'd found them all excessive and self-aggran- dizing, reactions of women who couldn't have been too stable to begin with, who clearly harboured some very bad notions about themselves as sexual beings. For years that was what she thought.

But the older she gets, clutching her secret to herself, the less sure she is that those women were wrong, and that her reac- tion—to keep silent, not to think about it, to count herself lucky among those who'd been raped—is perhaps the less rational approach after all, and that maybe *she* is the one who values her- self too little, who suffers from an absence of self-esteem, and a badly developed sexuality. They'd been outraged at their viola- tion; she hadn't even been surprised; she'd resisted till she saw resistance was useless, then she'd gone limp till he was done. All those years, whenever it popped into her mind, she'd quickly thought of how she was lucky compared to being a concubine or forced to commit suttee or being a tribal slave. Even now, when she's learned to value herself quite a lot, she's still not outraged and isn't sure why not.

And, she tells herself, if you never told anybody, you can hardly be the only raped woman who reacted that way. Remember dating when you were a college student? Most dates wound up in wrestling matches. You expected them, there was an unspoken accord: he would try, you would say no, at a certain point you'd either give in or he would realize you meant it and stop. Sometimes he went further than the accord allowed, and if he did, you didn't go out with him again. It was a dangerous game, but the only one. Now she thinks that maybe she'd been lucky there too and her girlfriends were being raped and not telling anyone.

Besides, the only reason she didn't give in was that her mother had told her she shouldn't, so had the nuns and priests who'd educated her, and her girlfriends, and even the boys who were her friends, counselling her sagely and whispering about girls they all knew who were easy. If you didn't resist, it was absolutely clear, the life you were being groomed for would be over, and that was a price too high for anybody to pay.

Then, abruptly, when she was in her late twenties and newly divorced, all that ended. Suddenly, making love was socially acceptable, a positive good, everybody was doing it, it was expected. She thinks that probably almost nobody was doing it as much as they implied they were, she for one wasn't, but the point was that you could if you wanted to and nobody would call you slut or a whore or easy. Nobody would say anything at all.

I never even noticed him, she thinks. A dozen of them together in a club at one big table, her girlfriends, somebody's husband, a few male friends who were always around, and him, the rapist, a stranger, a house guest of one of the men. They hadn't even sat close together. When she thought about that night, she remembered he'd sat on the opposite side of the table at the far end, and when she thought harder about it, she'd remembered he'd asked her to dance, that he hadn't been a good dancer, that they'd danced once, then sat down. She hadn't even talked to him, and she hadn't liked him because he was so silent and his silence had a heavy impenetrableness to it that made her wonder why he'd asked her to dance.

The reason she didn't at first remember dancing with him was that sitting at a table behind them was a man she'd had an affair with and in a forlorn way was still in love with. He was sitting with a woman; by the way he was acting she could tell he was in love. When she'd noticed him and smiled and waved, he'd deliberately looked away without even nodding. She'd been so wounded by this unexpected, deliberate and undeserved slight that all enjoyment was leached from the evening and after a while, it was barely midnight, she'd gotten up, said goodnight, and left.

But then, she thinks, I do remember that the man I'd danced with stood up when he noticed I was leaving, that as I was walking away he was hastily trying to make change to settle his share of the bill. And I hurried out of the club, and I kept telling myself he wasn't leaving because of me. And yet, as I passed the shadowed street behind the club I thought seriously of stepping into it and hiding against a building till he'd gone by. I didn't, my training to stay on well-lit streets was too strong, and besides, I kept thinking I was imagining things, that he wasn't going to follow me, or if he was, it was only because my house and the house he was staying in were near each other.

Even now, after all these years, after all the times she's remembered the details of that night, she can still see the comforting shadows of that narrow side street. She remembers clearly how she hesitated, how close she came to taking those few quick steps that would have saved her, and how she didn't, telling herself not to be silly, not to be melodramatic.

I never told anyone, she thinks, because if I did how could I maintain my dignity, my good name, my social standing as a decent woman? I was a divorcee, I was in a nightclub unescorted, I'd had affairs, I'd slept with men I'd just met. I'd violated all the codes I was raised with, had become all the things a dozen years before I'd fought with my dates not to become. This is why for twenty-five years I couldn't tell this story. Because it was all my fault; I had been asking for it.

Is that why I refused to think about it? she asks herself. Because I couldn't face that awful truth? That everyone would think I should have expected it, given my lifestyle? That because of it nobody would care? She knows that was part of it: her pride kept her silent, and her stubborn belief in her own strength to endure even the worst that fate might have in store for her.

For all those years she hasn't allowed herself to think about it—except inadvertently, stopping herself as soon as she noticed she was—now, her dark secret out in the open at last, she's driven obsessively to remember it clearly, in every detail. Despite the new climate of opinion, she still suspects it really was her fault, as she'd thought for all these years, something she'd earned, and has no right to be troubled or angry about. She needs to know the truth about it, either to accept the blame or to at last feel the outrage she's told she has a right to.

No, it's more than that, she thinks. She's reached a time when she needs to study her rape from every possible angle in order to at last discover its true meaning; she's driven to gathering together all the details of her life, every single one. She's weaving them into a precise tapestry—her finished life—something, when she reaches old age, she'll be able to glance at with awe and in contentment, everything sorted and in its place, all passions wiped away, everything clearly what it is and nothing more.

She knows that what happened to her was trivial compared to the rapes other women have endured. She wasn't even really frightened, not at any time during the whole thing. He scared me, the way when I got my key out he stood close to me, and when I tried to slip inside first and shut the door on him, he put his leg in the gap, shoved, and was inside. Then I was scared, she thinks, but not terrified, just scared, because I knew he would try to force me to have sex. I didn't think beyond that, because he was a close friend of a man I trusted, and I couldn't believe anybody that man cared about would be capable of anything really bad like maybe—murder. As he pushed his way in, I believe I clung to that thought.

She remembers he put his arms around her and kissed her in the darkness of her living room—I don't remember anything about that part, she tells herself—and said, "Where's the bedroom?" He thought it was upstairs and was pushing her toward it and she said, "No, not upstairs," thinking if he couldn't find the bedroom she'd be safe, but the moon was so bright and they were at the bottom of the stairs and it was through the open door beside them, they could see the moonlight shining on the satin spread.

She can't remember about the clothes part. She would have been wearing jeans, she doesn't know how they came off. She remembers his belt buckle hurting her and his raising up to undo it while he kept one forearm across her chest. She fought with him, pushed against him, tried to hold her legs together, to bring her knees up, to shove him away, but it was hopeless. In the one effort when she used all her strength to throw him off, he responded by using his strength to hold her down. She knew when she felt his whole masculine power, if she didn't stop fighting him he not only could hurt her, he would. It seemed the only sensible thing to do was to give in.

Somehow the sex didn't matter much, not at the time, anyway. It was horrible and disgusting, but it was his action, not hers, so she wasn't disgusting, he was. That was what she was thinking as it happened, that it wasn't much, it wasn't anything. After, she pretended she was asleep. He pushed her a bit or something, she doesn't clearly remember what, and then he just left. Got up, pulled on his pants, walked out.

She remembers how the second she heard the door shut she leaped out of bed and locked it. She doesn't know if she saw this through the window or if she imagined it, but she sees him hesitate and look over his shoulder when he hears the bolt snap shut. Like it just occurred to him she might be mad at him or afraid of him, like up to that moment it never occurred to him that she had any feelings at all. Or maybe she was going to call the police. She remembers she thought of them for only one brief instant, shuddering at what they might say to her. No, she never seriously considered the police, but she thinks at that moment it might have crossed his mind, and for an instant he was afraid.

Then I just walked around the house in the dark, she remembers, didn't even put on any lights. Just walked around from room to room and looked out the windows at the moonlight. And I felt so bad. I felt like life was too awful to want to live. That I wasn't loved by anyone, that I wasn't—I was going to say, fit to live, she thinks, but that sounds like all those women on TV and radio and in magazines who are so excessive. Anyway, it wasn't quite like that.

I was fighting this terrible sense of loss and the ugliness of life. Like this I would never recover from because I had been so defiled, and all the things I'd believed in, all the things I'd tried to be, one silent, well-muscled stranger could destroy in a minute. Could make me feel I was a fool, and alien to the loving, clean world I was raised in because I was so bad, so guilty, so big a liar about myself.

Yet, as well as she can remember she didn't think of suicide. Instead, she'd been plunged down into an echoing underworld whose very air was made of something more resonant and more meaningful than mere pain, and the place was so far down and so dark she couldn't pull herself out of it, couldn't even think of escaping, couldn't think at all. Now she sees it was the place that at bottom holds death, and she'd been aware of it then, but beyond action of any kind.

Eventually she must have simply gone to sleep. The next day she got up and went to work and looked after her children when they returned from visiting their grandparents, and kept on going to work and doing all the things she was supposed to do—doing them badly sometimes, fitfully, failing as often as she succeeded, being an ordinary, normal human being, she supposes, and didn't even try to kill herself.

She regards it also as ironic that the night she heard herself say out loud she'd been raped, the mutual friend she and her new acquaintance had been talking about was the man who'd sat behind her in the club that night, the man she'd been in love with, who'd refused even to say hello. She remembers how his deliberate turning away from her had hurt as much as if he'd slapped her. Even now she can't think why he'd done that, and she's surprised to find it stands out in her memory as one of the worst hurts she's had to endure.

Nor did she once think *why me* as she'd heard victims of misfortune do: it was where she was headed, it was a fate she could foresee—not that she had, she doesn't mean that—but it hadn't surprised her, it hadn't seemed unfair, because it fit within the context of her life at that time.

This is why she feels no outrage, only this bottomless, unending sorrow whenever she thinks of it. That he had no right was never in question but—if only she could hold onto that glimmer she sometimes catches of some greater wisdom that might tell her what she really wonders: why so small a thing, that didn't even leave a bruise, made her feel so bad.

Now she remembers something else that hovered on the edge of her memory all these years. The day afterward, coming home from work to discover she'd forgotten her keys, she'd had to break a pane of glass in the French doors in the dining room to get in. A few nights later a male friend walked her home from the movie she'd been to with her friends. She must have invited him in, because she remembers, when he saw the broken glass lying where she'd left it on the dining-room floor, he'd picked up every shard and put it all in the garbage. She remembers the strange way he did it, glancing at her once, not listening to her feeble protest that she'd do it herself in the morning, but bending so quietly and carefully, with an air of the most complete gentleness, a sort of tenderness toward her for which she could find no explanation.

Neither of them spoke as he worked, but it was as if they both knew this was something she was unable to do herself, something she needed help with. Even now she doesn't know why she couldn't do it, and she remembers how as she watched him work she had been filled with gratitude, she nearly wept for his kindness. Yet try as she might, she can't remember his face or his name, only his gentleness, and the sound of his broom brushing over the hardwood floor, sweeping up the last particles of broken glass.

Margaret Gibson

The House That Stan and Rosie Built

The clock ticks. Ten minutes to nine, it says. The minute
hand is pale green and luminous. The clock is battery
operated so that there are no electrical cords stretched across the
bedside table. There are two side tables, one to either side of the
bed, one white, one brown. You can see that the white bedside
table used to have a brown finish and has been poorly painted
over. Splotches and streaks of the brown finish can be seen
through the white paint. The other bedside table, the one with
the brown finish, holds a small blue lamp. There is a tea stain, and
dust, on the pale blue lampshade, a plain black telephone sits just
in front of the lamp. The tea stain looks like a country marked
on a map, Italy maybe.

In between the two bedside tables is the bed. It is an unremarkable bed, narrow with a worn pink bedspread, worn so
badly that in some places the material is shiny, little balding
patches. Once the bed was a part of a set of twin beds. You could
buy it in any furniture store, a bed like that, or on the upstairs
floor of Simpson's in downtown Toronto. Little is expected of

this bed, not romance or dreams. The bed is only expected to provide sleep, oblivion for so many hours each night. Its occupant, her name is Rosie, scoffs at romance and dreams. They are for the young, she says.

This is what we have, this small, square, lifeless room, ordinary in every corner. The clock ticks. A very old dresser of dark wood with a small mirror is pushed against one wall opposite the foot of the bed. *This is what we have*, says Rosie, *this is all we have.* Rosie doesn't fear oblivion, she seeks it.

The clock ticks.

Rosie is old. Her long white hair which she pins up during her waking hours is fanned out across the pillowcase. The pillowcase is embroidered in tiny pink flowers like dewdrops in their shape. When you see the pink embroidered dewdrop flowers you might think to yourself that once someone tried to make this oh-so-ordinary room pretty, attractive, add light and air to it. Who? Rosie?

Rosie sleeps, her thin face pressed on one side into the pillow, one hand and arm flung out as if reaching for someone—or pushing them away. On the side of her face that is not pressed to the pillow can be seen one high cheekbone. High, and softly curving. Maybe a younger Rosie was once pretty, beautiful even, but Rosie never talks of it.

Her eyes, when open, show two watery blue pools, wrinkles snake across her pale complexioned skin, the skin itself seems fragile white and wafer-thin as if it could crumble into dry dust at any moment. You could stroke her skin, bunch it in your hand, and upon opening your hand it would be nothing but dust, white as chalk, sifting through your fingers. You can imagine it like that and expect to see light shining clear through Rosie's skin, in one side and out the other. One of Rosie's legs, the right one, is shorter than the other due to an unfortunate hip operation. Three-legged with a cane Rosie staggers through the days. She wears a plain blue flannel nightie with long sleeves, the sleeves come a little below her elbows where they are bunched and gathered in with elastic.

Outside it is March, and it is cold, Rosie knows that. She knows that because she heard the weather report on the CBC news at six o'clock. She has not set foot outside the house in over fifteen years, instead she stands in shadows, her old face pressed close to one window or another, an oval of steamy breath on the glass.

Rosie had a turkey leg and scalloped potatoes for dinner. It is getting harder and harder to prepare meals and wash up afterwards, she has always been an indifferent cook and housekeeper anyway.

Rosie's breathing is short and rapid, short, rapid spurts, little balloon puffs of breath. And she does not dream. Dreams are impractical, foolish things, and better left for the young. A younger Rosie had time to dream, now she is old and the minutes have exploded and there is not much time left, an urgency lives in those old and twisted fingers. Dream? she would ask. Dream of what? Once I dreamt of romance and love, and a husband, and children, and a little house filled with happy voices and laughter, isn't that what all young women dream of? But now she is old, and everything is already over, she'll tell you, except that final fact. The old carcass still breathes in-out, the pulse-beat measures time. It is already over. This is what we have. Little balloon puffs of breath.

Next door to Rosie's room is another bedroom. Stan, Rosie's husband of fifty years, sleeps. He has a long, thin face. His nose is long and a little hooked at the end, his eyes small and pale blue in colour, and his hair is a shock of white and sticks up from his head in little white, excited tufts. The right side of Stan's face is frozen into a slight grimace, one corner pulled downwards like the tail on a comma, and his right hand and arm twist out at an odd, awkward angle. Stan had a stroke last year. His bedroom, like Rosie's, is square with off-white walls. It is a replica of Rosie's room except there is no battery operated clock on the bedside table, and his bedspread is pale blue, not the pale pink of Rosie's. Both of the rooms have identical dressers of dark wood with the small mirror attached on top.

The house they live in is a tiny, narrow rectangle with tiny rooms. There is a kitchen, the two bedrooms, a living room, and a bathroom all on one floor. The kitchen is more like a small kitchenette in an apartment rather than the full-blown walk-around kitchen of a house. In the kitchen are the usual appliances, a stove, refrigerator, two metal sinks, a yellow Formica kitchen table wedged tightly against one wall opposite the avocado green refrigerator. The living room also is tiny with floor-length shiny gold drapes which are drawn, in fact, these curtains are never open no matter what the time of day or night. In the tiny living room there is a low beige couch, and two beige armchairs to either side of the couch. Pressed close to the couch, almost smack-up against it, is a honey-coloured Danish modern coffee table with untidy stacks of magazines and library books on it spilling out over the edge, a metal ashtray wedged in between the book and magazine piles with three squashed cigarette butts curled in it, fat and curling, like caterpillars. Rosie's old-fashioned treadle sewing machine is up against the end wall, and in one corner turned at an angle is an enormous coloured television set. Stan watches TV every day, all day. He can get over seventy channels because he has one of those satellite dishes. "Best investment I ever made," he told his nephew last week. Stan rises early—four a.m., or four-thirty at the latest—and he watches TV from the time he gets up until the time he switches off the set each night at nine when he gently touches the dials and strokes the knobs, then he goes to bed. He watches game shows and soap operas, sports and talk shows. His favourite soap opera is "The Young and the Restless," his favourite sport is golf.

There are no paintings on the walls, no plants on the windowsills, no photographs arranged on top of the television set bound neatly in gold frames. The house is a blanked face, an unfinished picture.

In this tiny, ordinary house, ordinary in every corner, there is all one needs to function: a dishwasher, white, and a garbage disposal unit, a small Moffat stove (avocado green) and the Frigidaire refrigerator (avocado green), Rosie's old treadle sewing machine, the two beds from the once twin set, and a cubbyhole bathroom, pink-tiled with a sink, a toilet, and tub, toilet paper, white, two-ply. They needn't ever go out. Stan has to use a walker now and a wheelchair since his stroke, and Rosie can no longer remember how cool air can feel, cool as silk, and summer dreams, and long drinks of water, instead she presses her face up against glass, steamy ovals of breath on windowpanes.

The house is built of rust-coloured bricks and is rectangular in shape, a bungalow in a suburb of Toronto, Scarboro. Rosie can remember when they used to spell Scarborough properly with the "ough." She still addresses her infrequent letters this way. There is a small off-white cement porch at the front of the house. The front door leading onto the porch is painted blue and white and there is an aluminum screen door, a black wrought-iron porch rail, a suburban patch of lawn, and a carport to the left-hand side of the house and a little way down from the house on a black tarred drive.

Not long ago a developer, a man in his mid-forties who smoked a pipe and drove a little Gremlin automobile, offered them a fairly large sum of money for their house and the patch of land it stands on. They wouldn't take it. If you were to ask them why they might shrug and say, "We've always lived here in the house. It is our house. This is what we have, this is all we have."

And you know it is.

This is the house that Stan and Rosie built.

Stan sits in the living room ensconced in his wheelchair. His old, arthritic hands rest on the arms and his feet dangle loosely on the footrest. He's had to use the wheelchair almost exclusively these past four months, the walker requires just more effort and energy than he's got. The television is turned on, Phil Donahue's on screen swinging his mike, and pulling up tufts of his thick white hair, and waving his arms in the air to accompany his histrionics for the audience which is made up mostly of women in their thirties and forties, a smattering of fifties. The very old, like Stan, watch Phil on the television from chairs and couches that smell of dust and lavender sachets.

Stan is smiling, and he thinks, Once Rosie'd have liked this show. Old bitch. I won't tell her he's having the male strippers on today. Let her find out herself. For a moment his smile fades. Did he detect a yearning in his silent voice, his deep-inside parts when he thinks about Rosie having liked this show once? A yearning for younger, gentler days when everything was softer, more rounded out somehow. Hell, the whole world once was softer and fuller. Nothin' soft and round now, all sharp angles and aches. No, no, he doesn't know if he's yearning, and wishing, and he's not about to think on it. He puts his mind on the television show. He likes Phil Donahue. He's a pretty smart guy, Stan thinks. An' you can learn about anything on his show from nuclear fission to the love life of necrophiliacs. Yeah, really educational. Commercial break.

Stan lights a cigarette with a disposable orange Bic lighter. This is done with some difficulty. It is hard to move three of the fingers on his right hand at all since the stroke. Finally, after several unsuccessful attempts, and some soft cursing, the cigarette is lighted. He holds the cigarette in his left hand between two nicotine-stained fingers.

The commercial is one for brass beds and a trumpet wails in the background of the commercial. Stan leans forward in the wheelchair listening carefully, an earnest, intent look on his face, and this time he knows he yearns, no doubt about it, this long sigh of a feeling. Stan remembers when he used to play the horn himself, that gold-yellow gleaming, notes like perfect jewels spiralling out. He sighs his sigh, the long sigh of this feeling, and he thinks of Ross and Eddie, and Donnie, and Gerald, the guys in the band he belonged to—oh, when?—way back—was that after the war or was it a little before? He cannot remember but he remembers the war. Single, he was, a bachelor, fancy-free, still a young man. "All my own teeth then," Stan says out loud, making a tooth-tooth grimace with a smacking sound and displaying several gaps in his gums, "an' two good arms an' hands."

He addresses this to the trumpet wailing in the commercial, to the dark ache and hollow inside him. How that horn used to howl! Nights spent with the boys in small night spots in Toronto, slippery neon signs flashing electric red and blue and gold on the downtown streets, the night jumping, the marquee flashing out the band's name—The Golden Notes, yeah, that was it, what we called ourselves. He remembers smoky rooms and glasses of gin and whisky, cigarette and hat-check girls, girls in tights and low-cut dresses.

Never wanted to marry, Stan thinks, nope, didn't want that—to be tied down to the same woman, the same woman's legs to lay between for fifty years. He just couldn't see that, he still can't. Rosie chased an' chased me till I was too worn out to protest. She was pretty enough, good enough to sleep with, strong legs, she had good, strong legs, but mean, she was always mean-spirited—oh, the booze, wished I had some now. That long, long sigh and ache of a feeling.

The commercial is over and Stan stares at the screen as the strippers' music begins. He thinks about his horn and how he used to wedge it between his lips and how his heart just soared and sang and howled out the night with the horn. The pretty girls, smoky blue rooms, the delicate clink of ice in cocktail glasses, smoke curling and hovering up around the ceiling in a midnight blue blanket. The war came along, or it didn't if the band was after the war, World War II—was there another?—that next war after the last...

He thinks of that. He thinks of the war years he spent on the submarine. Sometimes they were afraid, and being underwater, tons of it, got to some of the guys more than it got to others, but mostly he remembers the boredom, and restlessness. Lots of drinking then. Playing cards, girlie mags, and writing letters home, drinking and joking with the guys. Stan has always liked the company of men. Men are easier, have more determination and good-will than women, sharing their smokes and booze and jokes, women are all tight and controlled and ungiving just like the space between their legs is. Stan laughs a little at this observation.

The band was before the war, Stan remembers now, and continued for a few years after. He bought himself a motorcycle just after the war, a Harley, and the other guys in the band bought motorcycles too. Great big sputtering, muttering, roaring metal chariots spewing out clouds of dust, hair flying back and abandoned in the wind, the sun warm lemon pools on the backs of his hands, his horn in the sidecar. They rode everywhere on those bikes spewing out dirt and energy and reckless joy.

All the guys dead now, thinks Stan sadly, 'cept Ross. Hey, I should give old Ross a call one of these days, haven't talked to him since Rosie threw away my phone book, my little personalized address and phone directory, old bitch.

Stan watches as one of the male strippers thrusts his pelvis and genitalia forward, the music throbs and beats a sexual pulse in the background, the women shriek and giggle, and Stan thinks, God, I hate being an old man.

Rosie sits in the kitchen at the yellow Formica kitchen table. A blue plate with toast crumbs scattered on it sits on the table in front of her. She is drinking a cup of tea, coffee is too hard on her old stomach these days. The tea is in a thick blue coffee mug, a deep blue. Once she planned to buy curtain fabric in just that colour. It seems long ago now.

Her long white hair is gathered and pinned up in a chignon, little stray white hairs have slipped out from the pins here and there and curl in little commas against the back of her neck. A book by John Steinbeck, *Tortilla Flat*, lies on the table next to the blue china plate. Steinbeck is one of Rosie's favourite writers and she supposes *Of Mice and Men* is her all-time, all-out favourite Steinbeck piece. She likes the way George watches out for Lennie. And she likes the way they were always telling each other stories about the farm they'd have. They gave a hoot in hell about each other. "H-ummph," Rosie says in the space of that thought. "H-ummph."

This is what we have.

She remembers she wept at the end of the book when Lennie— well, who didn't know about Lennie. Wept because she could still weep, she was young and still had dreams, and hope. Haven't cried in I don't know how long, tears so rare they got a preciousness of jewels, catch 'em in a silver teaspoon and save 'em. Been a long time since I cried, my tears all withered up and dry like the rest of me, been a long, long time.

She'd cried the first time Stan hit her, and the second, but not after that, no, never again. She supposed that all in all he didn't hit her so often. But that wasn't the worst of it, no, not by a long shot. There was the drinking and every time he drank he turned mean, real nasty, and then his fists might fall like hammers, but even that was not the worst. When Stan had his stroke last year he was weak as a newborn kitten and blows would have been as insubstantial as dust motes spinning in a shaft of sun. He used to get the booze in, usually the rye whisky, once every two weeks or so.

She remembers years ago when she first met him—just out of the navy and so handsome in his uniform—he told her that he had the willpower of a tic flea when it came to the booze. Well, he'd been straight with her about that then, credit where due, fair and square. And she'd loved him and wanted him to be her husband, belong to her—to give a hoot in hell about him and her—and Stan so handsome, dashing even in the sailor uniform and jaunty hat. She supposed that maybe she did chase him a little but she doesn't remember so clearly because over the years the script has altered, shifted subtly like drifting dust, and the accounts are muddled. And this is what she has to remember with.

This is what I have, this is all I have, thinks Rosie.

Carefully she pours tea from the small two-cup brown pottery teapot. She is wearing a pale blue housedress with wide dark blue stripes on it and it hangs a couple of inches below her thin, bony knees. She sighs because she remembers when these thin sticks of legs were shapely and strong—could run, jump—*I'm the wind, I'm a top spinning, I'm a running rabbit.* Stan used to smile wide and tell her she looked delicious and he'd say, "I'm gonna give you a real good lovin'," and he lay between her legs, good legs, strong legs. Bodies, they had bodies then, not these white loose sacks of flesh hanging on brittle bone like now. Bodies, real bodies, trim and shapely, rocks, we were hard as two rocks back then.

She'd loved him and wanted children, boys, to look just like him, three, maybe four. And I coulda, she thinks, I coulda.

He can't get out of the house now, not with the wheelchair and how weak he is, so he can't get any rye whisky or any other boozy concoction. Sometimes his no-good nephew dropped by and snuck him a bottle but she always found the bottles hidden under cushions or stashed in side table drawers, or under couches, and she pitched them out.

That no-good nephew he dotes on, and I coulda given him five all told. But no. He has no children and he dotes on that nephew as if he'd sprung from his very own loins. I even had names—for some of them.

She sips her tea. Idly she thumbs through *Tortilla Flat. To give a hoot…* Three times a week a nurse comes in. She comes in the afternoons to do light housework and cook the dinner meal and do laundry and banking, grocery store errands. Sometimes the nurse drops by the library for Rosie, the library over there by Cedarbrae Mall. Rosie is reminded that she should make out a new list of books for the nurse, whose name is Mrs. Greene.

Rosie has never seen the library where her treasures of Steinbeck and odd thin volumes of poetry lie, or the dozens of biographies of famous people she likes to read about. She also likes those true-life, real crime books that give an account of the murderer and his crime; books like *Small Sacrifices*, and *Doc*, and *Helter Skelter*. Like that. She does not know and will never know if she'd like the library, if she would find a damp warm rain smell there between the towers of books, or some small peace between its sturdy brick walls and wide sunlit windows. No, she'll never know, don't go out any more, haven't in—years—ten—has it been ten—*more?*—years? Yes, more. Fifteen. Over that.

Fifteen.

Years.

Twenty minutes to ten. Rosie looks at the stove clock. The day has hardly begun and she wants it to be over. She rubs at her forehead with her fingertips, massaging it. Rubs the tissue pale white skin, and sighs. Coulda given him five all told. Her hand falls to her lap where it motions for a moment seeking out a phantom womb filled with child. His name, she thinks, the first one, his name was Eugene. *This is what we have.* The minute hand on the clock moves. Outside a cold, grim March rain falls. The Ides of March. She sees the Roman calendar crumpling into dust. She supposes that even way back then one day could seem like the next to an old person. *Old*, I'm *old*. No children now, no dreams. Old. She sees rivers of blood and elastic wombs, and nipples plump, swollen, and flowing milk.

I loved him and I just wasn't satisfied, wouldn't be until he slipped that ring on my finger. I thought I could change him, alter him pliable like potter's clay on a wheel, but I couldn't change a thing. And he said he'd leave if I didn't... leave... back then I couldn't bear... No use thinkin' about all that. Slowly, with an effort, Rosie's long, thin hands gripping the edges of the Formica table, she stands, and leans heavily on her cane navigating slowly over to the avocado green Frigidaire. She opens it. The freezer compartment. Yes, she better make out a grocery list for Mrs. Greene tomorrow. Tonight have a frozen chicken pot-pie and fry up some of those frozen french fries in a pan. Her skin looks transparent under the white kitchen ceiling light. You expect to see bones, her skeleton laid right out there under the bright electric ceiling light like in an X-ray, her skin pale white and fragile like white papier-mâché, but you don't. Instead you see white wrinkled folds of flesh-and-regrets.

Phil Donahue is winding down now. Once he had a really good show just like a tabloid newspaper, all the weird and wild guests he has on. The show on child abuse last week, well, he just couldn't believe it. This one child had to have her legs amputated on account of her mother left her in a deserted, freezing building for three days as a punishment for something or other and the child's legs got frozen and turned gangrenous, and the first person the child asked for after she come out of the anaesthetic from the operation was her mother. Good Christ! That was real interesting, Stan thinks, and it just goes to show you that some people are better off without.

Well, don't it?

Maybe he could get his nephew to come out this week and take him to the carport where he's got a mickey of rye whisky hid.

The old bitch don't know about that. What does she expect me to do, anyway, a prisoner like this? She threw out my personal address and phone book and she's driven all my friends away with her nastiness, and she listens in on the extension phone in her room to the few paltry calls I do get.

Ahh! Old bitch! At first I thought it was just kinda accidental destroying my sports magazines and throwing out my phone book but now I see it's systematic, this cruelty, she means to make my life miserable. And she has. Maybe I oughten' to have hit her ever, all told it wasn't so often, was it? You'd think her skull was a bone-china plate the way she carries on, an' she remembers every time, every goddamn little in-ci-dent. No, I suppose I shouldn'ta, but the booze does that sometimes, all that damn whining and crazy female dreams.

Sometimes now though I think maybe one kid woulda been kind of nice, company and all. If he were like my nephew I'd like him real fine. Someone to play gin rummy with and crack a few jokes and have a drink or two, me—I got nobody now—not with the way Rosie acts.

"Rosie!" Stan calls. His thin voice is raised with difficulty. "Rosie, would ya please do up my cuffs?"

Stan is wearing a white long-sleeved shirt and because of his stroke he can't button them or put in cufflinks, his right hand is pretty well useless. The cuffs dangle loose out at his wrists like white birds' wings.

"Rosie, ya hear me?"

But he keeps his voice polite, neutral, it doesn't do to rile her. He hears the slow tap of her cane and he brightens a little. Maybe she's in a good mood today and will be civil. Rosie stands in the doorway of the living room. She doesn't look directly at

Stan but instead fastens her gaze on the shiny gold curtains. Stan turns his head and tries to smile.

"Rosie, dear, would ya do up my cuffs?"

Rosie doesn't answer right away. She turns the knobbed cane in her hand. Oprah announces that they are going to talk with psychopaths today on the show. Stan waits. Somewhere a clock ticks.

Finally, "What do you want them done up for? It's not as if you was going anywhere."

"That's not the point, Rosie. They feel sloppy. I may be old but I'm no sloppy bum. Remember what a natty dresser I used to be? Sure ya do. All the time ya told me how swell I looked."

"Can't remember." Her mouth closes in a thin, stubborn line. The two pale blue sets of eyes find one another.

"Well ..." Stan says, impatient.

"Well nothin'."

"Please do 'em up, Rosie, and please remember to put my Belvederes down on the grocery list for Mrs. Greene. You forgot last time."

Oprah's audience applauds as the first guest comes on, a psychopathic fifteen-year-old black girl. The girl's face is blank, all other emotions having surrendered to an old anger, and now nothing but coldness shows from inside to the face out.

"I'll tell you," Rosie says, the thin stubborn line of mouth twisting into a small smile, "I didn't forget to put your smokes on the list, I just didn't put them on, and I'm not doin' up your damn cuffs. Be a slob, for all I care. Sit there, old man, sit there and rot. Fossilize, for all I care! Yeah, old man, just sit there and watch your TV 'cause you're not going to make any phone calls. I ripped up your phone book and there's no booze, and no more smokes, and no sports magazines, so sit there and stare at the idiot box and pretend you're alive! 'Cause that's all you're doing—pretending. This is it—all we have! Sit there and fossilize, you old bastard!"

"You old bitch," Stan says tearfully, one frail fist helplessly clenched. "You rotten old bitch!"

"That's right, that's right, that's the way," she says in a hiss and the hiss falters, dies.

Rosie turns, and slowly hobbles out of the room leaning on her cane. The fifteen-year-old girl is saying to Oprah, "And then I'd cut off her arms and knife her a little in the tits and I'd keep bringing her around when she passed out so that she'd feel the pain as much as possible."

The audience sits in silence, spellbound, and Stan shakes his head, *Christ, this crazy world, the whole world gone nuts.* Suddenly he feels very vulnerable and small and weak like a child, all bruised and ruined nerve-endings, no protective covering of skin, and every day it's the same, day in day out, no one to talk to, to share a joke and a good day, and his whole self is bruised and tender and vulnerable without protection, and a single tear rolls down his cheek.

Later, one p.m.

Rosie knows the time without looking at the clock on the Moffat stove. Stan's soap opera, "All My Children," is just beginning and she charts the time with that. Can set your clock by it. She can hear it blasting away from the living room. She is drinking more tea from the little brown two-cup teapot. She sketches on a white typewriter-sized tablet of paper. She draws roses and tulips by a stream. This is where she'd like to be, by the stream and smelling the flowers' perfume, but she doesn't think she'll go out this spring either, not even when it warms some—she might never be able to get back into the house. She is too feeble, too old, too afraid. She knows the map of the house, what it expects of her, where the walls and the detours are, where there is a corner, a turn, and all her friends dead anyway—where would she go if she did go out? There is nowhere.

Rosie has always liked sketching and she is really not half bad at it, not entirely unaccomplished. She draws a long curving line, and twists a stem. She remembers in a long-ago time when the minutes did not hang heavy like hours on the clock hand, and time, weighted, had not sagged with the burden of blank-white years laid end to end like empty white boxes, that she dreamt of being an artist of some sort. Later, when she was a young woman, she thought she might like to try designing fashions, be a clothing designer with her agile fingers, a talent in them, but the hands are old and twisted now, the bones inside the dry white skin aching with arthritis in the joints, and gnarled like old tree roots. Then, of course, she'd married Stan, and forgotten her dreams of sketching and designing or at the least pushed those ideas to the back of her mind.

She dreamt of babies when she married Stan.

Round, plump babies with Stan's shock of fine blond hair and blue eyes. His eyes had a brightness to them back then, they were two sparkling blue pools in that handsome face with the finely drawn, rather aristocratic nose. Eugene, she'd been in her sixth month with Eugene. Rosie counts it out on her fingers. Sixth, yes. Eugene formed right down to beautiful curved and pearly white fingernails, fingers as tiny as bits of thread. She remembers how she planned and planned his nursery. She cut out the coloured plastic shapes of a giraffe, an elephant with a hat, a tiger, and a hippopotamus. Eugene was the first. Her hair had been thick and black and long falling past her shoulders. She wore a summer frock, with lace, she recalls, and remembers sitting in that pretty pink and lace frock on the floor of the nursery, little Eugene's nursery, and she carefully cut out the animal shapes, patiently, hour after hour. The shapes, being plastic, were hard to cut, and put up a resistance to the scissors so that she cut and cut and cut for so long that every finger of her right hand ached. She only ceased cutting and laid down the scissors when her hand could not endure another moment of it. Her belly swollen, puffy and stretched, her womb elastic moving in-out to the rhythm of Eugene's tiny breaths. She bought a baby book, blue, she knew she was going to have a boy. She even bought the birth announcements, little bright gay cards at the Rexall Drugstore. The sky that day was the brightest blue, nearly a turquoise with dreamy white wisps of clouds floating in the blue. The sun shone on the sidewalk bright as a lemon peel.

It was on this most perfect of days in her sixth month, her belly heavy and ripe as a watermelon, that Stan came home from work early and told her he did not want the baby.

"But Stan," she said, "there's nothin' we can do about that and you'll love little Eugene fine. You'll love him fine, you'll see."

"Like hell I will! Some snivelling, dirty brat taking up all our time. I want no part of it!"

"Why did you wait so long to tell me this?" Tears rose in her eyes.

"I was tryin' to get used to the idea, being fair like I am, I tried to get used to it, and I can't. My mind's made up. Get rid of that miscarriage or I'm gone, lady, out the door!"

What could she have done? There was nothing…

She remembers lying on the table. It was a kitchen table but not Formica, it was a wooden kitchen table with a blue oilcloth in an alcove. There was a metal basin with warm water in it just beside her, a round, white light dangled above her. The man was cooking a steak. He was the abortionist and he was preparing his dinner. Steak, onions, a baked potato, chives. He was broiling the steak in the oven. The onions were sautéeing in butter in a pan on the stove burner. The smell of the onions mingled with the smell of the broiling steak. He was a man in his mid-fifties and around his waist he wore a gaily coloured chef's apron, the kind suburban husbands wear at backyard barbecues in the summers. He had a bushy, full white beard, and his black sweater and jacket smelt of cigarette smoke and onions. He chatted as he bustled around his kitchen, chatted amicably, even as he put his hand up inside of her. Up, way, way up where little Eugene lived like a sweet fairy child all hidden and warm inside her pink pearly shell-parts.

"This is your first," he said. It was not a question. "You know how I know?" Blind, and worse than blind, mute, she shook her head. "Well," he said, warming to his subject, "you're so tight there, you see? I knew right away. This one woman I've done so many times I can put half my arm up her, clear up to my elbow." He laughed companionably sharing the joke. The onions sputtered in the pan of butter on the stove. The steak smell wafted by the table, and the agony, the burning, and the searing began. All the time she screamed the steak broiled and the onions sputtered in the pan of butter.

Since Rosie had been six months along she went into labour right there on the kitchen table and though she did not want to she could not stop it, nothing could stop it now, and she pushed little Eugene, her first baby, into the outstretched, waiting arms of the abortionist. She saw Eugene in the basin. Before she climbed off the table and went home she forced herself to turn and look into the basin. She looked. There he was, her fairy child, tiny, round, pink with dark, dark blond hair like a mist atop his head, little threads of pink fingers. He would have made a beautiful child.

Rosie touched Eugene's tiny head, her hand wading through muck and blood and tissue in the basin. She screamed. She screamed at the man, in the chef's picnic apron, who was turning his steak over, the oven door open, the oven's heat filling up the room. "Take the blood off him! Take the blood off him!" She screamed and screamed. The onions sputtered frying a delicious gold.

Stan drove her home in their grey automobile with the running board. What was it? The Pontiac? The Plymouth? No matter, he drove her home cooing in her ear. She went straight to bed when they got home. She was bleeding, bleeding. And being seared with the burning pain. Stan sat on the edge of the bed as Rosie twisted and turned in agony, her fingers gripping the sheets. "Everything's fine now, everything's fine, just fine," Stan crooned over and over. The bedsheets were drenched with blood. Rosie had to ask Stan to get a towel from the bathroom and she staunched the blood flow with the towel pressed between her legs. "Everything's fine, just fine," Stan crooned. Rosie pressed the towel tight against her, and thought, *This is what we have. This is all we have.* Just her and Stan, and the tiny empty house, a moon rising blood, and nothing could be the same, after this nothing could be the same. There was no taking it back, getting back the dreams.

She was all grown-up now.

The second abortion was performed months earlier than the first. Stan hit her nevertheless when he learnt of the second pregnancy, a slap that stung like a whip, Stan sobbing, and dribbling whisky down his shirtfront, sobbing with pity for himself. "Please, Stan," she'd begged. They could not use any birth control methods since they were both Catholics. Maybe if she'd begged for little Eugene he'd be curled up in the crib in the nursery with the giraffe and the hippo, and the tiger in the forest, and the elephant wearing a pink hat and eating peanuts, all frolicking across the nursery wall. Stan, she begged. Please. It did no good. He hit her again and repeated his threat of leaving. And Rosie could not bear that, the thought of him gone, no Stan any more ... Please didn't help. The second child's name was Albert. There were five abortions in all over the years.

Stan was very solicitous after each abortion. He brought her aspirins and cups of steaming tea and told her how fine everything was and was going to be. Sometimes he even bought her flowers and chocolates. But the flowers withered untended in vases, the chocolates went uneaten and turned hard and stale.

The Past moves under Rosie's eyelids. Her head aches.

Stan comes into the kitchen. His wheelchair, protesting, squeaks a little. It is difficult for him to navigate the wheelchair here, the halls are narrow and corners are especially tricky to get around.

"Any lunch?" Stan wants to know.

Rosie looks up at him, massaging her temples. Her smile is unpleasant. "No."

Stan mutters under his breath and slowly wheels his chair over to the refrigerator. He opens the door. As he lifts out the Sara Lee chocolate cake, he says, "You plan to starve me to death?"

"I give you enough to eat. Just enough," and she laughs, her laugh as unpleasant as her smile.

"Cup a tea, it'd be nice." Stan reaches into a drawer beside the refrigerator for a knife, finds one, and cuts himself a big slice of Sara Lee cake.

"I'm not making anything now."

"Look," says Stan, his voice strained and high and thin, "I'm sorry I hit you those times but I haven't hit you in years. An' Rosie, you know it was just the booze talkin'. You know. I shouldn'ta done that, I know that now but hell, Rosie..."

A commercial for Comet cleanser blasts out of the TV in the living room. Rosie hears the peppy little commercial jingle and thinks of swollen nipples flowing milk, babies washed away down drains like bits of refuse, waste, she sees rivers flowing blood, basins with skulls and muck in them, and hears onions sputtering on a stove.

The Past shifts, and moves again in her tears.

Rosie heaves herself up from her kitchen chair with great effort, and she leans against her cane taking a step towards Stan.

"How would you like it, old man, if I hit you?! How'd you like that? Would you be quick to forgive me! I think not!" Rosie places one hand against the yellow Formica table and steadies herself. She picks up the teapot from the table and snakes it towards Stan with a menacing motion. "Let's see how much you like it! How quick you are to forgive me!"

"Rosie, for God's sake, I've had a stroke!"

The teapot menaces.

"That stroke can't have bothered you no more than those abortions bothered me!"

The clock on the avocado green Moffat stove indicates that it is one-fifteen p.m. Rosie flings the hot tea in Stan's face. Stan cries out. Rosie shifts her weight against the kitchen table. She raises her cane above Stan's head. Stan turns his face up towards her in wondering and fear. He puts out one old withered hand to stop the blow, deflect it, but he is old and enfeebled. The cane comes crashing down on his skull. "This is for Eugene!" Rosie screams. And the cane comes crashing down again, this time on his nose. And again. "For Albert!" The cane flails the air, flails Stan. "For Ernest!" The cane has blood stains on it. One by one

Rosie calls out the names of her children, the cane marks them off, one by one, with each blow.

Stan is crying out, "Rosie!" but Rosie no longer has a name. I am not exactly a person any more, Rosie thinks. She is a mass of withered pale avenging flesh and hate, hate as strong as the burning searing her tucked-up parts, a blue oilcloth spread out beneath her, the smell of steak and onions in the air.

It is three-fifteen p.m. Rosie is lying down on her narrow bed. The luminous green minute hand falls. Rosie lies carefully down on the worn pink bedspread. She made the bed up that morning and does not want it mussed up. She folds her long fingers across her chest.

This is what we have, this is all we have.

Stan is sitting bent over in his wheelchair by the gold curtains. His face is a mass of purple and black and yellow bruises, and jagged lines of crimson cuts, his shock of white hair is matted and crusted with blood. He is weeping. He is an old man, and he is alone, and he weeps. He pulls the gold curtain back a little. It is raining still, raining great, fat, angry drops.

The Past moves behind his eyelids as it earlier moved under Rosie's lids. He sees the Past obscured and scattered like bits of dry dust or autumn leaves in a wind. Who can remember exactly how things were? We have only our own versions in the end. Remembered in bits and pieces like an unfinished puzzle, not all the pieces there, or fitting, or making a proper sense.

He looks out the window through the little crack in the curtains he's made. He can see the black wrought-iron porch rail and the patch of suburban lawn. Carefully he brings his fingers, frail, white, to his face, and sketches there the wounds, the pain, the cuts and bruises and burns and bumps. The rain falls steadily against the pale grey shingles, hitting hard, determined like pebbles being tossed. What's he going to do now? he thinks. I'm a prisoner. Can't even phone a friend or have a drink and a talk and a laugh, and she doesn't give me enough to eat and now this. Good Christ, I'm at her mercy. He looks longingly out the window. For the first time he realizes just exactly how much of a prisoner he is. Maybe if we'd kept just one, let it not—die, he thinks. But it—died, they—all—just—died . . . *This is what we have*, he thinks, *this is all we have.*

This is the house that Stan and Rosie built.

Dorothy Speak

Stroke

Mrs. Hazzard's husband has been taken by ambulance to the hospital and now she has been allowed upstairs to see him. She finds their physician standing beside the bed in a cool glass-walled room. He is a lanky seven-foot man who dresses in heavy tweed suits like a country doctor. Mrs. Hazzard and her husband have always shared a belief that the doctor's height endowed him with extraordinary powers, but here among these machines and wires and beeping monitors he seems shockingly weakened, diminished, like a fallen god. For five years he has been pressing his stethoscope with his long beautiful fingers to their faulty hearts and talking to them in his grave respectful voice. But he never said things would come to this. This is not heart. Has someone played a trick on them all?

"Mr. Hazzard, you have had a stroke!" the doctor shouts so loudly that it startles Mrs. Hazzard. "Mr. Hazzard, you have had a stroke. Can you hear me? Do you understand?"

Mr. Hazzard opens his mouth eagerly to speak, but all that comes out is *jabber jabber jabber*. Mrs. Hazzard begins to cry.

"Now, now," says the doctor, laying a long hand on her shoulder. She cannot believe its terrible weight. She is certain it will crush her. He explains how strokes occur, how there is a blockage somewhere, an absence of blood supply, killing brain cells, which may or may not be replaced. Mrs. Hazzard cannot comprehend what he is saying. It is both too simple and too complicated an explanation. In the doctor's blue eyes is something deeper, some dark knowledge for which she is not ready. She senses that he is preparing to abandon her and Mr. Hazzard. Already, he seems to have retreated from them a measurable distance. His kind smile pains her. He rushes off to another part of the hospital. Mrs. Hazzard would like to run away too but she must stay here, where nurses in dazzling white uniforms pad efficiently from room to room in their crêpe-soled shoes. All the patients here are very sick. Mr. Hazzard is no more important or lucky than any other. This thought frightens Mrs. Hazzard. Dusk is falling. She sees herself and her husband reflected against the black window like two silent actors on a bright stage.

Mrs. Hazzard is calling her daughter Merilee far away in a part of the United States where there is never any snow. A male voice answers the phone. When Merilee comes on, Mrs. Hazzard asks, "Who was that?"

Merilee says coldly, "Just a friend." Mrs. Hazzard wonders if Merilee will marry this one. Merilee has had four husbands and is not yet thirty-five. Once, Mr. Hazzard asked her if she was trying to set some kind of record. They have not met the last three husbands and this has made it easier for them because they have been able to think of these men as thin characters in a series of entertaining American films. In these films love is amusing and not to be taken seriously.

Mrs. Hazzard tells Merilee what has happened to her father.

Merilee asks her a string of questions to which Mrs. Hazzard may as recently as yesterday have had the answers but now cannot remember them.

"I'll call the hospital," says Merilee.

"Oh, I wish you wouldn't," says Mrs. Hazzard. "They're doing everything they can." Merilee has a way of destroying things. Mrs. Hazzard has a superstitious fear that a call from Merilee might trigger something. At the moment everything is in delicate balance, like a feather poised on a fingertip. One puff of air could send it spinning.

"Should I come home now? I don't want to come home now," says Merilee. "I'm going crazy. I haven't made my monthly quota." Merilee has quit nursing and is now selling cosmetics for a big company. She has an expense account and a company car, a small white convertible. Mrs. Hazzard pictures Merilee driving in this convertible through the hot yellow palm-lined streets of a southern city, wearing dark glasses and a short skirt. Merilee has bleached her hair and fixes it in a cumbersome Dolly Parton style. She diets until she has the waistline of a little girl. She has had breast implants, a face-lift, an abortion. Of course, Mrs. Hazzard finds all of this disturbing.

Merilee herself is sick enough to be in the hospital. She has nervous rashes, a stomach ulcer. She is like a gypsy, moving from one apartment to another, one husband to another. She can't sit still or be alone for more than five minutes. "You are running away from yourself," they have told her, but she laughs, her face, caked with heavy orange makeup, breaking into cracks.

"You sound more Canadian every day," she has told them. "I'll never come back to Canada. Nothing there is worth what you pay for it."

Now, Merilee tells Mrs. Hazzard, "I'd rather come near the end."

"Near the end of what?" asks Mrs. Hazzard. "Near the end of the month?"

"No," says Merilee. "If Dad gets worse, I mean. I'd rather come closer to the end. It costs so much to fly up there."

It is a sunny afternoon and Mrs. Hazzard is walking to the hospital, a journey of approximately one mile, taking her down a gentle hill, over a thin fall of fresh snow. She walks cautiously, afraid of falling. She passes an elementary school. It is recess and the playground is swarming with noisy children. Mrs. Hazzard stops on the sidewalk to look at the children, amazed. What vitality! What wonderful chaos! She is joyous and grateful for the sight of the children, for the beautiful day, for the white roads and lawns, for the knowledge that Mr. Hazzard has been taken off intravenous. The tubes and wires are gone and so is the catheter but he is wearing a big adult diaper. Several times a day, his cold fingers close with great urgency on Mrs. Hazzard's wrist. She listens expectantly. He pushes his face close to hers and says, "See, I can't…" or "I want…" but that is as far as he can get. She can feel the pressure of the message trapped in his head, pushing like water behind a dam, bursting to break through. He does not like to look at her. When he does, his eyes are full of a sorrow so devastating that even Mrs. Hazzard, with a voice still at her command, could not have found words to describe it.

"What do you want?" she gently encourages him. "What do you want? Tell me."

He says what sounds like *kitchen kitchen kitchen*. He draws a U shape over and over on the table in front of him.

"A letter? The letter U?" Mrs. Hazzard guesses. "A cup? A curved road?" Mrs. Hazzard cannot understand. Mr. Hazzard pushes her away angrily.

"Ge out!" he shouts at her. "Ge out!" She blinks at him, a frozen smile on her face.

Later she walks in the hallway. This is a noisy, dirty part of the hospital. She does not like it here. After the bright and modern intensive care unit, this ward is wretched and grey. The nurses seem to be very angry. Mrs. Hazzard feels tension in the air. She wonders how a person is supposed to recuperate in such an environment. Surely this is not a healthy place!

"Will you bring my husband another blanket?" she asks a nurse. "It's so cold in this part of the hospital and the blankets are so thin."

"We can't be running after every little whim of the patients," the nurse tells her.

At dinnertime, tall, rattling trolleys are wheeled past the door and the smell of canned gravy fills the ward. A tray is brought in and placed on a table in front of Mr. Hazzard. Mrs. Hazzard lifts the stainless steel lids to reveal bowls of soft pale food. Mr. Hazzard stares down at the meal, uncomprehending. She gives him a cup of mushroom soup and he tries to drink it, using the hand that is not paralysed. The white soup runs in two rivers out of the corners of his mouth and down his chin. It gushes out his nose. Mrs. Hazzard takes the cup away from him. She feeds him small bites of custard with a child's spoon. He swallows with great gravity and concentration, his mouth working endlessly.

One day Mrs. Hazzard comes home from the hospital and sees her neighbour in the Hazzards' backyard, a widower named Conte McTavish. For thirty years this man and Mr. Hazzard carried on a silly feud, the origins of which they could not remember. When they retired they started to say good morning to each other and soon were talking in the driveway or over the hedge in a shy, embarrassed, happy way, like reunited friends. Mrs. Hazzard calls to him but he cannot hear her because he is swinging an axe. She makes her way slowly across the front lawn, past the house and into the back corner. The skies are heavy and the cold smell of snow is in the air. Her feet break through a granular crust to the powdery snow beneath, which is soft and dry and insulated from the winter by the brittle surface layer.

The snow is deep and some of it falls inside her boots. It makes her think of a day in her childhood when she was so angry with her mother that she walked through snow this deep to a park. There she sat on a swing anchored in a drift and cried and prayed that her mother would fall down dead. The force of this memory makes her stop in her tracks, dizzy with the power and malice of her childhood emotions. For a moment, the landscape tilts and spins. Then Conte appears again across the lawn, which is polished by the wind into sculpted waves, a white sea.

"Conte, what are you doing?" Mrs. Hazzard asks her neighbour.

He swings around, startled, a short heavy man with wire-rimmed glasses and a square red face. He says, "I couldn't sleep last night. I woke up thinking about the cherry tree. William and I were supposed to cut it down this fall. It's diseased. Don't you remember? I was going to help him, but then—" He looks down at the ground for a moment, shaking his head. "Tell him I've cut it down for him, would you? Tell him he doesn't have to worry about it any more."

Mrs. Hazzard does not say that Mr. Hazzard probably does not remember his neighbour or even know any more what a cherry tree is. Pale, meaty wood chips are scattered in a circle around them, like pieces of blasted flesh. The felled branches lie like charred limbs against the untouched snow. Mrs. Hazzard stares around at all of this in bewilderment and shock. She smells the sweet smell of the fresh wood. For a moment anger flares up in her like a flame in a lamp, protected from the winter wind. She is about to say to Conte: I wish you hadn't done this. I wish you'd let it stand. Perhaps it was not diseased at all but merely temporarily dormant. Perhaps it would have hung on much longer than you expected. You had no right. But when she opens her mouth to speak, Conte begins to weep, tears flowing easily down his vein-tracked cheeks. He stands with his hands, in thick stiff leather gloves, wrapped around the axe, sobbing like a boy, his breath coming out in white puffs of cloud.

"I'm just so sorry," he blubbers. "I'm so sorry about all those years we never spoke to each other. Such a loss. Such a stupid waste."

Mrs. Hazzard thinks about the sadness, the futility of everything. She thinks how ridiculous she and her neighbour are, two old people standing in the snow.

The country doctor is transferring Mr. Hazzard to a rehab centre.

"Is this a step forward or a step back?" Mrs. Hazzard asks him.

He smiles at her gently, as though she is a child.

"Let's just think of it as a step," he says.

Always now, Mrs. Hazzard has the feeling that people are not telling her the truth. Or perhaps they are telling her the truth over and over in different ways but she cannot hear it. Mr. Hazzard grips the bed gate and shakes with tearless weeping.

"This may not be grief at all," the nurses tell Mrs. Hazzard. "It may be a nervous reflex, wires crossed somewhere."

Mrs. Hazzard does not believe this. "You are going to get better," she tells him. He looks up at her, his eyes so full of betrayal that she realizes now it is she who is telling the lies.

Mrs. Hazzard is playing bridge. All afternoon she has listened to the *slap slap slap* of the cards falling on the table like waves lapping at a shore. She has played more brilliantly than ever before in her life but she has played blindly, like a person under hypnosis. She can scarcely remember a single hand. Today the cards seem to her mysterious and powerful. They have some message for her. The faces of the heavy-lidded queen, the unhappy king, the weak prince hold some complex secret. She stares at their gay geometric jackets in black, red and gold, at the stiff gestures of their tiny prophetic hands. As the cards spin into a soft pile, the red spots of the diamonds and hearts swim in her vision like drops of blood. Again and again today the ace of spades has turned up in Mrs. Hazzard's hand. What does this mean? She gazes at the spade and sees a gravedigger's shovel.

The women with whom she plays are bloated with widowhood. After their husbands died, they ate and ate until they swelled up like slugs, expanding to fill the void. She senses them waiting for her to join them in widowhood. These are her friends but today Mrs. Hazzard notices things about them: powder settling like sand in the creases of their faces, their bracelets jangling with potent charms, their pink hair, lipstick bleeding in rivers around their mouths.

"Mr. Hazzard has been transferred to White Oaks," she tells them.

"Oh, White Oaks," they say gravely. "Nobody ever comes out of there. How *is* Mr. Hazzard?" they ask.

She feels their eyes burning into her forehead. "He is thin," she tells them.

"How much longer?" they ask.

"How much longer for what?" she says.

A silence falls in the room. The women stare at Mrs. Hazzard, smug as fortune tellers behind cards fanned out in their hands. She can feel the force of their desire like something evil, a deadly spell. The room is hot and filled with their flowery perfume. Mrs. Hazzard cannot breathe. She rises suddenly, tipping the table. The cards slide sideways. The women's eyes grow wide with alarm. Mrs. Hazzard hurries down a hall to the bathroom, where she locks the door behind her. The women follow. They try the doorknob. They tap gently with their lacquered nails.

"Come out of there," they tell her. Mrs. Hazzard imagines them on the other side of the door, their soft bodies pressed together in the narrow hallway.

"I could not live without William," she tells them through the door. "If William dies, I will die."

"You will not be permitted to die," they tell her. "You will have to go on. There is nothing special about you. You will have to get through it just as we have. Then you will become one of us."

Outside it is cold. Dusk is falling. The snow on the ground is turning blue.

It is nearly Christmas, and Mrs. Hazzard comes home and sees Conte McTavish's grandchildren building a snowman in front of his house. She stands on Conte's driveway and watches them, pleased to see something being created in this season of death. When she arrives the children have just mounted the head on the snowman. They add snow, packing it on where the spheres join. She watches them building up the body with handfuls, miracle of white flesh adhering to white flesh. It is a bright day. Mrs. Hazzard feels warmed by the life-giving sun. The snow is soft, the children's mittens stick to the snowman, pull off with difficulty. The snowman's curves are full and nourished, his belly swollen with health. He casts a robust shadow across the lawn.

Mrs. Hazzard stares at the children. They are amazing to her because they are so whole and lithe of limb, because they are so lucky, because they know little of their power to give life and to take it away. Above all, to take it away. The snowman belongs to the children, just as, in a way, Merilee holds the life of her father in her hands. It is within their means to create the snowman and to destroy him by their brief memories, their loss of faith, their susceptibility to distractions. The children inherit the earth.

"Hello," Mrs. Hazzard says, smiling at them.

"You are the woman whose husband is dying," they say.

"He is not dying," Mrs. Hazzard tells them. "He is only very ill."

The children stare at her. Their eyes grow wide, revealing the whites, so pure and unblemished, like the white of a hard-boiled egg, like snow before it has touched the ground. In their disbelief, the children are taking away with their hard-boiled eyes the life of my husband, Mrs. Hazzard thinks. The children's thick snowsuits distort their bodies, protecting them from the cold that Mrs. Hazzard feels and from something else within her, some fallacy.

The children go to the side of the house looking for branches piled there by Conte from the cherry tree. They bring out two vein-red sticks, which are multibranched, so that when they are stuck into the snowman's sides, they do not look like arms at all, but like whole circulatory systems.

"Do you have eyes for the snowman?" Mrs. Hazzard asks the children. She goes into her house and brings out a bowl of bright gumdrops she bought for Christmas though there is no one to eat them, she will have no visitors.

"I have brought you some eyes," she tells the children, holding out the bowl. The children look at the glittery orbs and begin to tremble. They run into the house, their scarves flying behind them like flags.

Dusk is falling. Lights come on up and down the street. Mrs. Hazzard stands in the snow with her bowl of candies, looking at the replete, sightless snowman.

Mrs. Hazzard has made for dinner a baked potato and a fried egg. This is a simple and healthy meal but she does not feel hungry. She is thinking about the pounds Mr. Hazzard has lost. Reaching for the telephone, she dials the long-distance number that will connect her with her daughter. The phone rings and rings. Finally Merilee answers breathlessly. She says she was on her way out, she was in fact in her car with the key in the ignition when she heard the phone ringing and came running back in. She thought it might have been someone important. Mrs. Hazzard looks out her kitchen window and tells Merilee that a heavy rain has been falling for several hours, though in Canada it should be snowing on the second day of January.

Merilee says, "God! I wish we had some of that where I am. The ground is cracking. We haven't had rain in three months. Water is rationed. What do you want, Mother? I'm late for my aerobics class."

Mrs. Hazzard tells Merilee that she has asked for an operation to put a tube in Mr. Hazzard's stomach because he cannot swallow food. Merilee is very angry.

"This is an artificial means to sustain him," she says. "We agreed not to do anything like this."

"I cannot sit here and watch him starve to death," says Mrs. Hazzard with emotion.

"Under the circumstances it would be the kindest thing," says Merilee. "You are doing this for yourself, not for him. You are being selfish."

"He's going to get better," Mrs. Hazzard insists.

"Oh, Mother," says Merilee bitterly, "you have always been so unrealistic."

"After the operation," says Mrs. Hazzard, "he's in God's hands."

Merilee snorts. "There must be somebody better than God we could put in charge of this," she says.

Mrs. Hazzard hangs up, quite shaken. She looks down at the potato and egg, solitary and undefiled on the plate. The egg yolk is the sun and Mrs. Hazzard will not break it, will not turn it into a watery eye. She puts the plate in the refrigerator.

She thinks about Merilee going out again to her car, walking across earth cracked like the surface of an overbaked cake. She pictures her at her aerobics class wearing one of those bright skin-tight costumes, and others in similar attire, young men and women leaning, bending trancelike before a wide mirror, stretching their firm, glistening, immortal limbs.

Dusk has fallen. Mrs. Hazzard goes out on to her porch with a bag of garbage. She sees the blind snowman, illuminated by Conte's porch light. The rain beats hard and steady on his shoulders, washing him away. It runs down his shrinking belly. His arms droop, loosened in their sockets. His flesh has become translucent as alabaster. It glows with a gentle but extraordinary quality, like a fading light bulb.

It is the morning of the operation and Mrs. Hazzard comes outside on her way to the hospital. She looks for the snowman in the neighbour's yard but he is gone. She stands on the white lawn, looking down at all that is left of him: the cherry tree branches lying on the ground.

At the hospital, a young intern intercepts Mrs. Hazzard on her way to Mr. Hazzard's room. He is tall and narrow-chested, with beautiful eyes and a woman's long lashes. Mrs. Hazzard does not know how such a thin, delicate man will be strong enough to save Mr. Hazzard.

"How is my husband?" she asks him. The intern tells her that Mr. Hazzard is dying. It is not the operation that is killing him, the intern explains, but pneumonia. He says pneumonia is something to be grateful for. It is known as the friend of the elderly. Mr. Hazzard will now die quickly. He will probably not live through the day.

"Death is very efficient," the intern says. "First the lungs shut down, then the kidneys, then the heart. *Bam bam bam*," he says, emphasizing his words by striking his fist in his hand. Mrs. Hazzard decides she does not like these young modern doctors. They are too smart, too confident, too unscathed.

A nurse indicates Mr. Hazzard's room. At first Mrs. Hazzard thinks they are playing a joke on her. You have shown me to the wrong room, she is going to say. This is not my husband. She is stunned by his appearance. He is unconscious and wearing an oxygen mask, through which Mrs. Hazzard can see his tongue rising and falling in his throat like a ship bobbing on a sea. Everything about his body now seems out of proportion. Parts of him have withered away and other parts look larger. His ears are like monarch butterflies, his nose is the size of a potato, his labourer's chest is massive, heaving beneath his hospital gown. His hands have grown puffy, filling up with fluid like the balloon hands in a child's drawing. He looks, thinks Mrs. Hazzard, like a clown. It seems that he is mocking her, with this droll exterior, this transformation. You have left me, William, she thinks. You have turned into someone else.

Mrs. Hazzard thinks about her daughter. She feels Merilee willing Mr. Hazzard to die. Merilee has more power from a thousand miles away than Mrs. Hazzard has standing here, beside her husband's bed. How foolish I have been, she thinks. No one ever told her hope could be so cruel. Hope seems to be killing her now, at the same time that it is making it difficult for Mr. Hazzard to die. She thinks about calling the doctor back, calling Merilee, calling Conte McTavish. Yes, she would tell Conte. Yes, you were right. Better to cut the tree down than to hold out hope. "It's all right, William," she says to her husband now. "It's all right. You can let go. You can stop breathing." Suddenly, Mrs. Hazzard feels a tension flowing out of herself and the onset of a terrible, comforting fatigue.

Mrs. Hazzard walks in the dim yellow light of the hallways in her heavy zipped boots. Though people die here every day, every hour, the nurses, rushing past her, do not seem to grasp the magnitude of what is happening to her. She is filled up, Mrs. Hazzard is brimming with the knowledge of Mr. Hazzard's death. She is like a cup gently running over, yet there is no one to catch the precious overflow.

Now Mrs. Hazzard is down on the first floor looking for the cafeteria, with her stiff square purse over her arm. She will buy a muffin. She must keep up her strength for the vigil. The big front doors swing open letting in warm air that sweeps around Mrs. Hazzard like a healing river. Hospital staff are coming in from the outdoors, coatless. They have been walking in the warm sunny streets carrying their winter coats over their arms here in January in the centre of the city in an old neighbourhood of sturdy brick homes. They are astounded, grateful, lightened by the springlike temperatures. It is my husband, Mrs. Hazzard wants to tell them. It is my husband who has brought this weather. He is dying and his body is absorbing all the cold.

Carol Shields

Hazel

After a man has mistreated a woman he feels a need to do something nice which she must accept.

In line with this way of thinking, Hazel has accepted from her husband, Brian, sprays of flowers, trips to Hawaii, extravagant compliments on her rather ordinary cooking, bracelets of dull-coloured silver and copper, a dressing gown in green tartan wool, a second dressing gown with maribou trim around the hem and sleeves, dinners in expensive revolving restaurants and, once, a tender kiss, tenderly delivered, on the instep of her right foot.

But there will be no more such compensatory gifts, for Brian died last December of heart failure.

The heart failure, as Hazel, even after all these years, continues to think of it. In her family, the family of her girlhood that is, a time of gulped confusion in a place called Porcupine Falls, all familiar diseases were preceded by the horrific article: *the* measles, *the* polio, *the* rheumatism, *the* cancer, and—to come down to her husband Brian and his final thrashing with life—*the* heart failure.

He was only fifty-five. He combed his uncoloured hair

smooth and wore clothes made of gabardinelike materials, a silky exterior covering a complex core. It took him ten days to die after the initial attack, and during the time he lay there, all his minor wounds healed. He was a careless man who bumped into things, shrubbery, table legs, lighted cigarettes, simple curbstones. Even the making of love seemed to him a labour and a recovery, attended by scratches, bites, effort, exhaustion and, once or twice, a mild but humiliating infection. Nevertheless, women found him attractive. He had an unhurried, good-humoured persistence about him and could be kind when he chose to be.

The night he died Hazel came home from the hospital and sat propped up in bed till four in the morning, reading a trashy, fast-moving New York novel about wives who lived in spacious duplexes overlooking Central Park, too alienated to carry on properly with their lives. They made salads with rare kinds of lettuce and sent their apparel to the dry cleaners, but they were bitter and helpless. Frequently they used the expression "fucked up" to describe their malaise. Their mothers or their fathers had fucked them up, or jealous sisters or bad-hearted nuns, but mainly they had been fucked up by men who no longer cared about them. These women were immobilized by the lack of love and kept alive only by a reflexive bounce between new ways of arranging salad greens and fantasies of suicide. Hazel wondered as she read how long it took for the remembered past to sink from view. A few miserable tears crept into her eyes, her first tears since Brian's initial attack, that shrill telephone call, the unearthly hour. Impetuously she wrote on the book's flyleaf the melodramatic words "I am alone and suffering unbearably." Not her best handwriting, not her usual floating morning-glory tendrils. Her fingers cramped at this hour. The cheap ball-point pen held back its ink, and the result was a barely legible scrawl that she nevertheless underlined twice.

By mid-January she had taken a job demonstrating kitchenware in department stores. The ad in the newspaper promised on-the-job training, opportunities for advancement and contact with the public. Hazel submitted to a short, vague, surprisingly painless interview, and was rewarded the following morning by a telephone call telling her she was to start immediately. She suspected she was the sole applicant, but nevertheless went numb with shock. Shock and also pleasure. She hugged the elbows of her dressing gown and smoothed the sleeves flat. She was fifty years old and without skills, a woman who had managed to avoid most of the arguments and issues of the world. Asked a direct question, her voice wavered. She understood nothing of the national debt or the situation in Nicaragua, nothing. At ten-thirty most mornings she was still in her dressing gown and had the sense to know this was shameful. She possessed a softened, tired body and rubbed-looking eyes. Her posture was only moderately good. She often touched her mouth with the back of her hand. Yet someone, some person with a downtown commercial address and an official letterhead and a firm telephone manner had seen fit to offer her a job.

Only Hazel, however, thought the job a good idea.

Brian's mother, a woman in her eighties living in a suburban retirement centre called Silver Oaks, said, "Really, there is no need, Hazel. There's plenty of money if you live reasonably. You have your condo paid for, your car, a good fur coat that'll last for years. Then there's the insurance and Brian's pension, and when you're sixty-five—now don't laugh, sixty-five will come, it's not that far off—you'll have your social security. You have a first-rate lawyer to look after your investments. There's no need."

Hazel's closest friend, Maxine Forestadt, a woman of her own age, a demon bridge player, a divorcée, a woman with a pinkish powdery face loosened by too many evenings of soft drinks and potato chips and too much cigarette smoke flowing up toward her eyes, said, "Look. You're not the type, Hazel. Period. I know the type and you're not it. Believe me. All right, so you feel this urge to assert yourself, to try to prove something. I know, I went through it myself, wanting to show the world I wasn't just this dipsy pushover and hanger-oner. But this isn't for you, Haze, this eight-to-five purgatory, standing on your feet, and especially *your* feet, your arches, your arches act up just shopping. I know what you're trying to do, but in the long run, what's the point?"

Hazel's older daughter, Marilyn, a pathologist, and possibly a lesbian, living in a women's co-op in the east end of the city, phones and, drawing on the sort of recollection that Hazel already had sutured, said, "Dad would not have approved. I know it, you know it. I mean, Christ, flogging pots and pans, it's so public. People crowding around. Idle curiosity and greed, a free show, just hanging in for a teaspoon of bloody quiche lorraine or whatever's going. Freebies. People off the street, bums, anybody. Christ. Another thing, you'll have to get a whole new wardrobe for a job like that. Eye shadow so thick it's like someone's given you a punch. Just ask yourself what Dad would have said. I know what he would have said, he would have said thumbs down, nix on it."

Hazel's other daughter, Rosie, living in British Columbia, married to a journalist, wrote: "Dear Mom, I absolutely respect what you're doing and admire your courage. But Robin and I can't help wondering if you've given this decision enough thought. You remember how after the funeral, back at your place with Grandma and Auntie Maxine and Marilyn, we had that long talk about the need to lie fallow for a bit and not rush headlong into things and making major decisions, just letting the grieving process take its natural course. Now here it is, a mere six weeks later, and you've got yourself involved with these cookware people. I just hope you haven't signed anything. Robin says he never heard of Kitchen Kult and it certainly isn't listed on the boards. We're just anxious about you, that's all. And this business of working on commission is exploitative to say the least. Ask

Marilyn. You've still got your shorthand and typing and, with a refresher course, you probably could find something, maybe Office Overload would give you a sense of your own independence and some spending money besides. We just don't want to see you hurt, that's all."

At first, Hazel's working day went more or less like this: at seven-thirty her alarm went off; the first five minutes were the worst; such a steamroller of sorrow passed over her that she was left as flat and lifeless as the queen-size mattress that supported her. Her squashed limbs felt emptied of blood, her breath came out thin and cool and quiet as ether. What was she to do? How was she to live her life? She mouthed these questions to the silky blanket binding, rubbing her lips frantically back and forth across the stitching. Then she got up, showered, did her hair, made coffee and toast, took a vitamin pill, brushed her teeth, made up her face (going easy on the eye shadow), and put on her coat. By eight-thirty she was in her car and checking her city map.

Reading maps, the tiny print, the confusion, caused her headaches. And she had trouble with orientation, turning the map first this way, then that, never willing to believe that north must lie at the top. North's natural place should be toward the bottom, past the Armoury and stockyards where a large cold lake bathed the city edges. Once on a car trip to the Indian River country early in their married life, Brian had joked about her lack of map sense. He spoke happily of this failing, proudly, giving her arm a squeeze, and then had thumped the cushioned steering wheel. Hazel, thinking about the plushy thump, wished she hadn't. To recall something once was to remember it forever; this was something she had only recently discovered, and she felt that the discovery might be turned to use.

The Kitchen Kult demonstrations took her on a revolving cycle of twelve stores, some of them in corners of the city where she'd seldom ventured. The Italian district. The Portuguese area.

Chinatown. A young Kitchen Kult salesman named Peter Lemmon broke her in, *familiarizing* her as he put it with the Kitchen Kult product. He taught her the spiel, the patter, the importance of keeping eye contact with customers at all times, how to draw on the mood and size of the crowd and play, if possible, to its ethnic character, how to make Kitchen Kult products seem like large beautiful toys, easily mastered and guaranteed to win the love and admiration of friends and family.

"That's what people out there really want," Peter Lemmon told Hazel, who was surprised to hear this view put forward so undisguisedly. "Lots of love and truckloads of admiration. Keep that in mind. People can't get enough."

He had an aggressive pointed chin and ferocious red sideburns, and when he talked he held his lips together so that the words came out with a soft zitherlike slur. Hazel noticed his teeth were discoloured and badly crowded, and she guessed that this accounted for his guarded way of talking. Either that or a nervous disposition. Early on, to put him at his ease, she told him of her small-town upbringing in Porcupine Falls, how her elderly parents had never quite recovered from the surprise of having a child. How at eighteen she came to Toronto to study stenography. That she was now a widow with two daughters, one of whom she suspected of being unhappily married and one who was undergoing a gender crisis. She told Peter Lemmon that this was her first real job, that at the age of fifty she was out working for the first time. She talked too much, babbled in fact—why? She didn't know. Later she was sorry.

In return he confided, opening his mouth a little wider, that he was planning to have extensive dental work in the future if he could scrape the money together. More than nine thousand dollars had been quoted. A quality job cost quality cash, that was the long and short of it, so why not take the plunge. He hoped to go right to the top with Kitchen Kult. Not just sales, but the real top, and that meant management. It was a company, he told her, with a forward-looking sales policy and sound product.

It disconcerted Hazel at first to hear Peter Lemmon speak of the Kitchen Kult product without its grammatical article, and she was jolted into the remembrance of how she had had to learn to suppress the article that attached to bodily ailments. When demonstrating product, Peter counselled, keep it well in view, repeating product's name frequently and withholding product's retail price until the actual demo and tasting has been concluded.

After two weeks Hazel was on her own, although Peter Lemmon continued to meet her at the appointed "sales venue" each morning, bringing with him in a company van the equipment to be demonstrated and helping her "set up" for the day. She slipped into her white smock, the same one every day, a smooth permapress blend with grommets down the front and Kitchen Kult in red script across the pocket, and stowed her pumps in a plastic bag, putting on the white crepe-soled shoes Peter Lemmon had recommended. "Your feet, Hazel, are your capital." He also produced, of his own volition, a tall collapsible stool on which she could perch in such a way that she appeared from across the counter to be standing unsupported.

She started each morning with a demonstration of the Jiffy-Sure-Slicer, Kitchen Kult's top seller, accounting for some sixty per cent of total sales. For an hour or more, talking to herself, or rather to the empty air, she shaved hillocks of carrots, beets, parsnips and rutabagas into baroque curls or else she transformed them into little star-shaped discs or elegant matchsticks. The use of cheap root vegetables kept the demo costs down, Peter Lemmon said, and presented a less threatening challenge to the average shopper, Mrs. Peas and Carrots, Mrs. Corn Niblets.

As Hazel warmed up, one or two shoppers drifted toward her, keeping her company—she learned she could count on these one or two who were elderly women for the most part, puffy of face and bulgy of eye. Widows, Hazel decided. The draggy-hemmed coats and beige tote bags gave them away. Like herself, though perhaps a few years older, these women had taken their toast and coffee early and had been driven out into the cold in search of diversion. "Just set the dial, ladies and gentlemen," Hazel told the discomfited two or three voyeurs, "and press gently on the Jiffy lever. Never requires sharpening, never rusts."

By mid-morning she generally had fifteen people gathered about her, by noon as many as forty. No one interrupted her, and why should they? She was free entertainment. They listened, they exchanged looks, they paid attention, they formed a miniature, temporary colony of good will and consumer seriousness waiting to be instructed, initiated into Hazel's rituals and promises.

At the beginning of her third week, going solo for the first time, she looked up to see Maxine in her long beaver coat, gawking. "Now this is just what you need, madam," Hazel sang out, not missing a beat, an uncontrollable smile on her face. "In no time you'll be making more nutritious, appealing salads for your family and friends and for those bridge club get-togethers."

Maxine had been offended. She complained afterward to Hazel that she found it embarrassing being picked out in a crowd like that. It was insulting, especially to mention the bridge club as if she did nothing all day long but shuffle cards. "It's a bit thick, Hazel, especially when you used to enjoy a good rubber yourself. And you know I only play cards as a form of social relaxation. You used to enjoy it, and don't try to tell me otherwise because I won't buy it. We miss you, we really do. I know perfectly well it's not easy for you facing Francine. She was always a bit of a you-know-what, and Brian was, God knows, susceptible, though I have to say you've put a dignified face on the whole thing. I don't think I could have done it, I don't have your knack for looking the other way, never have had, which is why I'm where I'm at, I suppose. But who are you really cheating, dropping out of the bridge club like this? I think, just between the two of us, that Francine's a bit hurt, she thinks you hold her responsible for Brian's attack, even though we all know that when our time's up, it's up. And besides, it takes two."

In the afternoon, after a quick pick-up lunch (leftover grated raw vegetables usually or a hard-boiled egg), Hazel demonstrated Kitchen Kult's all-purpose non-stick fry pan. The same crowds that admired her julienne carrots seemed ready to be mesmerized by the absolute roundness of her crepes and omelets, their uniform gold edges and the ease with which they came pulling away at a touch of her spatula. During the early months, January, February, Hazel learned just how easily people could be hypnotized, how easily, in fact, they could be put to sleep. Their mouths sagged. They grew dull-eyed and immobile. Their hands went hard into their pockets. They hugged their purses tight.

Then one afternoon a small fortuitous accident occurred: a crepe, zealously flipped, landed on the floor. Because of the accident, Hazel discovered how a rupture in routine could be turned to her advantage. "Whoops-a-daisy," she said that first day, stooping to recover the crepe. People laughed out loud. It was as though Hazel's mild exclamation had a forgotten period fragrance to it. "I guess I don't know my own strength," she said, shaking her curls and earning a second ripple of laughter.

After that she began, at least once or twice a day, to misdirect a crepe. Or overcook an omelet. Or bring herself to a state of comic tears over her plate of chopped onions. "Not my day," she would croon. Or "good grief" or "sacred rattlesnakes" or a shrugging, cheerful, "who ever promised perfection on the first try." Some of the phrases that came out of her mouth reminded her of the way people talked in Porcupine Falls back in a time she could not possibly have remembered. Gentle, unalarming expletives calling up wells of good nature and neighbourliness. She wouldn't have guessed she had this quality of rubbery humour inside her.

After a while she felt she could get away with anything as long as she kept up her line of chatter. That was the secret, she saw—never to stop talking. That was why these crowds gave her their attention: she could perform miracles (with occasional calculated human lapses) and keep right on talking at the same time. Words, a river of words. She had never before talked at such length, as though she were driving a wedge of air ahead of her. It was easy, *easy*. She dealt out repetitions, little punchy pushes of emphasis, and an ever growing inventory of affectionate declarations directed toward her vegetable friends. "What a devil!" she said, holding aloft a head of bulky cauliflower. "You darling radish, you!" She felt foolish at times, but often exuberant, like a semi-retired, slightly eccentric actress. And she felt, oddly, that she was exactly as strong and clever as she need be.

But the work was exhausting. She admitted it. Every day the crowds had to be wooed afresh. By five-thirty she was too tired to do anything more than drive home, make a sandwich, read the paper, rinse out her Kitchen Kult smock and hang it over the shower rail, then get into bed with a thick paperback. Propped up in bed reading, her book like a wimple at her chin, she seemed to have flames on her feet and on the tips of her fingers, as though she'd burned her way through a long blur of a day and now would burn the night behind her too. January, February, the first three weeks of March. So this was what work was: a two-way bargain people made with the world, a way to reduce time to rubble.

The books she read worked braids of panic into her consciousness. She'd drifted toward historical fiction, away from Central Park and into the Regency courts of England. But were the queens and courtesans any happier than the frustrated New York wives? Were they less lonely, less adrift? So far she had found no evidence of it. They wanted the same things more or less: abiding affection, attention paid to their moods and passing thoughts, their backs rubbed and, now and then, the tender grateful application of hands and lips. She remembered Brian's back turned toward her in sleep, well covered with flesh in his middle years. He had never been one for pajamas, and she had often been moved to reach out and stroke the smooth mound of flesh. She had not found his extra weight disagreeable, far from it.

In Brian's place there remained now only the rectangular softness of his allergy-free pillow. Its smooth casing, faintly puckered at the corners, had the feel of mysterious absence.

"But why does it always have to be one of my *friends!*" she had cried out at him once at the end of a long quarrel. "Don't you see how humiliating it is for me?"

He had seemed genuinely taken aback, and she saw in a flash it was only laziness on his part, not express cruelty. She recalled his solemn promises, his wet eyes, new beginnings. She fondly recalled, too, the resonant pulmonary sounds of his night breathing, the steep climb to the top of each inhalation and the tottery stillness before the descent. How he used to lull her to sleep with this nightly music! Compensations. But she had not asked for enough, hadn't known what to ask for, what was owed her.

It was because of the books she read, their dense complications and sharp surprises, that she had applied for a job in the first place. She had a sense of her own life turning over page by page, first a girl, then a young woman, then married with two young daughters, then a member of a bridge club and a quilting club, and now, too soon for symmetry, a widow. All of it fell into small childish paragraphs, the print over-large and blocky like a school reader. She had tried to imagine various new endings or turnings for herself—she might take a trip around the world or sign up for a course in ceramics—but could think of nothing big enough to fill the vacant time left to her—except perhaps an actual job. This was what other people did, tucking in around the edges those little routines—laundry, meals, errands—that had made up her whole existence.

"You're wearing yourself out," Brian's mother said when Hazel arrived for an Easter Sunday visit, bringing with her a double-layered box of chocolate almond bark and a bouquet of tulips. "Tearing all over town every day, on your feet, no proper lunch arrangements. You'd think they'd give you a good hour off and maybe a lunch voucher, give you a chance to catch your breath. It's hard on the back, standing. I always feel my tension in my back. These are delicious, Hazel, not that I'll eat half of them, not with my appetite, but it'll be something to pass round to the other ladies. Everyone shares here, that's one thing. And the flowers, tulips! One or the other would have more than sufficed, Hazel, you've been extravagant. I suppose now that you're actually earning, it makes a difference. You feel differently, I suppose, when it's your own money. Brian's father always saw that I had everything I needed, wanted for nothing, but I wouldn't have minded a little money of my own, though I never said so, not in so many words."

One morning Peter Lemmon surprised Hazel, and frightened her too, by saying, "Mr. Cortland wants to see you. The big boss himself. Tomorrow at ten-thirty. Downtown office. Headquarters. I'll cover the venue for you."

Mr. Cortland was the age of Hazel's son-in-law, Robin. She couldn't have said why, but she had expected someone theatrical and rude, not this handsome curly-haired man unwinding himself from behind a desk that was not really a desk but a gate-legged table, shaking her hand respectfully and leading her toward a soft brown easy chair. There was genuine solemnity to his jutting chin and a thick brush of hair across his quizzing brow. He offered her a cup of coffee. "Or perhaps you would prefer tea," he said, very politely, with a shock of inspiration.

She looked up from her shoes, her good polished pumps, not her nurse shoes, and saw a pink conch shell on Mr. Cortland's desk. It occurred to her it must be one of the things that made him happy. Other people were made happy by music or flowers or bowls of ice cream—enchanted, familiar things. Some people collected china, and when they found a long-sought piece, *that* made them happy. What made *her* happy was the obliteration of time, burning it away so cleanly she hardly noticed it. Not that she said so to Mr. Cortland. She said, in fact, very little, though some dragging filament of intuition urged her to accept tea rather than coffee, to forgo milk, to shake her head sadly over the proffered sugar.

"We are more delighted than I can say with your sales performance," Mr. Cortland said. "We are a small but growing firm and, as you know"—Hazel did not know, how could she?—"we are a family concern. My maternal grandfather studied commerce at McGill and started this business as a kind of hobby. Our aim, the family's aim, is a reliable product, but not a hard sell. I can't stress this enough to our sales people. We are anxious to avoid a crude hectoring approach or tactics that are in any way manipulative, and we are in the process of developing a quality sales force that matches the quality of our product line. This may surprise you, but it is difficult to find people like yourself who possess, if I may say so, your gentleness of manner. People like yourself transmit a sense of trust to the consumer. We've heard very fine things about you, and we have decided, Hazel—I do hope I may call you Hazel—to put you on regular salary, in addition of course to an adjusted commission. And I would like also to present you with this small brooch, a glazed ceramic K for Kitchen Kult, which we give each quarter to our top sales person."

"Do you realize what this means?" Peter Lemmon asked later

that afternoon over a celebratory drink at Mr. Duck's Happy Hour. "Salary means you're on the team, you're a Kitchen Kult player. Salary equals professional, Hazel. You've arrived, and I don't think you even realize it."

Hazel thought she saw flickering across Peter's guarded, eager face, like a blade of sunlight through a thick curtain, the suggestion that some privilege had been carelessly allocated. She pinned the brooch on the lapel of her good spring coat with an air of bafflement. Beyond the simple smoothness of her pay cheque, she perceived dark squadrons of planners and decision makers who had brought this teasing irony forward. She was being rewarded—a bewildering turn of events—for her timidity, her self-effacement, for what Maxine called her knack for looking the other way. She was a shy, ineffectual, untrained, neutral looking woman, and for this she was being kicked upstairs, or at least this was how Peter translated her move from commission to salary. He scratched his neck, took a long drink of his beer, and said it a third time, with a touch of belligerence it seemed to Hazel, "a kick upstairs." He insisted on paying for the drinks, even though Hazel pressed a ten-dollar bill into his hand. He shook it off.

"This place is bargain city," he assured her, opening the orange cave of his mouth, then closing it quickly. He came here often after work, he said, taking advantage of the two-for-one happy hour policy. Not that he was tight with his money, just the opposite, but he was setting aside a few dollars a week for his dental work in the summer. The work was mostly cosmetic, caps and spacers, and therefore not covered by Kitchen Kult's insurance scheme. The way he saw it, though, was as an investment in the future. If you were going to go to the top, you had to be able to open your mouth and project. "Like this brooch, Hazel, it's a way of projecting. Wearing the company logo means you're one of the family and that you don't mind shouting it out."

That night, when she whitened her shoes, she felt a sort of love for them. And she loved, too, suddenly, her other small tasks, rinsing out her smock, setting her alarm, settling into bed with her book, resting her head against Brian's little fibre-filled pillow with its stitched remnant of erotic privilege and reading herself out of her own life, leaving behind her cut-out shape, so bulky, rounded and unimaginably mute, a woman who swallowed her tongue, got it jammed down her throat and couldn't make a sound.

Marilyn gave a shout of derision on seeing the company brooch pinned to her mother's raincoat. "The old butter-up trick. A stroke here, a stroke there, just enough to keep you going and keep you grateful. But at least they had the decency to get you off straight commission, for that I have to give them some credit."

"Dear Mother," Rosie wrote from British Columbia. "Many thanks for the waterless veg cooker which is surprisingly well made and really very attractive too, and Robin feels that it fulfils a real need, nutritionally speaking, and also aesthetically."

"You're looking better," Maxine said. "You look as though you've dropped a few pounds, have you? All those grated carrots. But do you ever get a minute to yourself? Eight hours on the job plus commuting. I don't suppose they even pay for your gas, which adds up, and your parking. You want to think about a holiday, people can't be buying pots and pans three hundred and sixty-five days a year. JoAnn and Francine and I are thinking seriously of getting a cottage in Nova Scotia for two weeks. Let me know if you're interested, just tell those Kitchen Kult moguls you owe yourself a little peace and quiet by the seaside, ha! Though you do look more relaxed than the last time I saw you, you looked wrung out, completely."

In early May Hazel had an accident. She and Peter were setting up one morning, arranging a new demonstration, employing the usual cabbage, beets and onions, but adding a few spears of spring asparagus and a scatter of chopped chives. In the interest of economy she'd decided to split the asparagus lengthwise, bringing her knife first through the tender tapered head and down the woody stem. Peter was talking away about a new suit he was thinking of buying, asking Hazel's advice—should he go all out for a fine summer wool or compromise on wool and viscose? The knife slipped and entered the web of flesh between Hazel's thumb and forefinger. It sliced further into the flesh than she would have believed possible, so quickly, so lightly that she could only gaze at the spreading blood and grieve about the way it stained and spoiled her perfect circle of cucumber slices.

She required twelve stitches and, at Peter's urging, took the rest of the day off. Mr. Cortland's secretary telephoned and told her to take the whole week off if necessary. There were insurance forms to sign, but those could wait. The important thing was—but Hazel couldn't remember what the important thing was; she had been given some painkillers at the hospital and was having difficulty staying awake. She slept the afternoon away, dreaming of green fields and a yellow sun, and would have slept all evening too if she hadn't been wakened around eight o'clock by the faint buzz of her doorbell. She pulled on a dressing gown, a new one in flowered seersucker, and went to the door. It was Peter Lemmon with a clutch of flowers in his hand. "Why Peter," she said, and could think of nothing else.

The pain had left her hand and moved to the thin skin of her scalp. Its remoteness as much as its taut bright shine left her confused. She managed to take Peter's light jacket—though he protested, saying he had only come for a moment—and steered him toward a comfortable chair by the window. She listened as the cushions subsided under him, and hurried to put the flowers, already a little limp, into water, and to offer a drink—but what did she have on hand? No beer, no gin, and she knew better than to suggest sherry. Then the thought came: what about a glass of red wine?

He accepted twitchily. He said, "You don't have to twist my arm."

"You'll have to uncork it," Hazel said, gesturing at her bandaged hand. She felt she could see straight into his brain where there was nothing but rags and old plastic. But where had *this* come from, this sly, unpardonable superiority of hers?

He lurched forward, nearly falling. "Always happy to do the honours." He seemed afraid of her, of her apartment with its settled furniture, lamps and end tables and china cabinet, regarding these things first with a strict, dry, inquiring look. After a few minutes, he resettled in the soft chair with exaggerated respect.

"To your career," Peter said, raising his glass, appearing not to notice how the word career entered Hazel's consciousness, waking her up from her haze of painkillers and making her want to laugh.

"To the glory of Kitchen Kult," she said, suddenly reckless. She watched him, or part of herself watched him, as he twirled the glass and sniffed its contents. She braced herself for what would surely come.

"An excellent vin—" he started to say, but was interrupted by the doorbell.

It was only Marilyn, dropping in as she sometimes did after her self-defence course. "Already I can break a collarbone," she told Peter after a flustered introduction, "and next week we're going to learn how to go for the groin."

She looked surprisingly pretty with her pensive, wet, youthful eyes and dusty lashes. She accepted some wine and listened intently to the story of Hazel's accident, then said, "Now listen, Mother, don't sign a release with Kitchen Kult until I have Edna look at it. You remember Edna, she's the lawyer. She's sharp as a knife; she's the one who did our lease for us, and it's airtight. You could develop blood poisoning or an infection, you can't tell at this point. You can't trust these corporate entities when it comes to—"

"Kitchen Kult," Peter said, twirling his glass in a manner Hazel found silly, "is more like a family."

"Balls."

"We've decided," Maxine told Hazel a few weeks later, "against the cottage in Nova Scotia. It's too risky, and the weather's only so-so according to Francine. And the cost of air fare and then renting a car, we just figured it's too expensive. My rent's going up starting in July and, well, I took a look at my bank balance and said, Maxine kid, you've got to tighten the old belt. As a matter of fact, I thought—now this may surprise you—I'm thinking of looking for a job."

Hazel set up an interview for Maxine through Personnel, and in a week's time Maxine did her first demonstration. Hazel helped break her in. As a result of a dimly perceived office shuffle, she had been promoted to Assistant Area Manager, freeing Peter Lemmon for what was described as "Creative Sales Outreach." The promotion worried her slightly and she wondered if she were being compensated for the nerve damage in her hand, which was beginning to look more or less permanent. "Thank God you didn't sign the release," was all Marilyn said.

"Congrats," Rosie wired from British Columbia after hearing about the promotion. Hazel had not received a telegram for some years. She was surprised that this austere printed sheet went by the name of telegram. Where was the rough grey paper and the little pasted together words? She wondered who had composed the message, Robin or Rosie, and whose idea it had been to abbreviate the single word and if thrift were involved. *Congrats.* What a hard little hurting pellet to find in the middle of a smooth sheet of paper.

"Gorgeous," Brian's mother said of Hazel's opal-toned silk

suit with its scarf of muted pink, pearl and lemon. Her lips moved appreciatively. "Ah, gorgeous."

"A helluva improvement over a bloody smock," Maxine sniffed, looking sideways.

"Most elegant!" said Mr. Cortland, who had called Hazel into his office to discuss her future with Kitchen Kult. "The sort of image we hope and try to project. Elegance and understatement." He presented her with a small box in which rested, on a square of textured cotton, a pair of enamelled earrings with the flying letter K for Kitchen Kult.

"Beautiful," said Hazel, who never wore earrings. The clip-on sort hurt her, and she had never got around to piercing her ears. "For my sake," Brian had begged her when he was twenty-five and she was twenty and about to become his wife, "don't ever do it. I can't bear to lose a single bit of you."

Remembering this, the tone of Brian's voice, its rushing, foolish sincerity, Hazel felt her eyes tingle. "My handbag," she said, groping blindly.

Mr. Cortland misunderstood. He leaped up, touched by his own generosity, a Kleenex in hand. "We simply wanted to show our appreciation," he said, or rather sang.

Hazel sniffed, more loudly than she intended, and Mr. Cortland pretended not to hear. "We especially appreciate your filling in for Peter Lemmon during his leave of absence."

At this Hazel nodded. Poor Peter. She must phone tonight. He was finding the aftermath of his dental surgery painful and prolonged, and she had been looking, every chance she had, for a suitable convalescent card, something not too effusive and not too mocking—Peter took his teeth far too seriously. Perhaps she would just send one of her blurry impressionistic hasty notes, or better yet, a jaunty postcard saying she hoped he'd be back soon.

Mr. Cortland fingered the pink conch shell on his desk. He picked it up between his two hands and rocked it gently to and fro, then said, "Mr. Lemmon will not be returning. We have already sent him a letter of termination and, of course, a generous severance settlement. It was decided that his particular kind of personality, though admirable, was not quite in line with the Kitchen Kult approach, and we feel that you yourself have already demonstrated your ability to take over his work and perhaps even extend the scope of it."

"I don't believe you're doing this," Marilyn shouted over the phone to Hazel. "And Peter doesn't believe it either."

"How do you know what Peter thinks?"

"I saw him this afternoon. I saw him yesterday afternoon. I see him rather often if you want to know the truth."

Hazel offered the Kitchen Kult earrings to Maxine who snorted and said, "Come off it, Hazel."

Rosie in Vancouver sent a short note saying, "Marilyn phoned about your new position, which is really marvellous, though Robin and I are wondering if you aren't getting in deeper than you really want to at this time."

Brian's mother said nothing. A series of small strokes had taken her speech away and also her ability to leave her bed. Nothing Hazel brought her aroused her interest, not chocolates, not flowers, not even the fashion magazines she used to love.

Hazel phoned and made an appointment to see Mr. Cortland. She invented a pretext, one or two ideas she and Maxine had worked out to tighten up the demonstrations. Mr. Cortland listened to her and nodded approvingly. Then she sprang. She had been thinking about Peter Lemmon, she said, how much the sales force missed him, missed his resourcefulness and his attention to details. He had a certain imaginative flair, a peculiar usefulness. Some people had a way of giving energy to others, it was uncanny, it was a rare gift. She didn't mention Peter's dental work; she had some sense.

Mr. Cortland sent her a shrewd look, a look she would not

have believed he had in his repertoire. "Well, Hazel," he said at last, "in business we deal in hard bargains. Maybe you and I can come to some sort of bargain."

"Bargain?"

"That insurance form, the release. The one you haven't got round to signing yet. How would it be if you signed it right now on the promise that I find some slot or other for Peter Lemmon by the end of the week? You are quite right about his positive attributes, quite astute of you, really, to point them out. I can't promise anything in sales though. The absolute bottom end of management might be the best we can do."

Hazel considered. She stared at the conch shell for a full ten seconds. The office lighting coated it with a pink, even light, making it look like a piece of unglazed pottery. She liked the idea of bargains. She felt she understood them. "I'll sign," she said. She had her pen in her hand, poised.

On Sunday, a Sunday at the height of summer in early July, Hazel drives out to Silver Oaks to visit her ailing mother-in-law. All she can do for her now is sit by her side for an hour and hold her hand, and sometimes she wonders what the point is of these visits. Her mother-in-law's face is impassive and silken, and occasionally driblets of spittle, thin and clear as tears, run from the corners of her mouth. It used to be such a strong, organized face with its firm mouth and steady eyes. But now she doesn't recognize anyone, with the possible exception of Hazel.

Some benefit appears to derive from these hand-holding sessions, or so the nurses tell Hazel. "She's calmer after your visits," they say. "She struggles less."

Hazel is calm too. She likes sitting here and feeling the hour unwind like thread from a spindle. She wishes it would go on and on. A week ago she had come away from Mr. Cortland's office irradiated with the conviction that her life was going to be possible after all. All she had to do was bear in mind the bargains she made. This was an obscene revelation, but Hazel was excited by it. Everything could be made accountable, added up and balanced and fairly, evenly, shared. You only had to pay attention and ask for what was yours by right. You could be clever, dealing in sly acts of surrender, but holding fast at the same time, negotiating and measuring the tying up your life in useful bundles.

But she was wrong. It wasn't true. Her pride had misled her. No one has that kind of power, no one.

She looks around the little hospital room and marvels at the accident of its contents, its bureau and tumbler and toothbrush and folded towel. The open window looks out on to a parking lot filled with rows of cars, all their shining roofs baking in the light. Next year there will be different cars, differently ordered. The shrubs and trees, weighed down with their millions of new leaves, will form a new dark backdrop.

It is an accident that she should be sitting in this room, holding the hand of an old, unblinking, unresisting woman who had once been sternly disapproving of her, thinking her countrified and clumsy. "Hazel!" she had sometimes whispered in the early days. "Your slip strap! Your salad fork!" Now she lacks even the power to wet her lips with her tongue; it is Hazel who touches the lips with a damp towel from time to time, or applies a bit of Vaseline to keep them from cracking. But she can feel the old woman's dim pulse, and imagines that it forms a code of acknowledgment or faintly telegraphs certain perplexing final questions—how did all this happen? How did we get here?

Everything is an accident, Hazel would be willing to say if asked. Her whole life is an accident, and by accident she has blundered into the heart of it.

Jane Urquhart

Storm Glass

From where she lay she could see the lake. It seemed to her to be heading east, as if it had a definite destination in mind and would someday be gone altogether from the place where it was now. But it was going nowhere; though diminished by sun, replenished by rain and pushed around by strong winds, it was always a lake. And always there. God knows it had its twentieth-century problems; its illnesses, its weaknesses. Some had even said it was dying. But she knew better. She was dying, and although she felt as close as a cousin to the lake, she did not sense that it shared with her this strong, this irreversible decline. It would always be a lake, and always there, long after she had gone somewhere else. Alone.

She was alone in the room now. As alone as she would be a few months later when the brightness of the last breath closed on the dark, forever. She had imagined the voyage in that dark— her thoughts speaking in an alien tongue—textural black land-scape—non-visual—swimming towards the change. And then she had hoped that she would be blessed with some profound last words, some small amount of theatre to verify the end of things. But somehow she sensed it would be more of a letting go, slipping right through the centre of the concentric circles that are the world and into a private and inarticulate focus, and then ... the shore had changed again and again since her first summers there. One year there had been unexpected sand for her babies to play in. She remembered fine grains clinging to their soggy diapers, and their flat sturdy footprints which had existed for seconds only before the lake gathered them up. But a storm the following winter had altered the patterns of the water and the next year her small children had staggered over beach stones to the edge. In subsequent weeks their bare feet had toughened, allowing them to run over rocks and pebbles without pain. Her own feet had resisted the beach stones summer after summer, forcing her to wear some kind of shoes until she left the land for the smooth softness of the water.

Her husband, larger, more stubborn, less willing to admit to weaknesses than she, would brave the distance of the beach, like the children, barefoot. But his feet had never toughened, and standing, as she sometimes had, on the screened veranda, she had watched the pain move through his stiffened legs and up his back until, like a large performing animal, he had fallen, backwards and laughing, into the lake.

He was not there now, unwilling to admit to this, her last, most impossible weakness.

Yet he came and went, mostly at mealtimes, when a hired woman came to cook for them. He came in heavy with the smell of the farm where he had worked and worked, making things come to be; a field of corn, a litter of pigs, or even a basket of smooth, brown eggs. The farm took all of his time now, as if, as she moved down this isolated tunnel towards that change, it was even more important that he make things come to be. And though this small summer cottage was only minutes away from the earth that he worked, the fact of her lying there had made it a distance too great for him to travel except for the uncontrol-lable and predictable necessities of hunger and of sleep.

The beach was smaller this year, and higher. Strong spring winds had urged the lake to push the stones into several banks, like large steps, up to the grass. These elevations curved in a reg-ular way around the shoreline as if a natural amphitheatre had been mysteriously provided so that audiences of pilgrims might come and sit and watch the miracle of the lake. They never arrived, of course, but she sometimes found it fun to conjure the image of the beach filled with spectators, row on row, cheering on the glide of a wave, the leap of a fish, the flash of a white sail on the horizon. In her imagination she could see their backs, an array of colourful shirts, covering the usual solid grey of the stones.

And yet, even without the imaginary spectators, the grey was not entirely solid. Here and there a white stone shone amongst the others, the result of some pre-Cambrian magic. In other years the children had collected these and old honey pails full of them still lined the windowsills on the porch. The children had changed, had left, had disappeared into adult-hood, lost to cities and success. And yet they too came and went with smiles and gifts and offers of obscure and indefinite forms of help. She remembered mending things for them; a toy, a scratch on the skin, a piece of clothing, and she understood their helpless, inarticulate desire to pretend that now they could somehow mend her.

In her room there were two windows. One faced the lake, the other the weather, which always seemed to come in from the east. In the mornings when the sun shone, a golden rectangle appeared like an extra blanket placed on the bed by some anony-mous benevolent hand. On those days her eyes moved from the small flame of her opal ring to the millions of diamonds scat-tered on the lake and she wished that she could lie out there among them, rolling slightly with the current until the sun moved to the other side of the sky. During the heat of all those summers she had never strayed far from the water, teaching her children to swim or swimming herself in long graceful strokes, covering the distance from one point of land to another, until she knew by heart the shoreline and the horizon visible from the small bay where the cottage was situated. And many times she had laughed and called until at last, with a certain reluctance, her husband had stumbled over the stones to join her.

He seldom swam now, and if he did it was early in the morning before she was awake. Perhaps he did not wish to illustrate to her his mobility, and her lack of it. Or perhaps, growing older, he wished his battle with the lake to be entirely private. In other times she had laughed at him for his method of attacking the lake, back bent, shoulders drawn forward, like a determined prize fighter, while she slipped effortlessly by, as fluid as the water, and as relaxed. His moments in the lake were tense, and quickly finished; a kind of enforced pleasure, containing more comedy than surrender.

But sometimes lately she had awakened to see him, shivering and bent, scrambling into his overalls in some far corner of the room and knowing he had been swimming, she would ask the customary questions about the lake. "Was it cold? Was there much of an undertow?" and he had replied with the customary answers. "Not bad, not really, once you are in, once you are used to it."

That morning he had left her early, without swimming. The woman had made her bed, bathed her and abandoned her to the warm wind that drifted in one window and the vision of the beach and the lake that occupied the other. Her eyes scanned the stones beyond the glass trying to remember the objects that, in the past, she had found among them. Trying to remember, for instance, the look and then the texture of the clean dry bones of seagulls; more delicate than the dried stems of chrysanthemums and more pleasing to her than that flower in full bloom. These precise working parts of once animate things were so whole in themselves that they left no evidence of the final breakdown of flesh and feather. They were suspended somewhere between being and non-being like the documentation of an important event and their presence somehow justified the absence of all that had gone before.

But then, instead of bone, she caught sight of a minuscule edge of colour, blue-green, a dusty shine, an irregular shape sur-rounded by rounded rocks—so small she ought not to have seen it, she ought to have overlooked it altogether.

"Storm glass," she whispered to herself, and then she laughed realizing that she had made use of her husband's words without thinking, without allowing the pause of reason to interrupt her response as it so often did. When they spoke together she some-times tried expressly to avoid his words, to be in possession of her own, hard thoughts. Those words and thoughts, she believed, were entirely her own. They were among the few things he had no ability to control with either his force or his tenderness.

It must have been at least fifteen summers before, when the children, bored and sullen in the clutches of early adolescence, had sat day after day like ominous boulders on the beach, until she, remembering the honey pails on the windowsills, had sug-gested that they collect the small pieces of worn glass that were sometimes scattered throughout the stones. Perhaps, she had remarked, they could do something with them; build a small patio or path, or fill glass Mason jars to decorate their bedrooms. It would be better, at least, than sitting at the water's edge won-dering what to do with the endless summer days that stretched before them.

The three children had begun their search almost immedi-ately; their thin backs brown and shining in the hot sun. Most of the pieces they found were a dark ochre colour, beer bottles no doubt, thrown into the lake by campers from the provincial park fifteen miles down the road. But occasionally they would come across a rarer commodity, a kind of soft turquoise glass similar to the colour of bottles they had seen in antique shops with their mother. These fragments sometimes caused disputes over who had spotted them first but, as often as not, there were enough pieces to go fairly around. Still rarer and smaller were the particles of emerald green and navy blue, to be found among the tiny damp pebbles at the very edge of the shore, the remnants of bottles even more advanced in age than those that were available in the shops. But the children had seen these intact as well, locked behind the glass of display cases in the county museum. Often the word *poison* or a skull and crossbones would be visible in raised relief across the surface of this older, darker glassware. Their mother knew that the bottles had held cleaning fluid, which was as toxic now in its cheerful tin and plastic containers as it had been then housed in dark glass, but the children associated it with dire and passionate plots, perhaps involving pirates, and they held it up to their parents as the most important prize of all.

The combing of the beach had lasted two days, maybe three, and had become, for a while, the topic of family conversations. But one evening, she remembered, when they were all seated at the table, her husband had argued with her, insisting as he often did on his own personal form of definition—even in the realm of the activities of children.

"It's really storm glass," he had announced to the children who had been calling it by a variety of different names, "that's what I always called it."

"But," she had responded, "I remember a storm glass from high school, from physics, something to do with predicting weather, I don't know just what. But that's what it is, not the glass out there on the beach."

"No," he had continued, "storms make it with waves and stones. That wears down the edges. You can't take the edge off a piece of glass that lies at the bottom of a bird bath. Storms make it, it's storm glass."

"Well, we always called it beach glass, or sometimes water glass when we were children, and the storm glass came later when we were in high school."

"It is storm glass," he said, with the kind of grave finality she had come to know; a statement you don't retract, a place you don't return from.

It was after these small, really insignificant, disputes that they would turn silently away from each other for a while; she holding fiercely, quietly, to her own privacy, her own person. To him it seemed she refused out of stubbornness to accept his simplified sense of the order of things, that she wished to confuse him by leaning towards the complexities of alternatives. He was not a man of great intellect. Almost every issue that he had questioned had settled into fact and belief in early manhood. He clung to the predictability of these preordained facts with such tenacity that when she became ill the very enormity of the impending disorder frightened him beyond words and into the privacy of his own belief that it was not so, could not be happening to her, or, perhaps more importantly, to him. They did not speak of it but turned instead quietly from each other, she not wishing to defend her own tragedy, and he not wishing to submit to any reference to such monumental change.

But fifteen years before, in the small matter of the glass, the children had submitted easily, as children will, to the sound of his authority; and storm glass it had become. Within a week, however, their project had been abandoned in favour of boredom and neither path nor patio had appeared. Nevertheless, the glass itself appeared year after year among the stones on the beach and, try as she might, she could never quite control the impulse to pick it up. The desire to collect it was with her even now, creating an invisible tension, like a slim, taut wire, from her eyes to her hands to the beach as she lay confined within her room. It was, after all, a small treasure, an enigma; broken glass robbed by time of one of its more important qualities, the ability to cut. And though she could no longer rub it between her palms she knew it would be as firm and as strong as ever. And as gentle.

From where she lay she could see the lake and she knew that this was good; to be able to see the land and the end of the land, to be able to see the vast indefinite bowl of the lake. And she was pleased that she had seen the storm glass. She felt she understood the evolution of its story. What had once been a shattered dangerous substance now lay upon the beach, harmless, inert and beautiful after being tossed and rubbed by the real weather of the world. It had, with time, become a pastel memory of a useful vessel, to be carried, perhaps in a back pocket, and brought out and examined now and then. It was a relic of that special moment when the memory and the edge of the break softened and combined in order to allow preservation.

How long, she wondered, did it take, from the break on the rocks, through the storms of different seasons, to the change? When did the edges cease to cut?

That night he came in tired and heavy, followed by the smell of making things come to be. He spoke of problems with the farm, of obstinate machinery that refused to function or of crops with inexplicable malformations—events that, even in the power of his stubbornness, he could never hope to control. And when he turned to look at her his eyes were like fresh broken glass: sharp, dangerous, alive. She answered him with kindness, though, knowing the storm ahead and then the softening of edges yet to come.

"There's storm glass on the beach," she said.

Copyright Acknowledgments

FRANCES ITANI. "Marx & Co." by Frances Itani is reprinted from *Pack Ice* by permission of Oberon Press.

JOYCE MARSHALL. "Blood and Bone" from *Blood and Bone* by Joyce Marshall (Mosaic Press, 1995), copyright © Joyce Marshall, 1995. Reprinted by permission of Mosaic Press, 1252 Speers Road, Oakville.

SHANI MOOTOO. "A Garden of Her Own" from *Out on Main Street and Other Stories* by Shani Mootoo (Press Gang, 1993), copyright © 1993 Shani Mootoo. Reprinted by permission of Press Gang Publishers.

ALICE MUNRO. "Miles City, Montana" from *The Progress of Love* by Alice Munro. Used by permission, McClelland & Stewart, Inc. *The Canadian Publishers*.

MONIQUE PROULX. "Leah and Paul, for Example" from *Aurora Montrealis* by Monique Proulx, translated by Matt Cohen. Originally published as *Les Aurores Montréales* in 1996 by Les Éditions du Boréal. Translation copyright © 1997 by Matt Cohen. Reprinted by permission of Douglas & McIntyre.

HÉLÈNE RIOUX. "Opening Night" by Hélène Rioux, translated by Diane Schoemperlen, is reprinted from *Parallel Voices*, edited by André Carpentier and Matt Cohen, by permission of Quarry Press Inc.

EDEN ROBINSON. "Queen of the North" extracted from *Traplines* by Eden Robinson. Copyright © 1996. Reprinted by permission of Alfred A. Knopf Canada Limited.

HOLLEY RUBINSKY. "Rapid Transits" is reprinted from the collection *Rapid Transits and Other Stories* by Holley Rubinsky, published by Polestar Book Publishers, Victoria, B.C. Reprinted with permission.

JANE RULE. "Lilian" from *Outlander* by Jane Rule (Naiad Press, 1982), copyright © 1981 by Jane Rule.

DIANE SCHOEMPERLEN. "She Wants to Tell Me" by Diane